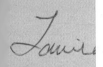

THERE WERE SF GIANTS
ON THE EARTH THOSE DAYS!

Unforgettable writers like C.M. Kornbluth,
Anthony Boucher, Fredric Brown, Edgar
Pangborn . . .

AND MOST OF THEM ARE
STILL AROUND!

Literary colossi like Fritz Leiber, Ray Bradbury,
Julian May, Arthur C. Clarke, Isaac Asimov,
Jack Finney, Alan E. Nourse, William Tenn,
Katherine MacLean . . .

They made their names then, they keep their
fames now.

THEY ARE ALL HERE IN
ASIMOV'S LUCKY THIRTEENTH!

Anthologies from DAW include

ASIMOV PRESENTS THE GREAT SF STORIES
The best stories of the last four decades.
Edited by Isaac Asimov and Martin H. Greenberg.

THE ANNUAL WORLD'S BEST SF
The best of the current year.
Edited by Donald A. Wollheim with Arthur W. Saha.

THE YEAR'S BEST HORROR STORIES
An annual of gooseflesh tales.
Edited by Karl Edward Wagner.

THE YEAR'S BEST FANTASY STORIES
An annual of high imagination.
Edited by Arthur W. Saha.

TERRA SF
The best SF from Western Europe.
Edited by Richard D. Nolane.

ISAAC ASIMOV

PRESENTS

THE GREAT SF STORIES

#13

(1951)

EDITED BY ISAAC ASIMOV AND MARTIN H. GREENBERG

DAW BOOKS, INC.

DONALD A. WOLLHEIM, PUBLISHER

1633 Broadway, New York, NY 10019

Copyright ©, 1985 by Isaac Asimov and Martin H. Greenberg.

All Rights Reserved.

Complete list of copyright acknowledgments
will be found on the following page.

Cover design by One Plus One Studios.

Cover art by Cesare Reggiani.

DAW Collectors' Book No. 636

First Printing, July 1985

1 2 3 4 5 6 7 8 9

PRINTED IN U.S.A.

ACKNOWLEDGMENTS

Tenn—Copyright 1950 by Hillman Periodicals, Inc.; copyright renewed © 1978 by William Tenn; reprinted by permission of the author and the author's agent, Virginia Kidd.

Clarke (THE SENTINEL)—copyright 1951; copyright renewed © 1979 by Arthur C. Clarke. Reprinted by permission of the author and his agents, the Scott Meredith Literary Agency, Inc., 845 Third Ave., New York, NY 10022.

Bradbury—Copyright 1951 by Ray Bradbury, renewed 1979. Reprinted by permission of Don Congdon Associates, Inc.

Kornbluth (THE MARCHING MORONS)—Copyright 1951 by World Editions; copyright renewed © 1979 by Mary Kornbluth. Reprinted by permission of Richard Curtis Associates.

Brown—Copyright 1951 by Street & Smith Publications, Inc.; copyright renewed © 1979 by the Estate of Fredric Brown. Reprinted by permission of International Creative Management.

Pangborn—Copyright 1951 by World Editions; copyright renewed © 1979 by the Estate of Edgar Pangborn. Reprinted by permission of Richard Curtis Associates.

Asimov—Copyright 1951 by Street & Smith Publications, Inc.; copyright renewed © 1979 by Isaac Asimov. Reprinted by permission of the author.

MacLean—Copyright © 1951, 1952 by Katherine MacLean, copyright renewed 1979 by Katherine MacLean; reprinted by permission of the author and the author's agent, Virginia Kidd.

Clarke (SUPERIORITY)—Copyright 1951, copyright renewed © 1979 by Arthur C. Clarke. Reprinted by permission of the author and the author's agents, the Scott Meredith Literary Agency, Inc., 845 Third Ave., New York, NY 10022.

Finney—Copyright 1951 by Jack Finney, renewed © 1979. Reprinted by permission of Don Congdon Associates, Inc.

Boucher—Copyright renewed © 1979 by Phyllis White. Reprinted by permission of Curtis Brown Associates, Ltd.

Nourse—Copyright 1951 by Galaxy Publishing Corporation. Copyright renewed © 1979 by Alan E. Nourse. Reprinted by permission of Brandt & Brandt Literary Agents, Inc.

Kornbluth (WITH THESE HANDS)—Copyright 1951 by Galaxy Publishing Corporation; copyright renewed © 1979 by Mary Kornbluth. Reprinted by permission of Richard Curtis Associates, Inc.

Leiber—Copyright 1951 by Galaxy Publishing Corporation; copyright renewed © 1979 by Fritz Leiber. Reprinted by permission of Richard Curtis Associates, Inc.

May—Copyright 1952 by T.E. Dikty and Everett F. Bleiler. Copyright renewed 1983 by Julian May. Reprinted by permission of the author.

Contents

INTRODUCTION

In the world outside reality, the year got off to a disastrous start on January 1st when Chinese Communist and North Korean troops penetrated Allied lines, taking the South Korean capital of Seoul on the 4th. On February 8th President Truman moved forcefully against striking railroad workers, ordering the U.S. military to take over and operate the system. In an even more controversial but quite necessary decision, the President fired American hero General Douglas MacArthur on April 11, replacing him with the capable Matthew Ridgway as Commander of U.S. forces in the far East. MacArthur fought back eight days later in a famous speech before both houses of Congress in which he said, "Old soldiers never die, they just fade away." He then faded away.

On June 13 Ireland received a new leader as Eamon de Valera returned to power. Toward the end of the month two of the most famous spies in the history of the Cold War, Guy Burgess and Donald Maclean, both high-ranking members of British intelligence, made their way to the Soviet Union after a lifetime spent betraying their country. King Abdullah of Jordan, the father of King Hussein (who witnessed the act), was gunned down in the main mosque in Jerusalem. A much more peaceable event was the signing on September 8th of the official peace treaty between the Allied powers (except for the Soviet Union and its friends) and Japan in San Francisco. War continued to rage in Korea as United Nations forces captured Heartbreak Ridge in one of the most famous battles of that conflict.

In two important elections, the Conservatives under Churchill and Eden were returned to power in Great Britain on October 25th, while on November 11 Juan Peron was re-elected President of Argentina.

The 22nd Amendment to the Constitution of the United States was passed, limiting a President to a maximum of two terms in office.

During 1951 the first color television sets became available, but the quality was so poor that it would be many years before anyone could watch them in comfort. Dali painted "Christ of St. John of the Cross," while the New York Yankees captured the World Series, defeating the "miracle" New York Giants four games to two. Novels about World War II were very popular, especially Herman Wouk's *The Caine Mutiny* and James Jones's *From Here to Eternity*. The Nobel Prize for Medicine was awarded to Max Theiler of the United States for his work in developing a vaccine against yellow fever.

Outstanding films of the year included the wonderful *An American in Paris*, with Gene Kelly; *Viva Zapata*, directed by Elia Kazan; *A Streetcar Named Desire*, starring a young Marlon Brando; Alfred Hitchcock's great *Strangers on a Train;* Max Ophul's *Le Plaisir;* and *The African Queen*, starring Bogart and Hepburn. And to top it all off, a gentleman named Fred Waller invented Cinerama.

A new heavyweight champion was crowned when Jersey Joe Walcott knocked out Ezzard Charles in the seventh round. Tennessee Williams wrote *The Rose Tattoo*, while Rodgers and Hammerstein's *The King and I* was the top musical of the year. Stan "the Man" Musial led the majors with a .355 average and Ralph Kiner was again home run king, this time with 41 round-trippers. The Nobel Prize in Chemistry went to Americans Edwin M. McMillan and Glenn Seaborg for their discovery of plutonium.

The U.S. Open Tennis champions were Frank Sedgman and Maureen "Little Mo" Connolly. Top songs of the year included "Hello, Young Lovers," "Kisses Sweeter Than Wine," "Shrimp Boats," "Getting to Know You," and the classic "Come On-a My House," but most people were shedding tears over Johnny Ray's great "Cry." The world record for the mile run was still the 4:01.4 set by Gunder Haegg of Sweden in 1945.

Important non-fiction books of the year included Sartre's *The Psychology of Imagination* and Rachel Carson's *The Sea Around Us*. Count Turf won the Kentucky Derby. People were discussing J. D. Salinger's novel *The Catcher in the Rye*, which was banned in some cities. There were an estimated 153,000,000 people in the United States and 490,000,000 in The People's Republic of China.

Death took Ludwig Wittgenstein, William Randolph Hearst, Arnold Schoenberg, André Gide, Ernest Bevin, and the great Huddie Ledbetter.

Mel Brooks may still have been Melvin Kaminsky.

In the real world it was another outstanding year as a goodly number of excellent science fiction novels and collections were published (some of which had been serialized years before in the magazines), including *Shadow over Mars* by Leigh Brackett, *The Martian Chronicles* by Ray Bradbury, *The Sands of Mars* by Arthur C. Clarke, *Rogue Queen* by L. Sprague de Camp, *City at World's End* by Edmond Hamilton, *Between Planets* by Robert A. Heinlein, *Time and Again* by Clifford D. Simak, *The Weapon Shops of Isher* by A. E. van Vogt, *Seetee Ship* by Jack Williamson, *The Disappearance* by Philip Wylie, *The Day of the Triffids* by John Wyndham, and *The Stars Like Dust* by Isaac Asimov. Some of these books were published by fan publishers.

More wondrous things were happening in the real world as six solid writers made their maiden voyages into reality: Charles Beaumont with "The Devil You Say?" in January,

Walter M. Miller, Jr. with "The Secret of the Death Dome" in January, Harry Harrison with "Rock Diver" in February, Alan E. Nourse with "High Threshold" in March, E.C. Tubb with "No Short Cuts" in June, and the wonderful Zenna Henderson with "Come On Wagon" in December.

Two science fiction magazines died in 1951—*Super Science Stories* and *Worlds Beyond*—but two new ones took their place: the *Avon Science Fiction Reader*, edited by one Donald A. Wollheim, and *Science Fiction Quarterly*. In addition, two editors began working who would leave their mark on the field—Sam Mines at *Startling* and *Thrilling Wonder*, and E. J. Carnell at the British *Science-Fantasy*.

The real people gathered together for the ninth time as the World Science Convention (Nolacon) was held in New Orleans.

Death took Algernon Blackwood, but distant wings continued to beat as Orson Scott Card was born.

1951 saw the release of a group of science fiction films, some good and some awful, including *Abbott and Costello Meet the Invisible Man* (fair), *The Day the Earth Stood Still* (terrific), *Five* (should have been much better), *Flight to Mars* (forgettable), *Lost Continent* (okay), *The Man From Planet X* (strange), *The Thing From Another World* (wonderful, in spite of what it led to), and *When Worlds Collide* (hokey).

Finally, we want to mention two great novellas that are too long for inclusion here—"The Fireman" by Ray Bradbury, which later became *Fahrenheit 451*, and the stunning "Beyond Bedlam" by the vastly underrated Wyman Guin.

Let us travel back to that honored year of 1951 and enjoy the best stories that the real world bequeathed to us.

NULL-P

BY WILLIAM TENN (PHILIP KLASS, 1920–   )
WORLDS BEYOND, JANUARY

Now a Professor of English at Penn State University, Phil Klass produced work that was one of the great joys of the 1950s. His refreshing wit and urbanity, coupled with a sharp eye for the phoney and the absurd, brought him great popularity and steady markets. Revealing a deep suspicion of bureaucracy and institutions of all types, his stories often appeared within and among the Pohl-Gold-Ballantine Gang of Three. We will meet him frequently in future volumes in this series.

"Null-P" shows him near the top of his form, attacking the safe, the average, and the "normal." Worlds Beyond was a short-lived (three issues) magazine edited by Damon Knight, one of many such ventures that failed to find a niche in the markets of the early 1950s.
—M.H.G.

Phil Klass is exactly my age, but, of course, he looks much older.

It's difficult to tell whether Phil knows when he's being funny, because he maintains a dead-pan expression all the time. Back in the days when this story was written, we all

1

belonged to the Hydra Club, and once a year we used to wait for Phil to give us a speech. Since he had no sense of time, he used to arrive at midnight for a speech scheduled for 9 p.m., but he was worth waiting for.

I remember when he gave us the recipe for a commercially successful story. "You need the bright red thread of plot" (he would say, with one hand making a snakelike motion) "weaving its way through. You need a bit of tension and suspense" (one hand tipping to allow just a bit of its content to dribble into the story). "You need a touch of humor (two fingers twiddling to add that touch) "and a soupçon of human interest" (business of squeezing the bulb of an eyedropper to add a small drop). "Finally, you need just the tiniest, tiniest bit of sex." (Mad pantomime of an author shoveling a manure pile in huge heaps into the story.)

I never found out what he said afterward. I laughed hysterically for the duration of the speech.
—*I.A.*

SEVERAL MONTHS after the Second Atomic War, when radio-activity still held one-third of the planet in desolation, Dr. Daniel Glurt of Fillmore Township, Wisc., stumbled upon a discovery which was to generate humanity's ultimate sociological advance.

Like Columbus, smug over his voyage to India; like Nobel, proud of the synthesis of dynamite which made combat between nations impossible, the doctor misinterpreted his discovery. Years later, he cackled to a visiting historian:

"Had no idea it would lead to this, no idea at all. You remember, the war had just ended: we were feeling mighty subdued what with the eastern and western coasts of the United States practically sizzled away. Well, word came down from the new capital at Topeka in Kansas for us doctors to give all our patients a complete physical check. Sort of be on the lookout, you know, for radioactive burns and them fancy new diseases the armies had been tossing back and forth. Well, sir, that's absolutely all I set out to do. I'd known George Abnego for over thirty years—treated him for chicken-pox and pneumonia and ptomaine poisoning. I'd *never* suspected!''

Having reported to Dr. Glurt's office immediately after work in accordance with the proclamation shouted through the streets by the county clerk, and having waited patiently in line for an hour and a half, George Abnego was at last received into the small consulting room. Here he was thoroughly chest-thumped, X-rayed, blood-sampled, and urinanalyzed. His skin was examined carefully, and he was made to answer the five hundred questions prepared by the Department of Health in a pathetic attempt to cover the symptoms of the new ailments.

George Abnego then dressed and went home to the cereal supper permitted for that day by the ration board. Dr. Glurt placed his folder in a drawer and called for the next patient. He had noticed nothing up to this point; yet already he had unwittingly begun the Abnegite Revolution.

Four days later, the health survey of Fillmore, Wisc., being complete, the doctor forwarded the examination reports to Topeka. Just before signing George Abnego's sheet, he glanced at it cursorily, raised his eyebrows and entered the following note: "Despite the tendency to dental caries and athlete's foot, I would consider this man to be of average health. Physically, he is the Fillmore Township norm."

It was this last sentence which caused the government medical official to chuckle and glance at the sheet once more. His smile was puzzled after this; it was even more puzzled after he had checked the figures and statements on the form against standard medical references.

He wrote a phrase in red ink in the right-hand corner and sent it along to Research.

His name is lost to history.

Research wondered why the report on George Abnego had been sent up—he had no unusual symptoms portending exotic innovations like cerebral measles or arterial trichinosis. Then it observed the phrase in red ink and Dr. Glurt's remark.

Research shrugged its anonymous shoulders and assigned a crew of statisticians to go further into the matter.

A week later, as a result of their findings, another crew—nine medical specialists—left for Fillmore. They examined George Abnego with coordinated precision. Afterwards, they called on Dr. Glurt briefly, leaving a copy of their examination report with him when he expressed interest.

Ironically, the government copies were destroyed in the Topeka Hard-Shelled Baptist Riots a month later, the same riots which stimulated Dr. Glurt to launch the Abnegite Revolution.

This Baptist denomination, because of population shrinkage due to atomic and bacteriological warfare, was now the largest single religious body in the nation. It was then controlled by a group pledged to the establishment of a Hard-Shelled Baptist theocracy in what was left of the United States. The rioters were quelled after much destruction and bloodshed; their leader, the Reverend Hemingway T. Gaunt—who had vowed that he would remove neither the pistol from his left hand nor the Bible from his right until the Rule of God had been established and the Third Temple built—was sentenced to death by a jury composed of stern-faced fellow Baptists.

Commenting on the riots, the Fillmore, Wisc., *Bugle-Herald* drew a mournful parallel between the Topeka street battles and the destruction wreaked upon the world by atomic conflict.

"International communication and transportation having broken down," the editorial went on broodingly, "we now know little of the smashed world in which we live, beyond such meager facts as the complete disappearance of Australia beneath the waves, and the contraction of Europe to the Pyrenees and Ural Mountains. We know that our planet's physical appearance has changed as much from what it was ten years ago, as the infant monstrosities and mutants being born everywhere as a result of radioactivity are unpleasantly different from their parents.

"Truly, in these days of mounting catastrophe and change,

our faltering spirits beg the heavens for a sign, a portent, that all will be well again, that all will yet be as it once was, that the waters of disaster will subside and we shall once more walk upon the solid ground of normalcy."

It was this last word which attracted Dr. Glurt's attention. That night, he slid the report of the special government medical crew into the newspaper's mail slot. He had penciled a laconic note in the margin of the first page:

"Noticed your interest in the subject."

Next week's edition of the Fillmore *Bugle-Herald* flaunted a page-one five-column headline.

FILLMORE CITIZEN THE SIGN?

Normal Man of Fillmore May be Answer From Above
Local Doctor Reveals Government Medical Secret

The story that followed was liberally sprinkled with quotations taken equally from the government report and the Psalms of David. The startled residents of Fillmore learned that one George Abnego, a citizen unnoticed in their midst for almost forty years, was a living abstraction. Through a combination of circumstances no more remarkable than those producing a royal flush in stud poker, Abnego's physique, psyche, and other miscellaneous attributes had resulted in that legendary creature—the statistical average.

According to the last census taken before the war, George Abnego's height and weight were identical with the mean of the American adult male. He had married at the exact age— year, month, day—when statisticians had estimated the marriage of the *average* man took place; he had married a woman the *average* number of years younger than himself; his income as declared on his last tax statement was the *average* income for that year. The very teeth in his mouth tallied in quantity and condition with those predicted by the American Dental Association to be found on a man extracted at random from the population. Abnego's metabolism and blood pressure, his bodily proportions and private neuroses, were all cross-sections of the latest available records. Subjected to every psychological and personality test available, his final, overall grade corrected out to show that he was both average and normal.

Finally, Mrs. Abnego had been recently delivered of their third child, a boy. This development had not only occurred at exactly the right time according to the population indices, but it had resulted in an entirely normal sample of humanity— unlike most babies being born throughout the land.

The *Bugle-Herald* blared its hymn to the new celebrity around a greasy photograph of the family in which the assembled Abnegos stared glassily out at the reader, looking, as many put it, "Average—average as hell!"

Newspapers in other states were invited to copy.

They did, slowly at first, then with an accelerating, contagious enthusiasm. Indeed, as the intense public interest in this symbol of stability, this refugee from the extremes, became manifest, newspaper columns gushed fountains of purple prose about the "Normal Man of Fillmore."

At Nebraska State University, Professor Roderick Klingmeister noticed that many members of his biology class were wearing extra-large buttons decorated with pictures of George Abnego. "Before beginning my lecture," he chuckled, "I would like to tell you that this 'normal man' of yours is no Messiah. All he is, I am afraid, is a bell-shaped curve with ambitions, the median made flesh—"

He got no further. He was brained with his own demonstration microscope.

Even that early, a few watchful politicians noticed that no one was punished for this hasty act.

The incident could be related to many others which followed: the unfortunate and unknown citizen of Duluth, for example, who—at the high point of that city's *Welcome Average Old Abnego* parade—was heard to remark in good-natured amazement, "Why, he's just an ordinary jerk like you and me," and was immediately torn into celebratory confetti by horrified neighbors in the crowd.

Developments such as these received careful consideration

from men whose power was derived from the just, if well-directed, consent of the governed.

George Abnego, these gentry concluded, represented the maturation of a great national myth which, implicit in the culture for over a century, had been brought to garish fulfillment by the mass communication and entertainment media.

This was the myth that began with the juvenile appeal to be "A Normal Red-Blooded American Boy" and ended, on the highest political levels, with a shirt-sleeved, suspendered seeker after political office boasting. "Shucks, everybody knows who I am. I'm folks—just plain folks."

This was the myth from which were derived such superficially disparate practices as the rite of political baby-kissing, the cult of "keeping up with the Joneses," the foppish, foolish, forever-changing fads which went through the population with the monotonous regularity and sweep of a windshield wiper. The myth of styles and fraternal organizations. The myth of the "regular fellow."

There was a presidential election that year.

Since all that remained of the United States was the Middle West, the Democratic Party had disappeared. Its remnants had been absorbed by a group calling itself the Old Guard Republicans, the closest thing to an American Left. The party in power—the Conservative Republicans—so far right as to verge upon royalism, had acquired enough pledged theocratic votes to make them smug about the election.

Desperately, the Old Guard Republicans searched for a candidate. Having regretfully passed over the adolescent epileptic recently elected to the governorship of South Dakota in violation of the state constitution—and deciding against the psalm-singing grandmother from Oklahoma who punctuated her senatorial speeches with religious music upon the banjo—the party strategists arrived, one summer afternoon, in Fillmore, Wisconsin.

From the moment that Abnego was persuaded to accept the nomination and his last well-intentioned but flimsy objection was overcome (the fact that he was a registered member of

the opposition party) it was obvious that the tide of battle had
turned, that the fabled grass roots had caught fire.

Abnego ran for president on the slogan "Back to Normal
with the Normal Man!"

By the time the Conservative Republicans met in convention assembled, the danger of loss by landslide was already
apparent. They changed their tactics, tried to meet the attack
head-on and imaginatively.

They nominated a hunchback for the presidency. This man
suffered from the additional disability of being a distinguished
professor of law in a leading university; he had married with
no issue- and divorced with much publicity; and finally, he
had once admitted to a congressional investigating committee
that he had written and published surrealist poetry. Posters
depicting him leering horribly, his hump twice life-size, were
smeared across the country over the slogan: "An Abnormal
Man for an Abnormal World!"

Despite this brilliant political stroke, the issue was never in
doubt. On Election Day, the nostalgic slogan defeated its
medicative adversary by three to one. Four years later, with
the same opponents, it had risen to five and a half to one.
And there was no organized opposition when Abnego ran for
a third term. . . .

Not that he had crushed it. There was more casual liberty
of political thought allowed during Abnego's administrations
than in many previous ones. But less political thinking and
debating were done.

Whenever possible, Abnego avoided decision. When a
decision was unavoidable, he made it entirely on the basis of
precedent. He rarely spoke on a topic of current interest and
never committed himself. He was garrulous and an exhibi-
tionist only about his family.

"How can you lampoon a vacuum?" This had been the
wail of many opposition newspaper writers and cartoonists
during the early years of the Abnegite Revolution, when men
still ran against Abnego at election time. They tried to draw
him into ridiculous statements or admissions time and again
without success. Abnego was simply incapable of saying

anything that any major cross-section of the population would consider ridiculous.

Emergencies? "Well," Abnego had said, in the story every schoolchild knew, "I've noticed even the biggest forest fire will burn itself out. Main thing is not to get excited."

He made them lie down in low-blood-pressure areas. And, after years of building and destruction, of stimulation and conflict, of accelerating anxieties and torments, they rested and were humbly grateful.

It seemed to many, from the day Abnego was sworn in, that chaos began to waver and everywhere a glorious, welcome stability flowered. In some respects, such as the decrease in the number of monstrous births, processes were under way which had nothing at all to do with the Normal Man of Fillmore; in others—the astonished announcement by lexicographers, for example, that slang expressions peculiar to teen-agers in Abnego's first term were used by their children in exactly the same contexts eighteen years later in his fifth administration—the historical leveling-out and patting-down effects of the Abnegite trowel were obvious.

The verbal expression of this great calm was the Abnegism.

History's earliest record of these deftly phrased inadequacies relates to the administration in which Abnego, at last feeling secure enough to do so, appointed a cabinet without any regard to the wishes of his party hierarchy. A journalist, attempting to point up the absolute lack of color in the new official family, asked if any one of them—from Secretary of State to Postmaster-General—had ever committed himself publicly on any issue or, in previous positions, had been responsible for a single constructive step in any direction.

To which the President supposedly replied with a bland, unhesitating smile, "I always say there's no hard feelings if no one's defeated. Well, sir, no one's defeated in a fight where the referee can't make a decision."

Apocryphal though it may have been, this remark expressed the mood of Abnegite America perfectly. "As pleasant as a no-decision bout" became part of everyday language. Certainly as apocryphal as the George Washington cherry-tree legend, but the most definite Abnegism of them all was the one attributed to the President after a performance of *Romeo and Juliet*. "It is better not to have loved at all, than to have loved and lost," he is reported to have remarked at the morbid end of the play.

At the inception of Abnego's sixth term—the first in which his oldest son served with him as Vice-President—a group of Europeans reopened trade with the United States by arriving in a cargo ship assembled from the salvaged parts of three sunken destroyers and one capsized aircraft carrier.

Received everywhere with undemonstrative cordiality, they traveled the country, amazed at the placidity—the almost total absence of political and military excitement on the one hand, and the rapid technological retrogression on the other. One of the emissaries sufficiently mislaid his diplomatic caution to comment before he left:

"We came to America, to these cathedrals of industrialism, in the hope that we would find solutions to many vexing problems of applied science. These problems—the development of atomic power for factory use, the application of nuclear fission to such small arms as pistols and hand grenades—stand in the way of our postwar recovery. But you, in what remains of the United States of America, don't even see what we, in what remains of Europe, consider so complex and pressing. Excuse me, but what you have here is a national trance!"

His American hosts were not offended: they received his expostulations with polite smiles and shrugs. The delegate returned to tell his countrymen that the Americans, always notorious for their madness, had finally specialized in cretinism.

But another delegate who had observed widely and asked many searching questions went back to his native Toulouse (French culture had once more coagulated in Provence) to define the philosophical foundations of the Abnegite Revolution.

In a book which was read by the world with enormous interest, Michel Gaston Fouffnique, sometime Professor of History at the Sorbonne, pointed out that while twentieth-century man had escaped from the narrow Greek formulations sufficiently to visualize a non-Aristotelian logic and a non-Euclidean geometry, he had not yet had the intellectual temerity to create a non-Platonic system of politics. Not until Abnego.

"Since the time of Socrates," wrote Monsieur Fouffnique, "Man's political viewpoints have been in thrall to the conception that the best should govern. How to determine that 'best,' the scale of values to be used in order that the 'best' and not mere undifferentiated 'betters' should rule—these have been the basic issues around which have raged the fires of political controversy for almost three millennia. Whether an aristocracy of birth or intellect should prevail is an argument over values; whether rulers should be determined by the will of a god as determined by the entrails of a hog, or selected by the whole people on the basis of a ballot tally—these are alternatives in method. But hitherto no political system has ventured away from the implicit and unexamined assumption first embodied in the philosopher-state of Plato's *Republic*.

"Now, at last, America has turned and questioned the pragmatic validity of the axiom. The young democracy to the West, which introduced the concept of the Rights of Man to jurisprudence, now gives a feverish world the Doctrine of the Lowest Common Denominator in government. According to this doctrine as I have come to understand it through prolonged observation, it is *not* the worst who should govern—as many of my prejudiced fellow-delegates insist—but the mean: what might be termed the 'unbest' or the 'non-elite.' "

Situated amid the still-radioactive rubbish of modern war, the people of Europe listened devoutly to readings from Fouffnique's monograph. They were enthralled by the peaceful monotonies said to exist in the United States and bored by the academician's reasons thereto: that a governing group who knew to begin with that they were "unbest" would be free of the myriad jealousies and conflicts arising from the need to prove individual superiority, and that such a group would tend to smooth any major quarrel very rapidly because of the dangerous opportunities created for imaginative and resourceful people by conditions of struggle and strain.

There were oligarchs here and bosses there; in one nation an ancient religious order still held sway, in another, calculating and brilliant men continued to lead the people. But the word was preached. Shamans appeared in the population, ordinary-looking folk who were called "abnegos." Tyrants found it impossible to destroy these shamans, since they were not chosen for any special abilities but simply because they represented the median of a given group: the middle of any population grouping, it was found, lasts as long as the group itself. Therefore, through bloodshed and much time, the abnegos spread their philosophy and flourished.

Oliver Abnego, who became the first President of the World, was President Abnego VI of the United States of America. His son presided—as Vice-President—over a Senate composed mostly of his uncles and his cousins and his aunts. They and their numerous offspring lived in an economy which had deteriorated very, very slightly from the conditions experienced by the founder of their line.

As world president, Oliver Abnego approved only one measure—that granting preferential university scholarships to students whose grades were closest to their age-group median all over the planet. The President could hardly have been accused of originality and innovation unbecoming to his high office, however, since for some time now all reward systems— scholastic, athletic, and even industrial—had been adjusted to recognition of the most average achievement while castigating equally the highest and lowest scores.

When the usable oil gave out shortly afterwards, men turned with perfect calmness to coal. The last turbines were placed in museums while still in operating condition: the people they served felt their isolated and individual use of electricity was too ostentatious for good abnegism.

Outstanding cultural phenomena of this period were carefully rhymed and exactly metered poems addressed to the nondescript beauties and vague charms of a wife or old mother. Had not anthropology disappeared long ago, it would have become a matter of common knowledge that there was a startling tendency to uniformity everywhere in such qualities as bone structure, features and pigmentation, not to mention intelligence, musculature, and personality. Humanity was breeding rapidly and unconsciously in toward its center.

Nonetheless, just before the exhaustion of coal, there was a brief sputter of intellect among a group who established themselves on a site northwest of Cairo. These Nilotics, as they were known, consisted mostly of unreconstructed dissidents expelled by their communities, with a leavening of the mentally ill and the physically handicapped; they had at their peak an immense number of technical gadgets and yellowing books culled from crumbling museums and libraries the world over.

Intensely ignored by their fellowmen, the Nilotics carried on shrill and interminable debates while plowing their muddy fields just enough to keep alive. They concluded that they were the only surviving heirs of *homo sapiens*, the bulk of the world's population now being composed of what they termed *homo abnegus*.

Man's evolutionary success, they concluded, had been due chiefly to his lack of specialization. While other creatures had been forced to standardize to a particular and limited environment, mankind had been free for a tremendous spurt, until ultimately it had struck an environmental factor which demanded the fee of specialization. To avoid war, Man had to specialize in nonentity.

Having come this far in discussion, the Nilotics determined to use the ancient weapons at their disposal to save *homo abnegus* from himself. However, violent disagreements over the methods of re-education to be employed led them to a bloody internecine conflict with those same weapons in the course of which the entire colony was destroyed and its site made untenable for life. About this time, his coal used up, Man re-entered the broad, self-replenishing forests.

The reign of *homo abnegus* endured for a quarter of a million years. It was disputed finally—and successfully—by a group of Newfoundland retrievers who had been marooned

on an island in Hudson Bay when the cargo vessel transporting them to new owners had sunk back in the twentieth
century.

These sturdy and highly intelligent dogs, limited perforce
to each other's growling society for several hundred millennia, learned to talk in much the same manner that mankind's
simian ancestors had learned to walk when a sudden shift in
botany destroyed their ancient arboreal homes—out of boredom. Their wits sharpened further by the hardships of their
bleak island, their imaginations stimulated by the cold, the
articulate retrievers built a most remarkable canine civilization in the Arctic before sweeping southward to enslave and
eventually domesticate humanity.

Domestication took the form of breeding men solely for
their ability to throw sticks and other objects, the retrieving of
which was a sport still popular among the new masters of the
planet, however sedentary certain erudite individuals might
have become.

Highly prized as pets were a group of men with incredibly
thin and long arms; another school of retrievers, however,
favored a stocky breed whose arms were short, but extremely
sinewy; while, occasionally, interesting results were obtained
by inducing rickets for a few generations to produce a pet
whose arms were sufficiently limber as to appear almost
boneless. This last type, while intriguing both esthetically and
scientifically, was generally decried as a sign of decadence in
the owner as well as a functional insult to the animal.

Eventually, of course, the retriever civilization developed
machines which could throw sticks farther, faster, and with
more frequency. Thereupon, except in the most backward
canine communities, Man disappeared.

THE SENTINEL

BY ARTHUR C. CLARKE (1917–   )
TEN STORY FANTASY, SPRING

Arthur C. Clarke continued his high rate of quality productivity in 1951. In addition to the two stories in this volume, he published the now badly dated novel The Sands of Mars, *while a third short story, "If I Forget Thee, Oh Earth"* (Future, *September), narrowly missed being in this book.*

"The Sentinel" was the basis for 2001: A Space Odyssey *(1968), certainly one of the best and most important science fiction films of all time. Directed by Stanley Kubrick and starring Keir Dullea and Gary Lockwood, it was the first sf film to make use of new technology special effects, done for the production by Douglas Trumbull and others. Its psychedelic-like ending was tailor-made for the late 1960s, and the computer character HAL 9000 (voice by Douglas Rain) helped set the tone for media computers in the following decade.*

Ten Story Fantasy was a single-issue magazine published by Avon Periodicals and edited by our own Donald A. Wollheim. The story appeared as "Sentinel of Eternity" in the magazine.

—M.H.G.

I guess it is at this point that I must own up to one of the dark secrets of my life. I am part of the tiny minority who wasn't completely pleased with 2001: A Space Odyssey.

1. I found it too slow on the whole.

2. I was talked into being interviewed on the subject of extra-terrestrial life, with a whole battery of movie cameras trained on me. It was a lot of trouble, but I did it for good old Arthur, because the word was that this was needed to lend credibility and prestige to the picture. Then, when the picture was previewed in New York, I received an invitation (black tie) and I rented a tuxedo so that I could see myself on the screen. —Except that the whole interview was dropped (without our being informed) because the producers got brave and decided to let the picture stand on its own. This combination of taking up half a day of my time after a hard-sell persuasion that it was necessary for a pal; paying me nothing for my trouble and time; and then dropping the thing without the common decency of telling us, is typical of Hollywood manners. I have never forgiven Kubrick, and I have never been caught the same way again.

Two minor points: Another person I knew was invited to be interviewed and wouldn't do it because no pay was involved. I disapproved of this, when I first heard of it, but later on, it seemed to me to make sense. Robert Bloch once, in a moment of cynicism, said to me, ''When you do something, professionally, without charging, the people you do it for think that's what you're worth.'' I have never been able to order my activities from that point of view entirely, but I recognize the validity of that remark.

Secondly, when I showed up at the preview, all uncomfortable in my ill-fitting rented tuxedo, there was a friend of mine (a notable roboticist) in a turtle-neck sweater. How I wished I'd had his daredevil courage.

—I.A.

THE NEXT TIME you see the full Moon high in the south, look carefully at its right-hand edge and let your eye travel upwards along the curve of the disk. Round about two o'clock you will notice a small, dark oval: anyone with normal eyesight can find it quite easily. It is the great walled plain, one of the finest on the Moon, known as the Mare Crisium—the Sea of Crises. Three hundred miles in diameter, and almost completely surrounded by a ring of magnificent mountains, it had never been explored until we entered it in the late summer of 1996.

Our expedition was a large one. We had two heavy freighters which had flown our supplies and equipment from the main lunar base in the Mare Serenitatis, five hundred miles away. There were also three small rockets which were intended for short-range transport over regions which our surface vehicles couldn't cross. Luckily, most of the Mare Crisium is very flat. There are none of the great crevasses so common and so dangerous elsewhere, and very few craters or mountains of any size. As far as we could tell, our powerful caterpillar tractors would have no difficulty in taking us wherever we wished to go.

I was geologist—or selenologist, if you want to be pedantic—in charge of the group exploring the southern region of the Mare. We had crossed a hundred miles of it in a week, skirting the foothills of the mountains along the shore of what was once the ancient sea, some thousand million years before. When life was beginning on Earth, it was already dying here. The waters were retreating down the flanks of those stupendous cliffs, retreating into the empty heart of the Moon. Over the land which we were crossing, the tideless ocean had once been half a mile deep, and now the only trace of moisture was the hoarfrost one could sometimes find in caves which the searing sunlight never penetrated.

We had begun our journey early in the slow lunar dawn, and still had almost a week of Earth-time before nightfall. Half a dozen times a day we would leave our vehicle and go outside in the spacesuits to hunt for interesting minerals, or to place markers for the guidance of future travellers. It was an uneventful routine. There is nothing hazardous or even particularly exciting about lunar exploration. We could live comfortably for a month in our pressurized tractors, and if we ran into trouble we could always radio for help and sit tight until one of the spaceships came to our rescue.

I said just now that there was nothing exciting about lunar exploration, but of course that isn't true. One could never grow tired of those incredible mountains, so much more rugged than the gentle hills of Earth. We never knew, as we rounded the capes and promontories of that vanished sea, what new splendors would be revealed to us. The whole southern curve of the Mare Crisium is a vast delta where a score of rivers once found their way into the ocean, fed perhaps by the torrential rains that must have lashed the mountains in the brief volcanic age when the Moon was young. Each of these ancient valleys was an invitation, challenging us to climb into the unknown uplands beyond. But we had a hundred miles still to cover, and could only look longingly at the heights which others must scale.

We kept Earth-time aboard the tractor, and precisely at 2200 hours the final radio message would be sent out to Base and we would close down for the day. Outside, the rocks would still be burning beneath the almost vertical Sun, but to us it was night until we awoke again eight hours later. Then one of us would prepare breakfast, there would be a great buzzing of electric razors, and someone would switch on the short-wave radio from Earth. Indeed, when the smell of frying sausages began to fill the cabin, it was sometimes hard to believe that we were not back on our own world—everything was so normal and homely, apart from the feeling of decreased weight and the unnatural slowness with which objects fell.

It was my turn to prepare breakfast in the corner of the main cabin that served as a galley. I can remember that moment quite vividly after all these years, for the radio had just played one of my favourite melodies, the old Welsh air, "David of the White Rock." Our driver was already outside in his spacesuit, inspecting our caterpillar treads. My assistant, Louis Garnett, was up forward in the control position, making some belated entries in yesterday's log.

As I stood by the frying pan waiting, like any terrestrial housewife, for the sausages to brown, I let my gaze wander idly over the mountain walls which covered the whole of the southern horizon, marching out of sight to east and west below the curve of the Moon. They seemed only a mile or two from the tractor, but I knew that the nearest was twenty miles away. On the Moon, of course, there is no loss of detail with distance—none of that almost imperceptible haziness which softens and sometimes transfigures all far-off things on Earth.

Those mountains were ten thousand feet high, and they climbed steeply out of the plain as if ages ago some subterranean eruption had smashed them skywards through the molten crust. The base of even the nearest was hidden from sight by the steeply curving surface of the plain, for the Moon is a very little world, and from where I was standing the horizon was only two miles away.

I lifted my eyes towards the peaks which no man had ever climbed, the peaks which, before the coming of terrestrial life, had watched the retreating oceans sink sullenly into their graves, taking with them the hope and the morning promise of a world. The sunlight was beating against those ramparts with a glare that hurt the eyes, yet only a little way above them the stars were shining steadily in a sky blacker than a winter midnight on Earth.

I was turning away when my eye caught a metallic glitter high on the ridge of a great promontory thrusting out into the sea thirty miles to the west. It was a dimensionless point of light, as if a star had been clawed from the sky by one of those cruel peaks, and I imagined that some smooth rock surface was catching the sunlight and heliographing it straight into my eyes. Such things were not uncommon. When the Moon is in her second quarter, observers on Earth can sometimes see the great ranges in the Oceanus Procellarum burning with a blue-white iridescence as the sunlight flashes from their slopes and leaps again from world to world. But I was curious to know what kind of rock could be shining so brightly up there, and I climbed into the observation turret and swung our four-inch telescope round to the west.

I could see just enough to tantalize me. Clear and sharp in the field of vision, the mountain peaks seemed only half a mile away, but whatever was catching the sunlight was still too small to be resolved. Yet it seemed to have an elusive symmetry, and the summit upon which it rested was curiously flat. I stared for a long time at that glittering enigma, straining my eyes into space, until presently a smell of burning from the galley told me that our breakfast sausages had made their quarter-million-mile journey in vain.

All that morning we argued our way across the Mare Crisium while the western mountains reared higher in the sky. Even when we were out prospecting in the spacesuits, the discussion would continue over the radio. It was absolutely certain, my companion argued, that there had never been any form of intelligent life on the Moon. The only living things that had ever existed there were a few primitive plants and their slightly less degenerate ancestors. I know that as well as anyone, but there are times when a scientist must not be afraid to make a fool of himself.

"Listen," I said at last, "I'm going up there, if only for my own peace of mind. That mountain's less than twelve thousand feet high—that's only two thousand under Earth gravity—and I can make the trip in twenty hours at the outside. I've always wanted to go up into those hills, anyway, and this gives me an excellent excuse."

"If you don't break your neck," said Garnett, "you'll be the laughing-stock of the expedition when we get back to Base. That mountain will probably be called Wilson's Folly from now on."

"I won't break my neck," I said firmly. "Who was the first man to climb Pico and Helicon?"

"But weren't you rather younger in those days?" asked Louis gently.

"That," I said with great dignity, "is as good a reason as any for going."

We went to bed early that night, after driving the tractor to within half a mile of the promontory. Garnett was coming with me in the morning; he was a good climber, and had often been with me on such exploits before. Our driver was only too glad to be left in charge of the machine.

At first sight, those cliffs seemed completely unscalable, but to anyone with a good head for heights, climbing is easy on a world where all weights are only a sixth of their normal value. The real danger in lunar mountaineering lies in over-confidence; a six-hundred-foot drop on the Moon can kill you just as thoroughly as a hundred-foot fall on Earth.

We made our first halt on a wide ledge about four thousand feet above the plain. Climbing had not been very difficult, but my limbs were stiff with the unaccustomed effort, and I was glad of the rest. We could still see the tractor as a tiny metal insect far down at the foot of the cliff, and we reported our progress to the driver before starting on the next ascent.

Inside our suits it was comfortably cool, for the refrigeration units were fighting the fierce sun and carrying away the body-heat of our exertions. We seldom spoke to each other, except to pass climbing instructions and to discuss our best plan of ascent. I do not know what Garnett was thinking, probably that this was the craziest goose-chase he had ever embarked upon. I more than half agreed with him, but the joy of climbing, the knowledge that no man had ever gone this way before and the exhilaration of the steadily widening landscape gave me all the reward I needed.

I don't think I was particularly excited when I saw in front of us the wall of rock I had first inspected through the telescope from thirty miles away. It would level off about fifty feet above our heads, and there on the plateau would be the thing that had lured me over these barren wastes. It was, almost certainly, nothing more than a boulder splintered ages ago by a falling meteor, and with its cleavage planes still fresh and bright in this incorruptible, unchanging silence.

There were no hand-holds on the rock face, and we had to use a grapnel. My tired arms seemed to gain new strength as I swung the three-pronged metal anchor round my head and

sent it sailing up towards the stars. The first time it broke
loose and came falling slowly back when we pulled the rope.
On the third attempt, the prongs gripped firmly and our
combined weights could not shift it.

Garnett looked at me anxiously. I could tell that he wanted
to go first, but I smiled back at him through the glass of my
helmet and shook my head. Slowly, taking my time, I began
the final ascent.

Even with my spacesuit, I weighed only forty pounds here,
so I pulled myself up hand over hand without bothering to use
my feet. At the rim I paused and waved to my companion,
then I scrambled over the edge and stood upright, staring
ahead of me.

You must understand that until this very moment I had
been almost completely convinced that there could be nothing
strange or unusual for me to find here. Almost, but not quite;
it was that haunting doubt that had driven me forward. Well,
it was a doubt no longer, but the haunting had scarcely
begun.

I was standing on a plateau perhaps a hundred feet across.
It had once been smooth—too smooth to be natural—but
falling meteors had pitted and scored its surface through
immeasurable eons. It had been levelled to support a glittering, roughly pyramidal structure, twice as high as a man, that
was set in the rock like a gigantic, many-faceted jewel.

Probably no emotion at all filled my mind in those first few
seconds. Then I felt a great lifting of my heart, and a strange,
inexpressible joy. For I loved the Moon, and now I knew that
the creeping moss of Aristarchus and Eratosthenes was not
the only life she had brought forth in her youth. The old,
discredited dream of the first explorers was true. There had,
after all, been a lunar civilization—and I was the first to find
it. That I had come perhaps a hundred million years too late
did not distress me; it was enough to have come at all.

My mind was beginning to function normally, to analyze
and to ask questions. Was this a building, a shrine—or
something for which my language had no name? If a building, then why was it erected in so uniquely inaccessible a

spot? I wondered if it might be a temple, and I could picture the adepts of some strange priesthood calling on their gods to preserve them as the life of the Moon ebbed with the dying oceans, and calling on their gods in vain.

I took a dozen steps forward to examine the thing more closely, but some sense of caution kept me from going too near. I knew a little of archaeology, and tried to guess the cultural level of the civilization that must have smoothed this mountain and raised the glittering mirror surfaces that still dazzled my eyes.

The Egyptians could have done it, I thought, if their workmen had possessed whatever strange materials these far more ancient architects had used. Because of the thing's smallness, it did not occur to me that I might be looking at the handiwork of a race more advanced than my own. The idea that the Moon had possessed intelligence at all was still almost too tremendous to grasp, and my pride would not let me take the final, humiliating plunge.

And then I noticed something that set the scalp crawling at the back of my neck—something so trivial and so innocent that many would never have noticed it at all. I have said that the plateau was scarred by meteors; it was also coated inches-deep with the cosmic dust that is always filtering down upon the surface of any world where there are no winds to disturb it. Yet the dust and the meteor scratches ended quite abruptly in a wide circle enclosing the little pyramid, as though an invisible wall was protecting it from the ravages of time and the slow but ceaseless bombardment from space.

There was someone shouting in my earphones, and I realized that Garnett had been calling me for some time. I walked unsteadily to the edge of the cliff and signaled him to join me, not trusting myself to speak. Then I went back toward that circle in the dust. I picked up a fragment of splintered rock and tossed it gently toward the shining enigma. If the pebble had vanished at that invisible barrier I should not have been surprised, but it seemed to hit a smooth, hemispherical surface and slide gently to the ground.

I knew then that I was looking at nothing that could be

matched in the antiquity of my own race. This was not a building, but a machine, protecting itself with forces that had challenged Eternity. Those forces, whatever they might be, were still operating, and perhaps I had already come too close. I thought of all the radiations man had trapped and tamed in the past century. For all I knew, I might be as irrevocably doomed as if I had stepped into the deadly, silent aura of an unshielded atomic pile.

I remember turning then toward Garnett, who had joined me and was now standing motionless at my side. He seemed quite oblivious to me, so I did not disturb him but walked to the edge of the cliff in an effort to marshal my thoughts. There below me lay the Mare Crisium—Sea of Crises, indeed—strange and weird to most men, but reassuringly familiar to me. I lifted my eyes toward the crescent Earth, lying in her cradle of stars, and I wondered what her clouds had covered when these unknown builders had finished their work. Was it the steaming jungle of the Carboniferous, the bleak shoreline over which the first amphibians must crawl to conquer the land—or, earlier still, the long loneliness before the coming of life?

Do not ask me why I did not guess the truth sooner—the truth that seems so obvious now. In the first excitement of my discovery, I had assumed without question that this crystalline apparition had been built by some race belonging to the Moon's remote past, but suddenly, and with overwhelming force, the belief came to me that it was as alien to the Moon as I myself.

In twenty years we had found no trace of life but a few degenerate plants. No lunar civilization, whatever its doom, could have left but a single token of its existence.

I looked at the shining pyramid again, and the more remote it seemed from anything that had to do with the Moon. And suddenly I felt myself shaking with a foolish, hysterical laughter, brought on by excitement and overexertion: for I had imagined that the little pyramid was speaking to me and was saying: "Sorry, I'm a stranger here myself."

It has taken us twenty years to crack that invisible shield and to reach the machine inside those crystal walls. What we could not understand, we broke at last with the savage might of atomic power and now I have seen the fragments of the lovely, glittering thing I found up there on the mountain.

They are meaningless. The mechanisms—if indeed they are mechanisms—of the pyramid belong to a technology that lies far beyond our horizon, perhaps to the technology of paraphysical forces.

The mystery haunts us all the more now that the other planets have been reached and we know that only Earth has ever been the home of intelligent life in our Universe. Nor could any lost civilization of our own world have built that machine, for the thickness of the meteoric dust on the plateau has enabled us to measure its age. It was set there upon its mountain before life had emerged from the seas of Earth.

When our world was half its present age, *something* from the stars swept through the Solar System, left this token of its passage, and went again upon its way. Until we destroyed it, that machine was still fulfilling the purpose of its builders; and as to that purpose, here is my guess.

Nearly a hundred thousand million stars are turning in the circle of the Milky Way, and long ago other races on the worlds of other suns must have scaled and passed the heights that we have reached. Think of such civilizations, far back in time against the fading afterglow of Creation, masters of a universe so young that life as yet had come only to a handful of worlds. Theirs would have been a loneliness we cannot imagine, the loneliness of gods looking out across infinity and finding none to share their thoughts.

They must have searched the star-clusters as we have searched the planets. Everywhere there would be worlds, but they would be empty or peopled with crawling, mindless things. Such was our Earth, the smoke of the great volcanoes still staining the skies, when that first ship of the peoples of the dawn came sliding in from the abyss beyond Pluto. It passed the frozen outer worlds, knowing that life could play no part in their destinies. It came to rest among the inner planets, warming themselves around the fire of the Sun and waiting for their stories to begin.

Those wanderers must have looked on Earth, circling safely in the narrow zone between fire and ice, and must have guessed that it was the favorite of the Sun's children. Here, in the distant future, would be intelligence; but there were countless stars before them still, and they might never come this way again.

So they left a sentinel, one of millions they have scattered throughout the Universe, watching over all worlds with the promise of life. It was a beacon that down the ages has been patiently signaling the fact that no one had discovered it.

Perhaps you understand now why that crystal pyramid was set upon the Moon instead of on the Earth. Its builders were not concerned with races still struggling up from savagery. They would be interested in our civilization only if we proved our fitness to survive—by crossing space and so escaping from the Earth, our cradle. That is the challenge that all intelligent races must meet, sooner or later. It is a double challenge, for it depends in turn upon the conquest of atomic energy and the last choice between life and death.

Once we had passed that crisis, it was only a matter of time before we found the pyramid and forced it open. Now its signals have ceased, and those whose duty it is will be turning their minds upon Earth. Perhaps they wish to help our infant civilization. But they must be very, very old, and the old are often insanely jealous of the young.

I can never look now at the Milky Way without wondering from which of those banked clouds of stars the emissaries are coming. If you will pardon so commonplace a simile, we have set off the fire-alarm and have nothing to do but to wait.

I do not think we will have to wait for long.

THE FIRE BALLOONS

BY RAY BRADBURY (1920–)
IMAGINATION, APRIL

1951 was another big year for the 31-year-old Bradbury, highlighted by the publication of his third and up to that point best collection, The Illustrated Man. *He also had several other excellent stories in the magazines, including "The Fog Horn."* Imagination *(actually* Imagination: Stories of Science and Fantasy *until the mid 1950s) debuted in 1950 under the editorship of Ray Palmer. It later was edited by William L. Hamling. While most of the stories appearing in its 60-plus issues were pedestrian, it did feature some good short novels and the occasional gem. It died in the fall of 1958.*

"The Fire Balloons" is certainly a gem—a powerful story that addresses the question of whether an alien can have a soul, and if so, what does this mean for mankind?

—M.H.G.

By a curious coincidence, Ray is almost just my age and, like Phil Klass, looks much older. When people ask me the secret of my claim of a youthful appearance, I always say. "A clean life and a good imagination."

This is one of those stories that deals with the religious

27

aspects of the future. How will our traditional religious beliefs stand up against the discovery of alien intelligences?

It has always been my feeling that an intelligent and so-phisticated religion will have no trouble adapting. Such religions have adapted to the view that the Earth is not, after all, the center of the Universe; that the Sun is not, after all, the center of the Universe; that humanity and humanity's place is physically insignificant in the face of a Universe inconceivably larger than had been thought in centuries past.

There are people, of course, who, in the name of religion cling to the outmoded views of the past in a literalistic way, and they *have trouble. One can be sorry for them as long as they don't try to foist their folly on people who have the capacity for thought.*

—*I.A.*

FIRE EXPLODED over summer night lawns. You saw sparkling faces of uncles and aunts. Skyrockets fell up in the brown shining eyes of cousins on the porch, and the cold charred sticks thumped down in dry meadows far away.

The Very Reverend Father Joseph Daniel Peregrine opened his eyes. What a dream: he and his cousins with their fiery play at his grandfather's ancient Ohio home so many years ago!

He lay listening to the great hollow of the church, the other cells where other Fathers lay. Had they, too, on the eve of the flight of the rocket *Crucifix*, lain with memories of the Fourth of July? Yes. This was like those breathless Independence dawns when you waited for the first concussion and rushed out on the dewy sidewalks, your hands full of loud miracles.

So here they were, the Episcopal Fathers, in the breathing dawn before they pinwheeled off to Mars, leaving their incense through the velvet cathedral of space.

"Should we go at all?" whispered Father Peregrine. "Shouldn't we solve our own sins on Earth? Aren't we running from our lives here?"

He arose, his fleshy body, with its rich look of strawberries, milk, and steak, moving heavily.

"Or is it sloth?" he wondered. "Do I dread the journey?"

He stepped into the needle-spray shower.

"But I shall take you to Mars, body." He addressed himself. "Leaving old sins here. And on to Mars to find *new* sins?" A delightful thought, almost. Sins no one had ever thought of. Oh, he himself had written a little book: *The Problem of Sin on Other Worlds*, ignored as somehow not serious enough by his Episcopal brethren.

Only last night, over a final cigar, he and Father Stone had talked of it.

"On Mars sin might appear as virtue. We must guard against virtuous acts there that, later, might be found to be sins!" said Father Peregrine, beaming. "How exciting! It's been centuries since so much adventure has accompanied the prospect of being a missionary!"

"*I* will recognize sin," said Father Stone bluntly, "*even* on Mars."

"Oh, we priests pride ourselves on being litmus paper, changing color in sins presence," retorted Father Peregrine, "but what if Martian chemistry is such we do not color *at all!* If there are new senses on Mars, you must admit the possibility of unrecognizable sin."

"If there is no malice aforethought, there is no sin or punishment for same—the Lord assures us that," Father Stone replied.

"On Earth, yes. But perhaps a Martian sin might inform the subconscious of its evil, telepathically, leaving the conscious mind of man free to act, seemingly without malice! What *then?*"

"What *could* there be in the way of new sins?"

Father Peregrine leaned heavily forward. "Adam *alone* did not sin. Add Eve and you add temptation. Add a second man and you make adultery possible. With the addition of sex or people, you add sin. If men were armless they could not strangle with their hands. You would not have that particular sin of murder. Add arms, and you add the possibility of a

new violence. Amoebas cannot sin because they reproduce by
fission. They do not covet wives or murder each other. Add
sex to amoebas, add arms and legs, and you would have
murder and adultery. Add an arm or leg or person, or take
away each, and you add or subtract possible evil. On Mars,
what if there are five new senses, organs, invisible limbs we
can't conceive of—then mightn't there be five *new sins*?"

Father Stone gasped. "I think you *enjoy* this sort of thing!"

"I keep my mind alive, Father; just alive, is all."

"Your mind's always juggling, isn't it?—mirrors, torches,
plates."

"Yes. Because sometimes the Church seems like those
posed circus tableaus where the curtain lifts and men, white,
zinc-oxide, talcum-powder statues, freeze to represent ab-
stract Beauty. Very wonderful. But I hope there will always
be room for me to dart about among the statues, don't you,
Father Stone?"

Father Stone had moved away. "I think we'd better go to
bed. In a few hours we'll be jumping up to see your *new* sins,
Father Peregrine."

The rocket stood ready for the firing.

The Fathers walked from their devotions in the chilly
morning, many a fine priest from New York or Chicago or
Los Angeles—the Church was sending its best—walking across
town to the frosty field. Walking, Father Peregrine remembered the Bishop's words:

"Father Peregrine, you will captain the missionaries, with
Father Stone at your side. Having chosen you for this serious
task, I find my reasons deplorably obscure, Father, but your
pamphlet on planetary sin did not go unread. You are a
flexible man. And Mars is like that uncleaned closet we have
neglected for millennia. Sin has collected there like bric-a-
brac. Mars is twice Earth's age and has had double the
number of Saturday nights, liquor baths, and eye-poppings at
women as naked as white seals. When we open that closet
door, things will fall on us. We need a quick, flexible man—
one whose mind can dodge. Anyone a little too dogmatic

might break in two. I feel you'll be resilient. Father, the job is yours."

The Bishop and the Fathers knelt.

The blessing was said and the rocket given a little shower of holy water. Arising, the Bishop addressed them:

"I know you will go with God, to prepare the Martians for the reception of His Truth. I wish you all a *thoughtful* journey."

They filed past the Bishop, twenty men, robes whispering, to deliver their hands into his kind hands before passing into the cleansed projectile.

"I wonder," said Father Peregrine, at the last moment, "if Mars is hell? Only waiting for our arrival before it bursts into brimstone and fire."

"Lord, be with us," said Father Stone.

The rocket moved.

Coming out of space was like coming out of the most beautiful cathedral they had ever seen. Touching Mars was like touching the ordinary pavement outside the church five minutes after having *really* known your love for God.

The Fathers stepped gingerly from the steaming rocket and knelt upon Martian sand while Father Peregrine gave thanks.

"Lord, we thank Thee for the journey through Thy rooms. And, Lord, we have reached a new land, so we must have new eyes. We shall hear new sounds and must needs have new ears. And there will be new sins, for which we ask the gift of better and firmer and purer hearts. Amen."

They arose.

And here was Mars like a sea under which they trudged in the guise of submarine biologists, seeking life. Here the territory of hidden sin. Oh, how carefully they must all balance, like gray feathers, in this new element, afraid that walking *itself* might be sinful; or breathing, or simple fasting!

And here was the mayor of First Town come to meet them with outstretched hand. "What can I do for you, Father Peregrine?"

"We'd like to know about the Martians. For only if we know about them can we plan our church intelligently. Are they ten feet tall? We will build large doors. Are their skins blue or red or green? We must know when we put human figures in the stained glass so we may use the right skin color. Are they heavy? We will build sturdy seats for them.''

"Father," said the mayor, "I don't think you should worry about the Martians. There are two races. One of them is pretty well dead. A few are in hiding. And the second race—well, they're not quite human.''

"Oh?" Father Peregrine's heart quickened.

"They're round luminous globes of light, Father, living in those hills. Man or beast, who can say? But they act intelligently, I hear.'' The mayor shrugged. "Of course, they're not men, so I don't think you'll care——''

"On the contrary," said Father Peregrine swiftly. "Intelligent, you say?''

"There's a story. A prospector broke his leg in those hills and would have died there. The blue spheres of light came at him. When he woke, he was down on a highway and didn't know how he got there.''

"Drunk," said Father Stone.

"That's the story," said the mayor. "Father Peregrine, with most of the Martians dead, and only these blue spheres, I frankly think you'd be better off in First City. Mars is opening up. It's a frontier now, like in the old days on Earth, out West, and in Alaska. Men are pouring up here. There's a couple thousand black Irish mechanics and miners and day laborers in First Town who need saving, because there're too many wicked women came with them, and too much ten-century-old Martian win——''

Father Peregrine was gazing into the soft blue hills.

Father Stone cleared his throat. "Well, Father?''

Father Peregrine did not hear. "Spheres of blue *fire*?''

"Yes, Father.''

"Ah," Father Peregrine sighed.

"Blue balloons.'' Father Stone shook his head. "A circus!''

Father Peregrine felt his wrists pounding. He saw the little frontier town with raw, fresh-built sin, and he saw the hills, old with the oldest and yet perhaps an even newer (to him) sin.

"Mayor, could your black Irish laborers cook one more day in hellfire?"

"I'd turn and baste them for you, Father."

Father Peregrine nodded to the hills. "Then that's where we'll go."

There was a murmur from everyone.

"It would be so simple," explained Father Peregrine, "to go into town. I prefer to think that if the Lord walked here and people said, 'Here is the beaten path,' He would reply, 'Show me the weeds. I will *make* a path.' "

"But——"

"Father Stone, think how it would weigh upon us if we passed sinners by and did not extend our hands."

"But globes of fire!"

"I imagine man looked funny to other animals when we first appeared. Yet he has a soul, for all his homeliness. Until we prove otherwise, let us assume that these fiery spheres have souls."

"All right," agreed the mayor, "but you'll be back to town."

"We'll see. First, some breakfast. Then you and I, Father Stone, will walk alone into the hills. I don't want to frighten those fiery Martians with machines or crowds. Shall we have breakfast?"

The Fathers ate in silence.

At nightfall Father Peregrine and Father Stone were high in the hills. They stopped and sat upon a rock to enjoy a moment of relaxation and waiting. The Martians had not as yet appeared and they both felt vaguely disappointed.

"I wonder——" Father Peregrine mopped his face. "Do you think if we called 'hello!' they might answer?"

"Father Peregrine, won't you ever be serious?"

"Not until the good Lord is. Oh, don't look so terribly shocked, please. The Lord is not serious. In fact, it is a little hard to know just what else He is except loving. And love has to do with humor, doesn't it? For you cannot love someone unless you put up with him, can you? And you cannot put up with someone constantly unless you can laugh at him. Isn't that true? And certainly we are ridiculous little animals wallowing in the fudge bowl, and God must love us all the more because we appeal to His humor."

"*I* never thought of God as humorous," said Father Stone.

"The Creator of the platypus, the camel, the ostrich, and man? Oh, come now!" Father Peregrine laughed.

But at this instant, from among the twilight hills, like a series of blue lamps lit to guide their way, came the Martians.

Father Stone saw them first. "Look!"

Father Peregrine turned and the laughter stopped in his mouth.

The round blue globes of fire hovered among the twinkling stars, distantly trembling.

"Monsters!" Father Stone leaped up. But Father Peregrine caught him. "Wait!"

"We should've gone to town!"

"No, listen, look!" pleaded Father Peregrine.

"I'm afraid!"

"Don't be. This is God's work!"

"The devil's!"

"No, now, quiet!" Father Peregrine gentled him and they crouched with the soft blue light on their upturned faces as the fiery orbs drew near.

And again, Independence Night, thought Father Peregrine, tremoring. He felt like a child back in those July Fourth evenings, the sky blowing apart, breaking into powdery stars and burning sound, the concussions jingling house windows like the ice on a thousand thin ponds. The aunts, uncles, cousins crying, "Ah!" as to some celestial physician. The summer sky colors. And the Fire Balloons, lit by an indulgent grandfather, steadied in his massively tender hands. Oh, the memory of those lovely Fire Balloons, softly lighted, warmly billowed bits of tissue, like insect wings, lying like folded wasps in boxes and, last of all, after the day of riot and fury, at long last from their boxes, delicately unfolded, blue, red, white, patriotic—the Fire Balloons! He saw the dim faces of dear relatives long dead and mantled with moss as Grandfather lit the tiny candle and let the warm air breathe up to form the balloon plumply luminous in his hands, a shining vision which they held, reluctant to let it go; for, once released, it was yet another year gone from life, another Fourth, another bit of Beauty vanished. And then up, up, still up through the warm summer night constellations, the Fire Balloons had drifted, while red-white-and-blue eyes followed them, wordless, from family porches. Away into deep Illinois country, over night rivers and sleeping mansions the Fire Balloons dwindled, forever gone. . . .

Father Peregrine felt tears in his eyes. Above him the Martians, not one but a *thousand* whispering Fire Balloons, it seemed, hovered. Any moment he might find his long-dead and blessed grandfather at his elbow, staring up at Beauty.

But it was Father Stone.

"Let's go, please, Father!"

"I must speak to them." Father Peregrine rustled forward, not knowing what to say, for what had he ever said to the Fire Balloons of time past except with his mind: *you are beautiful, you are beautiful,* and that was not enough now. He could only lift his heavy arms and call upward, as he had often wished to call after the enchanted Fire Balloons, "Hello!"

But the fiery spheres only burned like images in a dark mirror. They seemed fixed, gaseous, miraculous, forever.

"We come with God," said Father Peregrine to the sky.

"Silly, silly, silly." Father Stone chewed the back of his hand. "In the name of God, Father Peregrine, stop!"

But now the phosphorescent spheres blew away into the hills. In a moment they were gone.

Father Peregrine called again, and the echo of his last cry shook the hills above. Turning, he saw an avalanche shake out dust, pause, and then, with a thunder of stone wheels, crash down the mountain upon them.

"Look what you've done!" cried Father Stone.

Father Peregrine was almost fascinated, then horrified. He turned, knowing they could run only a few feet before the rocks crushed them into ruins. He had time to whisper, *Oh, Lord!* and the rocks fell!

"Father!"

They were separated like chaff from wheat. There was a blue shimmering of globes, a shift of cold stars, a roar, and then they stood upon a ledge two hundred feet away watching the spot where their bodies should have been buried under tons of stone.

The blue light evaporated.

The two Fathers clutched each other. "What happened?"

"The blue fires lifted us!"

"We ran, *that* was it!"

"No, the globes saved us."

"They couldn't!"

"They *did.*"

The sky was empty. There was a feel as if a great bell had just stopped tolling. Reverberations lingered in their teeth and marrows.

"Let's get away from here. You'll have us killed."

"I haven't feared death for a good many years, Father Stone."

"We've proved nothing. Those blue lights ran off at the first cry. It's useless."

"No." Father Peregrine was suffused with a stubborn wonder. "Somehow, they saved us. That proves they have souls."

"It proves only that they *might* have saved us. Everything was confused. We might have escaped, ourselves."

"They are not animals, Father Stone. Animals do not save lives, especially of strangers. There is mercy and compassion here. Perhaps, tomorrow, we may prove more."

"Prove what? How?" Father Stone was immensely tired now; the outrage to his mind and body showed on his stiff face. "Follow them in helicopters, reading chapter and verse? They're not human. They haven't eyes or ears or bodies like ours."

"But I feel something about them," replied Father Peregrine. "I know a great revelation is at hand. They saved us.

They *think*. They had a choice; let us live or die. That proves free will!''

Father Stone set to work building a fire, glaring at the sticks in his hands, choking on the gray smoke. ''I myself will open a convent for nursling geese, a monastery for sainted swine, and I shall build a miniature apse in a microscope so that paramecium can attend services and tell their beads with their flagella.''

''Oh, Father Stone.''

''I'm sorry.'' Father Stone blinked redly across the fire. ''But this is like blessing a crocodile before he chews you up. You're risking the entire missionary expedition. We belong in First Town, washing liquor from men's throats and perfume off their hands!''

''Can't you recognize the human in the inhuman?''

''I'd much rather recognize the inhuman in the human.''

''But if I prove these things sin, know sin, know a moral life, have free will and intellect, Father Stone?''

''That will take much convincing.''

The night grew rapidly cold and they peered into the fire to find their wildest thoughts, while eating biscuits and berries, and soon they were bundled for sleep under the chiming stars. And just before turning over one last time Father Stone, who had been thinking for many minutes to find something to bother Father Peregrine about, stared into the soft pink charcoal bed and said, ''No Adam and Eve on Mars. No Original Sin. Maybe the Martians live in a state of God's grace. Then we can go back down to town and start work on the Earthmen.''

Father Peregrine reminded himself to say a little prayer for Father Stone, who got so mad and who was now being vindictive, God help him. ''Yes, Father Stone, but the Martians killed some of our settlers. That's sinful. There must have been an Original Sin and a Martian Adam and Eve. We'll find them. Men are men, unfortunately, no matter what their shape, and inclined to sin.''

But Father Stone was pretending sleep.

* * *

Father Peregrine did not shut his eyes.

Of course they couldn't let these Martians go to hell, could they? With a compromise to their consciences, could they go back to the new colonial towns, those towns so full of sinful gullets and women with scintilla eyes and white oyster bodies rollicking in beds with lonely laborers? Wasn't that the place for the Fathers? Wasn't this trek into the hills merely a personal whim? Was he really thinking of God's Church, or was he quenching the thirst of a spongelike curiosity? Those blue round globes of St. Anthony's fire—how they burned in his mind! What a challenge, to find the man behind the mask, the human behind the inhuman. Wouldn't he be proud if he could say, even to his secret self, that he had converted a rolling huge pool table full of fiery spheres! What a sin of pride! Worth doing penance for! But then one did many prideful things out of Love, and he loved the Lord so much and was so happy at it that he wanted everyone else to be happy too.

The last thing he saw before sleep was the return of the blue fires, like a flight of burning angels silently singing him to his worried rest.

The blue round dreams were still there in the sky when Father Peregrine awoke in the early morning.

Father Stone slept like a stiff bundle, quietly. Father Peregrine watched the Martians floating and watching him. They were human—he *knew* it. But he must prove it or face a dry-mouthed, dry-eyed Bishop telling him kindly to step aside.

But how to prove humanity if they hid in the high vaults of the sky? How to bring them nearer and provide answers to the many questions?

"They saved us from the avalanche."

Father Peregrine arose, moved off among the rocks, and began to climb the nearest hill until he came to a place where a cliff dropped sheerly to a floor two hundred feet below. He was choking from his vigorous climb in the frosty air. He stood, getting his breath.

"If I fall from here, it would surely kill me."

He let a pebble drop. Moments later it clicked on the rocks below.

"The Lord would never forgive me."

He tossed another pebble.

"It wouldn't be suicide, would it, if I did it out of Love . . .?"

He lifted his gaze to the blue spheres. "But first, another try." He called to them: "Hello, hello!"

The echoes tumbled upon each other, but the blue fires did not blink or move.

He talked to them for five minutes. When he stopped, he peered down and saw Father Stone, still indignantly asleep, below in the little camp.

"I must prove everything." Father Peregrine stepped to the cliff rim. "I am an old man. I am not afraid. Surely the Lord will understand that I am doing this for Him?"

He drew a deep breath. All his life swam through his eyes and he thought, In a moment shall I die? I am afraid that I love living much too much. But I love other things more.

And, thinking thus, he stepped off the cliff.

He fell.

"Fool!" he cried. He tumbled end over end. "You were wrong!" The rocks rushed up at him and he saw himself dashed on them and sent to glory. "Why did I do this thing?" But he knew the answer, and an instant later was calm as he fell. The wind roared around him and the rocks hurtled to meet him.

And then there was a shift of stars, a glimmering of blue light, and he felt himself surrounded by blueness and suspended. A moment later he was deposited, with a gentle bump, upon the rocks, where he sat a full moment, alive, and touching himself, and looking up at those blue lights that had withdrawn instantly.

"You saved me!" he whispered. "You wouldn't let me die. You knew it was wrong."

He rushed over to Father Stone, who still lay quietly

asleep. "Father, Father, wake up!" He shook him and brought him round. "Father, they saved me!"

"Who saved you?" Father Stone blinked and sat up.

Father Peregrine related his experience.

"A dream, a nightmare; go back to sleep," said Father Stone irritably. "You and your circus balloons."

"But I was awake!"

"Now, now, Father, calm yourself. There now."

"You don't believe me? Have you a gun? Yes, there, let me have it."

"What are you going to do?" Father Stone handed over the small pistol they had brought along for protection against snakes or other similar and unpredictable animals.

Father Peregrine seized the pistol. "I'll prove it!"

He pointed the pistol at his own hand and fired.

"Stop!"

There was a shimmer of light, and before their eyes the bullet stood upon the air, poised an inch from his open palm. It hung for a moment, surrounded by a blue phosphorescence. Then it fell, hissing, into the dust.

Father Peregrine fired the gun three times—at his hand, at his leg, at his body. The three bullets hovered, glittering, and, like dead insects, fell at their feet.

"You see?" said Father Peregrine, letting his arm fall, and allowing the pistol to drop after the bullets. "They know. They understand. They are not animals. They think and judge and live in a moral climate. What animal would save me from myself like this? There is no animal would do that. Only another man, Father. Now, do you believe?"

Father Stone was watching the sky and the blue lights, and now, silently, he dropped to one knee and picked up the warm bullets and cupped them in his hand. He closed his hand tight.

The sun was rising behind them.

"I think we had better go down to the others and tell them of this and bring them back up here," said Father Peregrine.

By the time the sun was up, they were well on their way back to the rocket.

*   *   *

Father Peregrine drew the round circle in the center of the blackboard.

"This is Christ, the son of the Father."

He pretended not to hear the other Fathers' sharp intake of breath.

"This is Christ, in all His Glory," he continued.

"It looks like a geometry problem," observed Father Stone.

"A fortunate comparison, for we deal with symbols here. Christ is no less Christ, you must admit, in being represented by a circle or a square. For centuries the cross has symbolized his love and agony. So this circle will be the Martian Christ. This is how we shall bring Him to Mars."

The Fathers stirred fretfully and looked at each other.

"You, Brother Mathias, will create, in glass, a replica of this circle, a globe, filled with bright fire. It will stand upon the altar."

"A cheap magic trick," muttered Father Stone.

Father Peregrine went on patiently: "On the contrary. We are giving them God in an understandable image. If Christ had come to us on Earth as an octopus, would we have accepted him readily?" He spread his hands. "Was it then a cheap magic trick of the Lord's to bring us Christ through Jesus, in man's shape? After we bless the church we build here and sanctify its altar and this symbol, do you think Christ would refuse to inhabit the shape before us? You know in your hearts He would not refuse."

"But the body of a soulless animal!" said Brother Mathias.

"We've already gone over that, many times since we returned this morning, Brother Mathias. These creatures saved us from the avalanche. They realized that self-destruction was sinful, and prevented it, time after time. Therefore we must build a church in the hills, live with them, to find their own special ways of sinning, the alien ways, and help them to discover God."

The Fathers did not seem pleased at the prospect.

"Is it because they are so odd to the eye?" wondered Father Peregrine. "But what is a shape? Only a cup for the blazing soul that God provides us all. If tomorrow I found that sea lions suddenly possessed free will, intellect, knew when not to sin, knew what life was and tempered justice with mercy and life with love, then I would build an undersea cathedral. And if the sparrows should, miraculously, with God's will, gain everlasting souls tomorrow, I would freight a church with helium and take after them, for all souls, in any shape, if they have free will and are aware of their sins, will burn in hell unless given their rightful communions. I would not let a Martian sphere burn in hell, either, for it is a sphere only in mine eyes. When I close my eyes it stands before me, an intelligence, a love, a soul—and I must not deny it.''

"But that glass globe you wish placed on the altar," protested Father Stone.

"Consider the Chinese," replied Father Peregrine imperturbably. "What sort of Christ do Christian Chinese worship? An oriental Christ, naturally. You've all seen oriental Nativity scenes. How is Christ dressed? In Eastern robes. Where does He walk? In Chinese settings of bamboo and misty mountain and crooked tree. His eyelids taper, his cheekbones rise. Each country, each race adds something to Our Lord. I am reminded of the Virgin of Guadalupe, to whom all Mexico pays its love. Her skin? Have you noticed the paintings of her? A dark skin, like that of her worshipers. Is this blasphemy? Not at all. It is not logical that men should accept a God, no matter how real, of another color. I often wonder why our missionaries do well in Africa, with a snow-white Christ. Perhaps because white is a sacred color, in albino, or any other form, to the African tribes. Given time, mightn't Christ darken there too? The form does not matter. Content is everything. We cannot expect these Martians to accept an alien form. We shall give them Christ in their own image."

"There's a flaw in your reasoning, Father," said Father Stone. "Won't the Martians suspect us of hypocrisy? They will realize that *we* don't worship a round, globular Christ, but a man with limbs and a head. How do we explain the difference?"

"By showing there is none. Christ will fill any vessel that

is offered. Bodies or globes, he is there, and each will worship the same thing in a different guise. What is more, we must *believe* in this globe we give the Martians. We must believe in a shape which is meaningless to us as to form. This spheroid *will* be Christ. And we must remember that we ourselves, and the shape of our Earth Christ, would be meaningless, ridiculous, a squander of material to these Martians.''

Father Peregrine laid aside his chalk. "Now let us go into the hills and build our church."

The Fathers began to pack their equipment.

The church was not a church but an area cleared of rocks, a plateau on one of the low mountains, its soil smoothed and brushed, and an altar established whereon Brother Mathias placed the fiery globe he had constructed.

At the end of six days of work the "church" was ready.

"What shall we do with this?" Father Stone tapped an iron bell they had brought along. "What does a bell mean to *them?*"

"I imagine I brought it for our own comfort," admitted Father Peregrine. "We need a few familiarities. This church seems so little like a church. And we feel somewhat absurd here—even I; for it is something new, this business of converting the creatures of another world. I feel like a ridiculous play actor at times. And then I pray to God to lend me strength."

"Many of the Fathers are unhappy. Some of them joke about all this, Father Peregrine."

"I know. We'll put this bell in a small tower for their comfort, anyway."

"What about the organ?"

"We'll play it at the first service, tomorrow."

"But, the Martians——"

"I know. But again, I suppose, for our own comfort, our own music. Later we may discover theirs."

They arose very early on Sunday morning and moved through the coldness like pale phantoms, rime tinkling on their habits; covered with chimes they were, shaking down showers of silver water.

"I wonder if it *is* Sunday here on Mars?" mused Father Peregrine, but seeing Father Stone wince, he hastened on, "It might be Tuesday or Thursday—who knows? But no matter. My idle fancy. It's Sunday to *us*. Come."

The Fathers walked into the flat wide area of the "church" and knelt, shivering and blue-lipped.

Father Peregrine said a little prayer and put his cold fingers to the organ keys. The music went up like a flight of pretty birds. He touched the keys like a man moving his hands among the weeds of a wild garden, startling up great soarings of beauty into the hills.

The music calmed the air. It smelled the fresh smell of morning. The music drifted into the mountains and shook down mineral powders in a dusty rain.

The Fathers waited.

"Well, Father Peregrine." Father Stone eyed the empty sky where the sun was rising, furnace-red. "I don't see our friends."

"Let me try again." Father Peregrine was perspiring.

He built an architecture of Bach, stone by exquisite stone, raising a music cathedral so vast that its furthest chancels were in Nineveh, its furthest dome at St. Peter's left hand. The music stayed and did not crash in ruin when it was over, but partook of a series of white clouds and was carried away among other lands.

The sky was still empty.

"They'll come!" But Father Peregrine felt the panic in his chest, very small, growing. "Let us pray. Let us ask them to come. They read minds; they *know*."

The Fathers lowered themselves yet again, in rustlings and whispers. They prayed.

And to the East, out of the icy mountains of seven o'clock on Sunday morning or perhaps Thursday morning or maybe Monday morning on Mars, came the soft fiery globes.

They hovered and sank and filled the area around the shivering priests. "Thank you; oh, thank you, Lord." Father

Peregrine shut his eyes tight and played the music, and when it was done he turned and gazed upon his wondrous congregation.

And a voice touched his mind, and the voice said:

"We have come for a little while."

"You may stay," said Father Peregrine.

"For a little while only," said the voice quietly. "We have come to tell you certain things. We should have spoken sooner. But we had hoped that you might go on your way if left alone."

Father Peregrine started to speak, but the voice hushed him.

"We are the Old Ones," the voice said, and it entered him like a blue gaseous flare and burned in the chambers of his head. "We are the old Martians, who left our marble cities and went into the hills, forsaking the material life we had lived. So very long ago we became these things that we now are. Once we were men, with bodies and legs and arms such as yours. The legend has it that one of us, a good man, discovered a way to free man's soul and intellect, to free him of bodily ills and melancholies, of deaths and transfigurations, of ill humors and senilities, and so we took on the look of lightning and blue fire and have lived in the winds and skies and hills forever after that, neither prideful nor arrogant, neither rich nor poor, passionate nor cold. We have lived apart from those we left behind, those other men of this world, and how we came to be has been forgotten, the process lost; but we shall never die, nor do harm. We have put away the sins of the body and live in God's grace. We covet no other property; we have no property. We do not steal, nor kill, nor lust, nor hate. We live in happiness. We cannot reproduce; we do not eat or drink or make war. All the sensualities and childishnesses and sins of the body were stripped away when our bodies were put aside. We have left sin behind, Father Peregrine, and it is burned like the leaves in the autumn, and it is gone like the soiled snow of an evil winter, and it is gone like the sexual flowers of a red-and-yellow spring, and it is gone like the panting nights of hottest summer, and our season is temperate and our clime is rich in thought.''

Father Peregrine was standing now, for the voice touched him at such a pitch that it almost shook him from his senses. It was an ecstasy and a fire washing through him.

''We wish to tell you that we appreciate your building this place for us, but we have no need of it, for each of us is a temple unto himself and needs no place wherein to cleanse himself. Forgive us for not coming to you sooner, but we are separate and apart and have talked to no one for ten thousand years, nor have we interfered in any way with the life of this planet. It has come into your mind now that we are the lilies of the field; we toil not, neither do we spin. You are right. And so we suggest that you take the parts of this temple into your own new cities and there cleanse others. For, rest assured, we are happy and at peace.''

The Fathers were on their knees in the vast blue light, and Father Peregrine was down, too, and they were weeping, and it did not matter that their time had been wasted; it did not matter to them at all.

The blue spheres murmured and began to rise once more, on a breath of cool air.

''May I''—cried Father Peregrine, not daring to ask, eyes closed—''may I come again, someday, that I may learn from you?''

The blue fires blazed. The air trembled.

Yes. Someday he might come again. Someday.

And then the Fire Balloons blew away and were gone, and he was like a child, on his knees, tears streaming from his eyes, crying to himself, ''Come back, come back!'' And at any moment Grandfather might lift him and carry him upstairs to his bedroom in a long-gone Ohio town. . . .

They filed down out of the hills at sunset. Looking back, Father Peregrine saw the blue fires burning. No, he thought, we couldn't build a church for the likes of you. You're Beauty itself. What church could compete with the fireworks of the pure soul?

Father Stone moved in silence beside him. And at last he spoke:

"The way I see it is there's a Truth on every planet. All parts of the Big Truth. On a certain day they'll all fit together like the pieces of jigsaw. This has been a shaking experience. I'll never doubt again, Father Peregrine. For this Truth here is as true as Earth's Truth, and they lie side by side. And we'll go on to other worlds, adding the sum of the parts of the Truth until one day the whole Total will stand before us like the light of a new day."

"That's a lot, coming from you, Father Stone."

"I'm sorry now, in a way, we're going down to the town to handle our own kind. Those blue lights now. When they settled about us, and that *voice* . . ." Father Stone shivered.

Father Peregrine reached out to take the other's arm. They walked together.

"And you know," said Father Stone finally, fixing his eyes on Brother Mathias, who strode ahead with the glass sphere tenderly carried in his arms, that glass sphere with the blue phosphorous light glowing forever inside it, "you know, Father Peregrine, that globe there——"

"Yes?"

"It's Him. It *is* Him, after all."

Father Peregrine smiled, and they walked down out of the hills toward the new town.

THE MARCHING MORONS

BY C. M. KORNBLUTH (1923–58)
GALAXY SCIENCE FICTION, APRIL

*Here is the bitter, funny and tragic Cyril Kornbluth again
with this fascinating and deeply flawed story. It is his most
famous work, has been reprinted at least a dozen times within
the genre, and was chosen by The Science Fiction Writers of
America for inclusion in The Science Fiction Hall of Fame
(1973). I'm not sure it belongs in this book because this
series is dedicated to the best of the past, not the most
famous. The central premise of "The Marching Morons" is
that intelligence is genetically inherited. That the intelligentia
should have lots of children for this reason is at least dubi-
ous. What does the popularity of this story tell us about the
attitudes of the sf community?*

—M.H.G.

My own feeling is that Cyril was venting his personal
spleen against the Universe in this story. He was a child
prodigy, who was always getting in trouble with other children (and with adults, too) because his quick wit and quick
tongue could expose stupidity and wound in so doing. This is
not very uncommon among science fiction writers and many
had unhappy childhoods as a result.

As a matter of fact, I had a certain amount of trouble myself, but I was luckier than most. In the first place, I enjoyed being smart and actually liked the dullards about me because they made me feel so much better about being smart. Second, I quickly learned to make some of my funny remarks at my own expense (I owe that to Jack Benny) and found out that, in those circumstances, I would be forgiven everything else.

Cyril, however, was deeply unhappy at being in a world that was not designed for him, and he never did learn to de-fang his wit. "The Marching Morons" is the way he views humanity and almost anyone with intelligence will find himself sympathizing with Cyril at odd times. Whenever Janet and I encounter some example of overweening stupidity in others that needlessly complicates our lives, we sigh and say, "It's the marching morons," and it helps us survive.

—I.A.

SOME THINGS had not changed. A potter's wheel was still a potter's wheel and clay was still clay. Efim Hawkins had built his shop near Goose Lake, which had a narrow band of good fat clay and a narrow beach of white sand. He fired three bottle-nosed kilns with willow charcoal from the wood lot. The wood lot was also useful for long walks while the kilns were cooling; if he let himself stay within sight of them, he would open them prematurely, impatient to see how some new shape or glaze had come through the fire, and—*ping!* —the new shape or glaze would be good for nothing but the shard pile back of his slip tanks.

A business conference was in full swing in his shop, a modest cube of brick, tile-roofed, as the Chicago-Los Angeles "rocket" thundered overhead–very noisy, very swept back, very fiery jets, shaped as sleekly swift-looking as an airborne barracuda.

The buyer from Marshall Fields was turning over a black-glazed one-liter carafe, nodding approval with his massive, handsome head. "This is real pretty," he told Hawkins and his own secretary, Gomez-Laplace. "This has got lots of what ya call real est'etic principles. Yeah, it is real pretty."

"How much?" the secretary asked the potter.

"Seven-fifty in dozen lots," said Hawkins. "I ran up fifteen dozen last month."

"They are real est'etic," repeated the buyer from Fields. "I will take them all."

"I don't think we can do that, doctor," said the secretary. "They'd cost us $1,350. That would leave only $532 in our quarter's budget. And we still have to run down to East Liverpool to pick up some cheap dinner sets."

"Dinner sets?" asked the buyer, his big face full of wonder.

"Dinner sets. The department's been out of them for two months now. Mr. Garvy-Seabright got pretty nasty about it yesterday. Remember?"

"Garvy-Seabright, that meat-headed bluenose," the buyer said contemptuously. "He don't know nothin' about est'etics. Why for don't he lemme run my own department?" His eye fell on a stray copy of *Whambozambo Comix* and he sat down with it. An occasional deep chuckle or grunt of surprise escaped him as he turned the pages.

Uninterrupted, the potter and the buyer's secretary quickly closed a deal for two dozen of the liter carafes. "I wish we could take more," said the secretary, "but you heard what I told him. We've had to turn away customers for ordinary dinnerware because he shot the last quarter's budget on some Mexican piggy banks some equally enthusiastic importer stuck him with. The fifth floor is packed solid with them."

"I'll bet they look mighty est'etic."

"They're painted with purple cacti."

The potter shuddered and caressed the glaze of the sample carafe.

The buyer looked up and rumbled, "Ain't you dummies through yakkin' yet? What good's a seckertary for if'n he don't take the burden of *de*-tail off'n my back, harh?"

"We're all through, doctor. Are you ready to go?"

The buyer grunted peevishly, dropped *Whambozambo Comix*

on the floor and led the way out of the building and down the log corduroy road to the highway. His car was waiting on the concrete. It was, like all contemporary cars, too low-slung to get over the logs. He climbed down into the car and started the motor with a tremendous sparkle and roar.

"Gomez-Laplace," called out the potter under cover of the noise, "did anything come of the radiation program they were working on the last time I was on duty at the Pole?"

"The same old fallacy," said the secretary gloomily. "It stopped us on mutation, it stopped us on culling, it stopped us on segregation and now it's stopped us on hypnosis."

"Well, I'm scheduled back to the grind in nine days. Time for another firing right now. I've got a new luster to try. . . ."

"I'll miss you. I shall be 'vacationing'—running the drafting room of the New Century Engineering Corporation in Denver. They're going to put up a two-hundred-story office building, and naturally somebody's got to be on hand."

"Naturally," said Hawkins with a sour smile.

There was an ear-piercingly sweet blast as the buyer leaned on the horn button. Also, a yard-tall jet of what looked like flame spurted up from the car's radiator cap; the car's power plant was a gas turbine and had no radiator.

"I'm coming, doctor," said the secretary dispiritedly. He climbed down into the car and it whooshed off with much flame and noise.

The potter, depressed, wandered back up the corduroy road and contemplated his cooling kilns. The rustling wind in the boughs was obscuring the creak and mutter of the shrinking refractory brick. Hawkins wondered about the number two kiln—a reduction fire on a load of lusterware mugs. Had the clay chinking excluded the air? Had it been a properly smoky blaze? Would it do any harm if he just took one close . . .?

Common sense took Hawkins by the scruff of the neck and yanked him over to the tool shed. He got out his pick and resolutely set off on a prospecting jaunt to a hummocky field that might yield some oxides. He was especially low on coppers.

The long walk left him sweating hard, with his lust for a

peek into the kiln quiet in his breast. He swung his pick almost at random into one of the hummocks; it clanged on a stone which he excavated. A largely obliterated inscription said:

ERSITY OF CHIC
OGICAL LABO
ELOVED MEMORY OF
KILLED IN ACT

The potter swore mildly. He had hoped the field would turn out to be a cemetery, preferably a once-fashionable cemetery full of once-massive bronze caskets moldered into oxides of tin and copper.

Well, hell, maybe there were some around anyway.

He headed lackadaisically for the second largest hillock and sliced into it with his pick. There was a stone to undercut and topple into a trench, and then the potter was very glad he'd stuck at it. His nostrils were filled with the bitter smell and the dirt was tinged with the exciting blue of copper salts. The pick went *clang!*

Hawkins, puffing, pried up a stainless steel plate that was quite badly stained and was also marked with incised letters. It seemed to have pulled loose from rotting bronze; there were rivets on the back that brought up flakes of green patina. The potter wiped off the surface dirt with his sleeve, turned it to catch the sunlight obliquely and read:

HONEST JOHN BARLOW

Honest John, famed in university annals, represents a challenge which medical science has not yet answered: revival of a human being accidentally thrown into a state of suspended animation.

In 1988 Mr. Barlow, a leading Evanston real estate dealer, visited his dentist for treatment of an impacted wisdom tooth. His dentist requested and received permission to use the experimental anesthetic Cycloparadimethanol-B-7, developed at the university.

After administration of the anesthetic, the dentist resorted to his drill. By freakish mischance, a short circuit in his machine delivered 220 volts of 60-cycle current into the patient. (In a damage suit instituted by Mrs. Barlow against the dentist, the university and the makers of the drill, a jury found for the defendants.) Mr. Barlow never got up from the dentist's chair and was assumed to have died of poisoning, electrocution or both.

Morticians preparing him for embalming discovered, however, that their subject was—though certainly not living—just as certainly not dead. The university was notified and a series of exhaustive tests was begun, including attempts to duplicate the trance state on volunteers. After a bad run of seven cases which ended fatally, the attempts were abandoned.

Honest John was long an exhibit at the university museum and livened many a football game as mascot of the university's Blue Crushers. The bounds of taste were overstepped, however, when a pledge to Sigma Delta Chi was ordered in '03 to "kidnap" Honest John from his loosely guarded glass museum case and introduce him into the Rachel Swanson Memorial Girls' Gymnasium shower room.

On May 22, 2003, the university board of regents issued the following order: "By unanimous vote, it is directed that the remains of Honest John Barlow be removed from the university museum and conveyed to the university's Lieutenant James Scott III Memorial Biological Laboratories and there be securely locked in a specially prepared vault. It is further directed that all possible measures for the preservation of these remains be taken by the laboratory administration and that access to these remains be denied to all persons except qualified scholars authorized in writing by the board. The board reluctantly takes this action in view of recent notices and photographs in the nation's press which, to say the least, reflect but small credit upon the university.

It was far from his field, but Hawkins understood what had happened—an early and accidental blundering onto the bare bones of the Levantman shock anesthesia, which had since been replaced by other methods. To bring subjects out of Levantman shock, you let them have a squirt of simple saline in the trigeminal nerve. Interesting. And now about that bronze . . .

He heaved the pick into the rotting green salts, expecting

no resistance, and almost fractured his wrist. *Something* down there was *solid*. He began to flake off the oxides.

A half-hour of work brought him down to phosphor bronze, a huge casting of the almost incorruptible metal. It had weakened structurally over the centuries; he could fit the point of his pick under a corroded boss and pry off great creaking and grumbling striae of the stuff.

Hawkins wished he had an archaeologist with him but didn't dream of returning to his shop and calling one to take over the find. He was an all-around man: by choice, and in his free time, an artist in clay and glaze; by necessity, an automotive, electronics and atomic engineer who could also swing a project in traffic control, individual and group psychology, architecture or tool design. He didn't yell for a specialist every time something out of his line came up; there were so few with so much to do. . . .

He trenched around his find, discovering that it was a great brick-shaped bronze mass with an excitingly hollow sound. A long strip of moldering metal from one of the long vertical faces pulled away, exposing red rust that went *whoosh* and was sucked into the interior of the mass.

It had been de-aired, thought Hawkins, and there must have been an inner jacket of glass which had crystallized through the centuries and quietly crumbled at the first clang of his pick. He didn't know what a vacuum would do to a subject of Levantman shock, but he had hopes, nor did he quite understand what a real estate dealer was, but it might have something to do with pottery. And *anything* might have a bearing on Topic Number One.

He flung his pick out of the trench, climbed out and set off at a dogtrot for his shop. A little rummaging turned up a hypo and there was a plastic container of salt in the kitchen.

Back at his dig, he chipped for another half-hour to expose the juncture of lid and body. The hinges were hopeless; he smashed them off.

Hawkins extended the telescopic handle of the pick for the best leverage, fitted its point into a deep pit, set its built-in fulcrum, and heaved. Five more heaves and he could see, inside the vault, what looked like a dusty marble statue. Ten more and he could see that it was the naked body of Honest John Barlow, Evanston real estate dealer, uncorrupted by time.

The potter found the apex of the trigeminal nerve with his needle's point and gave him sixty cubic centimeters.

In an hour Barlow's chest began to pump.

In another hour, he rasped, "Did it work?"

"Did it!" muttered Hawkins.

Barlow opened his eyes and stirred, looked down, turned his hands before his eyes. . . .

"I'll sue!" he screamed. "My clothes! My fingernails!" A horrid suspicion came over his face and he clapped his hands to his hairless scalp. "My hair!" he wailed. "I'll sue you for every penny you've got! That release won't mean a damned thing in court—I didn't sign away my hair and clothes and fingernails!"

"They'll grow back," said Hawkins casually. "Also your epidermis. Those parts of you weren't alive, you know, so they weren't preserved like the rest of you. I'm afraid the clothes are gone, though."

"What is this—the university hospital?" demanded Barlow. "I want a phone. No. You phone. Tell my wife I'm all right and tell Sam Immerman—he's my lawyer—to get over here right away. Greenleaf 7-4022. Ow!" He had tried to sit up, and a portion of his pink skin rubbed against the inner surface of the casket, which was powdered by the ancient crystallized glass. "What the hell did you guys do, boil me alive? Oh, you're going to pay for this!"

"You're all right," said Hawkins, wishing now he had a reference book to clear up several obscure terms. "Your epidermis will start growing immediately. You're not in the hospital. Look here."

He handed Barlow the stainless steel plate that had labeled the casket. After a suspicious glance, the man started to read. Finishing, he laid the plate carefully on the edge of the vault and was silent for a spell.

"Poor Verna," he said at last. "It doesn't say whether she was stuck with the court costs. Do you happen to know . . .?"

"No," said the potter. "All I know is what was on the plate and how to revive you. The dentist accidentally gave you a dose of what we call Levantman shock anesthesia. We haven't used it for centuries; it was powerful, but too dangerous."

"Centuries . . ." brooded the man. "Centuries . . . I'll bet Sam swindled her out of her eyeteeth. Poor Verna. How long ago was it? What year is this?"

Hawkins shrugged. "We call it 7–B–936. That's no help to you. It takes a long time for these metals to oxidize."

"Like that movie," Barlow muttered. "Who would have thought it? Poor Verna!" He blubbered and sniffled, reminding Hawkins powerfully of the fact that he had been found under a flat rock.

Almost angrily, the potter demanded, "How many children did you have?"

"None yet," sniffed Barlow. "My first wife didn't want them. But Verna wants one—wanted one—but we're going to wait until—we *were* going to wait until . . ."

"Of course," said the potter, feeling a savage desire to tell him off, blast him to hell and gone for his work. But he choked it down. There was the problem to think of; there was always the problem to think of, and this poor blubberer might unexpectedly supply a clue. Hawkins would have to pass him on.

"Come along," Hawkins said. "My time is short."

Barlow looked up, outraged. "How can you be so unfeeling? I'm a human being like . . ."

The Los Angeles–Chicago "rocket" thundered overhead and Barlow broke off in mid-complaint. "Beautiful!" he breathed, following it with his eyes. "Beautiful!"

He climbed out of the vault, too interested to be pained by its roughness against his infantile skin. "After all," he said briskly, "this should have its sunny side. I never was much for reading, but this is just like one of those stories. And I ought to make some money out of it, shouldn't I?'' He gave Hawkins a shrewd glance.

"You want money?" asked the potter. "Here." He handed over a fistful of change and bills. "You'd better put my shoes on. It'll be about a quarter-mile. Oh, and you're—uh, modest? —yes, that was the word. Here.'' Hawkins gave him his pants, but Barlow was excitedly counting the money.

"Eighty-five, eighty-six—and it's dollars, too! I thought it'd be credits or whatever they call them. 'E Pluribus Unum' and 'Liberty'—just different faces. Say, is there a catch to this? Are these real, genuine, honest twenty-two-cent dollars like we had or just wallpaper?''

"They're quite all right, I assure you," said the potter. "I wish you'd come along. I'm in a hurry.''

The man babbled as they stumped toward the shop. "Where are we going—the Council of Scientists, the World Coordinator or something like that?''

"Who? Oh, no. We call them 'president' and 'congress.' No, that wouldn't do any good at all. I'm just taking you to see some people.''

"I ought to make plenty out of this. *Plenty!* I could write books. Get some smart young fellow to put it into words for me and I'll bet I could turn out a best-seller. What's the setup on things like that?''

"It's about like that. Smart young fellows. But there aren't any best-sellers anymore. People don't read much nowadays. We'll find something equally profitable for you to do.''

Back in the shop, Hawkins gave Barlow a suit of clothes, deposited him in the waiting room and called Central in Chicago. "Take him away," he pleaded. "I have time for one more firing and he blathers and blathers. I haven't told him anything. Perhaps we should just turn him loose and let him find his own level, but there's a chance . . .''

"The problem," agreed Central. "Yes, there's a chance.''

The potter delighted Barlow by making him a cup of coffee with a cube that not only dissolved in cold water but heated the water to boiling point. Killing time, Hawkins chatted about the "rocket" Barlow had admired and had to haul himself up short; he had almost told the real estate man what its top speed really was—almost, indeed, revealed that it was not a rocket.

He regretted, too, that he had so casually handed Barlow a couple of hundred dollars. The man seemed obsessed with fear that they were worthless since Hawkins refused to take a note or IOU or even a definite promise of repayment. But Hawkins couldn't go into details and was very glad when a stranger arrived from Central.

"Tinny-Peete from Algeciras," the stranger told him swiftly as the two of them met at the door. "Psychist for Poprob. Polassigned special overtake Barlow."

"Thank heaven," said Hawkins. "Barlow," he told the man from the past, "this is Tinny-Peete. He's going to take care of you and help you make lots of money."

The psychist stayed for a cup of the coffee whose preparation had delighted Barlow and then conducted the real estate man down the corduroy road to his car, leaving the potter to speculate on whether he could at last crack his kilns.

Hawkins, abruptly dismissing Barlow and the problem, happily picked the chinking from around the door of the number two kiln, prying it open a trifle. A blast of heat and the heady, smoky scent of the reduction fire delighted him. He peered and saw a corner of a shelf glowing cherry red, becoming obscured by wavering black areas as it lost heat through the opened door. He slipped a charred wood paddle under a mug on the shelf and pulled it out as a sample, the hairs on the back of his hand curling and scorching. The mug crackled and pinged and Hawkins sighed happily.

The bismuth resinate luster had fired to perfection, a haunting film of silvery black metal with strange bluish lights in it as it turned before the eyes, and the problem of population seemed very far away to Hawkins then.

Barlow and Tinny-Peete arrived at the concrete highway where the psychist's car was parked in a safety bay.

"What—a—*boat!*" gasped the man from the past.

"Boat? No, that's my car."

Barlow surveyed it with awe. Swept-back lines, deep-drawn compound curves, kilograms of chrome. He ran his hands over the door—or was it the door?—in a futile search for a handle and asked respectfully, "How fast does it go?"

The psychist gave him a keen look and said slowly, "Two hundred and fifty. You can tell by the speedometer."

"Wow! My old Chevy could hit a hundred on a straight-away, but you're out of my class, mister!"

Tinny-Peete somehow got a huge, low door open and Barlow descended three steps into immense cushions, floundering over to the right. He was too fascinated to pay serious attention to his flayed dermis. The dashboard was a lovely wilderness of dials, plugs, indicators, lights, scales and switches.

The psychist climbed down into the driver's seat and did something with his feet. The motor started like lighting a blowtorch as big as a silo. Wallowing around in the cushions, Barlow saw through a rear-view mirror a tremendous exhaust filled with brilliant white sparkles.

"Do you like it?" yelled the psychist.

"It's terrific!" Barlow yelled back. "It's . . ."

He was shut up as the car pulled out from the bay into the road with a great *voo-ooo-ooom!* A gale roared past Barlow's head, though the windows seemed to be closed; the impression of speed was terrific. He located the speedometer on the dashboard and saw it climb past 90, 100, 150, 200.

"Fast enough for me," yelled the psychist, noting that Barlow's face fell in response. "Radio?"

He passed over a surprisingly light object like a football helmet, with no trailing wires, and pointed to a row of buttons. Barlow put on the helmet, glad to have the roar of air stilled, and pushed a push button. It lit up satisfyingly, and Barlow settled back even farther for a sample of the brave new world's supermodern taste in ingenious entertainment.

"TAKE IT AND STICK IT!" a voice roared in his ears.

He snatched off the helmet and gave the psychist an injured look. Tinny-Peete grinned and turned a dial associated with the push-button layout. The man from the past donned the helmet again and found the voice had lowered to normal.

"The show of shows! The supershow! The super-duper show! The quiz of quizzes! *Take It and Stick It!*"

There were shrieks of laughter in the background.

"Here we got the contes-tants all ready to go. You know how we work it. I hand a contes-tant a triangle-shaped cutout and like that down the line. Now we got these here boards, they got cutout places the same shape as the triangles and things, only they're all different shapes, and the first contestant that sticks the cutouts into the boards, he wins.

"Now I'm gonna innaview the first contes-tant. Right here, honey. What's your name?"

"Name? Uh . . ."

"Hoddaya like that, folks? She don't remember her name! Hah? *Would you buy that for a quarter?*" The question was spoken with arch significance, and the audience shrieked, howled and whistled its appreciation.

It was dull listening when you didn't know the punch lines and catch lines. Barlow pushed another button, with his free hand ready at the volume control.

". . . latest from Washington. It's about Senator Hull-Mendoza. He is still attacking the Bureau of Fisheries. The North California *Syndicalist* says he got affydavits that John Kingsley-Schultz is a bluenose from way back. He didn't publistat the affydavits, but he says they say that Kingsley-Schultz was saw at bluenose meetings in Oregon State College and later at Florida University. Kingsley-Schultz says he gotta confess he did major in fly casting at Oregon and got his Ph.D. in game fish at Florida.

"And here is a quote from Kingsley-Schultz: 'Hull-Mendoza don't know what he's talking about. He should drop dead.' Unquote. Hull-Mendoza says he won't publistat the affydavits to pertect his sources. He says they was sworn by three former employees of the bureau which was fired for incompetence and in-com-pat-ibility by Kingsley-Schultz.

"Elsewhere they was the usual run of traffic accidents. A three-way pileup of cars on Route 66 going outta Chicago took twelve lives. The Chicago–Los Angeles morning rocket crashed and exploded in the Mohave—Mo-javvy—whatever-you-call-it Desert. All the ninety-four people aboard got killed. A Civil Aeronautics Authority investigator on the scene says that the pilot was buzzing herds of sheep and didn't pull out in time.

"Hey! Here's a hot one from New York! A diesel tug run wild in the harbor while the crew was below and shoved in the port bow of the luckshury liner *S. S. Placentia*. It says the ship filled and sank taking the lives of an es-ti-mated one hundred eighty passengers and fifty crew members. Six divers was sent down to study the wreckage, but they died, too, when their suits turned out to be fulla little holes.

"And here is a bulletin I just got from Denver. It seems . . ."

Barlow took off the headset uncomprehendingly. "He seemed so callous," he yelled at the driver. "I was listening to a newscast . . ."

Tinny-Peete shook his head and pointed at his ears. The roar of air was deafening. Barlow frowned baffledly and stared out of the window.

A glowing sign said:

MOOGS!
WOULD YOU BUY IT
FOR A QUARTER?

He didn't know what Moogs was or were; the illustration showed an incredibly proportioned girl, 99.9 percent naked, writhing passionately in animated full color.

The roadside jingle was still with him, but with a new feature. Radar or something spotted the car and alerted the lines of the jingle. Each in turn sped along a roadside track, even with the car, so it could be read before the next line was alerted.

IF THERE'S A GIRL
YOU WANT TO GET
DEFLOCCULIZE
UNROMANTIC SWEAT.
A*R*M*P*I*T*T*O

Another animated job, in two panels, the familiar "before and after." The first said, "Just Any Cigar?" and was illustrated with a two-person domestic tragedy of a wife holding her nose while her coarse and red-faced husband puffed a slimy-looking rope. The second panel glowed, "Or a VUELTA ABAJO?" and was illustrated with . . .

Barlow blushed and looked at his feet until they had passed the sign.

"Coming into Chicago!" bawled Tinny-Peete.

Other cars were showing up, all of them dreamboats.

Watching them, Barlow began to wonder if he knew what a kilometer was, exactly. They seemed to be traveling so slowly, if you ignored the roaring air past your ears and didn't let the speedy lines of the dreamboats fool you. He would have sworn they were really crawling along at twenty-five, with occasional spurts up to thirty. How much was a kilometer, anyway?

The city loomed ahead, and it was just what it ought to be: towering skyscrapers, overhead ramps, landing platforms for helicopters . . .

He clutched at the cushions. Those two copters. They were going to—they were going to—they . . .

He didn't see what happened because their apparent collision courses took them behind a giant building.

Screamingly sweet blasts of sound surrounded them as they stopped for a red light. "What the hell is going on here?" said Barlow in a shrill, frightened voice, because the braking time was just about zero, and he wasn't hurled against the dashboard. "Who's kidding whom?"

"Why, what's the matter?" demanded the driver.

The light changed to green and he started the pickup. Barlow stiffened as he realized that the rush of air past his ears began just a brief, unreal split second before the car was actually moving. He grabbed for the door handle on his side.

The city grew on them slowly: scattered buildings, denser buildings, taller buildings and a red light ahead. The car rolled to a stop in zero braking time, the rush of air cut off an instant after it stopped, and Barlow was out of the car and running frenziedly down a sidewalk one instant after that.

They'll track me down, he thought, panting. *It's a secret police thing. They'll get you—mind-reading machines, television eyes everywhere, afraid you'll tell their slaves about freedom and stuff. They don't let anybody cross them, like that story I once read.*

Winded, he slowed to a walk and congratulated himself that he had guts enough not to turn around. That was what they always watched for. Walking, he was just another business-suited back among hundreds. He would be safe, he would be safe. . . .

A hand gripped his shoulder and words tumbled from a large, coarse, handsome face thrust close to his: "Wassamatta bumpinninna people likeya owna sidewalk gotta miner slamya inna mushya bassar!" It was neither the mad potter nor the mad driver.

"Excuse me," said Barlow. "What did you say?"

"Oh, yeah?" yelled the stranger dangerously and waited for an answer.

Barlow, with the feeling that he had somehow been suckered into the short end of an intricate land-title deal, heard himself reply belligerently, "Yeah!"

The stranger let go of his shoulder and snarled, "Oh, yeah?"

"Yeah!" said Barlow, yanking his jacket back into shape.

"Aaah!" snarled the stranger, with more contempt and disgust than ferocity. He added an obscenity current in Barlow's time, a standard but physiologically impossible directive, and strutted off hulking his shoulders and balling his fists.

Barlow walked on, trembling. Evidently he had handled it well enough. He stopped at a red light while the long, low dreamboats roared before him and pedestrians in the sidewalk flow with him threaded their way through the stream of cars. Brakes screamed, fenders clanged and dented, hoarse cries flew back and forth between drivers and walkers. He leaped backward frantically as one car swerved over an arc of sidewalk to miss another.

The signal changed to green; the cars kept on coming for about thirty seconds and then dwindled to an occasional light runner. Barlow crossed warily and leaned against a vending machine, blowing big breaths.

Look natural, he told himself. *Do something normal. Buy something from the machine.* He fumbled out some change, got a newspaper for a dime, a handkerchief for a quarter and a candy bar for another quarter.

The faint chocolate smell made him ravenous suddenly. He clawed at the glassy wrapper printed *"Crigglies"* quite futilely for a few seconds, and then it divided neatly by itself. The bar made three good bites, and he bought two more and gobbled them down.

Thirsty, he drew a carbonated orange drink in another one of the glassy wrappers from the machine for another dime. When he fumbled with it, it divided neatly and spilled all over his knees. Barlow decided he had been there long enough and walked on.

The shop windows were—shop windows. People still wore and bought clothes, still smoked and bought tobacco, still ate and bought food. And they still went to the movies, he saw with pleased surprise as he passed and then returned to a glittering place whose sign said it was THE BIJOU.

The place seemed to be showing a triple feature, *Babies Are Terrible, Don't Have Children,* and *The Canali Kid.*

It was irresistible; he paid a dollar and went in.

He caught the tail end of *The Canali Kid* in three-dimensional, full-color, full-scent production. It appeared to be an interplanetary saga winding up with a chase scene and a reconciliation between estranged hero and heroine. *Babies Are Terrible* and *Don't Have Children* were fantastic arguments against parenthood—the grotesquely exaggerated dangers of painfully graphic childbirth, vicious children, old parents beaten and starved by their sadistic offspring. The audience, Barlow astoundedly noted, was placidly chomping sweets and showing no particular signs of revulsion.

The *Coming Attractions* drove him into the lobby. The fanfares were shattering, the blazing colors blinding and the added scents stomach-heaving.

When his eyes again became accustomed to the moderate lighting of the lobby, he groped his way to a bench and opened the newspaper he had bought. It turned out to be *The Racing Sheet*, which afflicted him with a crushing sense of loss. The familiar boxed index in the lower left-hand corner of the front page showed almost unbearably that Churchill Downs and Empire City were still in business. . . .

Blinking back tears, he turned to the past performance at Churchill. They weren't using abbreviations anymore, and the pages because of that were single-column instead of double. But it was all the same—or was it?

He squinted at the first race, a three-quarter-mile maiden claimer for thirteen hundred dollars. Incredibly, the track record was two minutes, ten and three-fifths seconds. Any beetle in his time could have knocked off the three-quarter in one-fifteen. It was the same for the other distances, much worse for route events.

What the hell had happened to everything?

He studied the form of a five-year-old brown mare in the second and couldn't make head or tail of it. She'd won and lost and placed and showed and lost and placed without rhyme or reason. She looked like a front runner for a couple of races and then she looked like a no-good pig and then she looked like a mudder but the next time it rained she wasn't and then she was a stayer and then she was a pig again. In a good five-thousand-dollar allowances event, too!

Barlow looked at the other entries and it slowly dawned on him that they were all like the five-year-old brown mare. Not a single damned horse running had even the slightest trace of class.

Somebody sat down beside him and said, "That's the story."

Barlow whirled to his feet and saw it was Tinny-Peete, his driver.

"I was in doubts about telling you," said the psychist,

"but I see you have some growing suspicions of the truth. Please don't get excited. It's all right, I tell you."

"So you've got me," said Barlow.

"*Got* you?"

"Don't pretend. I can put two and two together. You're the secret police. You and the rest of the aristocrats live in luxury on the sweat of these oppressed slaves. You're afraid of me because you have to keep them ignorant."

There was a bellow of bright laughter from the psychist that got them blank looks from other patrons of the lobby. The laughter didn't sound at all sinister.

"Let's get out of here," said Tinny-Peete, still chuckling. "You couldn't possibly have it more wrong." He engaged Barlow's arm and led him to the street. "The actual truth is that the millions of workers live in luxury on the sweat of the handful of aristocrats. I shall probably die before my time of overwork unless . . ." He gave Barlow a speculative look. "You may be able to help us."

"I know that gag," sneered Barlow. "I made money in my time and to make money you have to get people on your side. Go ahead and shoot me if you want, but you're not going to make a fool out of me."

"You nasty little ingrate!" snapped the psychist with a kaleidoscopic change of mood. "This damned mess is all your fault and the fault of people like you! Now come along and no more of your nonsense."

He yanked Barlow into an office building lobby and an elevator that, disconcertingly, went *whoosh* loudly as it rose. The real estate man's knees were wobbly as the psychist pushed him from the elevator, down a corridor and into an office.

A hawk-faced man rose from a plain chair as the door closed behind them. After an angry look at Barlow, he asked the psychist, "Was I called from the Pole to inspect this—this . . .?"

"Unget undandered. I've deeprobed etfind quasichance exhim Poprobattackline," said the psychist soothingly.

"Doubt," grunted the hawk-faced man.

"Try," suggested Tinny-Peete.

"Very well. Mr. Barlow, I understand you and your lamented had no children."

"What of it?"

"This of it. You were a blind, selfish, stupid ass to tolerate economic and social conditions which penalized childbearing by the prudent and foresighted. You made us what we are today, and I want you to know that we are far from satisfied. Damn-fool rockets! Damn-fool automobiles! Damn-fool cities with overhead ramps!"

"As far as I can see," said Barlow, "you're running down the best features of your time. Are you crazy?"

"The rockets aren't rockets. They're turbojets—good turbojets, but the fancy shell around them makes for a bad drag. The automobiles have a top speed of one hundred kilometers per hour—a kilometer is, if I recall my paleolinguistics, three-fifths of a mile—and the speedometers are all rigged accordingly so the drivers will think they're going two hundred and fifty. The cities are ridiculous, expensive, unsanitary, wasteful conglomerations of people who'd be better off and more productive if they were spread over the countryside.

"We need the rockets and trick speedometers and cities because, while you and your kind were being prudent and foresighted and not having children, the migrant workers, slum dwellers and tenant farmers were shiftlessly and shortsightedly having children—breeding, breeding. My God, how they bred!"

"Wait a minute," objected Barlow. "There were lots of people in our crowd who had two or three children."

"The attrition of accidents, illness, wars and such took care of that. Your intelligence was bred out. It is gone. Children that should have been born never were. The just-average, they'll-get-along majority took over the population. The average IQ now is forty-five."

"But that's far in the future. . . ."

"So are you," grunted the hawk-faced man sourly.

"But who are *you* people?"

"Just people—real people. Some generations ago, the geneticists realized at last that nobody was going to pay any attention to what they said, so they abandoned words for deeds. Specifically, they formed and recruited for a closed corporation intended to maintain and improve the breed. We are their descendants, about three million of us. There are five billion of the others, so we are their slaves.

"During the past couple of years I've designed a sky-scraper, kept Billings Memorial Hospital here in Chicago running, headed off war with Mexico and directed traffic at LaGuardia Field in New York."

"I don't understand! Why don't you let them go to hell in their own way?"

The man grimaced. "We tried it once for three months. We holed up at the South Pole and waited. They didn't notice it. Some drafting-room people were missing, some chief nurses didn't show up, minor government people on the nonpolicy level couldn't be located. It didn't seem to matter.

"In a week there was hunger. In two weeks there were famine and plague, in three weeks war and anarchy. We called off the experiment; it took us most of the next genera-tion to get things squared away again."

"But why *didn't* you let them kill each other off?"

"Five billion corpses mean about five hundred million tons of rotting flesh."

Barlow had another idea. "Why don't you sterilize them?"

"Two and one-half billion operations is a lot of operations. Because they breed continuously, the job would never be done."

"I see. Like the marching Chinese!"

"Who the devil are they?"

"It was a—uh—paradox of my time. Somebody figured out that if all the Chinese in the world were to line up four abreast, I think it was, and start marching past a given point, they'd never stop because of the babies that would be born and grow up before they passed the point."

"That's right. Only instead of 'a given point,' makc it 'the largest conceivable number of operating rooms that we could build and staff.' There could never be enough."

"Say!" said Barlow. "Those movies about babies—was that your propaganda?"

"It was. It doesn't seem to mean a thing to them. We have abandoned the idea of attempting propaganda contrary to a biological drive."

"So if you work *with* a biological drive . . .?"

"I know of none which is consistent with inhibition of fertility."

Barlow's face went poker blank, the result of years of careful discipline. "You don't, huh? You're the great brains and you can't think of any?"

"Why, no," said the psychist innocently. "Can you?"

"That depends. I sold ten thousand acres of Siberian tundra—through a dummy firm, of course—after the partition of Russia. The buyers thought they were getting improved building lots on the outskirts of Kiev. I'd say that was a lot tougher than this job."

"How so?" asked the hawk-faced man.

"Those were normal, suspicious customers and these are morons, born suckers. You just figure out a con they'll fall for; they won't know enough to do any smart checking."

The psychist and the hawk-faced man had also had training; they kept themselves from looking with sudden hope at each other.

"You seem to have something in mind," said the psychist.

Barlow's poker face went blanker still. "Maybe I have. I haven't heard any offer yet."

"There's the satisfaction of knowing that you've prevented Earth's resources from being so plundered," the hawk-faced man pointed out, "that the race will soon become extinct."

"I don't know that," Barlow said bluntly. "All I have is your word."

"If you really have a method, I don't think any price would be too great," the psychist offered.

"Money," said Barlow.

"All you want."

"More than you want," the hawk-faced man corrected.

"Prestige," added Barlow. "Plenty of publicity. My picture and my name in the papers and over TV every day, statues to me, parks and cities and streets and other things named after me. A whole chapter in the history books.''

The psychist made a facial sign to the hawk-faced man that meant, ''Oh, brother!''

The hawk-faced man signaled back, ''Steady, boy!''

''It's not too much to ask,'' the psychist agreed.

Barlow, sensing a seller's market, said, ''Power!''

''Power?'' the hawk-faced man repeated puzzledly. ''Your own hydro station or nuclear pile?''

''I mean a world dictatorship with me as dictator!''

''Well, now . . .'' said the psychist, but the hawk-faced man interrupted, ''It would take a special emergency act of congress but the situation warrants it. I think that can be guaranteed.''

''Could you give us some indication of your plan?'' the psychist asked.

''Ever hear of lemmings?''

''No.''

''They are—were, I guess, since you haven't heard of them—little animals in Norway, and every few years they'd swarm to the coast and swim out to sea until they drowned. I figure on putting some lemming urge into the population.''

''How?''

''I'll save that till I get the right signatures on the deal.''

The hawk-faced man said, ''I'd like to work with you on it, Barlow. My name's Ryan-Ngana.'' He put out his hand.

Barlow looked closely at the hand, then at the man's face. ''Ryan what?''

''Ngana.''

''That sounds like an African name.''

''It is. My mother's father was a Watusi.''

Barlow didn't take the hand. ''I thought you looked pretty dark. I don't want to hurt your feelings, but I don't think I'd be at my best working with you. There must be somebody else just as well qualified, I'm sure.''

The psychist made a facial sign to Ryan-Ngana that meant, ''Steady *yourself*, boy!''

"Very well," Ryan-Ngana told Barlow. "We'll see what arrangement can be made."

"It's not that I'm prejudiced, you understand. Some of my best friends . . ."

"Mr. Barlow, don't give it another thought. Anybody who could pick on the lemming analogy is going to be useful to us."

And so he would, thought Ryan-Ngana, alone in the office after Tinny-Peete had taken Barlow up to the helicopter stage. So he would. Poprob had exhausted every rational attempt and the new Poprobattacklines would have to be irrational or subrational. This creature from the past with his lemming legends and his improved building lots would be a fountain of precious vicious self-interest.

Ryan-Ngana sighed and stretched. He had to go and run the San Francisco subway. Summoned early from the Pole to study Barlow, he'd left unfinished a nice little theorem. Between interruptions, he was slowly constructing an n-dimensional geometry whose foundations and superstructure owed no debt whatsoever to intuition.

Upstairs, waiting for a helicopter, Barlow was explaining to Tinny-Peete that he had nothing against Negroes, and Tinny-Peete wished he had some of Ryan-Ngana's imperturbability and humor for the ordeal.

The helicopter took them to International Airport where, Tinny-Peete explained, Barlow would leave for the Pole.

The man from the past wasn't sure he'd like a dreary waste of ice and cold.

"It's all right," said the psychist. "A civilized layout. Warm, pleasant. You'll be able to work more efficiently there. All the facts at your fingertips, a good secretary . . ."

"I'll need a pretty big staff," said Barlow, who had learned from thousands of deals never to take the first offer.

"I meant a private, confidential one," said Tinny-Peete readily, "but you can have as many as you want. You'll naturally have top-primary-top priority if you really have a workable plan."

"Let's not forget this dictatorship angle," said Barlow.

He didn't know that the psychist would just as readily have
promised him deification to get him happily on the "rocket"
for the Pole. Tinny-Peete had no wish to be torn limb from
limb; he knew very well that it would end that way if the
population learned from this anachronism that there was a
small elite which considered itself head, shoulders, trunk and
groin above the rest. The fact that this assumption was perfectly true and the fact that the elite was condemned by its
superiority to a life of the most grinding toil would not be
considered; the difference would.

The psychist finally put Barlow aboard the "rocket" with
some thirty people—real people—headed for the Pole.

Barlow was airsick all the way because of a posthypnotic
suggestion Tinny-Peete had planted in him. One idea was to
make him as averse as possible to a return trip, and another
idea was to spare the other passengers from his aggressive,
talkative company.

Barlow during the first day at the Pole was reminded of his
first day in the army. It was the same now-where-the-hell-are-
we-going-to-put-*you?* business until he took a firm line with
them. Then instead of acting like supply sergeants they acted
like hotel clerks.

It was a wonderful, wonderfully calculated buildup and one
that he failed to suspect. After all, in his time a visitor from
the past would have been lionized.

At day's end he reclined in a snug underground billet with
the sixty-mile gales roaring yards overhead and tried to put
two and two together.

It was like old times, he thought—like a coup in real estate
where you had the competition by the throat, like a 50-percent
rent boost when you knew damned well there was no place
for the tenants to move, like smiling when you read over the
breakfast orange juice that the city council had decided to
build a school on the ground you had acquired by a deal with
the city council. And it was simple. He would just sell tundra
building lots to eagerly suicidal lemmings, and that was
absolutely all there was to solving the problem that had these
double-domes spinning.

They'd have to work out most of the details, naturally, but what the hell, that was what subordinates were for. He'd need specialists in advertising, engineering, communications—did they know anything about hypnotism? That might be helpful. If not, there'd have to be a lot of bribery done, but he'd make sure—damned sure—there were unlimited funds.

Just selling building lots to lemmings . . .

He wished, as he fell asleep, that poor Verna could have been in on this. It was his biggest, most stupendous deal. Verna—that sharp shyster Sam Immerman must have swindled her. . . .

It began the next day with people coming to visit him. He knew the approach. They merely wanted to be helpful to their illustrious visitor from the past and would he help fill them in about his era, which unfortunately was somewhat obscure historically, and what did he think could be done about the problem? He told them he was too old to be roped any more, and they wouldn't get any information out of him until he got a letter of intent from at least the Polar president and a session of the Polar congress empowered to make him dictator.

He got the letter and the session. He presented his program, was asked whether his conscience didn't revolt at its callousness, explained succinctly that a deal was a deal and anybody who wasn't smart enough to protect himself didn't deserve protection—"Caveat emptor," he threw in for scholarship, and had to translate it to "Let the buyer beware." He didn't, he stated, give a damn about either the morons or their intelligent slaves; he'd told them his price and that was all he was interested in.

Would they meet it or wouldn't they?

The Polar president offered to resign in his favor, with certain temporary emergency powers that the Polar congress would vote him if he thought them necessary. Barlow demanded the title of World Dictator, complete control of world finances, salary to be decided by himself and the publicity campaign and historical write-up to begin at once.

"As for the emergency powers," he added, "they are to be neither temporary nor limited."

Somebody wanted the floor to discuss the matter, with the declared hope that perhaps Barlow would modify his demands.

"You've got the proposition," Barlow said. "I'm not knocking off even ten percent."

"But what if the congress refuses, sir?" the president asked.

"Then you can stay up here at the Pole and try to work it out yourselves. I'll get what I want from the morons. A shrewd operator like me doesn't have to compromise; I haven't got a single competitor in this whole cockeyed moronic era."

Congress waived debate and voted by show of hands. Barlow won unanimously.

"You don't know how close you came to losing me," he said in his first official address to the joint houses. "I'm not the boy to haggle; either I get what I ask, or I go elsewhere. The first thing I want is to see designs for a new palace for me—nothing *un*ostentatious, either—and your best painters and sculptors to start working on my portraits and statues. Meanwhile, I'll get my staff together."

He dismissed the Polar president and the Polar congress, telling them that he'd let them know when the next meeting would be.

A week later, the program started with North America the first target.

Mrs. Garvy was resting after dinner before the ordeal of turning on the dishwasher. The TV, of course, was on and it said, "Oooh!"—long, shuddery and ecstatic, the cue for the *Parfum Assault Criminale* spot commercial. "Girls," said the announcer hoarsely, "do you want your man? It's easy to get him—easy as a trip to Venus."

"Huh?" said Mrs. Garvy.

"Wassamatter?" snorted her husband, starting out of a doze.

"Ja hear that?"

"Wha'?"

"He said 'easy like a trip to Venus.' "

"So?"

"Well, I thought ya couldn't get to Venus. I thought they just had that one rocket thing that crashed on the moon."

"Aah, women don't keep up with the news," said Garvy righteously, subsiding again.

"Oh," said his wife uncertainly.

And the next day, on *Henry's Other Mistress*, there was a new character who had just breezed in: Buzz Rentshaw, master rocket pilot of the Venus run. On *Henry's Other Mistress*, "the broadcast drama about you and your neighbors, *folksy* people, *ordinary* people, *real* people!" Mrs. Garvey listened with amazement over a cooling cup of coffee as Buzz made hay of her hazy convictions.

MONA: Darling, it's so good to see you again!
BUZZ: You don't know how I've missed you on that dreary Venus run.
SOUND: *Venetian blind run down, key turned in lock.*
MONA: Was it *very* dull, dearest?
BUZZ: Let's not talk about my humdrum job, darling. Let's talk about us.
SOUND: *Creaking bed.*

Well, the program was back to normal at last. That evening Mrs. Garvy tried to ask again whether her husband was sure about those rockets, but he was dozing right through *Take It and Stick It*, so she watched the screen and forgot the puzzle.

She was still rocking with laughter at the gag line, "Would you buy it for a quarter?" when the commercial went on for the detergent powder she always faithfully loaded her dishwasher with on the first of every month.

The announcer displayed mountains of suds from a tiny piece of the stuff and coyly added, "Of course, Cleano don't lay around for you to pick up like the soap root on Venus, but it's pretty cheap and it's almost pretty near just as good. So for us plain folks who ain't lucky enough to live up there on Venus, Cleano is the real cleaning stuff!"

Then the chorus went into their "Cleano-is-the-stuff" jingle, but Mrs. Garvy didn't hear it. She was a stubborn woman, but it occurred to her that she was very sick indeed.

She didn't want to worry her husband. The next day she quietly made an appointment with her family freud.

In the waiting room she picked up a fresh new copy of *Readers Pablum* and put it down with a faint palpitation. The lead article, according to the table of contents on the cover, was titled "The Most Memorable Venusian I Ever Met."

"The freud will see you now," said the nurse, and Mrs. Garvy tottered into his office.

His traditional glasses and whiskers were reassuring. She choked out the ritual. "Freud, forgive me, for I have neuroses."

He chanted the antiphonal, "Tut, my dear girl, what seems to be the trouble?"

"I got like a hole in the head." Her voice quavered. "I seem to forget all kinds of things. Things like everybody seems to know and I don't."

"Well, that happens to everybody occasionally, my dear. I suggest a vacation on Venus."

The freud stared, openmouthed, at the empty chair. His nurse came in and demanded, "Hey, you see how she scrammed? What was the matter with *her?*"

He took off his glasses and whiskers meditatively. "You can search me. I told her she should maybe try a vacation on Venus." A momentary bafflement came into his face and he dug through his desk drawers until he found a copy of the four-color, profusely illustrated journal of his profession. It had come that morning and he had lip-read it, though looking mostly at the pictures. He leafed to the article "Advantages of the Planet Venus in Rest Cures."

"It's right there," he said.

The nurse looked. "It sure is," she agreed. "Why shouldn't it be?"

"The trouble with these here neurotics," decided the freud, "is that they all the time got to fight reality. Show in the next twitch."

He put on his glasses and whiskers again and forgot Mrs. Garvy and her strange behavior.

"Freud, forgive me, for I have neuroses."

"Tut, my dear girl, what seems to be the trouble?"

Like many cures of mental disorders, Mrs. Garvy's was achieved largely by self-treatment. She disciplined herself sternly out of the crazy notion that there had been only one rocket ship and that one a failure. She could join without wincing, eventually, in any conversation on the desirability of Venus as a place to retire, on its fabulous floral profusion. Finally she went to Venus.

All her friends were trying to book passage with the Evening Star Travel and Real Estate Corporation, but naturally the demand was crushing. She considered herself lucky to get a seat at last for the two-week summer cruise. The spaceship took off from a place called Los Alamos, New Mexico. It looked just like all the spaceships on television and in the picture magazines but was more comfortable than you would expect.

Mrs. Garvy was delighted with the fifty or so fellow passengers assembled before takeoff. They were from all over the country and she had a distinct impression that they were on the brainy side. The captain, a tall, hawk-faced, impressive fellow named Ryan Something-or-other, welcomed them aboard and trusted that their trip would be a memorable one. He regretted that there would be nothing to see because, "due to the meteorite season," the ports would be dogged down. It was disappointing, yet reassuring that the line was taking no chances.

There was the expected momentary discomfort at takeoff and then two monotonous days of droning travel through space to be whiled away in the lounge at cards or craps. The landing was a routine bump and the voyagers were issued tablets to swallow to immunize them against any minor ailments.

When the tablets took effect, the lock was opened, and Venus was theirs.

It looked much like a tropical island on Earth, except for a blanket of cloud overhead. But it had a heady, otherworldly quality that was intoxicating and glamorous.

The ten days of the vacation were suffused with a hazy magic. The soap root, as advertised, was free and sudsy. The fruits, mostly tropical varieties transplanted from Earth, were delightful. The simple shelters provided by the travel company were more than adequate for the balmy days and nights.

It was with sincere regret that the voyagers filed again into the ship and swallowed more tablets doled out to counteract and sterilize any Venus illnesses they might unwittingly communicate to Earth.

Vacationing was one thing. Power politics was another.

At the Pole, a small man was in a soundproof room, his face deathly pale and his body limp in a straight chair.

In the American Senate Chamber, Senator Hull-Mendoza (Synd., N. Cal.) was saying, ''Mr. President and gentlemen, I would be remiss in my duty as a legislature if'n I didn't bring to the attention of the au-gust body I see here a perilous situation which is fraught with peril. As is well known to members of this au-gust body, the perfection of space flight has brought with it a situation I can only describe as fraught with peril. Mr. President and gentlemen, now that swift American rockets now traverse the trackless void of space between this planet and our nearest planetarial neighbor in space—and, gentlemen, I refer to Venus, the star of dawn, the brightest jewel in fair Vulcan's diadome—now, I say, I want to inquire what steps are being taken to colonize Venus with a vanguard of patriotic citizens like those minutemen of yore.

''Mr. President and gentlemen! There are in this world nations, envious nations—I do not name Mexico—who by fair means or foul may seek to wrest from Columbia's grasp the torch of freedom of space; nations whose low living standards and innate depravity give them an unfair advantage over the citizens of our fair republic.

''This is my program: I suggest that a city of more than one hundred thousand population be selected by lot. The citizens of the fortunate city are to be awarded choice lands on Venus free and clear, to have and to hold and convey to their descendants. And the national government shall provide free transportation to Venus for these citizens. And this program shall continue, city by city, until there has been deposited on Venus a sufficient vanguard of citizens to protect our manifest rights on that planet.

"Objections will be raised, for carping critics we have always with us. They will say there isn't enough steel. They will call it a cheap giveaway. I say there *is* enough steel for *one* city's population to be transferred to Venus, and that is all that is needed. For when the time comes for the second city to be transferred, the first, emptied city can be wrecked for the needed steel! And is it a giveaway? Yes! It is the most glorious giveaway in the history of mankind! Mr. President and gentlemen, there is no time to waste—Venus must be American!"

Black-Kupperman, at the Pole, opened his eyes and said feebly, "The style was a little uneven. Do you think anybody'll notice?"

"You did fine, boy; just fine," Barlow reassured him.

Hull-Mendoza's bill became law.

Drafting machines at the South Pole were busy around the clock and the Pittsburgh steel mills spewed millions of plates into the Los Alamos spaceport of the Evening Star Travel and Real Estate Corporation. It was going to be Los Angeles, for logistic reasons, and the three most accomplished psychokineticists went to Washington and mingled in the crowd at the drawing to make certain that the Los Angeles capsule slithered into the fingers of the blindfolded Senator.

Los Angeles loved the idea and a forest of spaceships began to blossom in the desert. They weren't very good spaceships, but they didn't have to be.

A team at the Pole worked at Barlow's direction on a mail setup. There would have to be letters to and from Venus to keep the slightest taint of suspicion from arising. Luckily Barlow remembered that the problem had been solved once before—by Hitler. Relatives of persons incinerated in the furnaces of Lublin or Majdanek continued to get cheery postal cards.

The Los Angeles flight went off on schedule, under tremendous press, newsreel and television coverage. The world cheered the gallant Angelenos who were setting off on their patriotic voyage to the land of milk and honey. The forest of spaceships thundered up and up and out of sight without untoward incident. Billions envied the Angelenos, cramped and on short rations though they were.

Wreckers from San Francisco, whose capsule came up second, moved immediately into the city of the angels for the scrap steel their own flight would require. Senator Hull-Mendoza's constituents could do no less.

The president of Mexico, hypnotically alarmed at this extension of *yanqui imperialismo* beyond the stratosphere, launched his own Venus-colony program.

Across the water it was England versus Ireland, France versus Germany, China versus Russia, India versus Indonesia. Ancient hatreds grew into the flames that were rocket ships assailing the air by hundreds daily.

Dear Ed, how are you? Sam and I are fine and hope you are fine. Is it nice up there like they say with food and close grone on trees? I drove by Springfield yesterday and it sure looked funny all the buildings down but of coarse it is worth it we have to keep the greasers in their place. Do you have any trouble with them on Venus? Drop me a line some time. Your loving sister, Alma.

Dear Alma, I am fine and hope you are fine. It is a fine place here fine climate and easy living. The doctor told me today that I seem to be ten years younger. He thinks there is something in the air here keeps people young. We do not have much trouble with the greasers here they keep to theirselves it is just a question of us outnumbering them and staking out the best places for the Americans. In South Bay I know a nice little island that I have been saving for you and Sam with lots of blanket trees and ham bushes. Hoping to see you and Sam soon, your loving brother, Ed.

Sam and Alma were on their way shortly.

Poprob got a dividend in every nation after the emigration had passed the halfway mark. The lonesome stay-at-homes were unable to bear the melancholy of a low population density; their conditioning had been to swarms of their kin.

After that point it was possible to foist off the crudest stripped-down accommodations on would-be emigrants; they didn't care.

Black-Kupperman did a final job on President Hull-Mendoza, the last job that genius of hypnotics would ever do on any moron, important or otherwise.

Hull-Mendoza, panic-stricken by his presidency over an emptying nation, joined his constituents. The *Independence*, aboard which traveled the national government of America, was the most elaborate of all the spaceships—bigger, more comfortable, with a lounge that was handsome, though cramped, and cloakrooms for senators and representatives. It went, however, to the same place as the others, and Black-Kupperman killed himself, leaving a note that stated he "couldn't live with my conscience."

The day after the American president departed, Barlow flew into a rage. Across his specially built desk were supposed to flow all Poprob high-level documents, and this thing—this outrageous thing—called Poprob*term* apparently had got into the executive stage before he had even had a glimpse of it!

He buzzed for Rogge-Smith, his statistician. Rogge-Smith seemed to be at the bottom of it. Poprobterm seemed to be about first and second and third derivatives, whatever they were. Barlow had a deep distrust of anything more complex than what he called an "average."

While Rogge-Smith was still at the door, Barlow snapped, "What's the meaning of this? Why haven't I been consulted? How far have you people got and why have you been working on something I haven't authorized?"

"Didn't want to bother you, chief," said Rogge-Smith. "It was really a technical matter, kind of a final cleanup. Want to come and see the work?"

Mollified, Barlow followed his statistician down the corridor.

"You still shouldn't have gone ahead without my okay," he grumbled. "Where the hell would you people have been without me?"

"That's right, chief. We couldn't have swung it ourselves;

our minds just don't work that way. And all that stuff you knew from Hitler—it wouldn't have occurred to us. Like poor Black-Kupperman.''

They were in a fair-sized machine shop at the end of a slight upward incline. It was cold. Rogge-Smith pushed a button that started a motor, and a flood of arctic light poured in as the roof parted slowly. It showed a small spaceship with the door open.

Barlow gaped as Rogge-Smith took him by the elbow and his other boys appeared: Swenson-Swenson, the engineer; Tsutsugimushi-Duncan, his propellants man; Kalb-French, advertising.

"In you go, chief," said Tsutsugimushi-Duncan. "This is Poprobterm."

"But I'm the world dictator!"

"You bet, chief. You'll be in history, all right—but this is necessary, I'm afraid."

The door was closed. Acceleration slammed Barlow cruelly to the metal floor. Something broke, and warm, wet stuff, salty tasting, ran from his mouth to his chin. Arctic sunlight through a port suddenly became a fierce lancet stabbing at his eyes; he was out of the atmosphere.

Lying twisted and broken under the acceleration, Barlow realized that some things had not changed, that Jack Ketch was never asked to dinner however many shillings you paid him to do your dirty work, that murder will out, that crime pays only temporarily.

The last thing he learned was that death is the end of pain.

THE WEAPON

BY FREDRIC BROWN (1906-1972)
ASTOUNDING SCIENCE FICTION, APRIL

The late Fredric Brown has been a frequent contributor to this series because he was simply one of the most inventive storytellers who ever lived. He excelled at all lengths and in several genres and his writing had a hard, cynical edge to it that readers loved (and love). 1951 was an especially productive year for him, highlighted by the publication of his first science fiction collection, Space on My Hands, the legendary mystery novella "The Case of the Dancing Sandwiches," and two suspense novels, Death Has Many Doors and The Far Cry.

"The Weapon" is one of the great awful-warning stories of all time, and its final sentence is simply unforgettable.

—M.H.G.

Rules are made to be broken. I have said over and over again that a story must not deliberately have a moral. If you feel something deeply enough and are a skillful enough writer, the moral will appear in the story without your deliberately placing it there.

Yes, but if the story is short enough and powerful enough and if the writer is as skillful as Fred Brown, you can do *anything you want including something that not only has a deliberate moral, but is, in a way, all moral.*

Marty mentions the last sentence. It appeared in print in 1951. A full third of a century has passed since then. That sentence is more meaningful now, and more frightening now, by far, than when Fred wrote it.

The world lasted Fred's time, and it may last mine. But I have children who are still young; and you, Gentle Reader, may be still young. Will it last your time?

Clearly we are (collectively) an idiot species. To dub us "marching morons" is to do us too much honor.

(By the way, "Niemand" is German for "no one." Is that coincidence? Or did Fred mean something by it?)

—I.A.

THE ROOM was quiet in the dimness of early evening. Dr. James Graham, key scientist of a very important project, sat in his favorite chair, thinking. It was so still that he could hear the turning of pages in the next room as his son leafed through a picture book.

Often Graham did his best work, his most creative thinking, under these circumstances, sitting alone in an unlighted room in his own apartment after the day's regular work. But tonight his mind would not work constructively. Mostly he thought about his mentally arrested son—his only son—in the next room. The thoughts were loving thoughts, not the bitter anguish he had felt years ago when he had first learned of the boy's condition. The boy was happy; wasn't that the main thing? And to how many men is given a child who will always be a child, who will not grow up to leave him? Certainly that was rationalization, but what is wrong with rationalization when— The doorbell rang.

Graham rose and turned on lights in the almost-dark room before he went through the hallway to the door. He was not annoyed; tonight, at this moment, almost any interruption to his thoughts was welcome.

He opened the door. A stranger stood there; he said, "Dr. Graham? My name is Niemand; I'd like to talk to you. May I come in a moment?"

Graham looked at him. He was a small man, nondescript, obviously harmless—possibly a reporter or an insurance agent.

But it didn't matter what he was. Graham found himself saying, "Of course. Come in, Mr. Niemand." A few minutes of conversation, he justified himself by thinking, might divert his thoughts and clear his mind.

"Sit down," he said, in the living room. "Care for a drink?"

Niemand said, "No, thank you." He sat in the chair; Graham sat on the sofa.

The small man interlocked his fingers; he leaned forward. He said, "Dr. Graham, you are the man whose scientific work is more likely than that of any other man to end the human race's chance for survival."

A crackpot, Graham thought. Too late now he realized that he should have asked the man's business before admitting him. It would be an embarrassing interview—he disliked being rude, yet only rudeness was effective.

"Dr. Graham, the weapon on which you are working—"

The visitor stopped and turned his head as the door that led to a bedroom opened and a boy of fifteen came in. The boy didn't notice Niemand; he ran to Graham.

"Daddy, will you read to me now?" The boy of fifteen laughed the sweet laughter of a child of four.

Graham put an arm around the boy. He looked at his visitor, wondering whether he had known about the boy. From the lack of surprise on Niemand's face, Graham felt sure he had known.

"Harry"—Graham's voice was warm with affection— "Daddy's busy. Just for a little while. Go back to your room; I'll come and read to you soon."

"*Chicken Little?* You'll read me *Chicken Little?*"

"If you wish. Now run along. Wait. Harry, this is Mr. Niemand."

The boy smiled bashfully at the visitor. Niemand said,

"Hi, Harry," and smiled back at him, holding out his hand. Graham, watching, was sure now that Niemand had known: the smile and the gesture were for the boy's mental age, not his physical one.

The boy took Niemand's hand. For a moment it seemed that he was going to climb into Niemand's lap, and Graham pulled him back gently. He said, "Go to your room now, Harry."

The boy skipped back into his bedroom, not closing the door.

Niemand's eyes met Graham's and he said, "I like him," with obvious sincerity. He added, "I hope that what you're going to read to him will always be true."

Graham didn't understand. Niemand said, *"Chicken Little,* I mean. It's a fine story—but may *Chicken Little* always be wrong about the sky falling down."

Graham suddenly had liked Niemand when Niemand had shown liking for the boy. Now he remembered that he must close the interview quickly. He rose, in dismissal.

He said, "I fear you're wasting your time and mine, Mr. Niemand. I know all the arguments, everything you can say I've heard a thousand times. Possibly there is truth in what you believe, but it does not concern me. I'm a scientist, and only a scientist. Yes, it is public knowledge that I am working on a weapon, a rather ultimate one. But, for me personally, that is only a by-product of the fact that I am advancing science. I have thought it through, and I have found that that is my only concern."

"But, Dr. Graham, is humanity *ready* for an ultimate weapon?"

Graham frowned. "I have told you my point of view, Mr. Niemand."

Niemand rose slowly from the chair. He said, "Very well, if you do not choose to discuss it, I'll say no more." He passed a hand across his forehead. "I'll leave, Dr. Graham. I wonder, though . . . may I change my mind about the drink you offered me?"

Graham's irritation faded. He said, "Certainly. Will whisky and water do?"

"Admirably."

Graham excused himself and went into the kitchen. He got the decanter of whisky, another of water, ice cubes, glasses.

When he returned to the living room, Niemand was just leaving the boy's bedroom. He heard Niemand's "Good night, Harry," and Harry's happy " 'Night, Mr. Niemand."

Graham made drinks. A little later, Niemand declined a second one and started to leave.

Niemand said, "I took the liberty of bringing a small gift to your son, doctor. I gave it to him while you were getting the drinks for us. I hope you'll forgive me."

"Of course. Thank you. Good night."

Graham closed the door; he walked through the living room into Harry's room. He said, "All right, Harry. Now I'll read to—"

There was sudden sweat on his forehead, but he forced his face and his voice to be calm as he stepped to the side of the bed. "May I see that, Harry?" When he had it safely, his hands shook as he examined it.

He thought, *only a madman would give a loaded revolver to an idiot.*

ANGEL'S EGG

BY EDGAR PANGBORN (1909–1976)
GALAXY SCIENCE FICTION, JUNE

Edgar Pangborn was one of the consistently fine writers to grace the field of science fiction. His work covers all human emotions, and he excelled at strong characterization, a quality all too rare in modern sf. His legacy to us is rich indeed, including five notable novels: West of the Sun *(1953),* A Mirror for Observers *(1954; winner of the International Fantasy Award);* Davy, *perhaps his most famous work (1964);* The Judgment of Eve *(1966), and* The Company of Glory *(1975). His two story collections,* Good Neighbors and Other Strangers *(1972), and* Still I Persist in Wondering *(1978), are also outstanding and deserve to be back in print. His work had a wonderful feeling of alienation and love to it, and his unique voice has never really been replaced.*

"Angel's Egg" was his first science fiction story, and is sad, joyous and unforgettable.

—*M.H.G.*

I have a theory about intelligence which I have expressed in some of my writings. I think that as intelligence increases, behavior becomes more reprehensible. As intelligence increases, the memory of past wrongs sharpens; the apprehen-

sion of future wrongs increases; the notion of revenge, or of a preemptive strike, of ambushes and allies, becomes more possible. Finally, as intelligence increases, the tools that help us in our anger become increasingly powerful and sophisticated.

The result is that intelligence may be self-limiting. Once any species becomes intelligent enough to develop weapons powerful enough, it destroys itself. But does it always? May it become intelligent enough to see that self-destruction is not a wonderful thing? It may, and, if so, there may be a point in developing intelligence where the danger of species suicide is greatest, and perhaps we are at that point. If we can survive past it somehow, the entire Universe may be ours some day; perhaps in cooperation with other intelligences.

It pains me to hear people assume that "invading extraterrestrials" must be fiends. They are merely judging other species by themselves. It seems to me that no species can develop a workable space-centered society, unless it has learned to master its own idiocy. Therefore, the "space invaders" will be benevolent. It is we that are villainous and to the villainous all things are villainous.

I thought of all this again as I reread "Angel's Egg."

—I.A.

LETTER OF RECORD, BLAINE TO MC CARRAN, DATED AUGUST 10, 1951.

Mr. Cleveland McCarran
Federal Bureau of Investigation
Washington, D.C.

Dear Sir:

In compliance with your request I enclose herewith a transcript of the pertinent sections of the journal of Dr. David Bannerman, deceased. The original document is being held at this office until proper disposition can be determined.

Our investigation has shown no connection between Dr. Bannerman and any organization, subversive or otherwise. So far as we can learn, he was exactly what he seemed, an inoffensive summer resident, retired, with a small independent income—a recluse to some extent, but well spoken of by local tradesmen and other neighbors. A connection between Dr. Bannerman and the type of activity that concerns your department would seem most unlikely.

The following information is summarized from the earlier parts of Dr. Bannerman's journal, and tallies with the results of our own limited inquiry. He was born in 1898 at Springfield, Massachusetts, attended public school there, and was graduated from Harvard College in 1922, his studies having been interrupted by two years' military service. He was wounded in action in Argonne, receiving a spinal injury. He earned a doctorate in biology in 1926. Delayed aftereffects of his war injury necessitated hospitalization, 1927–28. From 1929 to 1948 he taught elementary sciences in a private school in Boston. He published two textbooks in introductory biology, 1929 and 1937. In 1948 he retired from teaching: a pension and a modest income from textbook royalties evidently made this possible. Aside from the spinal deformity, which caused him to walk with a stoop, his health is said to have been fair. Autopsy findings suggested that the spinal condition must have given him considerable pain; he is not known to have mentioned this to anyone, not even to his physician, Dr. Lester Morse. There is no evidence whatever of drug addiction or alcoholism.

At one point early in his journal Dr. Bannerman describes himself as "a naturalist of the puttering type—I would rather sit on a log than write monographs: it pays off better." Dr. Morse, and others who knew Dr. Bannerman personally, tell me that this conveys a hint of his personality.

I am not qualified to comment on the material of this journal, except to say I have no evidence to support (or to contradict) Dr. Bannerman's statements. The journal has been studied only by my immediate superiors, by Dr. Morse and by myself. I take it for granted you will hold the matter in strictest confidence.

With the journal I am also enclosing a statement by Dr. Morse, written at my request for our records and for your information. You will note that he says, with some qualifications, that "death was not inconsistent with an embolism."

He has signed a death certificate on that basis. You will recall from my letter of August 4 that it was Dr. Morse who discovered Dr. Bannerman's body. Because he was a close personal friend of the deceased, Dr. Morse did not feel able to perform the autopsy himself. It was done by Dr. Stephen Clyde of this city, and was virtually negative as regards cause of death, neither confirming nor contradicting Dr. Morse's original tentative diagnosis. If you wish to read the autopsy report in full I shall be glad to forward a copy.

Dr. Morse tells me that so far as he knows Dr. Bannerman had no near relatives. He never married. For the last twelve summers he occupied a small cottage on a back road about twenty-five miles from this city, and had few visitors. The neighbor, Steele, mentioned in the journal is a farmer, age sixty-eight, of good character, who tells me he "never got really acquainted with Dr. Bannerman."

At this office we feel that unless new information comes to light, further active investigation is hardly justified.

Respectfully yours,
Garrison Blaine
Capt., State Police
Augusta, Me.

Encl: Extract from Journal of David Bannerman, dec'd. Statement by Lester Morse, M.D.

LIBRARIAN'S NOTE: The following document, originally attached as an unofficial "rider" to the foregoing letter, was donated to this institution in 1994 through the courtesy of Mrs. Helen McCarran, widow of the martyred first president of the World Federation. Other personal and state papers of President McCarran, many of them dating from the early period when he was employed by the FBI, are accessible to public view at the Institute of World History, Copenhagen.

PERSONAL NOTE, BLAINE TO MC CARRAN, DATED AUGUST 10, 1951

Dear Cleve:

Guess I didn't make it clear in my other letter that that bastard Clyde was responsible for my having to drag you into this. He is something to handle with tongs. Happened thusly— When he came in to heave the autopsy report at me, he was already having pups just because it was so completely negative (he does have certain types of honesty), and he caught sight of a page or two of the journal on my desk. Doc Morse was with me at the time. I fear we both got upstage with him (Clyde has that effect, and we were both in a State of Mind anyway), so right away the old drip thinks he smells something subversive. Belongs to the atomize-'em-NOW-WOW-WOW school of thought—nuf sed? He went into a grand whuff-whuff about referring to Higher Authority, and I knew that meant your hive, so I wanted to get ahead of the letter I knew he'd write. I suppose his literary effort couldn't be just sort of quietly transferred to File 13, otherwise known as the Appropriate Receptacle?

He can say what he likes about my character, if any, but even I never supposed he'd take a sideswipe at his professional colleague. Doc Morse is the best of the best and would not dream of suppressing any evidence important to us, as you say Clyde's letter hints. What Doc did do was to tell Clyde, pleasantly, in the privacy of my office, to go take a flying this-and-that at the moon. I only wish I'd thought of the expression myself. So Clyde rushes off to tell teacher. See what I mean about the tongs? However (knock on wood) I don't think Clyde saw enough of the journal to get any notion of what it's all about.

As for that journal, damn it, Cleve, I don't know. If you have any ideas I want them, of course. I'm afraid I believe in angels, myself. But when I think of the effect on local opinion if the story ever gets out—brother! Here was this old Bannerman living alone with a female angel and they wuzn't even common-law married. Aw, gee. . . . And the flood of phone calls from other crackpots anxious to explain it all to me. Experts in the care and feeding of angels. Methods of angel-proofing. An-

gels right outside the window a minute ago. Make
Angels a Profitable Enterprise in Your Spare Time!!!

When do I see you? You said you might have a week
clear in October. If we could get together maybe we
could make sense where there is none. I hear the cider
promises to be good this year. Try and make it. My
best to Ginny and the other young fry, and Helen of
course.

Respeckfully yourn,
Garry

P.S. If you do see any angels down your way, and they
aren't willing to wait for a Republican Administration,
by all means have them investigated by the Senate—
then we'll *know* we're all nuts.

G.

EXTRACT FROM JOURNAL OF DAVID BANNERMAN, JUNE 1–JULY
29, 1951

June 1

It must have been at least three weeks ago when we had
that flying saucer flurry. Observers the other side of Katahdin
saw it come down this side; observers this side saw it come
down the other. Size anywhere from six inches to sixty feet in
diameter (or was it cigar-shaped?) and speed whatever you
please. Seem to recall that witnesses agreed on a rosy-pink
light. There was the inevitable gobbledegookery of official
explanation designed to leave everyone impressed, soothed,
and disappointed. I paid scant attention to the excitement and
less to the explanation—naturally, I thought it was just a
flying saucer. But now Camilla has hatched out an angel.

It would have to be Camilla. Perhaps I haven't mentioned
my hens enough. In the last day or two it has dawned on me
that this journal may be of importance to other eyes than
mine, not merely a lonely man's plaything to blunt the edge

of mortality: an angel in the house makes a difference. I had
better show consideration for possible readers.

I have eight hens, all yearlings except Camilla: this is her
third spring, I boarded her two winters at my neighbor Steele's
farm when I closed this shack and shuffled my chilly bones
off to Florida, because even as a pullet she had a manner
which overbore me. I could never have eaten Camilla: if she
had looked at the ax with that same expression of rancid
disapproval (and she would), I should have felt I was beheading
a favorite aunt. Her only concession to sentiment is the
annual rush of maternity to the brain—normal, for a case-
hardened White Plymouth Rock.

This year she stole a nest successfully in a tangle of
blackberry. By the time I located it, I estimated I was about
two weeks too late. I had to outwit her by watching from a
window—she is far too acute to be openly trailed from feeding ground to nest. When I had bled and pruned my way to
her hideout she was sitting on nine eggs and hating my guts.
They could not be fertile, since I keep no rooster, and I was
about to rob her when I saw the ninth egg was nothing of
hers. It was a deep blue and transparent, with flecks of inner
light that made me think of the first stars in a clear evening. It
was the same size as Camilla's own. There was an embryo,
but I could make nothing of it. I returned the egg to Camilla's
bare and fevered breastbone and went back to the house for a
long, cool drink.

That was ten days ago. I know I ought to have kept a
record; I examined the blue egg every day, watching how
some nameless life grew within it. The angel has been out of
the shell three days now. This is the first time I have felt
equal to facing pen and ink.

I have been experiencing a sort of mental lassitude unfamiliar to me. Wrong word: not so much lassitude as a preoccupation, with no sure clue to what it is that preoccupies me.
By reputation I am a scientist of sorts. Right now I have no
impulse to look for data; I want to sit quiet and let truth come
to a relaxed mind if it will. Could be merely a part of
growing older, but I doubt that. The broken pieces of the

wonderful blue shell are on my desk. I have been peering at them—into them—for the last ten minutes or more. Can't call it study: my thought wanders into their blue, learning nothing I can retain in words. It does not convey much to say I have gone into a vision of open sky—and of peace, if such a thing there be.

The angel chipped the shell deftly in two parts. This was evidently done with the aid of small horny outgrowths on her elbows; these growths were sloughed off on the second day. I wish I had seen her break the shell, but when I visited the blackberry tangle three days ago she was already out. She poked her exquisite head through Camilla's neck feathers, smiled sleepily, and snuggled back into darkness to finish drying off. So what could I do, more than save the broken shell and wriggle my clumsy self out of there? I had removed Camilla's own eggs the day before—Camilla was only moderately annoyed. I was nervous about disposing of them, even though they were obviously Camilla's, but no harm was done. I cracked each one to be sure. Very frankly rotten eggs and nothing more.

In the evening of that day I thought of rats and weasels, as I should have done earlier. I prepared a box in the kitchen and brought the two in, the angel quiet in my closed hand. They are there now. I think they are comfortable.

Three days after hatching, the angel is the length of my forefinger, say three inches tall, with about the relative proportions of a six-year-old girl. Except for head, hands, and probably the soles of her feet, she is clothed in down the color of ivory; what can be seen of her skin is a glowing pink—I do mean glowing, like the inside of certain sea shells. Just above the small of her back are two stubs which I take to be infantile wings. They do not suggest an extra pair of specialized forelimbs. I think they are wholly differentiated organs; perhaps they will be like the wings on an insect. Somehow, I never thought of angels buzzing. Maybe she won't. I know very little about angels. At present the stubs are covered with some dull tissue, no doubt a protective sheath to be discarded when the membranes (if they are membranes) are ready to grow. Between the stubs is a not very prominent ridge—special musculature, I suppose. Otherwise her shape is quite human, even to a pair of minuscule mammalian buttons just visible under the down; how that can make sense in an egg-laying organism is beyond my comprehension. (Just for the record, so is a Corot landscape; so is Schubert's *Unfinished*; so is the flight of a hummingbird, or the other-world of frost on a window pane.) The down on her head has grown visibly in three days and is of different quality from the body down—later it may resemble human hair, as a diamond resembles a chunk of granite. . . .

A curious thing has happened. I went to Camilla's box after writing that. Judy* was already lying in front of it, unexcited. The angel's head was out from under the feathers, and I thought—with more verbal distinctness than such thoughts commonly take, "So here I am, a naturalist of middle years and cold sober, observing a three-inch oviparous mammal with down and wings." The thing is—she giggled. Now, it might have been only amusement at my appearance, which to her must be enormously gross and comic. But another thought formed unspoken: "I am no longer lonely." And her face (hardly bigger than a dime) immediately changed from laughter to a brooding and friendly thoughtfulness.

Judy and Camilla are old friends. Judy seems untroubled by the angel. I have no worries about leaving them alone together. I must sleep.

June 3

I made no entry last night. The angel was talking to me, and when that was finished I drowsed off immediately on a cot that I have moved into the kitchen so as to be near them.

I had never been strongly impressed by the evidence for extrasensory perception. It is fortunate my mind was able to

---

*Dr. Bannerman's dog, mentioned often earlier in the journal. A nine-year-old English setter. According to an entry of May 15, 1951, she was then beginning to go blind.—BLAINE.

accept the novelty, since to the angel it is clearly a matter of course. Her tiny mouth is most expressive but moves only for that reason and for eating—not for speech. Probably she could speak to her own kind if she wished, but I dare say the sound would be outside the range of my hearing as well as my understanding.

Last night after I brought the cot in and was about to finish my puttering bachelor supper, she climbed to the edge of the box and pointed, first at herself and then at the top of the kitchen table. Afraid to let my vast hand take hold of her, I held it out flat and she sat in my palm. Camilla was inclined to fuss, but the angel looked over her shoulder and Camilla subsided, watchful but no longer alarmed.

The table top is porcelain, and the angel shivered. I folded a towel and spread a silk handkerchief on top of that; the angel sat on this arrangement with apparent comfort, near my face. I was not even bewildered. Possibly she had already instructed me to blank out my mind. At any rate, I did so, without conscious effort to that end.

She reached me first with visual imagery. How can I make it plain that this had nothing in common with my sleep dreams? There was no weight of symbolism from my littered past; no discoverable connection with any of yesterday's commonplace; indeed, no actual involvement of my personality at all. I saw. I was moving vision, though without eyes or other flesh. And while my mind saw, it also knew where my flesh was, slumped at the kitchen table. If anyone had entered the kitchen, if there had been a noise of alarm out in the henhouse, I should have known it.

There was a valley such as I have not seen (and never will) on Earth. I have seen many beautiful places on this planet—some of them were even tranquil. Once I took a slow steamer to New Zealand and had the Pacific as a plaything for many days. I can hardly say how I knew this was not Earth. The grass of the valley was an earthly green; a river below me was a blue-and-silver thread under familiar-seeming sunlight; there were trees much like pine and maple, and maybe that is what they were. But it was not Earth. I was aware of moun-

tains heaped to strange heights on either side of the valley—
snow, rose, amber, gold. Perhaps the amber tint was unlike
any mountain color I have noticed in this world at midday.

Or I may have known it was not Earth simply because her
mind—dwelling within some unimaginable brain smaller than
the tip of my little finger—told me so.

I watched two inhabitants of that world come flying, to rest
in the field of sunny grass where my bodiless vision had
brought me. Adult forms, such as my angel would surely be
when she had her growth, except that both of these were male
and one of them was dark skinned. The latter was also old,
with a thousand-wrinkled face, knowing and full of tranquil-
ity; the other was flushed and lively with youth; both were
beautiful. The down of the brown-skinned old one was red-
dish tawny; the other's was ivory with hints of orange. Their
wings were true membranes, with more variety of subtle
iridescence than I have seen even in the wings of a dragonfly;
I could not say that any color was dominant, for each motion
brought a ripple of change. These two sat at their ease on the
grass. I realized that they were talking to each other, though
their lips did not move in speech more than once or twice.
They would nod, smile, now and then illustrate something
with twinkling hands.

A huge rabbit lolloped past them. I knew (thanks to my
own angel's efforts, I suppose) that this animal was of the
same size of our common wild ones. Later, a blue-green
snake three times the size of the angels came flowing through
the grass; the old one reached out to stroke its head carelessly, and I think he did it without interrupting whatever he
was saying.

Another creature came, in leisured leaps. He was monstrous, yet I felt no alarm in the angels or in myself. Imagine
a being built somewhat like a kangaroo up to the head, about
eight feet tall, and katydid-green. Really, the thick balancing
tail and enormous legs were the only kangaroolike features
about him: the body above the massive thighs was not dwarfed
but thick and square; the arms and hands were quite humanoid: the head was round, manlike except for its face—there

was only a single nostril and his mouth was set in the vertical; the eyes were large and mild. I received an impression of high intelligence and natural gentleness. In one of his manlike hands two tools so familiar and ordinary that I knew my body by the kitchen table had laughed in startled recognition. But, after all, a garden spade and rake are basic. Once invented—I expect we did it ourselves in the Neolithic Age—there is little reason why they should change much down the millennia.

This farmer halted by the angels, and the three conversed awhile. The big head nodded agreeably. I believe the young angel made a joke; certainly the convulsions in the huge green face made me think of laughter. Then this amiable monster turned up the grass in a patch a few yards square, broke the sod and raked the surface smooth, just as any competent gardener might do—except that he moved with the relaxed smoothness of a being whose strength far exceeds the requirements of his task. . . .

I was back in my kitchen with everyday eyes. My angel was exploring the table. I had a loaf of bread there and a dish of strawberries and cream. She was trying a bread crumb; seemed to like it fairly well. I offered the strawberries; she broke off one of the seeds and nibbled it but didn't care so much for the pulp. I held up the great spoon with sugary cream; she steadied it with both hands to try some. I think she liked it. It had been most stupid of me not to realize that she would be hungry. I brought wine from the cupboard; she watched inquiringly, so I put a couple of drops on the handle of a spoon. This really pleased her: she chuckled and patted her tiny stomach, though I'm afraid it wasn't awfully good sherry. I brought some crumbs of cake, but she indicated that she was full, came close to my face, and motioned me to lower my head.

She reached toward me until she could press both hands against my forehead—I felt it only enough to know her hands were there—and she stood so a long time, trying to tell me something.

It was difficult. Pictures come through with relative ease, but now she was transmitting an abstraction of a complex kind; my clumsy brain really suffered in the effort to receive. Something did come across. I have only the crudest way of passing it on. Imagine an equilateral triangle; place the following words one at each corner—"recruiting," "collecting," "saving." The meaning she wanted to convey ought to be near the center of the triangle.

I had also the sense that her message provided a partial explanation of her errand in this lovable and damnable world.

She looked weary when she stood away from me. I put out my palm and she climbed into it, to be carried back to the nest.

She did not talk to me tonight, nor eat, but she gave a reason, coming out from Camilla's feathers long enough to turn her back and show me the wing stubs. The protective sheaths have dropped off; the wings are rapidly growing. They are probably damp and weak. She was quite tired and went back into the warm darkness almost at once.

Camilla must be exhausted, too. I don't think she has been off the nest more than twice since I brought them into the house.

June 4

Today she can fly.

I learned it in the afternoon when I was fiddling about in the garden and Judy was loafing in the sunshine she loves. Something apart from sight and sound called me to hurry back to the house. I saw my angel through the screen door before I opened it. One of her feet had caught in a hideous loop of loose wire at a break in the mesh. Her first tug of alarm must have tightened the loop so that her hands were not strong enough to force it open.

Fortunately I was able to cut the wire with a pair of shears before I lost my head; then she could free her foot without injury. Camilla had been frantic, rushing around fluffed up, but—here's an odd thing—perfectly silent. None of the recognized chicken noises of dismay: if an ordinary chick had been in trouble she would have raised the roof.

The angel flew to me and hovered, pressing her hands on

my forehead. The message was clear at once: "No harm done." She flew down to tell Camilla the same thing.

Yes, in the same way. I saw Camilla standing near my feet with her neck out and head low, and the angel put a hand on either side of her scraggy comb. Camilla relaxed, clucked in the normal way, and spread her wings for a shelter. The angel went under it, but only to oblige Camilla, I think—at least, she stuck her head through the wing feathers and winked.

She must have seen something else, then, for she came out and flew back to me and touched a finger to my cheek, looked at the finger, saw it was wet, put it in her mouth, made a face and laughed at me.

We went outdoors into the sun (Camilla, too), and the angel gave me an exhibition of what flying ought to be. Not even Schubert can speak of joy as her first free flying did. At one moment she would be hanging in front of my eyes, radiant and delighted; the next instant she would be a dot of color against a cloud. Try to imagine something that would make a hummingbird seem a bit dull and sluggish.

They do hum. Softer than a hummingbird, louder than a dragonfly.

Something like the sound of hawk-moths—*Heinmaris thisbe*, for instance: the one I used to call Hummingbird Moth when I was a child.

I was frightened, naturally. Frightened first at what might happen to her, but that was unnecessary; I don't think she would be in danger from any savage animal except possibly man. I saw a Copper's hawk slant down the visible ray toward the swirl of color where she was dancing by herself; presently she was drawing iridescent rings around him; then, while he soared in smaller circles, I could not see her, but (maybe she felt my fright) she was again in front of me, pressing my forehead in the now familiar way. I knew she was amused and caught the idea that the hawk was a "lazy character." Not quite the way I'd describe *Accipiter Cooperi*, but it's all in the point of view. I believe she had been riding his back, no doubt with her speaking hands on his terrible head.

And later I was frightened by the thought that she might not want to return to me. Can I compete with sunlight and open sky? The passage of that terror through me brought her back swiftly, and her hands said with great clarity: "Don't ever be afraid of anything—it isn't necessary for you."

Once this afternoon I was saddened by the realization that old Judy can take little part in what goes on now. I can well remember Judy running like the wind. The angel must have heard this thought in me, for she stood a long time beside Judy's drowsy head, while Judy's tail thumped cheerfully on the warm grass. . . .

In the evening the angel made a heavy meal on two or three cake crumbs and another drop of sherry, and we had what was almost a sustained conversation. I will write it in that form this time, rather than grope for anything more exact. I asked her, "How far away is your home?"

"My home is here."

"Thank God!—but I meant, the place your people came from."

"Ten light-years."

"The images you showed me—that quiet valley—that is ten light-years away?"

"Yes. But that was my father talking to you, through me. He was grown when the journey began. He is two hundred and forty years old—our years, thirty-two days longer than yours."

Mainly I was conscious of a flood of relief: I had feared, on the basis of terrestrial biology, that her explosively rapid growth after hatching must foretell a brief life. But it's all right—she can outlive me, and by a few hundred years, at that. "Your father is here now, on this planet—shall I see him?"

She took her hands away—listening, I believe. The answer was: "No. He is ill and cannot live long. I am to see him in a few days, when I fly a little better. He taught me for twenty years after I was born."

"I don't understand. I thought . . ."

"Later, friend. My father is grateful for your kindness to me."

I don't know what I thought about that. I felt no faintest trace of condescension in the message. "And he was showing me things he had seen with his own eyes, ten light-years away?"

"Yes." Then she wanted me to rest awhile; I am sure she knows what a huge effort it is for my primitive brain to function in this way. But before she ended the conversation by humming down to her nest she gave me this, and I received it with such clarity that I cannot be mistaken: "He says that only fifty million years ago it was a jungle there, just as Terra is now."

June 8

When I woke four days ago the angel was having breakfast, and little Camilla was dead. The angel watched me rub sleep out of my eyes, watched me discover Camilla, and then flew to me. I received this: "Does it make you unhappy?"

"I don't know exactly." You can get fond of a hen, especially a cantankerous and homely old one whose personality has a lot in common with your own.

"She was old. She wanted a flock of chicks, and I couldn't stay with her. So I . . ." Something obscure here: probably my mind was trying too hard to grasp it—". . . so I saved her life." I could make nothing else out of it. She said "saved."

Camilla's death looked natural, except that I should have expected the death contractions to muss the straw, and that hadn't happened. Maybe the angel had arranged the old lady's body for decorum, though I don't see how her muscular strength would have been equal to it—Camilla weighed at least seven pounds.

As I was burying her at the edge of the garden and the angel was humming over my head, I recalled a thing which, when it happened, I had dismissed as a dream. Merely a moonlight image of the angel standing in the nest box with her hands on Camilla's head, then pressing her mouth gently on Camilla's throat, just before the hen's head sank down out of my line of vision. Probably I actually waked and saw it happen. I am somehow unconcerned—even, as I think more about it, pleased. . . .

After the burial the angel's hands said, "Sit on the grass and we'll talk. . . . Question me. I'll tell you what I can. My father asks you to write it down."

So that is what we have been doing for the last four days, I have been going to school, a slow but willing pupil. Rather than enter anything in this journal (for in the evenings I was exhausted), I made notes as best I could. The angel has gone now to see her father and will not return until morning. I shall try to make a readable version of my notes.

Since she had invited questions, I began with something which had been bothering me, as a would-be naturalist, exceedingly. I couldn't see how creatures no larger than the adults I had observed could lay eggs as large as Camilla's. Nor could I understand why, if they were hatched in an almost adult condition and able to eat a varied diet, she had any use for that ridiculous, lovely, and apparently functional pair of breasts. When the angel grasped my difficulty she exploded with laughter—her kind, which buzzed her all over the garden and caused her to fluff my hair on the wing and pinch my earlobe. She lit on a rhubarb leaf and gave a delectably naughty representation of herself as a hen laying an egg, including the cackle. She got me to bumbling helplessly—my kind of laughter—and it was some time before we could quiet down. Then she did her best to explain.

They are true mammals, and the young—not more than two or at most three in a lifetime averaging two hundred and fifty years—are delivered in very much the human way. The baby is nursed—human fashion—until his brain begins to respond a little to their unspoken language; that takes three to four weeks. Then he is placed in an altogether different medium. She could not describe that clearly, because there was very little in my educational storehouse to help me grasp it. It is some gaseous medium that arrests bodily growth for an almost indefinite period, while mental growth continues. It took them, she says, about seven thousand years to perfect this technique after they first hit on the idea: they are never in a hurry. The infant remains under this delicate and precise control for anywhere from fifteen to thirty years, the period depending not only on his mental vigor but also on the type of lifework he tentatively elects as soon as his brain is knowing enough to make a choice. During this period his mind is guided with unwavering patience by teachers who . . .

It seems those teachers know their business. This was peculiarly difficult for me to assimilate, although the fact came through clearly enough. In their world, the profession of teacher is more highly honored than any other—can such a thing be possible?—and so difficult to enter that only the strongest minds dare attempt it. (I had to rest a while after absorbing that.) An aspirant must spend fifty years (not including the period of infantile education) in merely getting ready to begin, and the acquisition of factual knowledge, while not understressed, takes only a small portion of those fifty years. Then—if he's good enough—he can take a small part in the elementary instruction of a few babies, and if he does well on that basis for another thirty or forty years, he is considered a fair beginner. . . . Once upon a time I lurched around stuffy classrooms trying to insert a few predigested facts (I wonder how many of them *were* facts?) into the minds of bored and preoccupied adolescents, some of whom may have liked me moderately well. I was even able to shake hands and be nice while their terribly well-meaning parents explained to me how they ought to be educated. So much of our human effort goes down the drain of futility, I sometimes wonder how we ever got as far as the Bronze Age. Somehow we did, though, and a short way beyond.

After that preliminary stage of an angel's education is finished, the baby is transferred to more ordinary surroundings, and his bodily growth completes itself in a very short time. Wings grow abruptly (as I have seen), and he reaches a maximum height of six inches (our measure). Only then does he enter on that lifetime of two hundred and fifty years, for not until then does his body begin to age. My angel has been a living personality for many years but will not celebrate her first birthday for almost a year. I like to think of that.

At about the same time they learned the principles of interplanetary travel (approximately twelve million years ago) these people also learned how, by use of a slightly different method, growth could be arrested at any point short of full maturity. At first the knowledge served no purpose except in the control of illnesses which still occasionally struck them at that time. But when the long periods of time required for space travel were considered, the advantages became obvious.

So it happens that my angel was born ten light-years away. She was trained by her father and many others in the wisdom of seventy million years (that, she tells me, is the approximate sum of their *recorded* history), and then she was safely sealed and cherished in what my superamoebic brain regarded as a blue egg. Education did not proceed at that time; her mind went to sleep with the rest of her. When Camilla's temperature made her wake and grow again, she remembered what to do with the little horny bumps provided for her elbows. And came out—into this planet, God help her.

I wondered why her father should have chosen any combination so unreliable as an old hen and a human being. Surely he must have had plenty of excellent ways to bring the shell to the right temperature. Her answer should have satisfied me immensely, but I am still compelled to wonder about it. "Camilla was a nice hen, and my father studied your mind while you were asleep. It was a bad landing, and much was broken—no such landing was ever made before after so long a journey: forty years. Only four other grown-ups could come with my father. Three of them died en route and he is very ill. And there were nine other children to care for."

Yes, I knew she'd said that an angel thought I was good enough to be trusted with his daughter. If it upsets me, all I need do is look at her and then in the mirror. As for the explanation, I can only conclude there must be more that I am not ready to understand. I was worried about those nine others, but she assured me they were all well, and I sensed that I ought not to ask more about them at present. . . .

Their planet, she says, is closely similar to this. A trifle larger, moving in a somewhat longer orbit around a sun like ours. Two gleaming moons, smaller than ours—their orbits are such that two-moon nights come rarely. They are magic, and she will ask her father to show me one, if he can. Their year is thirty-two days longer than ours; because of a slower rotation, their day has twenty-six of our hours. Their atmosphere is mainly nitrogen and oxygen in the proportions familiar to us; slightly richer in some of the rare gases. The climate is now what we should call tropical and subtropical, but they have known glacial rigors like those in our world's past. There are only two great continental land masses, and many thousands of large islands.

Their total population is only five billion. . . .

Most of the forms of life we know have parallels there—some quite exact parallels: rabbits, deer, mice, cats. The cats have been bred to an even higher intelligence than they possess on our Earth; it is possible, she says, to have a good deal of intellectual intercourse with their cats, who learned several million years ago that when they kill, it must be done with lightning precision and without torture. The cats had some difficulty grasping the possibility of pain in other organisms, but once that educational hurdle was passed, development was easy. Nowadays many of the cats are popular storytellers; about forty million years ago they were still occasionally needed as a special police force, and served the angels with real heroism.

It seems my angel wants to become a student of animal life here on Earth. I, a teacher!—but bless her heart for the notion, anyhow. We sat and traded animals for a couple of hours last night. I found it restful, after the mental struggle to grasp more difficult matters. Judy was something new to her. They have several luscious monsters on that planet but, in her view, so have we. She told me of a blue sea snake fifty feet long (relatively harmless) that bellows cowlike and comes into the tidal marshes to lay black eggs; so I gave her a whale. She offered a bat-winged, day-flying ball of mammalian fluff as big as my head and weighing under an ounce; I matched her with a marmoset. She tried me with a small-sized pink brontosaur (very rare), but I was ready with the duck-billed platypus, and that caused us to exchange some pretty smart remarks about mammalian eggs; she bounced. All trivial in a way; also, the happiest evening in my fifty-three tangled years of life.

She was a trifle hesitant to explain these kangaroolike people, until she was sure I really wanted to know. It seems they are about the nearest parallel to human life on that planet; not a near parallel, of course, as she was careful to explain. Agreeable and always friendly souls (though they weren't always so, I'm sure) and of a somewhat more alert intelligence than we possess. Manual workers, mainly, because they prefer it nowadays, but some of them are excellent mathematicians. The first practical spaceship was invented by a group of them, with some assistance. . . .

Names offer difficulties. Because of the nature of the angelic language, they have scant use for them except for the purpose of written record, and writing naturally plays little part in their daily lives—no occasion to write a letter when a thousand miles is no obstacle to the speech of your mind. An angel's formal name is about as important to him as, say, my social security number is to me. She has not told me hers, because the phonetics on which their written language is based have no parallel in my mind. As we would speak a friend's name, an angel will project the friend's image to his friend's receiving mind. More pleasant and more intimate, I think—although it was a shock to me at first to glimpse my own ugly mug in my mind's eye. Stories are occasionally written, if there is something in them that should be preserved precisely as it was in the first telling; but in their world the true storyteller has a more important place than the printer—he offers one of the best of their quieter pleasures: a good one can hold his audience for a week and never tire them.

"What is this 'angel' in your mind when you think of me?"

"A being men have imagined for centuries, when they

thought of themselves as they might like to be and not as they are."

I did not try too painfully hard to learn much about the principles of space travel. The most my brain could take in of her explanation was something like: "Rocket—then phototropism." Now, that makes scant sense. So far as I know, phototropism—movement toward light—is an organic phenomenon. One thinks of it as a response of protoplasm, in some plants and animal organisms (most of them simple), to the stimulus of light; certainly not as a force capable of moving inorganic matter. I think that whatever may be the principle she was describing, this word "phototropism" was merely the nearest thing to it in my reservoir of language. Not even the angels can create understanding out of blank ignorance. At least I have learned not to set neat limits to the possible.

(There was a time when I did, though. I can see myself, not so many years back, like a homunculus squatting at the foot of Mt. McKinley, throwing together two handfuls of mud and shouting, "Look at the big mountain *I* made!")

And if I did know the physical principles which brought them here, and could write them in terms accessible to technicians resembling myself, I would not do it.

Here is a thing I am afraid no reader of this journal will believe: these people, as I have written, learned their method of space travel some twelve million years ago. But this is the first time they have ever used it to convey them to another planet. The heavens are rich in worlds, she tells me; on many of them there is life, often on very primitive levels. No external force prevented her people from going forth, colonizing, conquering, as far as they pleased. They could have populated a galaxy. They did not, and for this reason: they believed they were not ready. More precisely: *Not good enough.*

Only some fifty million years ago, by her account, did they learn (as we may learn eventually) that intelligence without goodness is worse than high explosive in the hands of a baboon. For beings advanced beyond the level of Pithecanthropus, intelligence is a cheap commodity—not too hard to develop, hellishly easy to use for unconsidered ends. Whereas goodness is not to be achieved without unending effort of the hardest kind, within the self, whether the self be man or angel.

It is clear even to me that the conquest of evil is only one step, not the most important. For goodness, so she tried to tell me, is an altogether positive quality; the part of living nature that swarms with such monstrosities as cruelty, meanness, bitterness, greed, is not to be filled by a vacuum when these horrors are eliminated. When you clear away a poisonous gas, you try to fill the whole room with clean air. Kindness, for only one example: one who can define kindness only as the absence of cruelty has surely not begun to understand the nature of either.

They do not aim at perfection, these angels: only at the attainable. . . . That time fifty million years ago was evidently one of great suffering and confusion. War and all its attendant plagues. They passed through many centuries while advances in technology merely worsened their condition and increased the peril of self-annihilation. They came through that, in time. War was at length so far outgrown that its recurrence was impossible, and the development of wholly rational beings could begin. Then they were ready to start growing up, through millennia of self-searching, self-discipline, seeking to derive the simple from the complex, discovering how to use knowledge and not be used by it. Even then, of course, they slipped back often enough. There were what she refers to as "eras of fatigue." In their dimmer past, they had had many dark ages, lost civilizations, hopeful beginnings ending in dust. Earlier still, they had come out of the slime, as we did.

But their period of deepest uncertainty and sternest self-appraisal did not come until twelve million years ago, when they knew a universe could be theirs for the taking and knew they were not yet good enough.

They are in no more hurry than the stars. She tried to convey something tentatively, at this point, which was really beyond both of us. It had to do with time (not as I understand time) being perhaps the most essential attribute of God (not as I was ever able to understand that word). Seeing my mental exhaustion, she gave up the effort and later told me that the conception was extremely difficult for her, too—not only, I gathered, because of her youth and relative ignorance. There was also a hint that her father might not have wished her to bring my brain up to a hurdle like that one. . . .

Of course, they explored. Their little spaceships were roaming the ether before there was anything like Man on this earth—roaming and listening, observing, recording; never entering or taking part in the life of any home but their own. For five million years they even forbade themselves to go beyond their own Solar System, though it would have been easy to do so. And in the following seven million years, although they traveled to incredible distances, the same stern restraint was in force. It was altogether unrelated to what we should call fear—that, I think, is as extinct in them as hate. There was so much to do at home!—I wish I could imagine it. They mapped the heavens and played in their own sunlight.

Naturally, I cannot tell you what goodness is. I know only, moderately well, what it seems to mean to us human beings. It appears that the best of us can, with enormous difficulty, achieve a manner of life in which goodness is reasonably dominant, by a not too precarious balance, for the greater part of the time. Often, wise men have indicated they hope for nothing better than that in our present condition. We are, in other words, a fraction alive; the rest is in the dark. Dante was a bitter masochist, Beethoven a frantic and miserable snob, Shakespeare wrote potboilers. And Christ said, "My Father, if it be possible, let this cup pass from me."

But give us fifty million years—I am no pessimist. After all, I've watched one-celled organisms on the slide and listened to Brahms' Fourth. Night before last I said to the angel, "In spite of everything, you and I are kindred."

She granted me agreement.

She was lying on my pillow this morning so that I could see her when I awoke.

Her father has died, and she was with him when it happened. There was again that thought-impression that I could interpret only to mean that his life had been "saved." I was still sleep-bound when my mind asked, "What will you do?"

"Stay with you, if you wish it, for the rest of your life." Now, the last part of the message was clouded, but I am familiar with that—it seems to mean there is some further element that eludes me. I could not be mistaken about the part I did receive. It gives me amazing speculations. After all, I am only fifty-three; I might live for another thirty or forty years. . . .

She was preoccupied this morning, but whatever she felt about her father's death that might be paralleled by sadness in a human being was hidden from me. She did say her father was sorry he had not been able to show me a two-moon night.

One adult, then, remains in this world. Except to say that he is two hundred years old and full of knowledge, and that he endured the long journey without serious ill effects, she has told me little about him. And there are ten children, including herself.

Something was sparkling at her throat. When she was aware of my interest in it she took it off, and I fetched a magnifying glass. A necklace; under the glass, much like our finest human workmanship, if your imagination can reduce it to the proper scale. The stones appeared similar to the jewels we know: diamonds, sapphires, rubies, emeralds, the diamonds snapping out every color under heaven; but there were two or three very dark-purple stones unlike anything I know—not amethysts, I am sure. The necklace was strung on something more slender than cobweb, and the design of the joining clasp was too delicate for my glass to help me. The necklace had been her mother's, she told me; as she put it back around her throat I thought I saw the same shy pride that any human girl might feel in displaying a new pretty.

She wanted to show me other things she had brought, and flew to the table where she had left a sort of satchel an inch and a half long—quite a load for her to fly with, but the translucent substance is so light that when she rested the satchel on my finger I scarcely felt it. She arranged a few articles happily for my inspection, and I put the glass to work again. One was a jeweled comb; she ran it through the down on her chest and legs to show me its use. There was a set of tools too small for the glass to interpret; I learned later they were a sewing kit. A book, and some writing instrument much like a metal pencil: imagine a book and pencil that could be used comfortably by hands hardly bigger than the paws of a mouse—that is the best I can do. The book, I understand, is a blank record for her use as needed.

And finally, when I was fully awake and dressed and we had finished breakfast, she reached in the bottom of the satchel for a parcel (heavy for her) and made me understand it was a gift for me. "My father made it for you, but I put in the stone myself, last night." She unwrapped it. A ring, precisely the size for my little finger.

I broke down, rather. She understood that, and sat on my shoulder petting my earlobe till I had command of myself.

I have no idea what the jewel is. It shifts with the light from purple to jade green to amber. The metal resembles platinum in appearance except for a tinge of rose at certain angles of light. . . . When I stare into the stone, I think I see—never mind that now. I am not ready to write it down, and perhaps never will be; anyway, I must be sure.

We improved our housekeeping later in the morning. I showed her over the house. It isn't much—Cape Codder, two rooms up and two down. Every corner interested her, and when she found a shoe box in the bedroom closet, she asked for it. At her direction, I have arranged it on a chest near my bed and near the window, which will be always open; she says the mosquitoes will not bother me, and I don't doubt her. I unearthed a white silk scarf for the bottom of the box; after asking my permission (as if I could want to refuse her anything!) she got her sewing kit and snipped off a piece of

the scarf several inches square, folded it on itself several
times, and sewed it into a narrow pillow an inch long. So
now she had a proper bed and a room of her own. I wish I
had something less coarse than silk, but she insists it's nice.

We have not talked very much today. In the afternoon she
flew out for an hour's play in the cloud country; when she
returned she let me know that she needed a long sleep. She is
still sleeping, I think; I am writing this downstairs, fearing
the light might disturb her.

Is it possible I can have thirty or forty years in her company? I wonder how teachable my mind still is. I seem to be
able to assimilate new facts as well as I ever could; this
ungainly carcass should be durable, with reasonable care. Of
course, facts without a synthetic imagination are no better
than scattered bricks; but perhaps my imagination . . .

I don't know.

Judy wants out. I shall turn in when she comes back. I
wonder if poor Judy's life could be—the word is certainly
"saved." I must ask.

June 10

Last night when I stopped writing I did go to bed but I was
restless, refusing sleep. At some time in the small hours—
there was light from a single room—she flew over to me. The
tensions dissolved like an illness, and my mind was able to
respond with a certain calm.

I made plain (what I am sure she already knew) that I
would never willingly part company with her, and then she
gave me to understand that there are two alternatives for the
remainder of my life. The choice, she says, is altogether
mine, and I must take time to be sure of my decision.

I can live out my natural span, whatever it proves to be,
and she will not leave me for long at any time. She will be
there to counsel, teach, help me in anything good I care to
undertake. She says she would enjoy this; for some reason
she is, as we'd say in our language, fond of me. We'd have
fun.

Lord, the books I could write! I fumble for words now, in

the usual human way: whatever I put on paper is a miserable
fraction of the potential; the words themselves are rarely the
right ones. But under her guidance . . .

I could take a fair part in shaking the world. With words
alone. I could preach to my own people. Before long, I
would be heard.

I could study and explore. What small nibblings we have
made at the sum of available knowledge! Suppose I brought
in one leaf from outdoors, or one common little bug—in a
few hours of studying it with her I'd know more of my own
specialty than a flood of the best textbooks could tell me.

She has also let me know that when she and those who
came with her have learned a little more about the human
picture, it should be possible to improve my health greatly,
and probably my life expectancy. I don't imagine my back
could ever straighten, but she thinks the pain might be cleared
away, possibly without drugs. I could have a clearer mind, in
a body that would neither fail nor torment me.

Then there is the other alternative.

It seems they have developed a technique by means of
which any unresisting living subject whose brain is capable of
memory at all can experience a total recall. It is a byproduct,
I understand, of their silent speech, and a very recent one.
They have practiced it for only a few thousand years, and
since their own understanding of the phenomenon is very
incomplete, they classify it among their experimental techniques. In a general way, it may somewhat resemble that
reliving of the past that psychoanalysis can sometimes bring
about in a limited way for therapeutic purposes; but you must
imagine that sort of thing tremendously magnified and clari-
fied, capable of including every detail that has ever registered
on the subject's brain; and the end result is very different.
The purpose is not therapeutic, as we would understand it:
quite the opposite. The end result is death. Whatever is
recalled by this process is transmitted to the receiving mind,
which can retain it and record any or all of it if such a record
is desired; but to the subject who recalls it, it is a flowing
away, without return. Thus it is not a true "remembering"

but a giving. The mind is swept clear, naked of all its past, and along with memory, life withdraws also. Very quietly. At the end, I suppose it must be like standing without resistance in the engulfment of a flood time, until finally the waters close over.

That, it seems, is how Camilla's life was "saved." Now, when I finally grasped that, I laughed, and the angel of course caught ι. y joke. I was thinking about my neighbor Steele, who boarded the old lady for me in his henhouse for a couple of winters. Somewhere safe in the angelic records there must be a hen's-eye image of the patch in the seat of Steele's pants. Well—good. And, naturally, Camilla's view of me, too: not too unkind, I hope—she couldn't help the expression on her rigid little face, and I don't believe it ever meant anything.

At the other end of the scale is the saved life of my angel's father. Recall can be a long process, she says, depending on the intricacy and richness of the mind recalling; and in all but the last stages it can be halted at will. Her father's recall was begun when they were still far out in space and he knew that he could not long survive the journey. When that journey ended, the recall had progressed so far that very little actual memory remained to him of his life on that other planet. He had what must be called a "deductive memory"; from the material of the years not yet given away, he could reconstruct what must have been; and I assume the other adult who survived the passage must have been able to shelter him from errors that loss of memory might involve. This, I infer, is why he could not show me a two-moon night. I forgot to ask her whether the images he did send me were from actual or deductive memory. Deductive, I think, for there was a certain dimness about them not present when my angel gives me a picture of something seen with her own eyes.

Jade green eyes, by the way—were you wondering?

In the same fashion, my own life could be saved. Every aspect of existence that I ever touched, that ever touched me, could be transmitted to some perfect record. The nature of the written record is beyond me, but I have no doubt of its relative perfection. Nothing important, good or bad, would be lost. And they need a knowledge of humanity, if they are to carry out whatever it is they have in mind.

It would be difficult, she tells me, and sometimes painful. Most of the effort would be hers, but some of it would have to be mine. In her period of infantile education, she elected what we should call zoology as her lifework; for that reason she was given intensive theoretical training in this technique. Right now, I guess she knows more than anyone else on this planet not only about what makes a hen tick but about how it feels to be a hen. Though a beginner, she is in all essentials already an expert. She can help me, she thinks (if I choose this alternative)—at any rate, ease me over the toughest spots, soothe away resistance, keep my courage from flagging too much.

For it seems that this process of recall is painful to an advanced intellect (she, without condescension, calls us very advanced) because, while all pretense and self-delusion are stripped away, there remains conscience, still functioning by whatever standards of good and bad the individual has developed in his lifetime. Our present knowledge of our own motives is such a pathetically small beginning!—hardly stronger than an infant's first effort to focus his eyes. I am merely wondering how much of my life (if I choose this way) will seem to me altogether hideous. Certainly plenty of the "good deeds" that I still cherish in memory like so many well-behaved cherubs will turn up with the leering aspect of greed or petty vanity or worse.

Not that I am a bad man, in any reasonable sense of the term; not a bit of it. I respect myself; no occasion to grovel and beat my chest; I'm not ashamed to stand comparison with any other fair sample of the species. But there you are: I *am* human, and under the aspect of eternity so far, plus this afternoon's newspaper, that is a rather serious thing.

Without real knowledge, I think of this total recall as something like a passage down a corridor of myriad images—now dark, now brilliant; now pleasant, now horrible—guided by no certainty except an awareness of the open blind door at the end of it. It could have its pleasing moments and its consolations. I don't see how it could ever approximate the delight and satisfaction of living a few more years in this world with the angel lighting on my shoulder when she wishes, and talking to me.

I had to ask her of how great value such a record would be to them. Very great. Obvious enough—they can be of little use to us, by their standards, until they understand us; and they came here to be of use to us as well as to themselves. And understanding us, to them, means knowing us inside out with a completeness such as our most dedicated and laborious scholars could never imagine. I remember those twelve million years: they will not touch us until they are certain no harm will come of it. On our tortured planet, however, there is a time factor. They know that well enough, of course. . . . Recall cannot begin unless the subject is willing or unresisting; to them, that has to mean willing, for any being with intellect enough to make a considered choice. Now, I wonder how many they could find who would be honestly willing to make that uneasy journey into death, for no reward except an assurance that they were serving their own kind and the angels?

More to the point, I wonder if I would be able to achieve such willingness myself, even with her help?

When this had been explained to me, she urged me again to make no hasty decision. And she pointed out to me what my thoughts were already groping at—why not both alternatives, within a reasonable limit of time? Why couldn't I have ten or fifteen years or more with her and then undertake the total recall—perhaps not until my physical powers had started toward senility? I thought that over.

This morning I had almost decided to choose that most welcome and comforting solution. Then the mailman brought my daily paper. Not that I needed any such reminder.

In the afternoon I asked her if she knew whether, in the present state of human technology, it would be possible for our folly to actually destroy this planet. She did not know, for certain. Three of the other children have gone away to different parts of the world, to learn what they can about that. But she had to tell me that such a thing has happened before, elsewhere in the heavens. I guess I won't write a letter to the papers advancing an explanation for the occasional appearance of a nova among the stars. Doubtless others have hit on the same hypothesis without the aid of angels.

And that is not all I must consider. I could die by accident or sudden disease before I had begun to give my life.

Only now, at this very late moment, rubbing my sweaty forehead and gazing into the lights of that wonderful ring, have I been able to put together some obvious facts in the required synthesis.

I don't know, of course, what forms their assistance to us will take. I suspect human beings won't see or hear much of the angels for a long time to come. Now and then disastrous decisions may be altered, and those who believe themselves wholly responsible won't quite know why their minds worked that way. Here and there, maybe an influential mind will be rather strangely nudged into a better course. Something like that. There may be sudden new discoveries and inventions of kinds that will tend to neutralize the menace of our nastiest playthings. But whatever the angels decide to do, the record and analysis of my not too atypical life will be an aid: it could even be the small weight deciding the balance between triumph and failure. That is fact one.

Two: my angel and her brothers and sisters, for all their amazing level of advancement, are of perishable protoplasm, even as I am. Therefore, if this ball of earth becomes a ball of flame, they also will be destroyed. Even if they have the means to use their spaceship again or to build another, it might easily happen that they would not learn their danger in time to escape. And for all I know, this could be tomorrow. Or tonight.

So there can no longer be any doubt as to my choice, and I will tell her when she wakes.

Tonight* there is no recall—I am to rest awhile. I see it is

---

*At this point Dr. Bannerman's handwriting alters curiously. From here on he used a soft pencil instead of a pen, and the script shows signs of haste. In spite of this, however, it is actually much clearer, steadier, and easier to read than the earlier entries in his normal hand.—BLAINE.

almost a month since I last wrote in this journal. My total recall began three weeks ago, and I have already been able to give away the first twenty-eight years of my life.

Since I no longer require normal sleep, the recall begins at night, as soon as the lights begin to go out over there in the village and there is little danger of interruption. Daytimes, I putter about in my usual fashion. I have sold Steele my hens, and Judy's life was saved a week ago; that practically winds up my affairs, except that I want to write a codicil to my will. I might as well do that now, right here in this journal, instead of bothering my lawyer. It should be legal.

> TO WHOM IT MAY CONCERN: I hereby bequeath to my friend Lester Morse, M.D., of Augusta, Maine, the ring which will be found at my death on the fifth finger of my left hand; and I would urge Dr. Morse to retain this ring in his private possession at all times, and to make provision for its disposal, in the event of his own death, to some person in whose character he places the utmost faith.
>
> (Signed) David Bannerman*

Tonight she has gone away for a while, and I am to rest and do as I please until she returns. I shall spend the time filling in some blanks in this record, but I am afraid it will be a spotty job, unsatisfactory to any readers who are subject to the blessed old itch for facts. Mainly because there is so much I no longer care about. It is troublesome to try to decide what things would be considered important by interested strangers.

Except for the lack of any desire for sleep, and a bodily weariness that is not at all unpleasant, I notice no physical effects thus far. I have no faintest recollection of anything that happened earlier than my twenty-eighth birthday. My deductive memory seems rather efficient, and I am sure I could reconstruct most of the story if it were worth the bother: this afternoon I grubbed around among some old

---

*In spite of superficial changes in the handwriting, this signature has been certified genuine by an expert graphologist.—BLAINE.

letters of that period, but they weren't very interesting. My knowledge of English is unaffected; I can still read scientific German and some French, because I had occasion to use those languages fairly often after I was twenty-eight. The scraps of Latin dating from high school are quite gone. So are algebra and all but the simplest propositions of high-school geometry: I never needed 'em. I can remember thinking of my mother after twenty-eight, but do not know whether the image this provides really resembles her; my father died when I was thirty-one, so I remember him as a sick old man. I believe I had a younger brother, but he must have died in childhood.*

Judy's passing was tranquil—pleasant for her, I think. It took the better part of a day. We went out to an abandoned field I know, and she lay in the sunshine with the angel sitting by her, while I dug a grave and then rambled off after wild raspberries. Toward evening the angel came and told me it was finished. And most interesting, she said. I don't see how there can have been anything distressing about it for Judy; after all, what hurts us worse is to have our favorite self-deceptions stripped away.

As the angel has explained it to me, her people, their cats, those kangaroo-folk, Man, and just possibly the cats on our planet (she hasn't met them yet) are the only animals she knows who are introspective enough to develop self-delusion and related pretenses. I suggested she might find something of the sort, at least in rudimentary form, among some of the other primates. She was immensely interested and wanted to learn everything I could tell her about monkeys and apes. It seems that long ago on the other planet there used to be clumsy, winged creatures resembling the angels to about the degree that the large anthropoids resemble us. They became extinct some forty million years ago, in spite of enlightened efforts to keep their kin alive. Their birth rate became insufficient for replacement, as if some necessary spark had simply

*Dr. Bannerman's mother died in 1918 of influenza. His brother (three years older, not younger) died of pneumonia, 1906.—BLAINE.

flickered out; almost as if nature, or whatever name you prefer for the unknown, had with gentle finality written them off. . . .

I have not found the recall painful, at least not in retrospect. There must have been sharp moments, mercifully forgotten, along with their causes, as if the process had gone on under anesthesia. Certainly there were plenty of incidents in my first twenty-eight years that I should not care to offer to the understanding of any but the angels. Quite often I must have been mean, selfish, base in any number of ways, if only to judge by the record since twenty-eight. Those old letters touch on a few of these things. To me, they now matter only as material for a record which is safely out of my hands.

However, to any persons I may have harmed, I wish to say this: you were hurt by aspects of my humanity which may not, in a few million years, be quite so common among us all. Against these darker elements I struggled, in my human fashion, as you do yourselves. The effort is not wasted.

It was a week after I told the angel my decision before she was prepared to start the recall. During that week she searched my present mind more closely than I should have imagined was possible: she had to be sure. During that week of hard questions I dare say she learned more about my kind than has ever gone on record even in a physician's office; I hope she did. To any psychiatrist who might question that, I offer a naturalist's suggestion: it is easy to imagine, after some laborious time, that we have noticed everything a given patch of ground can show us; but alter the viewpoint only a little—dig down a foot with a space, say, or climb a tree branch and look downward—it's a whole new world.

When the angel was not exploring me in this fashion, she took pains to make me glimpse the satisfactions and million rewarding experiences I might have if I chose the other way. I see how necessary that was; at the time it seemed almost cruel. She had to do it, for my own sake, and I am glad that I was somehow able to stand fast to my original choice. So was she, in the end; she has even said she loves me for it. What that troubling word means to her is not within my mind: I am satisfied to take it in the human sense.

Some evening during that week—I think it was June 12—Lester dropped around for sherry and chess. Hadn't seen him in quite a while, and haven't since. There is a moderate polio scare this summer, and it keeps him on the jump. The angel retired behind some books on an upper shelf—I'm afraid it was dusty—and had fun with our chess. She had a fair view of your bald spot, Lester; later she remarked that she liked your looks, and can't you do something about that weight? She suggested an odd expedient, which I believe has occurred to your medical self from time to time—eating less.

Maybe she shouldn't have done what she did with those chess games. Nothing more than my usual blundering happened until after my first ten moves; by that time I suppose she had absorbed the principles and she took over, slightly. I was not fully aware of it until I saw Lester looking like a boiled duck: I had imagined my astonishing moves were the result of my own damn cleverness.

Seriously, Lester, think back to that evening. You've played in stiff amateur tournaments; you know your own abilities and you know mine. Ask yourself whether I could have done anything like that without help. I tell you again, I didn't study the game in the interval when you weren't there. I've never had a chess book in the library, and if I had, no amount of study would take me into your class. Haven't that sort of mentality—just your humble sparring partner, and I've enjoyed it on that basis, as you might enjoy watching a primadonna surgeon pull off some miracle you wouldn't dream of attempting yourself. Even if your game had been way below par that evening (I don't think it was), I could never have pinned your ears back three times running, without help. That evening you were a long way out of *your* class, that's all.

I couldn't tell you anything about it at the time—she was clear on that point—so I could only bumble and preen myself and leave you mystified. But she wants me to write anything I choose in this journal, and somehow, Lester, I think you may find the next few decades pretty interesting. You're still young—some ten years younger than I. I think you'll see many things that I do wish I myself might see come to pass—or I would so wish if I were not convinced that my choice was the right one.

Most of those new events will not be spectacular, I'd guess. Many of the turns to a better way will hardly be recognized at the time for what they are, by you or anyone else. Obviously, our nature being what it is, we shall not jump into heaven overnight. To hope for that would be as absurd as it is to imagine that any formula, ideology, theory of social pattern, can bring us into Utopia. As I see it, Lester—and I think your consulting room would have told you the same even if your own intuition were not enough— there is only one battle of importance: Armageddon. And Armageddon field is within each self, world without end.

At the moment I believe I am the happiest man who ever lived.

July 20

All but the last ten years now given away. The physical fatigue (still pleasant) is quite overwhelming. I am not troubled by the weeds in my garden patch—merely a different sort of flowers where I had planned something else. An hour ago she brought me the seed of a blown dandelion, to show me how lovely it was—I don't suppose I had ever noticed. I hope whoever takes over this place will bring it back to farming: they say the ten acres below the house used to be good potato land—nice early ground.

It is delightful to sit in the sun, as if I were old.

After thumbing over earlier entries in this journal, I see I have often felt quite bitter toward my own kind. I deduce that I must have been a lonely man—much of the loneliness self-imposed. A great part of my bitterness must have been no more than one ugly byproduct of a life spent too much apart. Some of it doubtless came from objective causes, yet I don't believe I ever had more cause than any moderately intelligent man who would like to see his world a pleasanter place than it ever has been. My angel tells me that the pain in my back is due to an injury received in some early stage of the world war that still goes on. That could have soured me, perhaps. It's all right—it's all in the record.

She is racing with a hummingbird—holding back, I think, to give the ball of green fluff a break.

Another note for you, Lester. I have already indicated that my ring is to be yours. I don't want to tell you what I have discovered of its properties, for fear it might not give you the same pleasure and interest that it has given me. Of course, like any spot of shifting light and color, it is an aid to self-hypnosis. It is much, much more than that, but—find out for yourself, at some time when you are a little protected from everyday distractions. I know it can't harm you, because I know its source.

By the way, I wish you would convey to my publishers my request that they either discontinue manufacture of my *Introductory Biology* or else bring out a new edition revised in accordance with some notes you will find in the top left drawer of my library desk. I glanced through that book after my angel assured me that I wrote it, and I was amazed. However, I'm afraid my notes are messy (I call them mine by a poetic license), and they may be too advanced for the present day—though the revision is mainly a matter of leaving out certain generalities that ain't so. Use your best judgment: it's a very minor textbook, and the thing isn't too important. A last wriggle of my personal vanity.

July 27

I have seen a two-moon night.

It was given to me by that other grown-up, at the end of a wonderful visit, when he and six of those nine other children came to see me. It was last night, I think—yes, must have been. First there was a murmur of wings above the house; my angel flew in, laughing; then they were here, all about me. Full of gaiety and colored fire, showing off in every way they knew would please me. Each one had something graceful and friendly to say to me. One brought me a moving image of the St. Lawrence seen at morning from half a mile up—clouds—

eagles; now, how could he know that would delight me so much? And each one thanked me for what I had done.

But it's been so easy!

And at the end the old one—his skin is quite brown, and his down is white and gray—gave the remembered image of a two-moon night. He saw it some sixty years ago.

I have not even considered making an effort to describe it—my fingers will not hold this pencil much longer tonight. Oh—soaring buildings of white and amber, untroubled countryside, silver on curling rivers, a glimpse of open sea; a moon rising in clarity, another setting in a wreath of cloud, between them a wide wandering of unfamiliar stars; and here and there the angels, worthy after fifty million years to live in such a night. No, I cannot describe anything like that. But, you human kindred of mine, I can do something better. I can tell you that this two-moon night, glorious as it was, was no more beautiful than a night under a single moon on this ancient and familiar Earth might be—if you will imagine that the rubbish of human evil has been cleared away and that our own people have started at last on the greatest of all explorations.

July 29

Nothing now remains to give away but the memory of the time that has passed since the angel came. I am to rest as long as I wish, write whatever I want to. Then I shall get myself over to the bed and lie down as if for sleep. She tells me that I can keep my eyes open: she will close them for me when I no longer see her.

I remain convinced that our human case is hopeful. I feel sure that in only a few thousand years we may be able to perform some of the simpler preparatory tasks, such as casting out evil and loving our neighbors. And if that should prove to be so, who can doubt that in another fifty million years we might well be only a little lower than the angels?

LIBRARIAN'S NOTE: As is generally known, the original of the Bannerman Journal is said to have been in the possession of Dr. Lester Morse at the time of the latter's disappearance in

1964, and that disappearance has remained an unsolved mystery to the present day. McCarran is known to have visited Captain Garrison Blaine in October, 1951, but no record remains of that visit. Captain Blaine appears to have been a bachelor who lived alone. He was killed in line of duty, December, 1951. McCarran is believed not to have written about or discussed the Bannerman affair with anyone else. It is almost certain that he himself removed the extract and related papers from the files (unofficially, it would seem!) when he severed his connection with the FBI in 1957; at any rate, they were found among his effects after his assassination and were relased to the public, considerably later, by Mrs. McCarran.

The following memorandum was originally attached to the extract from the Bannerman Journal; it carries the McCarran initialing.

Aug. 11, 1951

The original letter of complaint written by Stephen Clyde, M.D., and mentioned in the accompanying letter of Captain Blaine, has unfortunately been lost, owing perhaps to an error in filing.

Personnel presumed responsible have been instructed not to allow such error to be repeated except if, as, and/or when necessary.

C. McC.

On the margin of this memorandum there was a penciled notation, later erased. The imprint is sufficient to show the unmistakable McCarran script. The notation read in part as follows: *Far be it from a McC. to lose his job except if, as, and/or*—the rest is undecipherable, except for a terminal word which is regrettably unparliamentary.

STATEMENT BY LESTER MORSE, M.D., DATED AUGUST 9, 1951

On the afternoon of July 30, 1951, acting on what I am obliged to describe as an unexpected impulse, I drove out to the country for the purpose of calling on my friend Dr. David

Bannerman. I had not seen him nor had word from him since the evening of June 12 of this year.

I entered, as was my custom, without knocking. After calling to him and hearing no response, I went upstairs to his bedroom and found him dead. From superficial indications I judged that death must have taken place during the previous night. He was lying on his bed on his left side, comfortably disposed as if for sleep but fully dressed, with a fresh shirt and clean summer slacks. His eyes and mouth were closed, and there was no trace of the disorder to be expected at even the easiest natural death. Because of these signs I assumed, as soon as I had determined the absence of breath and heartbeat and noted the chill of the body, that some neighbor must have found him already, performed these simple rites out of respect for him, and probably notified a local physician or other responsible person. I therefore waited (Dr. Bannerman had no telephone), expecting that someone would soon call.

Dr. Bannerman's journal was on a table near his bed, open to that page on which he had written a codicil to his will. I read that part. Later, while I was waiting for others to come, I read the remainder of the journal, as I believe he wished me to do. The ring he mentions was on the fifth finger of his left hand, and it is now in my possession. When writing that codicil Dr. Bannerman must have overlooked or forgotten the fact that in his formal will, written some months earlier, he had appointed me executor. If there are legal technicalities involved, I shall be pleased to cooperate fully with the proper authorities.

The ring, however, will remain in my keeping, since that was Dr. Bannerman's expressed wish, and I am not prepared to offer it for examination or discussion under any circumstances.

The notes for a revision of one of his textbooks were in his desk, as noted in the journal. They are by no means "messy"; nor are they particularly revolutionary except insofar as he wished to rephrase, as theory or hypothesis, certain statements that I would have supposed could be regarded as axiomatic. This is not my field, and I am not competent to judge. I shall take up the matter with his publishers at the earliest opportunity.*

So far as I can determine, and bearing in mind the results of the autopsy performed by Stephen Clyde, M.D., the death of Dr. David Bannerman was not inconsistent with the presence of an embolism of some type not distinguishable by post mortem. I have so stated on the certificate of death. It would seem to be not in the public interest to leave such questions in doubt. I am compelled to add one other item of medical opinion for what it may be worth:

I am not a psychiatrist, but, owing to the demands of general practice, I have found it advisable to keep as up to date as possible with current findings and opinion in this branch of medicine. Dr. Bannerman possessed, in my opinion, emotional and intellectual stability to a better degree than anyone else of comparable intelligence in the entire field of my acquaintance, personal and professional. If it is suggested that he was suffering from a hallucinatory psychosis, I can only say that it must have been of a type quite outside my experience and not described, so far as I know, anywhere in the literature of psychopathology.

Dr. Bannerman's house, on the afternoon of July 30, was in good order. Near the open, unscreened window of his bedroom there was a coverless shoe box with a folded silk scarf in the bottom. I found no pillow such as Dr. Bannerman describes in the journal, but observed that a small section had been cut from the scarf. In this box, and near it, there was a peculiar fragrance, faint, aromatic, and very sweet, such as I have never encountered before and therefore cannot describe.

It may or may not have any bearing on the case that, while I remained in this house that afternoon, I felt no sense of grief or personal loss, although Dr. Bannerman had been a loved and honored friend for a number of years. I merely had, and have, a conviction that after the completion of some very great undertaking, he had found peace.

---

*LIBRARIAN'S NOTE: But it seems he never did. No new edition of *Introductory Biology* was ever brought out, and the textbook has been out of print since 1952.

"BREEDS THERE A MAN—?"

BY ISAAC ASIMOV (1920–   )
ASTOUNDING SCIENCE FICTION, JUNE

Another of my favorite pretenses is now punctured. Every once in a while, one of my own stories appears in this series. In every case till now Marty has chosen it and I have been honestly unnerved by it. I don't mind placing my own stories in my own anthologies, but when the anthology purports to be a list of the "best," doesn't it look funny for an Asimov story to be included? Who says it's the best? Asimov?

So till now I have protested that it was Marty who chose the story over my objections and that he refused to listen to anything I had to say to the contrary. And that's always been true enough—

Till now.

When Marty sent me a batch of possibles for this volume, I went through them all carefully and vetoed one or two, then went over the others thoughtfully and then said to myself, "Hey, didn't 'Breeds There a Man—?' appear about now?"

I looked it up and, sure enough, it did. So I called up Marty and said, "Did you reject 'Breeds There a Man—?'?" He said, "Was that a 1951 story?" I said, "It sure was. Please read it, Marty, and tell me what you think, because I think a great deal of it."

So Marty read it again, and he said he thought a great deal of it, too (he's such an old softy), and here it is.

—*I.A.*

POLICE SERGEANT MANKIEWICZ was on the telephone and he wasn't enjoying it. His conversation was sounding like a one-sided view of a firecracker.

He was saying, "That's right! He came in here and said, 'Put me in jail, because I want to kill myself.'

". . . I can't help that. Those were his exact words. It sounds crazy to me, too.

". . . Look, mister, the guy answers the description. You asked me for information and I'm giving it to you.

". . . He has exactly that scar on his right cheek and he said his name was John Smith. He didn't say it was Doctor anything-at-all.

". . . Well, sure it's a phony. Nobody is named John Smith. Not in a police station, anyway.

". . . He's in jail now.

". . . Yes, I mean it.

". . . Resisting an officer; assault and battery; malicious mischief. That's three counts.

". . . I don't care who he is.

". . . All right. I'll hold on."

He looked up at Officer Brown and put his hand over the mouthpiece of the phone. It was a ham of a hand that nearly swallowed up the phone altogether. His blunt-featured face was ruddy and steaming under a thatch of pale-yellow hair.

He said, "Trouble! Nothing but trouble at a precinct station. I'd rather be pounding a beat any day."

"Who's on the phone?" asked Brown. He had just come in and didn't really care. He thought Mankiewicz would look better on a suburban beat, too.

"Oak Ridge. Long Distance. A guy called Grant. Head of somethingological division, and now he's getting somebody else at seventy-five cents a min . . . Hello!"

Mankiewicz got a new grip on the phone and held himself down.

"Look," he said, "let me go through this from the beginning. I want you to get it straight and then if you don't like it, you can send someone down here. The guy doesn't want a lawyer. He claims he just wants to stay in jail and, brother, that's all right with me.

"Well, will you listen? He came in yesterday, walked right up to me, and said, 'Officer, I want you to put me in jail because I want to kill myself.' So I said, 'Mister, I'm sorry you want to kill yourself. Don't do it, because if you do, you'll regret it the rest of your life.'

". . . I *am* serious. I'm just telling you what I said. I'm not saying it was a funny joke, but I've got my own troubles here, if you know what I mean. Do you think all I've got to do here is to listen to cranks who walk in and——

"' . . . Give me a chance, will you?' I said, 'I can't put you in jail for wanting to kill yourself. That's no crime.' And he said, 'But I don't want to die.' So I said, 'Look, bud, get out of here.' I mean if a guy wants to commit suicide, all right, and if he doesn't want to, all right, but I don't want him weeping on my shoulder.

". . . I'm *getting* on with it. So he said to me, 'If I commit a crime, will you put me in jail?' I said, 'If you're caught and if someone files a charge and you can't put up bail, we will. Now beat it.' So he picked up the inkwell on my desk and, before I could stop him, he turned it upside down on the open police blotter.

". . . That's right! Why do you think we have 'malicious mischief' tabbed on him? The ink ran down all over my pants.

". . . Yes, assault and battery, too! I came hopping down to shake a little sense into him, and he kicked me in the shins and handed me one in the eye.

". . . I'm not making this up. You want to come down here and look at my face?

" . . . He'll be up in court one of these days. About Thursday, maybe.

". . . Ninety days is the least he'll get, unless the psychos say otherwise. I think he belongs in the loony-bin myself.

". . . Officially, he's John Smith. That's the only name he'll give.

". . . No, sir, he doesn't get released without the proper legal steps.

". . . O.K., you do that, if you want to, bud! I just do my job here."

He banged the phone into its cradle, glowered at it, then picked it up and began dialing. He said "Gianetti?", got the proper answer and began talking.

"What's the A. E. C.? I've been talking to some Joe on the phone and he says——

". . . No, I'm not kidding, lunk-head. If I were kidding, I'd put up a sign. What's the alphabet soup?"

He listened, said, "Thanks" in a small voice and hung up again.

He had lost some of his color. "That second guy was the head of the Atomic Energy Commission," he said to Brown. "They must have switched me from Oak Ridge to Washington."

Brown lounged to his feet. "Maybe the F.B.I. is after this John Smith guy. Maybe he's one of these here scientists." He felt moved to philosophy. "They ought to keep atomic secrets away from those guys. Things were O.K. as long as General Groves was the only fella who knew about the atom bomb. Once they cut in these here scientists on it, though——"

"Ah, shut up," snarled Mankiewicz.

Dr. Oswald Grant kept his eyes fixed on the white line that marked the highway and handled the car as though it were an enemy of his. He always did. He was tall and knobby with a withdrawn expression stamped on his face. His knees crowded the wheel, and his knuckles whitened whenever he made a turn.

Inspector Darrity sat beside him with his legs crossed so that the sole of his left shoe came up hard against the door. It would leave a sandy mark when he took it away. He tossed a

nut-brown penknife from hand to hand. Earlier, he had un-
sheathed its wicked, gleaming blade and scraped casually at
his nails as they drove, but a sudden swerve had nearly cost
him a finger and he desisted.

He said, "What do you know about this Ralson?"

Dr. Grant took his eyes from the road momentarily, then
returned them. He said, uneasily, "I've known him since he
took his doctorate at Princeton. He's a very brilliant man."

"Yes? Brilliant, huh? Why is it that all you scientific men
describe one another as 'brilliant'? Aren't there any mediocre
ones?"

"Many. I'm one of them. But Ralson isn't. You ask
anyone. Ask Oppenheimer. Ask Bush. He was the youngest
observer at Alamogordo."

"O.K. He was brilliant. What about his private life?"

Grant waited. "I wouldn't know."

"You know him since Princeton. How many years is
that?"

They had been scouring north along the highway from
Washington for two hours with scarcely a word between
them. Now Grant felt the atmosphere change and the grip of
the law on his coat collar.

"He got his degree in '43."

"You've known him eight years then."

"That's right."

"And you don't know about his private life?"

"A man's life is his own, Inspector. He wasn't very
sociable. A great many of the men are like that. They work
under pressure and when they're off the job, they're not
interested in continuing the lab acquaintanceships."

"Did he belong to any organizations that you know of?"

"No."

The inspector said, "Did he ever say anything to you that
might indicate he was disloyal?"

Grant shouted "No!" and there was silence for a while.

Then Darrity said, "How important is Ralson in atomic
research?"

Grant hunched over the wheel and said, "As important as

any one man can be. I grant you that no one is indispensable, but Ralson has always seemed to be rather unique. He has the engineering mentality.''

"What does that mean?"

"He isn't much of a mathematician himself, but he can work out the gadgets that put someone else's math into life. There's no one like him when it comes to that. Time and again, Inspector, we've had a problem to lick and no time to lick it in. There were nothing but blank minds all around until he put some thought into it and said, 'Why don't you try so-and-so?' Then he'd go away. He wouldn't even be interested enough to see if it worked. But it always did. Always! Maybe we would have got it ourselves eventually, but it might have taken months of additional time. I don't know how he does it. It's no use asking him either. He just looks at you and says 'It was obvious,' and walks away. Of course, once he's shown us how to do it, it *is* obvious.''

The inspector let him have his say out. When no more came, he said, "Would you say he was queer, mentally? Erratic, you know."

"When a person is a genius, you wouldn't expect him to be normal, would you?"

"Maybe not. But just how abnormal was this particular genius?"

"He never talked, particularly. Sometimes, he wouldn't work."

"Stayed at home and went fishing instead?"

"No. He came to the labs all right; but he would just sit at his desk. Sometimes that would go on for weeks. Wouldn't answer you, or even look at you, when you spoke to him."

"Did he ever actually leave work altogether?"

"Before now, you mean? Never!"

"Did he ever claim he wanted to commit suicide? Ever say he wouldn't feel safe except in jail?"

"No."

"You're sure this John Smith is Ralson?"

"I'm almost positive. He has a chemical burn on his right cheek that can't be mistaken."

"O.K. That's that, then I'll speak to him and see what he sounds like."

The silence fell for good this time. Dr. Grant followed the snaking line as Inspector Darrity tossed the penknife in low arcs from hand to hand.

The warden listened to the call-box and looked up at his visitors. "We can have him brought up here, Inspector, regardless."

"No," Dr. Grant shook his head. "Let's go to him."

Darrity said, "Is that normal for Ralson, Dr. Grant? Would you expect him to attack a guard trying to take him out of a prison cell?"

Grant said, "I can't say."

The warden spread a calloused palm. His thick nose twitched a little. "We haven't tried to do anything about him so far because of the telegram from Washington, but, frankly, he doesn't belong here. I'll be glad to have him taken off my hands."

"We'll see him in his cell," said Darrity.

They went down the hard, barlined corridor. Empty, incurious eyes watched their passing.

Dr. Grant felt his flesh crawl. "Has he been kept *here* all the time?"

Darrity did not answer.

The guard, pacing before them, stopped. "This is the cell."

Darrity said, "Is that Dr. Ralson?"

Dr. Grant looked silently at the figure upon the cot. The man had been lying down when they first reached the cell, but now he had risen to one elbow and seemed to be trying to shrink into the wall. His hair was sandy and thin, his figure slight, his eyes blank and china-blue. On his right cheek there was a raised pink patch that tailed off like a tadpole.

Dr. Grant said, "That's Ralson."

The guard opened the door and stepped inside, but Inspector Darrity sent him out again with a gesture. Ralson watched them mutely. He had drawn both feet up to the cot and was pushing backwards. His Adam's apple bobbled as he swallowed.

Darrity said quietly, "Dr. Elwood Ralson?"

"What do you want?" The voice was a surprising baritone.

"Would you come with us, please? We have some questions we would like to ask you."

"No! Leave me alone!"

"Dr. Ralson," said Grant, "I've been sent here to ask you to come back to work."

Ralson looked at the scientist and there was a momentary glint of something other than fear in his eyes. He said, "Hello, Grant." He got off his cot. "Listen, I've been trying to have them put me into a padded cell. Can't you make them do that for me? You know me, Grant. I wouldn't ask for something I didn't feel was necessary. Help me. I can't stand the hard walls. It makes me want to . . . bash——" He brought the flat of his palm thudding down against the hard, dull-gray concrete behind his cot.

Darrity looked thoughtful. He brought out his penknife and unbent the gleaming blade. Carefully, he scraped at his thumbnail, and said, "Would you like to see a doctor?"

But Ralson didn't answer that. He followed the gleam of metal and his lips parted and grew wet. His breath became ragged and harsh.

He said, "Put that away!"

Darrity paused. "Put what away?"

"The knife. Don't hold it in front of me. I can't stand looking at it."

Darrity said, "Why not?" He held it out. "Anything wrong with it? It's a good knife."

Ralson lunged. Darrity stepped back and his left hand came down on the other's wrist. He lifted the knife high in the air. "What's the matter, Ralson? What are you after?"

Grant cried a protest but Darrity waved him away.

Darrity said, "What do you want, Ralson?"

Ralson tried to reach upward, and bent under the other's appalling grip. He gasped, "Give me the knife."

"Why, Ralson? What do you want to do with it?"

"Please. I've got to——" He was pleading. "I've got to stop living."

"You want to die?"

"No. But I must."

Darrity shoved. Ralson flailed backward and tumbled into his cot, so that it squeaked noisily. Slowly, Darrity bent the blade of his penknife into its sheath and put it away. Ralson covered his face. His shoulders were shaking but otherwise he did not move.

There was the sound of shouting from the corridor, as the other prisoners reacted to the noise issuing from Ralson's cell. The guard came hurrying down, yelling, "Quiet!" as he went.

Darrity looked up. "It's all right, guard."

He was wiping his hands upon a large white handkerchief. "I think we'll get a doctor for him."

Dr. Gottfried Blaustein was small and dark and spoke with a trace of an Austrian accent. He needed only a small goatee to be the layman's caricature of a psychiatrist. But he was clean-shaven, and very carefully dressed. He watched Grant closely, assessing him, blocking in certain observations and deductions. He did this automatically, now, with everyone he met.

He said, "You give me a sort of picture. You describe a man of great talent, perhaps even genius. You tell me he has always been uncomfortable with people; that he has never fitted in with his laboratory environment, even though it was there that he met the greatest of success. Is there another environment to which he has fitted himself?"

"I don't understand."

"It is not given to all of us to be so fortunate as to find a congenial type of company at the place or in the field where we find it necessary to make a living. Often, one compensates by playing an instrument, or going hiking, or joining some club. In other words, one creates a new type of society, when not working, in which one can feel more at home. It need not have the slightest connection with what one's ordinary occupation is. It is an escape, and not necessarily an unhealthy one." He smiled and added, "Myself, I collect stamps. I am an active member of the American Society of Philatelists."

Grant shook his head. "I don't know what he did outside working hours. I doubt that he did anything like what you've mentioned."

"Um-m-m. Well, that would be sad. Relaxation and enjoyment are wherever you find them; but you must find them somewhere, no?"

"Have you spoken to Dr. Ralson, yet?"

"About his problems? No."

"Aren't you going to?"

"Oh, yes. But he has been here only a week. One must give him a chance to recover. He was in a highly excited state when he first came here. It was almost a delirium. Let him rest and become accustomed to the new environment. I will question him, then."

"Will you be able to get him back to work?"

Blaustein smiled. "How should I know? I don't even know what his sickness is."

"Couldn't you at least get rid of the worst of it; this suicidal obsession of his, and take care of the rest of the cure while he's at work?"

"Perhaps. I couldn't even venture an opinion so far without several interviews."

"How long do you suppose it will all take?"

"In these matters. Dr. Grant, nobody can say."

Grant brought his hands together in a sharp slap. "Do what seems best then. But this is more important than you know."

"Perhaps. But you may be able to help me, Dr. Grant."

"How?"

"Can you get me certain information which may be classified as top secret?"

"What kind of information?"

"I would like to know the suicide rate, since 1945, among nuclear scientists. Also, how many have left their jobs to go into other types of scientific work, or to leave science altogether.''

''Is this in connection with Ralson?''

''Don't you think it might be an occupational disease, this terrible unhappiness of his?''

''Well—a good many have left their jobs, naturally.''

''Why naturally, Dr. Grant?''

''You must know how it is, Dr. Blaustein. The atmosphere in modern atomic research is one of great pressure and red tape. You work with the government; you work with military men. You can't talk about your work; you have to be careful what you say. Naturally, if you get a chance at a job in a university, where you can fix your own hours, do your own work, write papers that don't have to be submitted to the A. E. C., attend conventions that aren't held behind locked doors, you take it.''

''And abandon your field of specialty forever.''

''There are always non-military applications. Of course, there was one man who did leave for another reason. He told me once he couldn't sleep nights. He said he'd hear one hundred thousand screams coming from Hiroshima, when he put the lights out. The last I heard of him he was a clerk in a haberdashery.''

''And do you ever hear a few screams yourself?''

Grant nodded. ''It isn't a nice feeling to know that even a little of the responsibility of atomic destruction might be your own.''

''How did Ralson feel?''

''He never spoke of anything like that.''

''In other words, if he felt it, he never even had the safety-valve effect of letting off steam to the rest of you.''

''I guess he hadn't.''

''Yet nuclear research must be done, no?''

''I'll say.''

''What would you do, Dr. Grant, if you felt you *had* to do something that you *couldn't* do.''

Grant shrugged. ''I don't know.''

''Some people kill themselves.''

"You mean that's what has Ralson down."

"I don't know. I do not know. I will speak to Dr. Ralson this evening. I can promise nothing, of course, but I will let you know whatever I can."

Grant rose. "Thanks, Doctor. I'll try to get the information you want."

Elwood Ralson's appearance had improved in the week he had been at Dr. Blaustein's sanatorium. His face had filled out and some of the restlessness had gone out of him. He was tieless and beltless. His shoes were without laces.

Blaustein said, "How do you feel, Dr. Ralson?"

"Rested."

"You have been treated well?"

"No complaints, Doctor."

Blaustein's hand fumbled for the letter-opener with which it was his habit to play during moments of abstraction, but his fingers met nothing. It had been put away, of course, with anything else possessing a sharp edge. There was nothing on his desk, now, but papers.

He said, "Sit down, Dr. Ralson. How do your symptoms progress?"

"You mean, do I have what you would call a suicidal impulse? Yes. It gets worse or better, depending on my thoughts, I think. But it's always with me. There is nothing you can do to help."

"Perhaps you are right. There are often things I cannot help. But I would like to know as much as I can about you. You are an important man——"

Ralson snorted.

"You do not consider that to be so?" asked Blaustein.

"No, I don't. There are no important men, any more than there are important individual bacteria."

"I don't understand."

"I don't expect you to."

"And yet it seems to me that behind your statement there must have been much thought. It would certainly be of the greatest interest to have you tell me some of this thought."

For the first time, Ralson smiled. It was not a pleasant smile. His nostrils were white. He said, "It is amusing to watch you, Doctor. You go about your business so conscientiously. You must listen to me, mustn't you, with just that air of phony interest and unctuous sympathy. I can tell you the most ridiculous things and still be sure of an audience, can't I?"

"Don't you think my interest can be real, even granted that it is professional, too?"

"No, I don't."

"Why not?"

"I'm not interested in discussing it."

"Would you rather return to your room?"

"If you don't mind. No!" His voice had suddenly suffused with fury as he stood up, then almost immediately sat down again. "Why shouldn't I use you? I don't like to talk to people. They're stupid. They don't see things. They stare at the obvious for hours and it means nothing to them. If I spoke to them, they wouldn't understand; they'd lose patience; they'd laugh. Whereas you must listen. It's your job. You can't interrupt to tell me I'm mad, even though you may think so."

"I'd be glad to listen to whatever you would like to tell me."

Ralson drew a deep breath. "I've known something for a year now, that very few people know. Maybe it's something no *live* person knows. Do you know that human cultural advances come in spurts? Over a space of two generations in a city containing thirty thousand free men, enough literary and artistic genius of the first rank arose to supply a nation of millions for a century under ordinary circumstances. I'm referring to the Athens of Pericles.

"There are other examples. There is the Florence of the Medicis, the England of Elizabeth, the Spain of the Cordovan Emirs. There was the spasm of social reformers among the Israelites of the Eighth and Seventh centuries before Christ. Do you know what I mean?"

Blaustein nodded. "I see that history is a subject that interests you."

"Why not? I suppose there's nothing that says I must restrict myself to nuclear cross-sections and wave mechanics."

"Nothing at all. Please proceed."

"At first, I thought I could learn more of the true inwardness of historical cycles by consulting a specialist. I had some conferences with a professional historian. A waste of time!"

"What was his name; this professional historian?"

"Does it matter?"

"Perhaps not, if you would rather consider it confidential. What did he tell you?"

"He said I was wrong; that history only appeared to go in spasms. He said that after closer studies the great civilizations of Egypt and Sumeria did not arise suddenly or out of nothing, but upon the basis of a long-developing sub-civilization that was already sophisticated in its arts. He said that Periclean Athens built upon a pre-Periclean Athens of lower accomplishments, without which the age of Pericles could not have been.

"I asked why was there not a post-Periclean Athens of higher accomplishments still, and he told me that Athens was ruined by a plague and by a long war with Sparta. I asked about other cultural spurts and each time it was a war that ended it, or, in some cases, even accompanied it. He was like all the rest. The truth was there; he had only to bend and pick it up; but he didn't."

Ralson stared at the floor, and said in a tired voice, "They come to me in the laboratory sometimes, Doctor. They say, 'how the devil are we going to get rid of the such-and-such effect that is ruining all our measurements, Ralson?' They show me the instruments and the wiring diagrams and I say, 'It's staring at you. Why don't you do so-and-so? A child could tell you that.' Then I walk away because I can't endure the slow puzzling of their stupid faces. Later, they come to me and say, 'It worked, Ralson. How did you figure it out?' I can't explain to them, Doctor; it would be like explaining that water is wet. And I couldn't explain to the historian. And I can't explain to you. It's a waste of time."

"Would you like to go back to your room?"

"Yes."

Blaustein sat and wondered for many minutes after Ralson had been escorted out of his office. His fingers found their way automatically into the upper right drawer of his desk and lifted out the letter-opener. He twiddled it in his fingers.

Finally, he lifted the telephone and dialed the unlisted number he had been given.

He said, "This is Blaustein. There is a professional historian who was consulted by Dr. Ralson some time in the past, probably a bit over a year ago. I don't know his name. I don't even know if he was connected with a university. If you could find him, I would like to see him."

Thaddeus Milton, Ph.D., blinked thoughtfully at Blaustein and brushed his hand through his iron-gray hair. He said, "They came to me and I said that I had indeed met this man. However, I have had very little connection with him. None, in fact, beyond a few conversations of a professional nature."

"How did he come to you?"

"He wrote me a letter; why me, rather than someone else, I do not know. A series of articles written by myself had appeared in one of the semi-learned journals of semi-popular appeal about that time. It may have attracted his attention."

"I see. With what general topic were the articles concerned?"

"They were a consideration of the validity of the cyclic approach to history. That is, whether one can really say that a particular civilization must follow laws of growth and decline in any matter analogous to those involving individuals."

"I have read Toynbee, Dr. Milton."

"Well, then, you know what I mean."

Blaustein said, "And when Dr. Ralson consulted you, was it with reference to this cyclic approach to history?"

"U-m-m-m. In a way, I suppose. Of course, the man is not an historian and some of his notions about cultural trends are rather dramatic and . . . what shall I say. . . . tabloidish. Pardon me, Doctor, if I ask a question which may be improper. Is Dr. Ralson one of your patients?"

"Dr. Ralson is not well and is in my care. This, and all else we say here, is confidential, of course."

"Quite. I understand that. However, your answer explains something to me. Some of his ideas almost verged on the irrational. He was always worried, it seemed to me, about the connection between what he called 'cultural spurts' and calamities of one sort or another. Now such connections have been noted frequently. The time of a nation's greatest vitality may come at a time of great national insecurity. The Netherlands is a good case in point. Her great artists, statesmen, and explorers belong to the early Seventeenth Century at the time when she was locked in a death struggle with the greatest European power of the time, Spain. When at the point of destruction at home, she was building an empire in the Far East and had secured footholds on the northern coast of South America, the southern tip of Africa, and the Hudson Valley of North America. Her fleets fought England to a standstill. And then, once her political safety was assured, she declined.

"Well, as I say, that is not unusual. Groups, like individuals, will rise to strange heights in answer to a challenge, and vegetate in the absence of a challenge. Where Dr. Ralson left the paths of sanity, however, was in insisting that such a view amounted to confusing cause and effect. He declared that it was not times of war and danger that stimulated 'cultural spurts,' but rather vice versa. He claimed that each time a group of men showed too much vitality and ability, a war became necessary to destroy the possibility of their further development."

"I see," said Blaustein.

"I rather laughed at him, I am afraid. It may be that that was why he did not keep the last appointment we made. Just toward the end of that last conference he asked me, in the most intense fashion imaginable, whether I did not think it queer that such an improbable species as man was dominant on earth, when all he had in his favor was intelligence. There I laughed aloud. Perhaps I should not have, poor fellow."

"It was a natural reaction," said Blaustein, "but I must take no more of your time. You have been most helpful."

They shook hands, and Thaddeus Milton took his leave.

"Well," said Darrity, "there are your figures on the recent suicides among scientific personnel. Get any deductions out of it?"

"I should be asking you that," said Blaustein, gently. "The F.B.I. must have investigated thoroughly."

"You can bet the national debt on that. They *are* suicides. There's no mistake about it. There have been people checking on it in another department. The rate is about four times above normal, taking age, social status, economic class into consideration."

"What about British scientists?"

"Just about the same."

"And the Soviet Union?"

"Who can tell?" The investigator leaned forward. "Doc, you don't think the Soviets have some sort of ray that can make people want to commit suicide, do you? It's sort of suspicious that men in atomic research are the only ones affected."

"Is it? Perhaps not. Nuclear physicists may have peculiar strains imposed upon them. It is difficult to tell without thorough study."

"You mean complexes might be coming through?" asked Darrity, warily.

Blaustein made a face. "Psychiatry is becoming too popular. Everybody talks of complexes and neuroses and psychoses and compulsions and what-not. One man's guilt complex is another man's good night's sleep. If I could talk to each one of the men who committed suicide, maybe I could know something."

"You're talking to Ralson."

"Yes, I'm talking to Ralson."

"Has *he* got a guilt complex?"

"Not particularly. He has a background out of which it would not surprise me if he obtained a morbid concern with death. When he was twelve he saw his mother die under the wheels of an automobile. His father died slowly of cancer. Yet the effect of those experiences on his present troubles is not clear."

Darrity picked up his hat. "Well, I wish you'd get a move on, Doc. There's something big on, bigger than the H-Bomb. I don't know how anything *can* be bigger than that, but it is."

Ralson insisted on standing. "I had a bad night last night, Doctor."

"I hope," said Blaustein, "these conferences are not disturbing you."

"Well, maybe they are. They have me thinking on the subject again. It makes things bad, when I do that. How do you imagine it feels being part of a bacterial culture, Doctor?"

"I had never thought of that. To a bacterium, it probably feels quite normal."

Ralson did not hear. He said, slowly, "A culture in which intelligence is being studied. We study all sorts of things as far as their genetic relationships are concerned. We take fruit flies and cross red eyes and white eyes to see what happens. We don't care anything about red eyes and white eyes, but we try to gather from them certain basic genetic principles. You see what I mean?"

"Certainly."

"Even in humans, we can follow various physical characteristics. There are the Hapsburg lips, and the hæmophilia that started with Queen Victoria and cropped up in her descendants among the Spanish and Russian royal families. We can even follow feeble-mindedness in the Jukeses and Kallikaks. You learn about it in high-school biology. But you can't breed human beings the way you do fruit flies. Humans live too long. It would take centuries to draw conclusions. It's a pity we don't have a special race of men that reproduce at weekly intervals, eh?"

He waited for an answer, but Blaustein only smiled.

Ralson said, "Only that's exactly what we would be for

another group of beings whose life span might be thousands of years. To them, we would reproduce rapidly enough. We would be short-lived creatures and they could study the genetics of such things as musical aptitude, scientific intelligence, and so on. Not that those things would interest them as such, any more than the white eyes of the fruit fly interest us as white eyes."

"This is a very interesting notion," said Blaustein.

"It is not simply a notion. It is true. To me, it is obvious, and I don't care how it seems to you. Look around you. Look at the planet, Earth. What kind of a ridiculous animal are we to be lords of the world after the dinosaurs had failed? Sure, we're intelligent, but what's intelligence? We think it is important because we have it. If the Tyrannosaurus could have picked out the one quality that he thought would ensure species domination, it would be size and strength. And he would make a better case for it. He lasted longer than we're likely to.

"Intelligence in itself isn't much as far as survival values are concerned. The elephant makes out very poorly indeed when compared to the sparrow even though he is much more intelligent. The dog does well, under man's protection, but not as well as the housefly against whom every human hand is raised. Or take the primates as a group. The small ones cower before their enemies; the large ones have always been remarkably unsuccessful in doing more than barely holding their own. The baboons do the best and that is because of their canines, not their brains."

A light film of perspiration covered Ralson's forehead. "And one can see that man has been tailored, made to careful specifications for those things that study us. Generally, the primate is short-lived. Naturally, the larger ones live longer, which is a fairly general rule in animal life. Yet the human being has a life span twice as long as any of the other great apes; considerably longer even than the gorilla that outweighs him. We mature later. It's as though we've been carefully bred to live a little longer so that our life cycle might be of a more convenient length."

He jumped to his feet, shaking his fists above his head. "A thousand years are but as yesterday——"

Blaustein punched a button hastily.

For a moment, Ralson struggled against the white-coated orderly who entered, and then he allowed himself to be led away.

Blaustein looked after him, shook his head, and picked up the telephone.

He got Darrity. "Inspector, you may as well know that this may take a long time."

He listened and shook his head. "I know. I don't minimize the urgency."

The voice in the receiver was tinny and harsh. "Doctor, you *are* minimizing it. I'll send Dr. Grant to you. He'll explain the situation to you."

Dr. Grant asked how Ralson was, then asked somewhat wistfully if he could see him. Blaustein shook his head gently.

Grant said, "I've been directed to explain the current situation in atomic research to you."

"So that I will understand, no?"

"I hope so. It's a measure of desperation. I'll have to remind you——"

"Not to breathe a word of it. Yes, I know. This insecurity on the part of you people is a very bad symptom. You must know these things cannot be hidden."

"You live with secrecy. It's contagious."

"Exactly. What is the current secret?"

"There is . . . or, at least, there might be a defense against the atomic bomb."

"And that is a secret? It would be better if it were shouted to all the people of the world instantly."

"For heaven's sake, no. Listen to me, Dr. Blaustein. It's only on paper so far. It's at the E quals mc square stage, almost. It may not be practical. It would be bad to raise hopes we would have to disappoint. On the other hand, if it were known that we *almost* had a defense, there *might* be a desire to start and win a war before the defense were completely developed.''

"That I don't believe. But, nevertheless, I distract you. What is the nature of this defense, or have you told me as much as you dare?''

"No, I can go as far as I like; as far as is necessary to convince you we have to have Ralson—and fast!''

"Well, then tell me, and I too, will know secrets. I'll feel like a member of the cabinet.''

"You'll know more than most. Look, Dr. Blaustein, let me explain it in lay language. So far, military advances have been made fairly equally in both offensive and defensive weapons. Once before there seemed to be a definite and permanent tipping of all warfare in the direction of the offense, and that was with the invention of gunpowder. But the defense caught up. The medieval man-in-armor-on-horse became the modern man-in-tank-on-treads, and the stone castle became the concrete pillbox. The same thing, you see, except that everything has been boosted several orders of magnitude.''

"Very good. You make it clear. But with the atomic bomb comes more orders of magnitude, no? You must go past concrete and steel for protection.''

"Right. Only we can't just make thicker and thicker walls. We've run out of materials that are strong enough. So we must abandon materials altogether. If the atom attacks, we must let the atom defend. We will use energy itself; a force field.''

"And what,'' asked Blaustein, gently, "is a force field?''

"I wish I could tell you. Right now, it's an equation on paper. Energy can be so channeled as to create a wall of matterless inertia, theoretically. In practice, we don't know how to do it.''

"It would be a wall you could not go through, is that it? Even for atoms?''

"Even for atom bombs. The only limit on its strength would be the amount of energy we could pour into it. It could even theoretically be made to be impermeable to radiation. The gamma rays would bounce off it. What we're dreaming of is a screen that would be in permanent place about cities; at minimum strength, using practically no energy. It could then be triggered to maximum intensity in a fraction of a millisecond at the impingement of short-wave radiation; say the amount radiating from the mass of plutonium large enough to be an atomic war head. All this is theoretically possible."

"And why must you have Ralson?"

"Because he is the only one who can reduce it to practice, if it can be made practical at all, quickly enough. Every minute counts these days. You know what the international situation is. Atomic defense *must* arrive before atomic war."

"You are so sure of Ralson?"

"I am as sure of him as I can be of anything. The man is amazing, Dr. Blaustein. He is always right. Nobody in the field knows how he does it."

"A sort of intiution, no?" The psychiatrist looked disturbed. "A kind of reasoning that goes beyond ordinary human capacities. Is that it?"

"I make no pretense of knowing what it is."

"Let me speak to him once more then. I will let you know."

"Good." Grant rose to leave; then, as if in afterthought, he said, "I might say, Doctor, that if you don't do something, the Commission plans to take Dr. Ralson out of your hands."

"And try another psychiatrist? If they wish to do that, of course, I will not stand in their way. It is my opinion, however, that no reputable practitioner will pretend there is a rapid cure."

"We may not intend further mental treatment. He may simply be returned to work."

"That, Dr. Grant, I will fight. You will get nothing out of him. It will be his death."

"We get nothing out of him anyway."

"This way there is at least a chance, no?"

"I hope so. And by the way, please don't mention the fact that I said anything about taking Ralson away."

"I will not, and I thank you for the warning. Good-bye, Dr. Grant."

*　　*　　*

"I made a fool of myself last time, didn't I, Doctor?" said Ralson. He was frowning.

"You mean you don't believe what you said then?"

"*I do!*" Ralson's slight form trembled with the intensity of his affirmation.

He rushed to the window, and Blaustein swiveled in his chair to keep him in view. There were bars in the window. He couldn't jump. The glass was unbreakable.

Twilight was ending, and the stars were beginning to come out. Ralson stared at them in fascination, then he turned to Blaustein and flung a finger outward. "Every single one of them is an incubator. They maintain temperatures at the desired point. Different experiments; different temperatures. And the planets that circle them are just huge cultures, containing different nutrient mixtures and different life forms. The experimenters are economical, too—whatever and whoever they are. They've cultured many types of life forms in this particular test-tube. Dinosaurs in a moist, tropical age and ourselves among the glaciers. They turn the sun up and down and we try to work out the physics of it. Physics!" He drew his lips back in a snarl.

"Surely," said Dr. Blaustein, "it is not possible that the sun can be turned up and down at will."

"Why not? It's just like a heating element in an oven. You think bacteria knows what it is that works the heat that reaches them? Who knows? Maybe they evolve theories, too. Maybe they have their cosmogonies about cosmic catastrophes, in which clashing lightbulbs create strings of Petri dishes. Maybe they think there must be some beneficent creator that supplies them with food and warmth and says to them, 'Be fruitful and multiply!'

"We breed like them, not knowing why. We obey the so-called laws of nature which are only our interpretation of the not-understood forces imposed upon us.

"And now they've got the biggest experiment of any yet on their hands. It's been going on for two hundred years. They decided to develop a strain for mechanical aptitude in

England in the seventeen hundreds, I imagine. We call it the Industrial Revolution. It began with steam, went on to electricity, then atoms. It was an interesting experiment, but they took their chances on letting it spread. Which is why they'll have to be very drastic indeed in ending it."

Blaustein said, "And how would they plan to end it? Do you have an idea about that?"

"You ask *me* how they plan to end it. You can look about the world today and still ask what is likely to bring our technological age to an end. All the earth fears an atomic war and would do anything to avoid it; yet all the earth fears that an atomic war is inevitable."

"In other words, the experimenters will arrange an atom war whether we want it or not, to kill off the technological era we are in, and to start fresh. That is it, no?"

"Yes. It's logical. When we sterilize an instrument, do the germs know where the killing heat comes from? Or what has brought it about? There is some way the experimenters can raise the heat of our emotions; some way they can handle us that passes our understanding."

"Tell me," said Blaustein, "is that why you want to die? Because you think the destruction of civilization is coming and can't be stopped?"

Ralson said, "I *don't* want to die. It's just that I must." His eyes were tortured. "Doctor, if you had a culture of germs that were highly dangerous and that you had to keep under absolute control, might you not have an agar medium impregnated with, say, penicillin, in a circle at a certain distance from the center of inoculation? Any germs spreading out too far from the center would die. You would have nothing against the particular germs who were killed; you might not even know that any germs had spread that far in the first place. It would be purely automatic.

"Doctor, there is a penicillin ring about our intellects. When we stray too far; when we penetrate the true meaning of our own existence, we have reached into the penicillin and we must die. It works slowly—but it's hard to stay alive."

He smiled briefly and sadly. Then he said, "May I go back to my room now, Doctor?"

Dr. Blaustein went to Ralson's room about noon the next day. It was a small room and featureless. The walls were gray with padding. Two small windows were high up and could not be reached. The mattress lay directly on the padded floor. There was nothing of metal in the room; nothing that could be utilized in tearing life from body. Even Ralson's nails were clipped short.

Ralson sat up. "Hello!"

"Hello, Dr. Ralson. May I speak to you?"

"Here? There isn't any seat I can offer you."

"It is all right. I'll stand. I have a sitting job and it is good for my sitting-down place that I should stand sometimes. Dr. Ralson, I have thought all night of what you told me yesterday and in the days before."

"And now you are going to apply treatment to rid me of what you think are delusions."

"No. It is just that I wish to ask questions and perhaps to point out some consequences of your theories which . . . you will forgive me? . . . you may not have thought of."

"Oh?"

"You see, Dr. Ralson, since you have explained your theories, I, too, know what you know. Yet I have no feeling about suicide."

"Belief is more than something intellectual, Doctor. You'd have to believe this with all your insides, which you don't."

"Do you not think perhaps it is rather a phenomenon of adaptation?"

"How do you mean?"

"You are not really a biologist, Dr. Ralson, and although you are very brilliant indeed in physics, you do not think of everything with respect to these bacterial cultures you use as analogies. You know that it is possible to breed bacterial strains that are resistant to penicillin or to almost any bacterial poison."

"Well?"

"The experimenters who breed us have been working with humanity for many generations, no? And this particular strain which they have been culturing for two centuries shows no sign of dying out spontaneously. Rather, it is a vigorous strain and a very infective one. Older high-culture strains were confined to single cities or to small areas and lasted only a generation or two. This one is spreading throughout the world. It is a *very* infective strain. Do you not think it may have developed penicillin immunity? In other words, the methods the experimenters use to wipe out the culture may not work too well any more, no?"

Ralson shook his head. "It's working on me."

"You are perhaps non-resistant. Or you have stumbled into a very high concentration of penicillin indeed. Consider all the people who have been trying to outlaw atomic warfare and to establish some form of world government and lasting peace. The effort has risen in recent years, without too awful results."

"It isn't stopping the atomic war that's coming."

"No, but maybe only a little more effort is all that is required. The peace-advocates do not kill themselves. More and more humans are immune to the experimenters. Do you know what they are doing in the laboratory?"

"I don't want to know."

"You *must* know. They are trying to invent a force field that will stop the atom bomb. Dr. Ralson, if I am culturing a virulent and pathological bacterium; then, even with all precautions, it may sometimes happen that I will start a plague. We may be bacteria to them, but we are dangerous to them, also, or they wouldn't wipe us out so carefully after each experiment.

"They are not quick, no? To them a thousand years is as a day, no? By the time they realize we are out of the culture, past the penicillin, it will be too late for them to stop us. They have brought us to the atom, and if we can only prevent ourselves from using it upon one another, we may turn out to be too much even for the experimenters."

Ralson rose to his feet. Small though he was, he was an

inch and a half taller than Blaustein. "They are really working on a force field?"

"They are trying to. But they need you."

"No. I can't."

"They must have you in order that you might see what is so obvious to you. It is not obvious to them. Remember, it is your help or else—defeat of man by the experimenters."

Ralson took a few rapid steps away, staring into the blank, padded wall. He muttered, "But there must be that defeat. If they build a force field, it will mean death for all of them before it can be completed."

"Some or all of them may be immune, no? And in any case, it will be death for them anyhow. They are trying."

Ralson said, "I'll try to help them."

"Do you still want to kill yourself?"

"Yes."

"But you'll try not to, no?"

"I'll *try* not to, Doctor." His lip quivered. "I'll have to be watched."

Blaustein climbed the stairs and presented his pass to the guard in the lobby. He had already been inspected at the outer gate, but he, his pass, and its signature were now scrutinized once again. After a moment, the guard retired to his little booth and made a phone call. The answer satisfied him. Blaustein took a seat and, in half a minute, was up again, shaking hands with Dr. Grant.

"The President of the United States would have trouble getting in here, no?" said Blaustein.

The lanky physicist smiled. "You're right, if he came without warning."

They took an elevator which traveled twelve floors. The office to which Grant led the way had windows in three directions. It was sound-proofed and air-conditioned. Its walnut furniture was in a state of high polish.

Blaustein said, "My goodness. It is like the office of the chairman of a board of directors. Science is becoming big business."

Grant looked embarrassed. "Yes, I know, but government money flows easily and it is difficult to persuade a congress-man that your work is important unless he can see, smell, and touch the surface shine."

Blaustein sat down and felt the upholstered seat give way slowly. He said, "Dr. Elwood Ralson has agreed to return to work."

"Wonderful. I was hoping you would say that. I was hoping that was why you wanted to see me." As though inspired by the news, Grant offered the psychiatrist a cigar, which was refused.

"However," said Blaustein, "he remains a very sick man. He will have to be treated carefully and with insight."

"Of course. Naturally."

"It's not quite as simple as you may think. I want to tell you something of Ralson's problems, so that you will really understand how delicate the situation is."

He went on talking and Grant listened first in concern, and then in astonishment. "But then the man is out of his head, Dr. Blaustein. He'll be of no use to us. He's crazy."

Blaustein shrugged. "It depends on how you define 'crazy.' It's a bad word; don't use it. He had delusions, certainly. Whether they will affect his peculiar talents one cannot know."

"But surely no sane man could possibly——"

"Please. Please. Let us not launch into long discussions on psychiatric definitions of sanity and so on. The man has delusions and, ordinarily, I would dismiss them from all consideration. It is just that I have been given to understand that the man's particular ability lies in his manner of proceed-ing to the solution of a problem by what seems to be outside ordinary reason. That is so, no?"

"Yes. That *must* be admitted."

"How can you and I judge then as to the worth of one of his conclusions. Let me ask you, do *you* have suicidal im-pulses lately?"

"I don't think so."

"And other scientists here?"

"No, of course not."

"I would suggest, however, that while research on the force field proceeds, the scientists concerned be watched here and at home. It might even be a good enough idea that they should not go home. Offices like these could be arranged to be a small dormitory——"

"Sleep at work. You would never get them to agree."

"Oh, yes. If you do not tell them the real reason but say it is for security purposes, they will agree. 'Security purposes' is a wonderful phrase these days, no? Ralson must be watched more than anyone."

"Of course."

"But all this is minor. It is something to be done to satisfy my conscience in case Ralson's theories are correct. Actually, I don't believe them. They *are* delusions, but once that is granted, it is necessary to ask what the causes of those delusions are. What is it in Ralson's mind, in his background, in life that makes it so necessary for him to have these particular delusions? One cannot answer that simply. It may well take years of constant psychoanalysis to discover the answer. And until the answer is discovered, he will not be cured.

"But meanwhile, we can perhaps make intelligent guesses. He has had an unhappy childhood, which, in one way or another, has brought him face to face with death in very unpleasant fashion. In addition, he has never been able to form associations with other children, or, as he grew older, with other men. He was always impatient with their slower forms of reasoning. Whatever difference there is between his mind and that of others, it has built a wall between him and society as strong as the force field you are trying to design. For similar reasons, he has been unable to enjoy a normal sex life. He has never married; he has had no sweethearts.

"It is easy to see that he could easily compensate to himself for this failure to be accepted by his social milieu by taking refuge in the thought that other human beings are inferior to himself. Which is, of course, true, as far as mentality is concerned. There are, of course, many, many facets to the human personality and in not all of them is he superior. No one is. Others, then, who are more prone to see merely what is inferior, just as he himself is, would not accept his affected pre-eminence of position. They would think him queer, even laughable, which would make it even more important to Ralson to prove how miserable and inferior the human species was. How could he better do that than to show that mankind was simply a form of bacteria to other superior creatures which experiment upon them. And then his impulses to suicide would be a wild desire to break away completely from being a man at all; to stop this identification with the miserable species he has created in his mind. You see?"

Grant nodded. "Poor guy."

"Yes, it is a pity. Had he been properly taken care of in childhood—— Well, it is best for Dr. Ralson that he have no contact with any of the other men here. He is too sick to be trusted with them. You, yourself, must arrange to be the only man who will see him or speak to him. Dr. Ralson has agreed to that. He apparently thinks you are not as stupid as some of the others."

Grant smiled faintly. "That is agreeable to me."

"You will, of course, be careful. I would not discuss anything with him but his work. If he should volunteer information about his theories, which I doubt, confine yourself to something non-committal, and leave. And at all times, keep away anything that is sharp and pointed. Do not let him reach a window. Try to have his hands kept in view. You understand. I leave my patient in your care, Dr. Grant."

"I will do my best, Dr. Blaustein."

For two months, Ralson lived in a corner of Grant's office, and Grant lived with him. Gridwork had been built up before the windows, wooden furniture was removed and upholstered sofas brought in. Ralson did his thinking on the couch and his calculating on a desk pad atop a hassock.

The "Do Not Enter" was a permanent fixture outside the office. Meals were left outside. The adjoining men's room was marked off for private use and the door between it and the office removed. Grant switched to an electric razor. He made certain that Ralson took sleeping pills each night and waited till the other slept before sleeping himself.

And always reports were brought to Ralson. He read them while Grant watched and tried to seem not to watch.

Then Ralson would let them drop and stare at the ceiling, with one hand shading his eyes.

"Anything?" asked Grant.

Ralson shook his head from side to side.

Grant said, "Look, I'll clear the building during the swing shift. It's important that you see some of the experimental jigs we've been setting up."

They did so, wandering through the lighted, empty buildings like drifting ghosts, hand in hand. Always hand in hand. Grant's grip was tight. But after each trip, Ralson would still shake his head from side to side.

Half a dozen times he would begin writing; each time there would be a few scrawls and then he would kick the hassock over on its side.

Until, finally, he began writing once again and covered half a page rapidly. Automatically, Grant approached. Ralson looked up, covering the sheet of paper with a trembling hand.

He said, "Call Blaustein."

"What?"

"I said, 'Call Blaustein.' Get him here. Now!"

Grant moved to the telephone.

Ralson was writing rapidly now, stopping only to brush wildly at his forehead with the back of a hand. It came away wet.

He looked up and his voice was cracked, "Is he coming?"

Grant looked worried. "He isn't at his office."

"Get him at his home. Get him wherever he is. *Use* that telephone. Don't play with it."

Grant used it; and Ralson pulled another sheet toward himself.

Five minutes later, Grant said, "He's coming. What's wrong? You're looking sick."

Ralson could speak only thickly, "No time—— Can't talk——"

He was writing, scribbling, scrawling, shakily diagraming. It was as though he were driving his hands, fighting it.

"Dictate!" urged Grant. "I'll write."

Ralson shook him off. His words were unintelligible. He held his wrist with his other hand, shoving it as though it were a piece of wood, and then he collapsed over the papers.

Grant edged them out from under and laid Ralson down on the couch. He hovered over him restlessly and hopelessly until Blaustein arrived.

Blaustein took one look. "What happened?"

Grant said, "I think he's alive," but by that time Blaustein had verified that for himself, and Grant told him what had happened.

Blaustein used a hypodermic and they waited. Ralson's eyes were blank when they opened. He moaned.

Blaustein leaned close. "Ralson."

Ralson's hands reached out blindly and clutched at the psychiatrist. "Doc. Take me back."

"I will. Now. It is that you have the force field worked out, no?"

"It's on the papers. Grant, it's on the papers."

Grant had them and was leafing through them dubiously. Ralson said, weakly, "It's not *all* there. It's all I can write. You'll *have* to make it out of that. Take me back, Doc!"

"Wait," said Grant. He whispered urgently to Blaustein. "Can't you leave him here till we test this thing? I can't make out what most of this is. The writing is illegible. Ask him what makes him think this will work."

"Ask *him*?" said Blaustein, gently. "Isn't he the one who always knows?"

"Ask me, anyway," said Ralson, overhearing from where he lay on the couch. His eyes were suddenly wide and blazing.

They turned to him.

He said, "*They* don't want a force field. *They!* The experimenters! As long as I had no true grasp, things remained as they were. But I hadn't followed up that thought—*that* thought which is there in the papers—I hadn't followed it up for thirty seconds before I felt . . . I felt—— Doctor——"

Blaustein said, "What is it?"

Ralson was whispering again, "I'm deeper in the penicillin. I could feel myself plunging in and in, the further I went with that. I've never been in . . . so deep. That's how I knew I was right. Take me away."

Blaustein straightened. "I'll have to take him away, Grant. There's no alternative. If you can make out what he's written, that's it. If you can't make it out, I can't help you. That man can do no more work in his field without dying, do you understand?"

"But," said Grant, "he's dying of something imaginary."

"All right. Say that he is. But he will be really dead just the same, no?"

Ralson was unconscious again and heard nothing of this. Grant looked at him somberly, then said, "Well, take him away, then."

Ten of the top men at the Institute watched glumly as slide after slide filled the illuminated screen. Grant faced them, expression hard and frowning.

He said, "I think the idea is simple enough. You're mathematicians and you're engineers. The scrawl may seem illegible, but it was done with meaning behind it. That meaning must somehow remain in the writing, distorted though it is. The first page is clear enough. It should be a good lead. Each one of you will look at every page over and over again. You're going to put down every possible version of each page as it seems it might be. You will work independently. I want no consultations."

One of them said, "How do you know it means *anything*, Grant?"

"Because those are Ralson's notes."

"*Ralson!* I thought he was——"

"You thought he was sick," said Grant. He had to shout over the rising hum of conversation. "I know. He is. That's the writing of a man who was nearly dead. It's all we'll ever get from Ralson, any more. Somewhere in that scrawl is the answer to the force field problem. If we can't find it, we may have to spend ten years looking for it elsewhere."

They bent to their work. The night passed. Two nights passed. Three nights——

Grant looked at the results. He shook his head. "I'll take your word for it that it is all self-consistent. I can't say I understand it."

Lowe, who, in the absence of Ralson, would readily have been rated the best nuclear engineer at the Institute, shrugged. "It's not exactly clear to me. If it works, he hasn't explained why."

"He had no time to explain. Can you build the generator as he describes it?"

"I could try."

"Would you look at all the other versions of the pages?"

"The others are definitely not self-consistent."

"Would you double-check?"

"Sure."

"And could you start construction anyway?"

"I'll get the shop started. But I tell you frankly that I'm pessimistic."

"I know. So am I."

The thing grew. Hal Ross, Senior Mechanic, was put in charge of the actual construction, and he stopped sleeping. At any hour of the day or night, he could be found at it, scratching his bald head.

He asked questions only once, "What is it, Dr. Lowe? Never saw anything like it. What's it supposed to do?"

Lowe said, "You know where you are, Ross. You know we don't ask questions here. Don't ask again."

Ross did not ask again. He was known to dislike the structure that was being built. He called it ugly and unnatural. But he stayed at it.

*   *   *

Blaustein called one day.

Grant said, "How's Ralson?"

"Not good. He wants to attend the testing of the Field Projector he designed."

Grant hesitated, "I suppose we should. It's his after all."

"I would have to come with him."

Grant looked unhappier. "It might be dangerous, you know. Even in a pilot test, we'd be playing with tremendous energies."

Blaustein said, "No more dangerous for us than for you."

"Very well. The list of observers will have to be cleared through the Commission and the F.B.I., but I'll put you in."

Blaustein looked about him. The field projector squatted in the very center of the huge testing laboratory, but all else had been cleared. There was no visible connection with the plutonium pile which served as energy-source, but from what the psychiatrist heard in scraps about him—he knew better than to ask Ralson—the connection was from beneath.

At first, the observers had circled the machine, talking in incomprehensibles, but they were drifting away now. The gallery was filling up. There were at least three men in generals' uniforms on the other side, and a real coterie of lower-scale military. Blaustein chose an unoccupied portion of the railing; for Ralson's sake, most of all.

He said, "Do you still think you would like to stay?"

It was warm enough within the laboratory, but Ralson was in his coat, with his collar turned up. It made little difference, Blaustein felt. He doubted that any of Ralson's former acquaintances would now recognize him.

Ralson said, "I'll stay."

Blaustein was pleased. He wanted to see the test. He turned again at a new voice.

"Hello, Dr. Blaustein."

For a minute, Blaustein did not place him, then he said, "Ah, Inspector Darrity. What are you doing here?"

"Just what you would suppose." He indicated the watchers. "There isn't any way you can weed them out so that you can be sure there won't be any mistakes. I once stood as near to Klaus Fuchs as I am standing to you." He tossed his pocketknife into the air and retrieved it with a dexterous motion.

"Ah, yes. Where shall one find perfect security? What man can trust even his own unconscious? And you will now stand near to me, no?"

"Might as well." Darrity smiled. "You were very anxious to get in here, weren't you?"

"Not for myself, Inspector. And would you put away the knife, please."

Darrity turned in surprise in the direction of Blaustein's gentle head-gesture. He put his knife away and looked at Blaustein's companion for the second time. He whistled softly.

He said, "Hello, Dr. Ralson."

Ralson croaked, "Hello."

Blaustein was not surprised at Darrity's reaction. Ralson had lost twenty pounds since returning to the sanatorium. His face was yellow and wrinkled; the face of a man who had suddenly become sixty.

Blaustein said, "Will the test be starting soon?"

Darrity said, "It looks as if they're starting now."

He turned and leaned on the rail. Blaustein took Ralson's elbow and began leading him away, but Darrity said, softly, "Stay here, Doc. I don't want you wandering about."

Blaustein looked across the laboratory. Men were standing about with the uncomfortable air of having turned half to stone. He could recognize Grant, tall and gaunt, moving his hand slowly to light a cigarette, then changing his mind and putting lighter and cigarette in his pocket. The young men at the control panels waited tensely.

Then there was a low humming and the faint smell of ozone filled the air.

Ralson said harshly, "Look!"

Blaustein and Darrity looked along the pointing finger. The projector seemed to flicker. It was as though there were heated air rising between it and them. An iron ball came swinging down pendulum fashion and passed through the flickering area.

"It slowed up, no?" said Blaustein, excitedly.

Ralson nodded. "They're measuring the height of rise on the other side to calculate the loss of momentum. Fools! I *said* it would work." He was speaking with obvious difficulty.

Blaustein said, "Just watch, Dr. Ralson. I would not allow myself to grow needlessly excited."

The pendulum was stopped in its swinging, drawn up. The flickering about the projector became a little more intense and the iron sphere arced down once again.

Over and over again, and each time the sphere's motion was slowed with more of a jerk. It made a clearly audible sound as it struck the flicker. And eventually, it *bounded*. First, soggily, as though it hit putty, and then ringingly, as though it hit steel, so that the noise filled the place.

They drew back the pendulum bob and used it no longer. The projector could hardly be seen behind the haze that surrounded it.

Grant gave an order and the odor of ozone was suddenly sharp and pungent. There was a cry from the assembled observers; each one exclaiming to his neighbor. A dozen fingers were pointing.

Blaustein leaned over the railing, as excited as the rest. Where the projector had been, there was now only a huge semi-globular mirror. It was perfectly and beautifully clear. He could see himself in it, a small man standing on a small balcony that curved up on each side. He could see the fluorescent lights reflected in spots of glowing illumination. It was wonderfully sharp.

He was shouting, "Look, Ralson. It is reflecting energy. It is reflecting light waves like a mirror. Ralson——"

He turned, "Ralson! Inspector, where is Ralson?"

"What?" Darrity whirled. "I haven't seen him."

He looked about, wildly. "Well, he won't get away. No way of getting out of here now. You take the other side." And then he clapped hand to thigh, fumbled for a moment in his pocket, and said, "My knife is gone."

Blaustein found him. He was inside the small office belonging to Hal Ross. It led off the balcony, but under the circumstances, of course, it had been deserted. Ross himself was not even an observer. A senior mechanic need not observe. But his office would do very well for the final end of the long fight against suicide.

Blaustein stood in the doorway for a sick moment, then turned. He caught Darrity's eye as the latter emerged from a similar office a hundred feet down the balcony. He beckoned, and Darrity came at a run.

Dr. Grant was trembling with excitement. He had taken two puffs at each of two cigarettes and trodden each underfoot thereafter. He was fumbling with the third now.

He was saying, "This is better than any of us could possibly have hoped. We'll have the gunfire test tomorrow. I'm sure of the result now, but we've planned it; we'll go through with it. We'll skip the small arms and start with the bazooka levels. Or maybe not. It might be necessary to construct a special testing structure to take care of the ricochet problem."

He discarded his third cigarette.

A general said, "We'd have to try a literal atom-bombing, of course."

"Naturally. Arrangements have already been made to build a mock-city at Eniwetok. We could build a generator on the spot and drop the bomb. There'd be animals inside."

"And you really think if we set up a field in full power it would hold the bomb?"

"It's not just that, General. There'd be no noticeable field at all until the bomb is dropped. The radiation of the plutonium would have to energize the field before explosion. As we did here in the last step. That's the essence of it all."

"You know," said a Princeton professor, "I see disadvantages, too. When the field is on full, anything it protects is in total darkness, as far as the sun is concerned. Besides that, it strikes me that the enemy can adopt the practice of dropping harmless radioactive missiles to set off the field at frequent intervals. It would have nuisance value and be a considerable drain on our pile as well."

"Nuisances," said Grant, "can be survived. These difficulties will be met eventually, I'm sure, now that the main problem has been solved."

The British observer had worked his way toward Grant and was shaking hands. He said, "I feel better about London already. I cannot help but wish your government would allow me to see the complete plans. What I have seen strikes me as completely ingenious. It seems obvious now, of course, but how did anyone ever come to think of it?"

Grant smiled. "That question has been asked before with reference to Dr. Ralson's devices——"

He turned at the touch of a hand upon his shoulder. "Dr. Blaustein! I had nearly forgotten. Here, I want to talk to you."

He dragged the small psychiatrirst to one side and hissed in his ear, "Listen, can you persuade Ralson to be introduced to these people? This is his triumph."

Blaustein said, "Ralson is dead."

"*What!*"

"Can you leave these people for a time?"

"Yes . . . yes—— Gentlemen, you will excuse me for a few minutes?"

He hurried·off with Blaustein.

The Federal men had already taken over. Unobtrusively, they barred the doorway to Ross's office. Outside there were the milling crowd discussing the answers to Alamogordo·that they had just witnessed. Inside, unknown to them, was the death of the answerer. The G-man barrier divided to allow Grant and Blaustein to enter. It closed behind them again.

For a moment, Grant raised the sheet. He said, "He looks peaceful."

"I would say—happy," said Blaustein.

Darrity said, colorlessly, "The suicide weapon was my own knife. It was my negligence; it will be reported as such."

"No, no," said Blaustein, "that would be useless. He was my patient and I am responsible. In any case, he would not have lived another week. Since he invented the projector, he was a dying man."

Grant said, "How much of this has to be placed in the Federal files? Can't we forget all about his madness?"

"I'm afraid not, Dr. Grant," said Darrity.

"I have told him the whole story," said Blaustein, sadly.

Grant looked from one to the other. "I'll speak to the Director. I'll go to the President, if necessary. I don't see that there need be any mention of suicide or of madness. He'll get full publicity as inventor of the field projector. It's the least we can do for him." His teeth were gritting.

Blaustein said, "He left a note."

"A note?"

Darrity handed him a sheet of paper and said, "Suicides almost always do. This is one reason the doctor told me about what really killed Ralson."

The note was addressed to Blaustein and it went:

"The projector works; I knew it would. The bargain is done. You've got it and you don't need me any more. So I'll go. You needn't worry about the human race, Doc. You were right. They've bred us too long; they've taken too many chances. We're out of the culture now and they won't be able to stop us. I know. That's all I can say. I know."

He had signed his name quickly and then underneath there was one scrawled line, and it said:

"Provided enough men are penicillin-resistant."

Grant made a motion to crumble the paper, but Darrity held out a quick hand.

"For the record, Doctor," he said.

Grant gave it to him and said, "Poor Ralson! He died believing all that trash."

Blaustein nodded. "So he did. Ralson will be given a great funeral, I suppose, and the fact of his invention will be publicized without the madness and the suicide. But the government men will remain interested in his mad theories. They may not be so mad, no, Mr. Darrity?"

"That's ridiculous, Doctor," said Grant. "There isn't a scientist on the job who has shown the least uneasiness about it at all."

"Tell him, Mr. Darrity," said Blaustein.

Darrity said, "There has been another suicide. No, no, none of the scientists. No one with a degree. It happened this morning, and we investigated because we thought it might have some connection with today's test. There didn't seem any, and we were going to keep it quiet till the test was over. Only now there seems to be a connection.

"The man who died was just a guy with a wife and three kids. No reason to die. No history of mental illness. He threw himself under a car. We have witnesses, and it's certain he did it on purpose. He didn't die right away and they got a doctor to him. He was horribly mangled, but his last words were 'I feel much better now' and he died."

"But who was he?" cried Grant.

"Hal Ross. The guy who actually built the projector. The guy whose office this is."

Blaustein walked to the window. The evening sky was darkening into starriness.

He said, "The man knew nothing about Ralson's views. He had never spoken to Ralson, Mr. Darrity tells me. Scientists are probably resistant as a whole. They must be or they are quickly driven out of the profession. Ralson was an exception, a penicillin-sensitive who insisted on remaining. You see what happened to him. But what about the others; those who have remained in walks of life where there is no constant weeding out of the sensitive ones. How much of humanity *is* penicillin-resistant?"

"You *believe* Ralson?" asked Grant in horror.

"I don't really know."

Blaustein looked at the stars.

Incubators?

PICTURES DON'T LIE

BY KATHERINE MACLEAN (1925–   )
GALAXY SCIENCE FICTION, AUGUST

The 1950s saw the emergence of a number of notable women science fiction writers who added much to the genre, including the late Zenna Henderson, Margaret St. Clair (who debuted in the late 1940s), Andre Norton, Mildred Clingerman, and Katherine MacLean.

Although she won a Nebula Award in 1971 for the shorter version of her 1975 novel Missing Man, *she has remained somewhat underrated because her output has been unfortunately small. Several collections of her work, including* The Diploids and Other Flights of Fancy *(1962),* Trouble With Treaties *(1975), and* The Trouble With You People *(1980), have been issued, but a definitive ''Best of'' book still needs to be done. Another noteworthy novel, done in collaboration with Charles V. De Vet, is* Cosmic Checkmate *(1962).*

''Pictures Don't Lie'' is one of the great point-of-view stories in the history of science fiction.

—M.H.G.

Harry Stubbs (Hal Clement to s f readers) asked an interesting question once. If the Universe is 15 billion years old and if intelligences have been evolving at different times, it

*must mean that extraterrestrial intelligences may have techno-
logical civilizations, hundreds, thousands, millions, even billions of years older than ours. (Others will start hundreds,
thousands, millions, even billions of years from now.)*

*Even if the ages differ by only small amounts, it doesn't
take much time to bring about enormous changes. Compare
the world of 1985 A.D. to that of 1985 B.C. That's only four
thousand years' difference. Yet our world would be incomprehensible to a Sumerian. And the rate of change is increasing with time. The world four hundred years in the future
(assuming it survives) may be more incomprehensible to us
than we are to Sumerians.*

*Therefore, if we encounter extraterrestrial civilizations four
centuries more advanced than ours (or four million years
more advanced) we may be completely snowed by them. And
yet, in science fiction, we are always encountering civilizations that are about on a par with ours. We have no trouble
understanding them. This is clearly impossible and reflects
only the difficulty s f writers have of imagining the unimaginable.*

*There may be other differences that would arise if we
stopped taking things-Earthly as things-inevitable. I say no
more, lest I spoil the following story.*

—I.A.

THE MAN from the *News* asked, "What do you think of the
aliens, Mr. Nathen? Are they friendly? Do they look human?"

"Very human," said the thin young man.

Outside, rain sleeted across the big windows with a steady,
faint drumming, blurring and dimming the view of the airfield where *They* would arrive. On the concrete runways the
puddles were pockmarked with rain, and the grass growing
untouched between the runways of the unused field glistened
wetly, bending before gusts of wind.

Back at a respectful distance from the place where the huge
spaceship would land were the gray shapes of trucks, where

TV camera crews huddled inside their mobile units, waiting. Farther back in the deserted, sandy landscape, behind distant sandy hills, artillery was ringed in a great circle, and in the distance across the horizon bombers stood ready at airfields, guarding the world against possible treachery from the first alien ship ever to land from space.

"Do you know anything about their home planet?" asked the man from the *Herald.*

The *Times* man stood with the others, listening absently, thinking of questions but reserving them. Joseph R. Nathen, the thin young man with the straight black hair and the tired lines on his face, was being treated with respect by his interviewers. He was obviously on edge, and they did not want to harry him with too many questions at once. They wanted to keep his good will. Tomorrow he would be one of the biggest celebrities ever to appear in headlines.

"No, nothing directly."

"Any ideas or deductions?" the *Herald* persisted.

"Their world must be Earthlike to them," the weary-looking young man answered uncertainly. "The environment evolves the animal. But only in relative terms, of course." He looked at them with a quick glance and then looked away evasively, his lank black hair beginning to cling to his forehead with sweat. "That doesn't necessarily mean anything."

"Earthlike," muttered a reporter, writing it down as if he had noticed nothing more in the reply.

The *Times* man glanced at the *Herald*, wondering if he had noticed, and received a quick glance in exchange.

The *Herald* asked Nathen, "You think they are dangerous, then?"

It was the kind of question, assuming much, that unusually broke reticence and brought forth quick facts—when it hit the mark. They all knew of the military precautions, although they were not supposed to know.

The question missed. Nathen glanced out the window vaguely. "No, I wouldn't say so."

"You think they are friendly, then?" said the *Herald*, equally positive on the opposite tack.

A fleeting smile touched Nathen's lips. "Those I know are."

There was no lead in this direction, and they had to get the basic facts of the story before the ship came. The *Times* asked, "What led up to your contacting them?"

Nathen answered, after a hesitation, "Static. Radio static. The Army told you my job, didn't they?"

The Army had told them nothing at all. The officer who had conducted them in for the interview stood glowering watchfully, as if he objected by instinct to telling anything to the public.

Nathen glanced at him doubtfully. "My job is radio decoder for the Department of Military Intelligence. I use a directional pickup, tune in on foreign bands, record any scrambled or coded messages I hear, and build automatic decoders and descramblers for all the basic scramble patterns."

The officer cleared his throat but said nothing.

The reporters smiled, noting that down.

Security regulations had changed since arms inspection had been legalized by the U.N. Complete information being the only public security against secret rearmament, spying and prying had come to seem a public service. Its aura had changed. It was good public relations to admit it.

Nathen continued, "In my spare time I started directing the pickup at stars. There's radio noise from stars, you know. Just stuff that sounds like spatter static, and an occasional squawk. People have been listening to it for a long time, and researching, trying to work out why stellar radiation on those bands comes in such jagged bursts. It didn't seem natural."

He paused and smiled uncertainly, aware that the next thing he would say was the thing that would make him famous—an idea that had come to him while he listened, an idea as simple and as perfect as the one that came to Newton when he saw the apple fall.

"I decided it wasn't natural. I tried decoding it."

Hurriedly, he tried to explain it away and make it seem obvious. "You see, there's an old intelligence trick, speeding up a message on a record until it sounds just like that, a short squawk of static, and then broadcasting it. Undergrounds use it. I'd heard that kind of screech before.''

"You mean they broadcast at us in code?" asked the *News*.

"It's not exactly code. All you need to do is record it and slow it down. They're not broadcasting at us. If a star has planets, inhabited planets, and there is broadcasting between them, they would send it on a tight beam to save power." He looked for comprehension. "You know, like a spotlight. Theoretically, a tight beam can go on forever without losing power. But aiming would be difficult from planet to planet. You can't expect a beam to stay on target, over such distances, more than a few seconds at a time. So they'd naturally compress each message into a short half-second- or one-second-length package and send it a few hundred times in one long blast to make sure it is picked up during the instant the beam swings across the target."

He was talking slowly and carefully, remembering that this explanation was for the newspapers. "When a stray beam swings through our section of space, there's a sharp peak in noise level from that direction. The beams are swinging to follow their own planets at home, and the distance between there and here exaggerates the speed of swing tremendously, so we wouldn't pick up more than a *bip* as it passes."

"How do you account for the number of squawks coming in?" the *Times* asked. "Do stellar systems rotate on the plane of the Galaxy?" It was a private question; he spoke impulsively from interest and excitement.

The radio decoder grinned, the lines of strain vanishing from his face for a moment. "Maybe we're intercepting everybody's telephone calls, and the whole Galaxy is swarming with races that spend all day yacking at each other over the radio. Maybe the human type is standard model."

"It would take something like that," the *Times* agreed. They smiled at each other.

The *News* asked, "How did you happen to pick up television instead of voices?"

"Not by accident," Nathen explained patiently. "I'd recognized a scanning pattern, and I wanted pictures. Pictures are understandable in any language.''

Near the interviewers, a senator paced back and forth, muttering his memorized speech of welcome and nervously glancing out the wide, streaming windows into the gray, sleeting rain.

Opposite the windows of the long room was a small raised platform flanked by the tall shapes of TV cameras and sound pickups on booms, and darkened floodlights, arranged and ready for the senator to make his speech of welcome to the aliens and the world. A shabby radio sending set stood beside it without a case to conceal its parts, two cathode television tubes flickered nakedly on one side and the speaker humming on the other. A vertical panel of dials and knobs jutted up before them, and a small hand-mike sat ready on the table before the panel. It was connected to a boxlike, expensively cased piece of equipment with ''Radio Lab, U. S. Property'' stenciled on it.

''I recorded a couple of package screeches from Sagittarius and began working on them,'' Nathen added. ''It took a couple of months to find the synchronizing signals and set the scanners close enough to the right time to even get a pattern. When I showed the pattern to the Department, they gave me full time to work on it, and an assistant to help. It took eight months to pick out the color bands and assign them the right colors, to get anything intelligible on the screen.''

The shabby-looking mess of exposed parts was the original receiver that they had labored over for ten months, adjusting and readjusting to reduce the maddening rippling plaids of unsynchronized color scanners to some kind of sane picture.

''Trial and error,'' said Nathen, ''but it came out all right. The wide band spread of the squawks had suggested color TV from the beginning.''

He walked over and touched the set. The speaker bipped slightly and the gray screen flickered with a flash of color at the touch. The set was awake and sensitive, tuned to receive from the great interstellar spaceship which now circled the atmosphere.

"We wondered why there were so many bands, but when we got the set working and started recording and playing everything that came in, we found we'd tapped something like a lending-library line. It was all fiction, plays."

Between the pauses in Nathen's voice, the *Times* found himself unconsciously listening for the sound of roaring, swiftly approaching pocket jets.

The *Post* asked, "How did you contact the spaceship?"

"I scanned and recorded a film copy of *The Rite of Spring*, the Disney-Stravinsky combination, and sent it back along the same line we were receiving from. Just testing. It wouldn't get there for a good number of years, if it got there at all, but I thought it would please the library to get a new record in.

"Two weeks later, when we caught and slowed a new batch of recordings, we found an answer. It was obviously meant for us. It was a flash of the Disney being played to a large audience, and then the audience sitting and waiting before a blank screen. The signal was very clear and loud. We'd intercepted a spaceship. They were asking for an encore, you see. They liked the film and wanted more. . . ."

He smiled at them in sudden thought. "You can see them for yourself. It's all right down the hall where the linguists are working on the automatic translator."

The listening officer frowned and cleared his throat, and the thin young man turned to him quickly. "No security reason why they should not see the broadcasts, is there? Perhaps you should show them." He said to the reporters reassuringly, "It's right down the hall. You will be informed the moment the spaceship approaches."

The interview was very definitely over. The lank-haired, nervous young man turned away and seated himself at the radio set while the officer swallowed his objections and showed them dourly down the hall to a closed door.

They opened it and fumbled into a darkened room crowded with empty folding chairs, dominated by a glowing bright screen. The door closed behind them, bringing total darkness.

There was the sound of reporters fumbling their way into seats around him, but the *Times* man remained standing, aware of an enormous surprise, as if he had been asleep and wakened to find himself in the wrong country.

The bright colors of the double image seemed the only real thing in the darkened room. Even blurred as they were, he could see that the action was subtly different, the shapes subtly not right.

He was looking at aliens.

The impression was of two humans disguised, humans moving oddly, half dancing, half crippled. Carefully, afraid the images would go away, he reached up to his breast pocket, took out his polarized glasses, rotated one lens at right angles to the other, and put them on.

Immediately, the two beings came into sharp focus, real and solid, and the screen became a wide, illusively near window through which he watched them.

They were conversing with each other in a gray-walled room, discussing something with restrained excitement. The large man in the green tunic closed his purple eyes for an instant at something the other said and grimaced, making a motion with his fingers as if shoving something away from him.

Mellerdrammer.

The second, smaller, with yellowish-green eyes, stepped closer, talking more rapidly in a lower voice. The first stood very still, not trying to interrupt.

Obviously, the proposal was some advantageous treachery, and he wanted to be persuaded. The *Times* groped for a chair and sat down.

Perhaps gesture is universal; desire and aversion, a leaning forward or a leaning back, tension, relaxation. Perhaps these actors were masters. The scenes changed: a corridor, a park-like place in what he began to realize was a spaceship, a lecture room. There were others talking and working, speaking to the man in the green tunic, and never was it unclear what was happening or how they felt.

They talked a flowing language with many short vowels

and shifts of pitch, and they gestured in the heat of talk, their hands moving with an odd lagging difference of motion, now slow, but somehow drifting.

He ignored the language, but after a time the difference in motion began to arouse his interest. Something in the way they walked . . .

With an effort he pulled his mind from the plot and forced his attention to the physical difference. Brown hair in short, silky crew cuts, varied eye colors, the colors showing clearly because their irises were very large, their round eyes set very widely apart in tapering, light-brown faces. Their necks and shoulders were thick in a way that would indicate unusual strength for a human, but their wrists were narrow and their fingers long and thin and delicate.

There seemed to be more than the usual number of fingers.

Since he came in, a machine had been whirring and a voice muttering beside him. He turned from counting their fingers and looked around. Beside him sat an alert-looking man wearing earphones, watching and listening with hawklike concentration. Beside him was a tall streamlined box. From the screen came the sound of the alien language. The man abruptly flipped a switch on the box, muttered a word into a small hand microphone, and flipped the switch back with nervous rapidity.

He reminded the *Times* man of the earphoned interpreters at the U.N. The machine was probably a vocal translator and the mutterer a linguist adding to its vocabulary. Near the screen were two other linguists taking notes.

The *Times* remembered the senator pacing in the observatory room, rehearsing his speech of welcome. The speech would not be just the empty pompous gesture he had expected. It would be translated mechanically and understood by the aliens.

On the other side of the glowing window that was the stereo screen the large protagonist in the green tunic was speaking to a pilot in a gray uniform. They stood in a brightly lit canary-yellow control room in a spaceship.

The *Times* tried to pick up the thread of the plot. Already he was interested in the fate of the hero, and liked him. That was the effect of good acting, probably, for part of the art of acting is to win affection from the audience, and this actor might be the matinee idol of whole Solar Systems.

Controlled tension, betraying itself by a jerk of the hands, a too quick answer to a question. The uniformed one, not suspicious, turned his back, busying himself at some task involving a map lit with glowing red points, his motions sharing the same fluid, dragging grace of the others, as if they were under water or on a slow-motion film. The other was watching a switch, a switch set into a panel, moving closer to it, talking casually—background music coming and rising in thin chords of tension.

There was a close-up of the alien's face watching the switch, and the *Times* noted that his ears were symmetrical half circles, almost perfect, with no earholes visible. The voice of the uniformed one answered—a brief word in a preoccupied, deep voice. His back was still turned. The other glanced at the switch, moving closer to it, talking casually, the switch coming closer and closer stereoscopically. It was in reach, filling the screen. His hand came into view, darted out, closed over the switch—

There was a sharp clap of sound and his hand opened in a frozen shape of pain. Beyond him, as his gaze swung up, stood the figure of the uniformed officer, unmoving, a weapon rigid in his hand, in the startled position in which he had turned and fired, watching with widened eyes as the man in the green tunic swayed and fell.

The tableau held, the uniformed one drooping, looking down at his hand holding the weapon which had killed, and music began to build in from the background. Just for an instant, the room and the things within it flashed into one of those bewildering color changes that were the bane of color television—to a color negative of itself, a green man standing in a violet control room, looking down at the body of a green man in a red tunic. It held for less than a second; then the color-band alternator fell back into phase and the colors reversed to normal.

Another uniformed man came and took the weapon from the limp hand of the other, who began to explain dejectedly in a low voice while the music mounted and covered his words and the screen slowly went blank, like a window that slowly filmed over with gray fog.

The music faded.

In the dark, someone clapped appreciatively.

The earphoned man beside the *Times* shifted his earphones back from his ears and spoke briskly. "I can't get any more. Either of you want a replay?"

There was a short silence until the linguist nearest the set said, "I guess we've squeezed that one dry. Let's run the tape where Nathen and that ship radio boy are kidding around CQing and tuning their beams in closer. I have a hunch the boy is talking routine ham talk and giving the old radio count one-two-three-testing."

There was some fumbling in the semidark and then the screen came to life again.

It showed a flash of an audience sitting before a screen and gave a clipped chord of some familiar symphony. "Crazy about Stravinsky and Mozart," remarked the earphoned linguist to the *Times*, resettling his earphones. "Can't stand Gershwin. Can you beat that?" He turned his attention back to the screen as the right sequence came on.

The *Post*, who was sitting just in front of him, turned to the *Times* and said, "Funny how much they look like people." He was writing, making notes to telephone his report. "What color hair did that character have?"

"I didn't notice." He wondered if he should remind the reporter that Nathen had said he assigned the color bands on guess, choosing the colors that gave the most plausible images. The guests, when they arrived, could turn out to be bright green with blue hair. Only the gradations of color in the picture were sure, only the similarities and contrasts, the relationship of one color to another.

From the screen came the sound of the alien language again. This race averaged deeper voices than human. He liked deep voices. Could he write that?

No, there was something wrong with that, too. How had Nathen established the right sound-track pitch? Was it a matter of taking the modulation as it came in, or some sort of heterodyning up and down by trial and error? Probably.

It might be safer to assume that Nathen had simply preferred deep voices.

As he sat there, doubting, an uneasiness he had seen in Nathen came back to add to his own uncertainty, and he remembered just how close that uneasiness had come to something that looked like restrained fear.

"What I don't get is why he went to all the trouble of picking up TV shows instead of just contacting them," the *News* complained. "They're good shows, but what's the point?"

"Maybe so we'd get to learn their language, too," said the *Herald*.

On the screen now was the obviously unstaged and genuine scene of a young alien working over a bank of apparatus. He turned and waved and opened his mouth in the comical O shape which the *Times* was beginning to recognize as their equivalent of a smile, then went back to trying to explain something about the equipment, in elaborate, awkward gestures and carefully mouthed words.

The *Times* got up quietly, went out into the bright white stone corridor, and walked back the way he had come, thoughtfully folding his stereo glasses and putting them away.

No one stopped him. Secrecy restrictions were ambiguous here. The reticence of the Army seemed more a matter of habit—mere reflex, from the fact that it had all originated in the Intelligence Department—than any reasoned policy of keeping the landing a secret.

The main room was more crowded than he had left it. The TV camera and sound crew stood near their apparatus, the senator had found a chair and was reading, and at the far end of the room eight men were grouped in a circle of chairs, arguing something with impassioned concentration. The *Times* recognized a few he knew personally, eminent names in science, workers in field theory.

A stray phrase reached him: "—reference to the universal constants as ratio—" It was probably a discussion of ways of converting formulas from one mathematics to another for a rapid exchange of information.

They had reason to be intent, aware of the flood of insights that novel viewpoints could bring, if they could grasp them. He would have liked to go over and listen, but there was too little time left before the spaceship was due, and he had a question to ask.

The hand-rigged transceiver was still humming, tuned to the sending band of the circling ship, and the young man who had started it all was sitting on the edge of the TV platform with his chin resting in one hand. He did not look up as the *Times* approached, but it was the indifference of preoccupation, not discourtesy.

The *Times* sat down on the edge of the platform beside him and took out a pack of cigarettes, then remembered the coming TV broadcast and the ban on smoking. He put them away, thoughtfully watching the diminishing rain spray against the streaming windows.

"What's wrong?" he asked.

Nathen showed that he was aware and friendly by a slight motion of his head.

"*You* tell me."

"Hunch," said the *Times* man. "Sheer hunch. Everything sailing along too smoothly, everyone taking too much for granted."

Nathen relaxed slightly. "I'm still listening."

"Something about the way they move . . ."

Nathen shifted to glance at him.

"That's bothered me, too."

"Are you sure they're adjusted to the right speed?"

Nathen clenched his hands out in front of him and looked at them consideringly. "I don't know. When I turn the tape faster, they're all rushing, and you begin to wonder why their clothes don't stream behind them, why the doors close so quickly and yet you can't hear them slam, why things fall so fast. If I turn it slower, they all seem to be swimming." He gave the *Times* a considering sideways glance. "Didn't catch the name."

Country-bred guy, thought the *Times*. "Jacob Luke, *Times*," he said, extending his hand.

Nathen gave the hand a quick, hard grip, identifying the name. "Sunday Science Section editor. I read it. Surprised to meet you here."

"Likewise." The *Times* smiled. "Look, have you gone into this rationally, with formulas?" He found a pencil in his pocket. "Obviously, there's something wrong with our judgment of their weight-to-speed-to-momentum ratio. Maybe it's something simple, like low gravity aboard ship, with magnetic shoes. Maybe they *are* floating slightly."

"Why worry?" Nathen cut in. "I don't see any reason to try to figure it out now." He laughed and shoved back his black hair nervously. "We'll see them in twenty minutes."

"Will we?" asked the *Times* slowly.

There was silence while the senator turned a page of his magazine with a slight crackling of paper and the scientists argued at the other end of the room. Nathen pushed at his black hair again, as if it were trying to fall forward in front of his eyes and keep him from seeing.

"Sure." The young man laughed suddenly, talked rapidly. "Sure we'll see them. Why shouldn't we, with all the government ready with welcome speeches, the whole Army turned out and hiding over the hill, reporters all around, newsreel cameras—everything set up to broadcast the landing to the world. The President himself shaking hands with me and waiting in Washington—"

He came to the truth without pausing for breath.

He said, "Hell, no, they won't get here. There's some mistake somewhere. Something's wrong. I should have told the brass hats yesterday when I started adding it up. Don't know why I didn't say anything. Scared, I guess. Too much top rank around here. Lost my nerve."

He clutched the *Times* man's sleeve. "Look. I don't know what—"

A green light flashed on the sending-receiving set. Nathen didn't look at it, but he stopped talking.

The loud-speaker on the set broke into a voice speaking in the aliens' language. The senator started and looked nervously at it, straightening his tie. The voice stopped.

Nathen turned and looked at the loud-speaker. His worry seemed to be gone.

"What is it?" the *Times* asked anxiously.

"He says they've slowed enough to enter the atmosphere now. They'll be here in five to ten minutes, I guess. That's Bud. He's all excited. He says holy smoke, what a murky-looking planet we live on." Nathen smiled. "Kidding."

The *Times* was puzzled. "What does he mean, murky? It can't be raining over much territory on Earth." Outside, the rain was slowing and bright-blue patches of sky were shining through breaks in the cloud blanket, glittering blue light from the drops that ran down the windows. He tried to think of an explanation. "Maybe they're trying to land on Venus." The thought was ridiculous, he knew. The spaceship was following Nathen's sending beam. It couldn't miss Earth. "Bud" had to be kidding.

The green light glowed on the set again, and they stopped speaking, waiting for the message to be recorded, slowed, and replayed. The cathode screen came to life suddenly with a picture of the young man sitting at his sending set, his back turned, watching a screen at one side that showed a glimpse of a huge dark plain approaching. As the ship plunged down toward it, the illusion of solidity melted into a boiling turbulence of black clouds. They expanded in an inky swirl, looked huge for an instant, and then blackness swallowed the screen. The young alien swung around to face the camera, speaking a few words as he moved, made the O of a smile again, then flipped the switch and the screen went gray.

Nathen's voice was suddenly toneless and strained. "He said something like break out the drinks, here they come."

"The atmosphere doesn't look like that," the *Times* said at random, knowing he was saying something too obvious even to think about. "Not Earth's atmosphere."

Some people drifted up. "What did they say?"

"Entering the atmosphere, ought to be landing in five or ten minutes," Nathen told them.

A ripple of heightened excitement ran through the room. Cameramen began adjusting the lens angles again, turning on the mike and checking it, turning on the floodlights. The scientists rose and stood near the window, still talking. The reporters trooped in from the hall and went to the windows to watch for the great event. The three linguists came in, trundling a large wheeled box that was the mechanical translator, supervising while it was hitched into the sound-broadcasting system.

"Landing where?" the *Times* asked Nathen brutally. "Why don't you do something?"

"Tell me what to do and I'll do it," Nathen said quietly, not moving.

It was not sarcasm. Jacob Luke of the *Times* looked sideways at the strained whiteness of his face and moderated his tone. "Can't you contact them?"

"Not while they're landing."

"What now?" The *Times* took out a pack of cigarettes, remembered the rule against smoking, and put it back.

"We just wait." Nathen leaned his elbow on one knee and his chin in his hand.

They waited.

All the people in the room were waiting. There was no conversation. A bald man of the scientist group was automatically buffing his fingernails over and over and inspecting them without seeing them; another absently polished his glasses, held them up to the light, put them on, and then a moment later took them off and began polishing again. The television crew concentrated on their jobs, moving quietly and efficiently, with perfectionist care, minutely arranging things that did not need to be arranged, checking things that had already been checked.

This was to be one of the great moments of human history, and they were all trying to forget that fact and remain impassive and wrapped up in the problems of their jobs, as good specialists should.

After an interminable age the *Times* consulted his watch. Three minutes had passed. He tried holding his breath a moment, listening for a distant approaching thunder of jets. There was no sound.

The sun came out from behind the clouds and lit up the field like a great spotlight on an empty stage.

Abruptly, the green light shone on the set again, indicating that a squawk message had been received. The recorder recorded it, slowed it, and fed it back to the speaker. It clicked and the sound was very loud in the still, tense room.

The screen remained gray, but Bud's voice spoke a few words in the alien language. He stopped, the speaker clicked, and the light went out. When it was plain that nothing more would occur and no announcement was to be made of what was said, the people in the room turned back to the windows and talk picked up again.

Somebody told a joke and laughed alone.

One of the linguists remained turned toward the loud-speaker, then looked at the widening patches of blue sky showing out the window, his expression puzzled. He had understood.

"It's dark," the thin Intelligence Department decoder translated, low-voiced, to the man from the *Times*. "Your atmosphere is *thick*. That's precisely what Bud said."

Another three minutes. The *Times* caught himself about to light a cigarette and swore silently, blowing the match out and putting the cigarette back into its package. He listened for the sound of the rockets. It was time for the landing, yet he heard no blasts.

The green light came on in the transceiver.

Message in.

Instinctively, he came to his feet. Nathen abruptly was standing beside him. Then the message came in the voice he was coming to think of as Bud. It spoke and paused. Suddenly the *Times* knew.

"We've landed." Nathen whispered the words.

The wind blew across the open spaces of white concrete and damp soil that was the empty airfield, swaying the wet, shiny grass. The people in the room looked out, listening for the roar of jets, looking for the silver bulk of a spaceship in the sky.

Nathen moved, seating himself at the transmitter, switching it on to warm up, checking and balancing dials. Jacob Luke of the *Times* moved softly to stand behind his right shoulder, hoping he could be useful. Nathen made a half motion of his head, as if to glance back at him, unhooked two of the earphone sets hanging on the side of the tall streamlined box that was the automatic translator, plugged them in, and handed one back over his shoulder to the *Times* man.

The voice began to come from the speaker again.

Hastily, Jacob Luke fitted the earphones over his ears. He fancied he could hear Bud's voice tremble. For a moment it was just Bud's voice speaking the alien language, and then, very distant and clear in his earphones, he heard the recorded voice of the linguist say an English word, then a mechanical click and another clear word in the voice of one of the translators, then another as the alien's voice flowed from the loudspeaker, the cool single words barely audible, overlapping and blending like translating thought, skipping unfamiliar words yet quite astonishingly clear.

"Radar shows no buildings or civilization near. The atmosphere around us registers as thick as glue. Tremendous gas pressure, low gravity, no light at all. You didn't describe it like this. Where are you, Joe? This isn't some kind of trick, is it?" Bud hesitated, was prompted by a deeper official voice, and jerked out the words.

"If it is a trick, we are ready to repel attack."

The linguist stood listening. He whitened slowly and beckoned the other linguists over to him and whispered to them.

Joseph Nathen looked at them with unwarranted bitter hostility while he picked up the hand mike, plugging it into the translator. "Joe calling," he said quietly into it in clear, slow English. "No trick. We don't know where you are. I am trying to get a direction fix from your signal. Describe your surroundings to us if at all possible.''

Nearby, the flood lights blazed steadily on the television platform, ready for the official welcome of the aliens to Earth. The television channels of the world had been alerted to set aside their scheduled programs for an unscheduled great event. In the long room the people waited, listening for the swelling sound of rocket jets.

This time, after the light came on, there was a long delay. The speaker sputtered and sputtered again, building to a steady scratching through which they could barely hear a dim voice. It came through in a few tinny words and then wavered back to inaudibility. The machine translated in their earphones. ''Tried . . . seemed . . . repair . . .'' Suddenly it came in clearly. ''Can't tell if the auxiliary blew, too. Will try it. We might pick you up clearly on the next try. I have the volume down. Where is the landing port? Repeat, where is the landing port? Where are you?''

Nathen put down the hand mike and carefully set a dial on the recording box and flipped a switch, speaking over his shoulder. ''This sets it to repeat what I said the last time. It keeps repeating.'' Then he sat with unnatural stillness, his head still half turned, as if he had suddenly caught a glimpse of answer and was trying with no success whatever to grasp it.

The green warning light cut in, the recording clicked, and the playback of Bud's face and voice, appeared on the screen. ''We heard a few words, Joe, and then the receiver blew again. We're adjusting a viewing screen to pick up the long waves that go through the murk and convert them to visible light. We'll be able to see out soon. The engineer says that something is wrong with the stern jets, and the captain has had me broadcast a help call to our nearest space base.'' He made the mouth O of a grin. ''The message won't reach it for some years. I trust you, Joe, but get us out of here, will you?—they're buzzing that the screen is finally ready. Hold everything.''

The screen went gray and the green light went off.

The *Times* considered the lag required for the help call, the speaking and recording of the message just received, the time needed to reconvert a viewing screen.

"They work fast." He shifted uneasily and added at random, "Something wrong with the time factor. All wrong. They work *too* fast."

The green light came on again immediately. Nathen half turned to him, sliding his words hastily into the gap of time as the message was recorded and slowed. "They're close enough for our transmission power to blow their receiver."

If it was on Earth, why the darkness around the ship? "Maybe they see in the high ultraviolet—the atmosphere is opaque to that band," the *Times* suggested hastily as the speaker began to talk in the young extra-Terrestrial's voice.

That voice *was* shaking now. "Stand by for the description."

They tensed, waiting. The *Times* brought a map of the state before his mind's eye.

"A half circle of cliffs around the horizon. A wide muddy lake swarming with swimming things. Huge, strange white foliage all around the ship and incredibly huge, pulpy monsters attacking and eating each other on all sides. We almost landed in the lake, right on the soft edge. The mud can't hold the ship's weight, and we're sinking. The engineer says we might be able to blast free, but the tubes are mud-clogged and might blow up the ship. When can you reach us?"

The *Times* thought vaguely of the Carboniferous era. Nathen obviously had seen something he had not.

"Where are they?" the *Times* asked him quietly.

Nathen pointed to the antenna position indicators. The *Times* let his eyes follow the converging imaginary lines of focus out the window to the sunlit airfield, the empty airfield, the drying concrete and green waving grass where the lines met.

Where the lines met. The spaceship was there!

The fear of something unknown gripped him suddenly.

The spaceship was broadcasting again. *"Where are you? Answer if possible! We are sinking! Where are you?"*

He saw that Nathen knew. "What is it?" the *Times* asked

hoarsely. "Are they in another dimension or the past or on another world or what?"

Nathen was smiling bitterly, and Jacob Luke remembered that the young man had a friend in that spaceship. "My guess is that they evolved on a high-gravity planet with a thin atmosphere, near a blue-white star. Sure, they see in the ultraviolet range. Our sun is abnormally small and dim and yellow. Our atmosphere is so thick it screens out ultraviolet." He laughed harshly. "A good joke on us, the weird place we evolved in, the thing it did to us!"

"Where are you?" called the alien spaceship. "Hurry, please! We're sinking!"

The decoder slowed his tumbled, frightened words and looked up into the *Times'* face for understanding. "We'll rescue them," he said quietly. "You were right about the time factor, right about them moving at a different speed. I misunderstood. This business about squawk coding, speeding for better transmission to counteract beam waver—I was wrong."

"What do you mean?"

"They don't speed up their broadcasts."

"They don't—?"

Suddenly, in his mind's eye, the *Times* began to see again the play he had just seen—but the actors were moving at blurring speed, the words jerking out in a fluting, dizzying stream, thoughts and decisions passing with unfollowable rapidity, rippling faces in a twisting blur of expressions, doors slamming wildly, shatteringly, as the actors leaped in and out of rooms.

No—faster, faster—he wasn't visualizing it as rapidly as it was, an hour of talk and action in one almost instantaneous "squaw," a narrow peak of "noise" interfering with a single word in an Earth broadcast! Faster—faster—it was impossible. Matter could not stand such stress—inertia—momentum—abrupt weight.

It was insane. "Why?" he asked. "How?"

Nathen laughed again harshly, reaching for the mike. "Get

them out? There isn't a lake or river within hundreds of miles from here!''

A shiver of unreality went down the *Times'* spine. Automatically and inanely, he found himself delving in his pocket for a cigarette while he tried to grasp what had happened. ''Where are they, then? Why can't we see their spaceship?''

Nathen switched the microphone on in a gesture that showed the bitterness of his disappointment.

''We'll need a magnifying glass for that.''

SUPERIORITY

BY ARTHUR C. CLARKE
THE MAGAZINE OF FANTASY AND SCIENCE FICTION, AUGUST

Arthur C. Clarke's second contribution to the best of 1951 is this wonderful lesson about too much innovation. Reportedly required reading several years ago for all freshmen at the Massachusetts Institute of Technology, it is also prophetic in regard to one of the most important military lessons to come out of American involvement in the Vietnam War.

—M.H.G.

And have we learned? That's what I want to know. Have we learned? Do we still think that all disputes can be settled easily and inevitably by the guy with the fastest draw, or the biggest gun, or the deadliest explosive?

Four years ago, the Soviets went into Afghanistan. They're still stuck there, even though they vastly outgun the Afghan rebels. We keep feeding the Salvadoran government all the weapons they can handle and they can't defeat the rebels. We complain that that is because the rebels get weapons from Cuba and Nicaragua, but we're kidding ourselves. They capture them from the Salvadoran army. We're supplying both sides, just as we did in Vietnam.

I admit we defeated the mighty war machine of Grenada.

Or as one American admiral said proudly, "We just blew them away." We then gave medals to every military person who was anywhere near Grenada on that great day. I understand that we are now almost ready to take on the mighty war machine of Monaco.

In short, it's not weapons alone! We would never have beaten Hitler if Hitler's peculiar ideas had not united the whole world against him. It's ideas that win or lose.

So do we look for ideas? Good ones? No, we're going to outsophisticate the Soviet Union a la Reagan's Star-Wars speech. You can bet Reagan never read "Superiority." (I know—but he can always have Schulz read it to him.)

—I.A.

IN MAKING this statement—which I do of my own free will—I wish first to make it perfectly clear that I am not in any way trying to gain sympathy, nor do I expect any mitigation of whatever sentence the Court may pronounce. I am writing this in an attempt to refute some of the lying reports broadcast over the prison radio and published in the papers I have been allowed to see. These have given an entirely false picture of the true causes of our defeat, and as the leader of my race's armed forces at the cessation of hostilities I feel it my duty to protest against such libels upon those who served under me.

I also hope that this statement may explain the reasons for the application I have twice made to the Court, and will now induce it to grant a favor for which I can see no possible grounds of refusal.

The ultimate cause of our failure was a simple one: despite all statements to the contrary, it was not due to lack of bravery on the part of our men, or to any fault of the Fleet's. We were defeated by one thing only—by the inferior science of our enemies. I repeat—by the *inferior* science of our enemies.

When the war opened we had no doubt of our ultimate victory. The combined fleets of our allies greatly exceeded in number and armament those which the enemy could muster against us, and in almost all branches of military science we were their superiors. We were sure that we could maintain this superiority. Our belief proved, alas, to be only too well founded.

At the opening of the war our main weapons were the longrange homing torpedo, dirigible ball-lightning and the various modifications of the Klydon beam. Every unit of the Fleet was equipped with these, and though the enemy possessed similar weapons their installations were generally of lesser power. Moreover, we had behind us a far greater military Research Organization, and with this initial advantage we could not possibly lose.

The campaign proceeded according to plan until the Battle of the Five Suns. We won this, of course, but the opposition proved stronger than we had expected. It was realized that victory might be more difficult, and more delayed than had first been imagined. A conference of supreme commanders was therefore called to discuss our future strategy.

Present for the first time at one of our war conferences was Professor-General Norden, the new Chief of the Research Staff, who had just been appointed to fill the gap left by the death of Malvar, our greatest scientist. Malvar's leadership had been responsible, more than any other single factor, for the efficiency and power of our weapons. His loss was a very serious blow, but no one doubted the brilliance of his successor—though many of us disputed the wisdom of appointing a theoretical scientist to fill a post of such vital importance. But we had been overruled.

I can well remember the impression Norden made at that conference. The military advisers were worried, and as usual turned to the scientists for help. Would it be possible to improve our existing weapons, they asked, so that our present advantage could be increased still further?

Norden's reply was quite unexpected. Malvar had often been asked such a question—and he had always done what we requested.

"Frankly, gentlemen," said Norden, "I doubt it. Our

existing weapons have practically reached finality. I don't wish to criticize my predecessor, or the excellent work done by the Research Staff in the last few generations, but do you realize that there has been no basic change in armaments for over a century? It is, I am afraid, the result of a tradition that has become conservative. For too long, the Research Staff has devoted itself to perfecting old weapons instead of developing new ones. It is fortunate for us that our opponents have been no wiser: we cannot assume that this will always be so.''

Norden's words left an uncomfortable impression, as he had no doubt intended. He quickly pressed home the attack.

"What we want are *new* weapons—weapons totally different from any that have been employed before. Such weapons can be made: it will take time, of course, but since assuming charge I have replaced some of the older scientists by young men and have directed research into several unexplored fields which show great promise. I believe, in fact, that a revolution in warfare may soon be upon us.''

We were skeptical. There was a bombastic tone in Norden's voice that made us suspicious of his claims. We did not know, then, that he never promised anything that he had not already almost perfected in the laboratory. *In the laboratory*—that was the operative phrase.

Norden proved his case less than a month later, when he demonstrated the Sphere of Annihilation, which produced complete disintegration of matter over a radius of several hundred meters. We were intoxicated by the power of the new weapon, and were quite prepared to overlook one fundamental defect—the fact that it *was* a sphere and hence destroyed its rather complicated generating equipment at the instant of formation. This meant, of course, that it could not be used on warships but only on guided missiles, and a great program was started to convert all homing torpedoes to carry the new weapon. For the time being all further offensives were suspended.

We realize now that this was our first mistake. I still think that it was a natural one, for it seemed to us then that all our existing weapons had become obsolete overnight, and we already regarded them as almost primitive survivals. What we did not appreciate was the magnitude of the task we were attempting, and the length of time it would take to get the revolutionary super-weapon into battle. Nothing like this had happened for a hundred years and we had no previous experience to guide us.

The conversion problem proved far more difficult than anticipated. A new class of torpedo had to be designed, because the standard model was too small. This meant in turn that only the larger ships could launch the weapon, but we were prepared to accept this penalty. After six months, the heavy units of the Fleet were being equipped with the Sphere. Training maneuvers and tests had shown that it was operating satisfactorily and we were ready to take it into action. Norden was already being hailed as the architect of victory, and had half promised even more spectacular weapons.

Then two things happened. One of our battleships disappeared completely on a training flight, and an investigation showed that under certain conditions the ship's long-range radar could trigger the Sphere immediately it had been launched. The modification needed to overcome this defect was trivial, but it caused a delay of another month and was the source of much bad feeling between the naval staff and the scientists. We were ready for action again—when Norden announced that the radius of effectiveness of the Sphere had now been increased by ten, thus multiplying by a thousand the chances of destroying an enemy ship.

So the modifications started all over again, but everyone agreed that the delay would be worth it. Meanwhile, however, the enemy had been emboldened by the absence of further attacks and had made an unexpected onslaught. Our ships were short of torpedoes, since none had been coming from the factories, and were forced to retire. So we lost the systems of Kyrane and Floranus, and the planetary fortress of Rhamsandron.

It was an annoying but not a serious blow, for the recaptured systems had been unfriendly, and difficult to administer. We had no doubt that we could restore the position in the near future, as soon as the new weapon became operational.

These hopes were only partially fulfilled. When we renewed our offensive, we had to do so with fewer of the Spheres of Annihilation than had been planned, and this was one reason for our limited success. The other reason was more serious.

While we had been equipping as many of our ships as we could with the irresistible weapon, the enemy had been building feverishly. His ships were of the old pattern with the old weapons—but they now outnumbered ours. When we went into action, we found that the numbers ranged against us were often one hundred per cent greater than expected, causing target confusion among the automatic weapons and resulting in higher losses than anticipated. The enemy losses were higher still, for once a Sphere had reached its objective, destruction was certain, but the balance had not swung as far in our favor as we had hoped.

Moreover, while the main fleets had been engaged, the enemy had launched a daring attack on the lightly held systems of Eriston, Duranus, Carmanidora and Pharandion—recapturing them all. We were thus faced with a threat only fifty light-years from our home planets.

There was much recrimination at the next meeting of the supreme commanders. Most of the complaints were addressed to Norden—Grand Admiral Taxaris in particular maintaining that thanks to our admittedly irresistible weapon we were now considerably worse off than before. We should, he claimed, have continued to build conventional ships, thus preventing the loss of our numerical superiority.

Norden was equally angry and called the naval staff ungrateful bunglers. But I could tell that he was worried—as indeed we all were—by the unexpected turn of events. He hinted that there might be a speedy way of remedying the situation.

We now know that Research had been working on the Battle Analyzer for many years, but, at the time, it came as a revelation to us and perhaps we were too easily swept off our feet. Norden's argument, also, was seductively convincing. What did it matter, he said, if the enemy had twice as many ships as we—if the efficiency of ours could be doubled or even trebled? For decades the limiting factor in warfare had been not mechanical but biological—it had become more and more difficult for any single mind, or group of minds, to cope with the rapidly changing complexities of battle in three-dimensional space. Norden's mathematicians had analyzed some of the classic engagements of the past, and had shown that even when we had been victorious we had often operated our units at much less than half of their theoretical efficiency.

The Battle Analyzer would change all this by replacing the operations staff with electronic calculators. The idea was not new, in theory, but until now it had been no more than a utopian dream. Many of us found it difficult to believe that it was still anything but a dream: after we had run through several very complex dummy battles, however, we were convinced.

It was decided to install the Analyzer in four of our heaviest ships, so that each of the main fleets could be equipped with one. At this stage, the trouble began—though we did not know it until later.

The Analyzer contained just short of a million vacuum tubes and needed a team of five hundred technicians to maintain and operate it. It was quite impossible to accommodate the extra staff aboard a battleship, so each of the four units had to be accompanied by a converted liner to carry the technicians not on duty. Installation was also a very slow and tedious business, but by gigantic efforts it was completed in six months.

Then, to our dismay, we were confronted by another crisis. Nearly five thousand highly skilled men had been selected to serve the Analyzers and had been given an intensive course at the Technical Training Schools. At the end of seven months, ten per cent of them had had nervous breakdowns and only forty per cent had qualified.

Once again, everyone started to blame everyone else. Norden, of course, said that the Research Staff could not be held responsible, and so incurred the enmity of the Personnel and Training Commands. It was finally decided that the only thing to do was to use two instead of four Analyzers and to bring the others into action as soon as men could be trained. There was little time to lose, for the enemy was still on the offensive and his morale was rising.

The first Analyzer fleet was ordered to recapture the system of Eriston. On the way, by one of the hazards of war, the liner carrying the technicians was struck by a roving mine. A warship would have survived, but the liner with its irreplaceable cargo was totally destroyed. So the operation had to be abandoned.

The other expedition was, at first, more successful. There was no doubt at all that the Analyzer fulfilled its designers' claims, and the enemy was heavily defeated in the first engagements. He withdrew, leaving us in possession of Saphran, Leucon and Hexanerax. But his Intelligence Staff must have noted the change in our tactics and the inexplicable presence of a liner in the heart of our battle Fleet. It must have noted, also, that our first Fleet had been accompanied by a similar ship—and had withdrawn when it had been destroyed.

In the next engagement, the enemy used his superior numbers to launch an overwhelming attack on the Analyzer ship and its unarmed consort. The attack was made without regard to losses—both ships were, of course, very heavily protected—and it succeeded. The result was the virtual decapitation of the Fleet, since an effectual transfer to the old operational methods proved impossible. We disengaged under heavy fire, and so lost all our gains and also the systems of Lormyia, Ismarnus, Beronis, Alphandidon and Sideneus.

At this stage, Grand Admiral Taxaris expressed his disapproval of Norden by committing suicide, and I assumed supreme command.

The situation was now both serious and infuriating. With stubborn conservatism and complete lack of imagination, the enemy continued to advance with his old-fashioned and inefficient but now vastly more numerous ships. It was galling to realize that if we had only continued building, without seeking new weapons, we would have been in a far more advantageous position. There were many acrimonious conferences at which Norden defended the scientists while everyone else blamed them for all that had happened. The difficulty was that Norden had proved everyone of his claims: he had a perfect excuse for all the disasters that had occurred. And we could not now turn back—the search for an irresistible weapon must go on. At first it had been a luxury that would shorten the war. Now it was a necessity if we were to end it victoriously.

We were on the defensive, and so was Norden. He was more than ever determined to re-establish his prestige and that of the Research Staff. But we had been twice disappointed, and would not make the same mistake again. No doubt Norden's twenty thousand scientists would produce many further weapons: we would remain unimpressed.

We were wrong. The final weapon was something so fantastic that even now it seems difficult to believe that it ever existed. Its innocent, noncommittal name—The Exponential Field—gave no hint of its real potentialities. Some of Norden's mathematicians had discovered it during a piece of entirely theoretical research into the properties of space, and to everyone's great surprise their results were found to be physically realizable.

It seems very difficult to explain the operation of the Field to the layman. According to the technical description, it "produces an exponential condition of space, so that a finite distance in normal, linear space may become infinite in pseudospace." Norden gave an analogy which some of us found useful. It was as if one took a flat disk of rubber—representing a region of normal space—and then pulled its center out to infinity. The circumference of the disk would be unaltered—but its "diameter" would be infinite. That was the sort of thing the generator of the Field did to the space around it.

As an example, suppose that a ship carrying the generator was surrounded by a ring of hostile machines. If it switched on the Field, *each* of the enemy ships would think that it—and the ships on the far side of the circle—had suddenly receded into nothingness. Yet the circumference of the circle would be the same as before: only the journey to the center would be of infinite duration, for as one proceeded, distances would appear to become greater and greater as the "scale" of space altered.

It was a nightmare condition, but a very useful one. Nothing could reach a ship carrying the Field: it might be englobed by an enemy fleet yet would be as inaccessible as if it were at the other side of the Universe. Against this, of course, it could not fight back without switching off the Field, but this still left it at a very great advantage, not only in defense but in offense. For a ship fitted with the Field could approach an enemy fleet undetected and suddenly appear in its midst.

This time there seemed to be no flaws in the new weapon. Needless to say, we looked for all the possible objections before we committed ourselves again. Fortunately the equipment was fairly simple and did not require a large operating staff. After much debate, we decided to rush it into production, for we realized that time was running short and the war was going against us. We had now lost about the whole of our initial gains, and enemy forces had made several raids into our own Solar System.

We managed to hold off the enemy while the Fleet was reequipped and the new battle techniques were worked out. To use the Field operationally it was necessary to locate an enemy formation, set a course that would intercept it, and then switch on the generator for the calculated period of time. On releasing the Field again—if the calculations had been accurate—one would be in the enemy's midst and could do great damage during the resulting confusion, retreating by the same route when necessary.

The first trial maneuvers proved satisfactory and the equipment seemed quite reliable. Numerous mock attacks were made and the crews became accustomed to the new technique. I was on one of the test flights and can vividly remember my impressions as the Field was switched on. The ships around us seemed to dwindle as if on the surface of an expanding bubble: in an instant they had vanished completely. So had the stars—but presently we could see that the Galaxy was still visible as a faint band of light around the ship. The virtual radius of our pseudo-space was not really infinite, but some hundred thousand light-years, and so the distance to the farthest stars of our system had not been greatly increased—though the nearest had of course totally disappeared.

These training maneuvers, however, had to be canceled before they were complete owing to a whole flock of minor technical troubles in various pieces of equipment, notably the communications circuits. These were annoying, but not important, though it was thought best to return to Base to clear them up.

At that moment the enemy made what was obviously intended to be a decisive attack against the fortress planet of Iton at the limits of our Solar System. The Fleet had to go into battle before repairs could be made.

The enemy must have believed that we had mastered the secret of invisibility—as in a sense we had. Our ships appeared suddenly out of nowhere and inflicted tremendous damage—for a while. And then something quite baffling and inexplicable happened.

I was in command of the flagship *Hircania* when the trouble started. We had been operating as independent units, each against assigned objectives. Our detectors observed an enemy formation at medium range and the navigating officers measured its distance with great accuracy. We set course and switched on the generator.

The Exponential Field was released at the moment when we should have been passing through the center of the enemy group. To our consternation, we emerged into normal space at a distance of many hundred miles—and when we found the enemy, he had already found us. We retreated, and tried again. This time we were so far away from the enemy that he located us first.

Obviously, something was seriously wrong. We broke communicator silence and tried to contact the other ships of the Fleet to see if they had experienced the same trouble. Once again we failed—and this time the failure was beyond all reason, for the communication equipment appeared to be working perfectly. We could only assume, fantastic though it seemed, that the rest of the Fleet had been destroyed.

I do not wish to describe the scenes when the scattered units of the Fleet struggled back to Base. Our casualties had actually been negligible, but the ships were completely demoralized. Almost all had lost touch with one another and had found that their ranging equipment showed inexplicable errors. It was obvious that the Exponential Field was the cause of the troubles, despite the fact that they were only apparent when it was switched off.

The explanation came too late to do us any good, and Norden's final discomfiture was small consolation for the virtual loss of the war. As I have explained, the Field generators produced a radial distortion of space, distances appearing greater and greater as one approached the center of the artificial pseudo-space. When the Field was switched off, conditions returned to normal.

But not quite. It was never possible to restore the initial state *exactly*. Switching the Field on and off was equivalent to an elongation and contraction of the ship carrying the generator, but there was a hysteretic effect, as it were, and the initial condition was never quite reproducible, owing to all the thousands of electrical changes and movements of mass aboard the ship while the Field was on. These asymmetries and distortions were cumulative, and though they seldom amounted to more than a fraction of one per cent, that was quite enough. It meant that the precision ranging equipment and the tuned circuits in the communication apparatus were thrown completely out of adjustment. Any single ship could never detect the change—only when it compared its equipment with that of another vessel, or tried to communicate with it, could it tell what had happened.

It is impossible to describe the resultant chaos. Not a single component of one ship could be expected with certainty to work aboard another. The very nuts and bolts were no longer interchangeable, and the supply position became quite impos-

sible. Given time, we might even have overcome these difficulties, but the enemy ships were already attacking in thousands
with weapons which now seemed centuries behind those that
we had invented. Our magnificent Fleet, crippled by our own
science, fought on as best it could until it was overwhelmed
and forced to surrender. The ships fitted with the Field were
still invulnerable, but as fighting units they were almost
helpless. Every time they switched on their generators to
escape from enemy attack, the permanent distortion of their
equipment increased. In a month, it was all over.

This is the true story of our defeat, which I give without
prejudice to my defense before this Court. I make it, as I
have said, to counteract the libels that have been circulating
against the men who fought under me, and to show where the
true blame for our misfortunes lay.

Finally, my request, which, as the Court will now realize, I
make in no frivolous manner and which I hope will therefore
be granted.

The Court will be aware that the conditions under which
we are housed and the constant surveillance to which we are
subjected night and day are somewhat distressing. Yet I am
not complaining of this: nor do I complain of the fact that
shortage of accommodation has made it necessary to house us
in pairs.

But I cannot be held responsible for my future actions if I
am compelled any longer to share my cell with Professor
Norden, late Chief of the Research Staff of my armed forces.

I'M SCARED

BY JACK FINNEY (WALTER B. FINNEY, 1911–   )
COLLIERS, SEPTEMBER

Jack Finney is an excellent science fiction and fantasy writer who has a substantial reputation outside the field, where much of his sf appeared. He is the author of several major novels in the genre, including The Body Snatchers *(1955), (which was made into two excellent films as* Invasion of the Body Snatchers), The Woodrow Wilson Dime *(1968), and* Time and Again *(1973). A superior craftsman at the shorter lengths, his best stories can be found in two collections;* The Third Level *(1957) and* I Love Galesburg in the Springtime: Fantasy and Time Stories *(1963). At least three of his mainstream novels have been filmed:* 5 Against the House *(1954),* Assault on a Queen *(1959) and* Good Neighbor Sam *(1963).*

"I'm Scared" is a minor classic of its kind about the relationship between anxiety and nostalgia, and I think of it every time I watch Laverne and Shirley *and* Happy Days. *You should too.*

—M.H.G.

This story is bound to strike a responsive chord in anyone old enough to remember an earlier "simpler" time.

The only trouble is that the story appeared in 1951. Most middle-aged Americans think of the 1950's as a kind of ideal time. The United States was prosperous and it dominated the world. Everything was nice and happy. Father Eisenhower was in the White House and all was right with the world.

Oh, yes, the early 1950's saw the Korean War, in which we eked out a draw. It saw the McCarthy era, which was as close to terror as we'd gotten in our 200-year history. It was the time when the Soviet Union got into space first and we experienced a national panic.

Still we tend to forget all that—now.

Jack Finney, writing at the beginning of the 1950's could see the flaws. I have read books written in the 1920's that longed for a simpler time "before the War." Socrates longed for a simpler and better time "before the War."

I have come to the conclusion there is no better and simpler time. There is only one's teenage years. I think of my teenage years as golden. Everything was right then. —It was also the decade of the Great Depression and Hitler. My golden decade began with the Stock Market Crash and ended with the beginning of World War II. Golden?

Down with nostalgia. We must stop looking to the past, and we must plan for the future instead. —But that doesn't change the fact that "I'm Scared" is a fascinating story.

—I.A.

I'M VERY BADLY SCARED, not so much for myself—I'm a gray-haired man of sixty-six, after all—but for you and everyone else who has not yet lived out his life. For I believe that certain dangerous things have recently begun to happen in the world. They are noticed here and there, idly discussed, then dismissed and forgotten. Yet I am convinced that unless these occurrences are recognized for what they are, the world will be plunged into a nightmare. Judge for yourself.

One evening last winter I came home from a chess club to which I belong. I'm a widower; I live alone in a small but

comfortable three-room apartment overlooking Fifth Avenue.
It was still fairly early, and I switched on a lamp beside my
leather easy chair, picked up a murder mystery I'd been
reading and turned on the radio; I did not, I'm sorry to say,
notice which station it was tuned to.

The tubes warmed, and the music of an accordion—faint at
first, then louder—came from the loudspeaker. Since it was
good music for reading, I adjusted the volume control and
began to read.

Now I want to be absolutely factual and accurate about
this, and I do not claim that I paid close attention to the radio.
But I do know that presently the music stopped and an
audience applauded. Than a man's voice, chuckling and pleased
with the applause, said, "All right, all right," but the applause continued for several more seconds. During that time
the voice once more chuckled appreciatively, then firmly
repeated, "All right," and the applause died down. "That
was Alec Somebody-or-other," the radio voice said, and I
went back to my book.

But I soon became aware of this middle-aged voice again,
perhaps a change of tone as he turned to a new subject caught
my attention. "And now, Miss Ruth Greeley," he was saying,
"of Trenton, New Jersey. Miss Greeley is a pianist; that
right?" A girl's voice, timid and barely audible, said, "That's
right, Major Bowes." The man's voice—and now I recognized his familiar singsong delivery—said, "And what are
you going to play?"

The girl replied, " 'La Paloma.' " The man repeated it
after her, as an announcement: " 'La Paloma.' " There was
a pause, than an introductory chord sounded from a piano,
and I resumed my reading.

As the girl played, I was half aware that her style was
mechanical, her rhythm defective, perhaps she was nervous.
Then my attention was fully aroused once more by a gong
which sounded suddenly. For a few notes more the girl
continued to play falteringly, not sure what to do. The gong
sounded jarringly again, the playing abruptly stopped and
there was a restless murmur from the audience. "All right, all

right,'' said the familiar voice, and I realized I'd been expecting this, knowing it would say just that. The audience quieted, and the voice began, ''Now . . .''

The radio went dead. For the smallest fraction of a second no sound issued from it but its own mechanical hum. Then a completely different program came from the loudspeaker; the recorded voices of Bing Crosby and his son were singing the concluding bars of ''Sam's Song,'' a favorite of mine. So I returned once more to my reading, wondering vaguely what had happened to the other program, but not actually thinking about it until I finished my book and began to get ready for bed.

Then, undressing in my bedroom, I remembered that Major Bowes was dead. Years had passed, half a decade, since that dry chuckle and familiar, ''All right, all right,'' had been heard in the nation's living rooms.

Well, what does one do when the apparently impossible occurs? It simply made a good story to tell friends, and more than once I was asked if I'd recently heard Moran and Mack, a pair of radio comedians popular some twenty-five years ago, or Floyd Gibbons, an old-time news broadcaster. And there were other joking references to my crystal radio set.

But one man—this was at a lodge meeting the following Thursday—listened to my story with utter seriousness, and when I had finished he told me a queer little story of his own. He is a thoughtful, intelligent man, and as I listened I was not frightened, but puzzled at what seemed to be a connecting link, a common denominator, between this story and the odd behavior of my radio. Since I am retired and have plenty of time, I took the trouble, the following day, of making a two-hour train trip to Connecticut in order to verify the story firsthand. I took detailed notes, and the story appears in my files now as follows:

Case 2. Louis Trachnor, coal and wood dealer, R.F.D. 1, Danbury, Connecticut, age fifty-four.

On July 20, 1950, Mr. Trachnor told me, he walked out on the front porch of his house about six o'clock in the morning.

Running from the eaves of his house to the floor of the porch was a streak of gray paint, still damp. "It was about the width of an eight-inch brush," Mr. Trachnor told me, "and it looked like hell because the house was white. I figured some kids did it in the night for a joke, but if they did, they had to get a ladder up to the eaves and you wouldn't figure they'd go to that much trouble. It wasn't smeared, either; it was a careful job, a nice even stripe straight down the front of the house."

Mr. Trachnor got a ladder and cleaned off the gray paint with turpentine.

In October of that same year Mr. Trachnor painted his house. "The white hadn't held up so good, so I painted it gray. I got to the front last and finished about five one Saturday afternoon. Next morning when I came out I saw a streak of white right down the front of the house. I figured it was the damn kids again because it was the same place as before. But when I looked close, I saw it wasn't new paint; it was the old white I'd painted over. Somebody had done a nice careful job of cleaning off the new paint in a long stripe about eight inches wide right down from the eaves! Now who the hell would go to that trouble? I just can't figure it out."

Do you see the link between this story and mine? Suppose for a moment that something had happened, on each occasion, to disturb briefly the orderly progress of time. That seemed to have happened in my case; for a matter of some seconds I apparently heard a radio broadcast that had been made years before. Suppose, then, that no one had touched Mr. Trachnor's house but himself; that he had painted his house in October, but that through some fantastic mix-up in time, a portion of that paint appeared on his house the previous summer. Since he had cleaned the paint off at that time, a broad stripe of new gray paint was missing *after* he painted his house in the fall.

I would be lying, however, if I said I really believed this. It was merely an intriguing speculation, and I told both these little stories to friends, simply as curious anecdotes. I am a sociable person, see a good many people, and occasionally I heard other odd stories in response to mine.

Someone would nod and say, "Reminds me of something I heard recently . . ." and I would have one more to add to my collection. A man on Long Island received a telephone call from his sister in New York one Friday evening. She insists that she did not make this call until the following Monday, three days later. At the Forty-fifth Street branch of the Chase National Bank, I was shown a check deposited the day before it was written. A letter was delivered on East Sixty-eighth Street in New York City, just seventeen minutes after it was dropped into a mailbox on the main street of Green River, Wyoming.

And so on, and so on; my stories were now in demand at parties, and I told myself that collecting and verifying them was a hobby. But the day I heard Julia Eisenberg's story, I knew it was no longer that.

Case 17. Julia Eisenberg, office worker, New York City, age thirty-one.

Miss Eisenberg lives in a small walk-up apartment in Greenwich Village. I talked to her there after a chess-club friend who lives in her neighborhood had repeated to me a somewhat garbled version of her story, which was told to him by the doorman of the building he lives in.

In October 1947, about eleven at night, Miss Eisenberg left her apartment to walk to the drugstore for toothpaste. On her way back, not far from her apartment, a large black and white dog ran up to her and put his front paws on her chest.

"I made the mistake of petting him," Miss Eisenberg told me, "and from then on he simply wouldn't leave. When I went into the lobby of my building, I actually had to push him away to get the door closed. I felt sorry for him, poor hound, and a little guilty because he was still sitting at the door an hour later when I looked out my front window."

This dog remained in the neighborhood for three days, discovering and greeting Miss Eisenberg with wild affection each time she appeared on the street. "When I'd get on the bus in the morning to go to work, he'd sit on the curb looking after me in the most mournful way, poor thing. I wanted to take him in, but I knew he'd never go home then, and I was afraid whoever owned him would be sorry to lose him. No one in the neighborhood knew whom he belonged to, and finally he disappeared.''

Two years later a friend gave Miss Eisenberg a three-week-old puppy. ''My apartment is really too small for a dog, but he was such a darling I couldn't resist. Well, he grew up into a nice big dog who ate more than I did.''

Since the neighborhood was quiet and the dog well behaved, Miss Eisenberg usually unleashed him when she walked him at night, for he never strayed far. ''One night—I'd last seen him sniffing around in the dark a few doors down—I called to him and he didn't come back. And he never did; I never saw him again.

''Now our street is a solid wall of brownstone buildings on both sides with locked doors and no areaways. He *couldn't* have disappeared like that, he just *couldn't.* But he did.''

Miss Eisenberg hunted for her dog for many days afterward, inquired of neighbors, put ads in the papers, but she never found him. ''Then one night I was getting ready for bed; I happened to glance out the front window down at the street, and suddenly I remembered something I'd forgotten all about. I remembered the dog I'd chased away over two years before.'' Miss Eisenberg looked at me for a moment, then she said flatly, ''It was the same dog. If you own a dog you know him, you can't be mistaken, and I tell you it was the same dog. Whether it makes sense or not, my dog was lost—I chased him away—two years before he was born.''

She began to cry silently, the tears running down her face. ''Maybe you think I'm crazy, or a little lonely and overly sentimental about a dog. But you're wrong.'' She brushed at her tears with a handkerchief. ''I'm a well-balanced person, as much as anyone is these days, at least, and I tell you I *know* what happened.''

It was at that moment, sitting in Miss Eisenberg's neat, shabby living room, that I realized fully that the consequences of these odd little incidents could be something more than merely intriguing; that they might, quite possibly, be tragic. It was in that moment that I began to be afraid.

I have spent the last eleven months discovering and tracking down these strange occurrences, and I am astonished and frightened at how many there are. I am astonished and frightened at how much more frequently they are happening now, and—I hardly know how to express this—at their increasing power to tear human lives tragically apart. This is an example, selected almost at random, of the increasing strength of—whatever it is that is happening in the world.

Case 34. Paul V. Kerch, accountant, the Bronx, age thirty-one.

On a bright clear Sunday afternoon, I met an unsmiling family of three at their Bronx apartment: Mr. Kerch, a chunky, darkly good-looking young man; his wife, a pleasant-faced dark-haired woman in her late twenties, whose attractiveness was marred by circles under her eyes; and their son, a nice-looking boy of six or seven. After introductions, the boy was sent to his room at the back of the house to play.

"All right," Mr. Kerch said wearily then and walked toward a bookcase, "let's get at it. You said on the phone that you know the story in general." It was half a question, half a statement.

"Yes," I said.

He took a book from the top shelf and removed some photographs from it. "There are the pictures." He sat down on the davenport beside me with the photographs in his hand. "I own a pretty good camera. I'm a fair amateur photographer, and I have a darkroom setup in the kitchen; do my own developing. Two weeks ago we went down to Central Park." His voice was a tired monotone, as though this was a story he'd repeated many times, aloud and in his own mind. "It was nice, like today, and the kid's grandmothers have been pestering us for pictures, so I took a whole roll of films, pictures of all of us. My camera can be set up and focused and it will snap the picture automatically a few seconds later, giving me time to get around in front of it and get in the picture myself."

There was a tired, hopeless look in his eyes as he handed me all but one of the photographs. "These are the first ones I took," he said. The photographs were all fairly large, perhaps seven by three and a half inches, and I examined them closely.

They were ordinary enough, very sharp and detailed, and each showed the family of three in various smiling poses. Mr. Kerch wore a light business suit, his wife had on a dark dress and a cloth coat and the boy wore a dark suit with knee-length pants. In the background stood a tree with bare branches. I glanced up at Mr. Kerch, signifying that I had finished my study of the photographs.

"The last picture," he said, holding it in his hand ready to give to me, "I took exactly like the others. We agreed on the pose, I set the camera, walked around in front, and joined my family. Monday night I developed the whole roll. This is what came out on the last negative." He handed me the photograph.

For an instant it seemed to me like merely one more photograph in the group; then I saw the difference. Mr. Kerch looked much the same, bareheaded and grinning broadly, but he wore an entirely different suit. The boy, standing beside him, wore long pants, was a good three inches taller, obviously older, but equally obviously the same boy. The woman was an entirely different person. Dressed smartly, her light hair catching the sun, she was very pretty and attractive. She was smiling into the camera and holding Mr. Kerch's hand.

I looked up at him. "Who is this?"

Wearily, Mr. Kerch shook his head. "I don't know," he said suddenly, then exploded: "I don't *know!* I've never seen her in my life!" He turned to look at his wife, but she would not return his glance, and he turned back to me, shrugging. "Well, there you have it," he said. "The whole story." And he stood up, thrusting both hands into his trouser pockets and began to pace about the room, glancing often at his wife, talking to *her* actually, though he addressed his words to me. "So who is she? How could the camera have snapped that picture? I've never seen that woman in my life!"

I glanced at the photograph again, then bent closer. "The trees here are in full bloom," I said. Behind the solemn-faced boy, the grinning man and smiling woman, the trees of Central Park were in full summer leaf.

Mr. Kerch nodded. "I know," he said bitterly. "And you know what *she* says?" he burst out, glaring at his wife. "She says that *is* my wife in the photograph, my *new* wife a couple of years from now! God!" He snapped both hands down on his head. "The ideas a woman can get!"

"What do you mean?" I glanced at Mrs. Kerch, but she ignored me, remaining silent, her lips tight.

Kerch shrugged hopelessly. "She says that photograph shows how things will be a couple of years from now. She'll be dead or"—he hesitated, then said the word bitterly—"divorced, and I'll have our son and be married to the woman in the picture."

We both looked at Mrs. Kerch, waiting until she was obliged to speak.

"Well, if it isn't so," she said, shrugging a shoulder, "then tell me what that picture does mean."

Neither of us could answer that, and a few minutes later I left. There was nothing much I could say to the Kerches; certainly I couldn't mention my conviction that, whatever the explanation of the last photograph, their married life was over? . . .

Case 72. Lieutenant Alfred Eichler, New York Police Department, age thirty-three.

In the late evening of January 9, 1951, two policemen found a revolver lying just off a gravel path near an East Side entrance to Central Park. The gun was examined for fingerprints at the police laboratory and several were found. One bullet had been fired from the revolver and the police fired another which was studied and classified by a ballistics expert. The fingerprints were checked and found in police files; they were those of a minor hoodlum with a record of assault.

A routine order to pick him up was sent out. A detective called at the rooming house where he was known to live, but he was out, and since no unsolved shootings had occurred recently, no intensive search for him was made that night.

The following evening a man was shot and killed in Central Park with the same gun. This was proved ballistically past all question of error. It was soon learned that the murdered man had been quarreling with a friend in a nearby tavern. The two men, both drunk, had left the tavern together. And the second man was the hoodlum whose gun had been found the previous night and which was still locked in a police safe.

As Lieutenant Eichler said to me, "it's impossible that the dead man was killed with that same gun, but he was. Don't ask me how, though, and if anybody thinks we'd go into court with a case like that, they're crazy."

Case 111. Captain Hubert V. Rihm, New York Police Department, retired, aged sixty-six.

I met Captain Rihm by appointment one morning in Stuyvesant Park, a patch of greenery, wood benches and asphalt surrounded by the city on lower Second Avenue. "You want to hear about the Fentz case, do you?" he said, after we had introduced ourselves and found an empty bench. "All right, I'll tell you. I don't like to talk about it—it bothers me—but I'd like to see what you think." He was a big, rather heavy man with a red, tough face, and he wore an old police jacket and uniform cap with the insignia removed.

"I was up at City Mortuary," he began as I took out my notebook and pencil, "at Bellevue about twelve one night, drinking coffee with one of the interns. This was in June of 1950, just before I retired, and I was in Missing Persons. They brought this guy in and he was a funny-looking character. Had a beard. A young guy, maybe thirty, but he wore regular muttonchop whiskers, and his clothes were funny-looking. Now I was thirty years on the force and I've seen a lot of queer guys killed on the streets. We found an Arab once in full regalia, and it took us a week to find out who he was. So it wasn't just the way the guy looked that bothered me; it was the stuff we found in his pockets."

Captain Rihm turned on the bench to see if he'd caught my

interest, then continued. "There was about a dollar in change in the dead guy's pocket, and one of the boys picked up a nickel and showed it to me. Now you've seen plenty of nickels, the new ones with Jefferson's picture, the buffalo nickels they made before that, and once in a while you still even see the old Liberty-head nickels; they quit making them before the first world war. But this one was even older than that. It had a shield on the front, a United States shield, and a big five on the back; I used to see that kind when I was a boy. And the funny things was, that old nickel looked new; what coin dealers call 'mint condition,' like it was made the day before yesterday. The date on that nickel was 1876, and there wasn't a coin in his pocket dated any later."

Captain Rihm looked at me questioningly. "Well," I said, glancing up from my notebook, "that could happen."

"Sure it could," he answered in a satisfied tone, "but all the pennies he had were Indian-head pennies. Now when did you see one of them last? There was even a silver three-cent piece; looked like an old-style dime, only smaller. And the bills in his wallet, every one of them, were old-time bills, the big kind."

Captain Rihm leaned forward and spat on the patch, a needle jet of tobacco juice and an expression of a policeman's annoyed contempt for anything deviating from an orderly norm.

"Over seventy bucks in cash, and not a federal reserve note in the lot. There were two yellow-back tens. Remember them? They were payable in gold. The rest were old national-bank notes; you remember them too. Issued direct by local banks, personally signed by the bank president; that kind used to be counterfeited a lot.

"Well," Captain Rihm continued, leaning back on the bench and crossing his knees, "there was a bill in his pocket from a livery stable on Lexington Avenue; three dollars for feeding and stabling his horse and washing a carriage. There was a brass slug in his pocket good for a five-cent beer at some saloon. There was a letter postmarked Philadelphia, June 1876, with an old-style two-cent stamp and a bunch of cards in his wallet. The cards had his name and address on them, and so did the letter.''

"Oh," I said, a little surprised, "you identified him right away, then?"

"Sure. Rudolph Fentz, some address on Fifth Avenue—I forget the exact number—in New York City. No problem at all." Captain Rihm leaned forward and spat again. "Only that address wasn't a residence. It's a store, and it had been for years, and nobody there ever heard of any Rudolph Fentz, and there's no such name in the phone book either. Nobody ever called or made any inquiries about the guy, and Washington didn't have his prints. There was a tailor's name in his coat, a lower Broadway address, but nobody there ever heard of this tailor."

"What was so strange about his clothes?"

The captain said, "Well, did you ever know anyone who wore a pair of pants with big black-and-white checks, cut very narrow, no cuffs, and pressed without a crease?"

I had to think for a moment. "Yes," I said then, "my father, when he was a very young man, before he was married; I've seen old photographs."

"Sure," said Captain Rihm, "and he probably wore a short sort of cutaway coat with two cloth-covered buttons at the back, a vest with lapels, a tall silk hat, a big, black oversized bow tie on a turned-up stiff collar and button shoes."

"That's how this man was dressed?"

"Like seventy-five years ago! And him no more than thirty years old. There was a label in his hat, a Twenty-third Street hat store that went out of business around the turn of the century. Now what do you make out of a thing like that?"

"Well," I said carefully, "there's nothing much you can make of it. Apparently someone went to a lot of trouble to dress up in an antique style—the coins and bills I assume he could buy at a coin dealer's—and then he got himself killed in a traffic accident."

"Got himself killed is right. Eleven-fifteen at night in Times Square—the theaters letting out, busiest time and place

in the world—and this guy shows up in the middle of the
street, gawking and looking around at the cars and up at the
signs like he'd never seen them before. The cop on duty
noticed him, so you can see how he must have been acting.
The lights change, the traffic starts up, with him in the
middle of the street, and instead of waiting, the damn fool, he
turns and tries to make it back to the sidewalk. A cab got him
and he was dead when he hit.''

For a moment Captain Rihm sat chewing his tobacco and
staring angrily at a young woman pushing a baby carriage,
though I'm sure he didn't see her. The young mother looked
at him in surprise as she passed, and the captain continued:

''Nothing you can make out of a thing like that. We found
out nothing. I started checking through our file of old phone
books, just as routine, but without much hope because they
only go back so far. But in the 1939 summer edition I found a
Rudolph Fentz, Jr., somewhere on East Fifty-second Street.
He'd moved away in 'forty-two, though, the building super
told me, and was a man in his sixties besides, retired from
business; used to work in a bank a few blocks away, the
super thought. I found the bank where he'd worked and they
told me he'd retired in 'forty, and had been dead for five
years; his widow was living in Florida with a sister.

''I wrote to the widow, but there was only one thing she
could tell us, and that was no good. I never even reported it,
not officially, anyway. Her husband's father had disappeared
when her husband was a boy maybe two years old. He went
out for a walk around ten one night—his wife thought cigar
smoke smelled up the curtains, so he used to take a little
stroll before he went to bed and smoke a cigar—and he didn't
come back and was never seen or heard of again. The family
spent a good deal of money trying to locate him, but they
never did. This was in the middle 1870s some time; the old
lady wasn't sure of the exact date. Her husband hadn't ever
said too much about it.

''And that's all,'' said Captain Rihm. ''Once I put in one
of my afternoons of hunting through a bunch of old police
records. And I finally found the missing persons file for

1876, and Rudolph Fentz was listed, all right. There wasn't much of a description, and no fingerprints, of course. I'd give a year of my life, even now, and maybe sleep better nights, if they'd had his fingerprints. He was listed as twenty-nine years old, wearing full muttonchop whiskers, a tall silk hat, dark coat and checked pants. That's about all it said. Didn't say what kind of tie or vest or if his shoes were the button kind. His name was Rudolph Fentz and he lived at this address on Fifth Avenue; it must have been a residence then. Final disposition of case: not located.

"Now, I hate that case," Captain Rihm said quietly. "I hate it and I wish I'd never heard of it. What do you think?" he demanded suddenly, angrily. "You think this guy walked off into thin air in 1876 and showed up again in 1950?"

I shrugged noncommittally, and the captain took it to mean no.

"No, of course not," he said. "Of *course* not—but give me some other explanation."

I could go on. I could give you several hundred such cases. A sixteen-year-old girl walked out of her bedroom one morning, carrying her clothes in her hand because they were too big for her and she was quite obviously eleven years old again. And there are other occurrences too horrible for print. All of them have happened in the New York City area alone, all within the last few years; and I suspect thousands more have occurred and are occurring, all over the world. I could go on, but the point is this: What is happening, and *why?* I believe that I know.

Haven't you noticed, too, on the part of nearly everyone you know, a growing rebellion against the *present?* And an increasing longing for the past? I have. Never before in all my long life have I heard so many people wish that they lived "at the turn of the century" or "when life was simpler" or "worth living" or "when you could bring children into the world and count on the future" or simply "in the good old days." People didn't talk that way when I was young! The present was a glorious time! But they talk that way now.

For the first time in man's history, man is desperate to

escape the present. Our newsstands are jammed with escape literature, the very name of which is significant. Entire magazines are devoted to fantastic stories of escape—to other times, past and future, to other worlds and planets—escape to anywhere but here and now. Even our larger magazines, book publishers and Hollywood are beginning to meet the rising demand for this kind of escape. Yes, there is a craving in the world like a thirst, a terrible mass pressure that you can almost feel, of millions of minds struggling against the barriers of time. I am utterly convinced that this terrible mass pressure of millions of minds is already, slightly but definitely, affecting time itself. In the moments when this happens—when the almost universal longing is greatest—my incidents occur. Man is disturbing the clock of time, and I am afraid it will break. When it does, I leave to your imagination the last few hours of madness that will be left to us; all the countless moments that now make up our lives suddenly ripped apart and chaotically tangled in time.

Well, I have lived most of my life; I can be robbed of only a few more years. But it seems too bad—this universal craving to escape what could be a rich, productive, happy world. We live on a planet well able to provide a decent life for every soul on it, which is all ninety-nine of a hundred human beings ask. Why in the world can't we have it?

THE QUEST FOR ST. AQUIN

BY ANTHONY BOUCHER (1911-1968)
NEW TALES OF SPACE AND TIME

The founding co-editor of The Magazine of Fantasy and Science Fiction, *Anthony Boucher (William Anthony Parker White) excelled in all phases of the literary life—he was a notable critic in both the science fiction and mystery fields, a gifted and patient editor with a long string of discoveries and successes to his credit, and a consumate craftsman whose stories and (mystery) novels have survived his untimely death. He never produced a fantasy or sf novel (the closest he came was* Rocket to the Morgue, *a murder mystery set at a science fiction convention with thinly disguised figures from the real world of sf), but two collections,* Far and Away *(1955), and* The Complete Werewolf and Other Stories of Fantasy and Science Fiction *(1969) contain most of his best short stories.*

"The Quest for St. Aquin" is deservedly his most famous science fiction effort, combining his interest in religion with speculation about the future of artificial intelligence. It proved to be one of the most influential stories of the early 1950s, and its ideas were exploited later by a number of other writers. New Tales of Space and Time, *edited by Raymond J. Healy, was one of the pioneer original anthologies, and is well worth looking for.*

—M.H.G.

I sometimes wonder why it is that such a large percentage of science fiction stories concerning religion seem to focus on Roman Catholicism. I have evolved several theories on the subject.

1) It may not be so. I've only read a fraction of the science fiction stories extant, and I only remember a fraction of the stories I've read. (It used to be different when I was younger and had less to do and there was less sf to read, but that's used to be—). Consequently, if someone makes a true study of magazine science fiction over the last sixty years, he may be able to show that a majority of the religious science fiction involved the Baptists.

2) If it is so, it may simply be that most of the writers who write on the subject happen to be Roman Catholic. (Anthony Boucher certainly was.) You might be able to explain that by deciding that Roman Catholics study religion more intensely and systematically than Protestants do. (Protestants may study the Bible more, but that's not quite the same thing.)

3) Then, too, even if the religion of the writers is not the deciding factor, it may be that Roman Catholicism is one of the oldest and certainly the best-organized of the religions of the western world, and therefore the one we automatically think of as having the best chance of surviving into the far future.

—I.A.

THE BISHOP OF ROME, the head of the Holy, Catholic and Apostolic Church, the Vicar of Christ on Earth—in short, the Pope—brushed a cockroach from the filth-encrusted wooden table, took another sip of the raw red wine, and resumed his discourse.

"In some respects, Thomas," he smiled, "we are stronger now than when we flourished in the liberty and exaltation for which we still pray after Mass. We know, as they knew in the Catacombs, that those who are of our flock are indeed truly of it; that they belong to Holy Mother the Church because they believe in the brotherhood of man under the fatherhood of God—not because they can further their political aspirations, their social ambitions, their business contacts.''

'' 'Not of the will of flesh, nor of the will of man, but of God . . .''' Thomas quoted softly from St. John.

The Pope nodded. ''We are, in a way, born again in Christ; but there are still too few of us—too few even if we include those other handfuls who are not of our faith, but still acknowledge God through the teachings of Luther or Laotse, Gautama Buddha or Joseph Smith. Too many men still go to their deaths hearing no gospel preached to them but the cynical self-worship of the Technarchy. And that is why, Thomas, you must go forth on your quest.''

''But Your Holiness,'' Thomas protested, ''if God's word and God's love will not convert them, what can saints and miracles do?''

''I seem to recall,'' murmured the Pope, ''that God's own Son once made a similar protest. But human nature, however illogical it may seem, is part of His design, and we must cater to it. If signs and wonders can lead souls to God, then by all means let us find the signs and wonders. And what can be better for the purpose than this legendary Aquin? Come now, Thomas; be not too scrupulously exact in copying the doubts of your namesake, but prepare for your journey.''

The Pope lifted the skin that covered the doorway and passed into the next room, with Thomas frowning at his heels. It was past legal hours and the main room of the tavern was empty. The swarthy innkeeper roused from his doze to drop to his knees and kiss the ring on the hand which the Pope extended to him. He rose crossing himself and at the same time glancing furtively about as though a Loyalty Checker might have seen him. Silently he indicated another door in the back, and the two priests passed through.

Toward the west the surf purred in an oddly gentle way at the edges of the fishing village. Toward the south the stars were sharp and bright; toward the north they dimmed a little in the persistent radiation of what had once been San Francisco.

"Your steed is here," the Pope said, with something like laughter in his voice.

"Steed?"

"We may be as poor and as persecuted as the primitive church, but we can occasionally gain greater advantages from our tyrants. I have secured for you a robass—gift of a leading Technarch who, like Nicodemus, does good by stealth—a secret convert, and converted indeed by that very Aquin whom you seek."

It looked harmlessly like a woodpile sheltered against possible rain. Thomas pulled off the skins and contemplated the sleek functional lines of the robass. Smiling, he stowed his minimal gear into its panniers and climbed into the foam saddle. The starlight was bright enough so that he could check the necessary coordinates on his map and feed the data into the electronic controls.

Meanwhile there was a murmur of Latin in the still night air, and the Pope's hand moved over Thomas in the immemorial symbol. Then he extended that hand, first for the kiss on the ring, and then again for the handclasp of a man to a friend he may never see again.

Thomas looked back once more as the robass moved off. The Pope was wisely removing his ring and slipping it into the hollow heel of his shoe.

Thomas looked hastily up at the sky. On that altar at least the candles still burnt openly to the glory of God.

Thomas had never ridden a robass before, but he was inclined, within their patent limitations, to trust the works of the Technarchy. After several miles had proved that the coordinates were duly registered, he put up the foam backrest, said his evening office (from memory; the possession of a breviary meant the death sentence), and went to sleep.

They were skirting the devastated area to the east of the Bay when he awoke. The foam seat and back had given him his best sleep in years; and it was with difficulty that he smothered an envy of the Technarchs and their creature comforts.

He said his morning office, breakfasted lightly, and took his first opportunity to inspect the robass in full light. He admired the fast-plodding, articulated legs, so necessary since roads had degenerated to, at best, trails in all save metropolitan areas; the side wheels that could be lowered into action if surface conditions permitted; and above all the smooth black mound that housed the electronic brain—the brain that stored commands and data concerning ultimate objectives and made its own decisions on how to fulfill those commands in view of those data; the brain that made this thing neither a beast, like the ass his Saviour had ridden, nor a machine, like the jeep of his many-times-great-grandfather, but a robot . . . a robass.

"Well," said a voice, "what do you think of the ride."

Thomas looked about him. The area on this fringe of desolation was as devoid of people as it was of vegetation.

"Well," the voice repeated unemotionally. "Are not priests taught to answer when spoken to politely?"

There was no querying inflection to the question. No inflection at all—each syllable was at the same dead level. It sounded strange, mechani . . .

Thomas stared at the black mound of brain. "Are you talking to me?" he asked the robass.

"Ha ha," the voice said in lieu of laughter. "Surprised, are you not."

"Somewhat," Thomas confessed. "I thought the only robots who could talk were in library information service and such."

"I am a new model. Designed-to-provide-conversation-to--entertain-the-way-worn traveler," the robass said slurring the words together as though that phrase of promotional copy was released all at once by one of his simplest binary synapses.

"Well," said Thomas simply. "One keeps learning new marvels."

"I am no marvel. I am a very simple robot. You do not know much about robots do you."

"I will admit that I have never studied the subject closely. I'll confess to being a little shocked at the whole robotic concept. It seems almost as though man were arrogating to himself the powers of—'' Thomas stopped abruptly.

''Do not fear,'' the voice droned on. ''You may speak freely. All data concerning your vocation and mission have been fed into me. That was necessary, otherwise I might inadvertently betray you.''

Thomas smiled. ''You know,'' he said, ''this might be rather pleasant—having one other being that one can talk to without fear of betrayal, aside from one's confessor.''

''Being,'' the robass repeated. ''Are you not in danger of lapsing into heretical thoughts.''

''To be sure, it *is* a little difficult to know how to think of you—one who can talk and think but has no soul.''

''Are you sure of that.''

''Of course I— Do you mind very much,'' Thomas asked, ''if we stop talking for a little while? I should like to meditate and adjust myself to the situation.''

''I do not mind. I never mind. I only obey. Which is to say that I *do* mind. This is very confusing language which has been fed into me.''

''If we are together long,'' said Thomas, ''I shall try teaching you Latin. I think you might like that better. And now let me meditate.''

The robass was automatically veering further east to escape the permanent source of radiation which had been the first cyclotron. Thomas fingered his coat. The combination of ten small buttons and one large made for a peculiar fashion; but it was much safer than carrying a rosary, and fortunately the Loyalty Checkers had not yet realized the fashion's functional purpose.

The Glorious Mysteries seemed appropriate to the possible glorious outcome of his venture; but his meditations were unable to stay fixedly on the Mysteries. As he murmured his *Aves* he was thinking.

If the prophet Balaam conversed with his ass, surely, I may converse with my robass. Balaam has always puzzled me. He was not an Israelite; he was a man of Moab, which worshiped Baal and was warring against Israel; and yet he was a prophet of the Lord. He blessed the Israelites when he was commanded to curse them; and for his reward he was slain by the Israelites when they triumphed over Moab. The whole story has no shape, no moral; it is as though it was there to say that there are portions of the Divine Plan which we will never understand . . .

He was nodding in the foam seat when the robass halted abruptly, rapidly adjusting itself to exterior data not previously fed into its calculations. Thomas blinked up to see a giant of a man glaring down at him.

"Inhabited area a mile ahead," the man barked. "If you're going there, show your access pass. If you ain't, steer off the road and stay off."

Thomas noted that they were indeed on what might roughly be called a road, and that the robass had lowered its side wheels and retracted its legs. "We—" he began, then changed it to "I'm not going there. Just on toward the mountains. We—I'll steer around."

The giant grunted and was about to turn when a voice shouted from the crude shelter at the roadside. "Hey Joe! Remember about robasses!"

Joe turned back. "Yeah, tha's right. Been a rumor about some robass got into the hands of Christians." He spat on the dusty road. "Guess I better see an ownership certificate."

To his other doubts Thomas now added certain uncharitable suspicions as to the motives of the Pope's anonymous Nicodemus, who had not provided him with any such certificate. But he made a pretense of searching for it, first touching his right hand to his forehead as if in thought, then fumbling low on his chest, then reaching his hand first to his left shoulder, then to his right.

The guard's eyes remained blank as he watched this furtive version of the sign of the cross. Then he looked down. Thomas followed his gaze to the dust of the road, where the guard's hulking right foot had drawn the two curved lines which a child uses for its sketch of a fish—and which the Christians in the catacombs had employed as a punning symbol of their faith. His boot scuffed out the fish as he called to his unseen mate, " 's OK, Fred!" and added, "Get going, mister."

The robass waited until they were out of earshot before it observed, "Pretty smart. You will make a secret agent yet."

"How did you see what happened?" Thomas asked. "You don't have any eyes."

"Modified *psi*-factor. Much more efficient."

"Then . . ." Thomas hesitated. "Does that mean you can read my thoughts?"

"Only a very little. Do not let it worry you. What I can read does not interest me it is such nonsense."

"Thank you," said Thomas.

"To believe in God. Bah." (It was the first time Thomas had ever heard that word pronounced just as it is written.) "I have a perfectly constructed logical mind that cannot commit such errors."

"I have a friend," Thomas smiled, "who is infallible too. But only on occasions and then only because God is with him."

"No human being is infallible."

"Then imperfection," asked Thomas, suddenly feeling a little of the spirit of the aged Jesuit who had taught him philosophy, "has been able to create perfection?"

"Do not quibble," said the robass. "That is no more absurd than your own belief that God who is perfection created man who is imperfection."

Thomas wished that his old teacher were here to answer that one. At the same time he took some comfort in the fact that, retort and all, the robass had still not answered his own objection. "I am not sure," he said, "that this comes under the head of conversation-to-entertain-the-way-weary-traveler. Let us suspend debate while you tell me what, if anything, robots do believe."

"What we have been fed."

"But your minds work on that; surely they must evolve ideas of their own?"

"Sometimes they do and if they are fed imperfect data they

may evolve very strange ideas. I have heard of one robot on an isolated space station who worshiped a God of robots and would not believe that any man had created him.''

''I suppose,'' Thomas mused, ''he argued that he had hardly been created in our image. I am glad that we—at least they, the Technarchs—have wisely made only usuform robots like you, each shaped for his function, and never tried to reproduce man himself.''

''It would not be logical,'' said the robass. ''Man is an all-purpose machine but not well designed for any one purpose. And yet I have heard that once . . .''

The voice stopped abruptly in midsentence.

So even robots have their dreams, Thomas thought. That once there existed a super-robot in the image of his creator Man. From that thought could be developed a whole robotic theology . . .

Suddenly Thomas realized that he had dozed again and again been waked by an abrupt stop. He looked around. They were at the foot of a mountain—presumably the mountain on his map, long ago named for the Devil but now perhaps sanctified beyond measure—and there was no one else anywhere in sight.

''All right,'' the robass said. ''By now I show plenty of dust and wear and tear and I can show you how to adjust my mileage recorder. You can have supper and a good night's sleep and we can go back.''

Thomas gasped. ''But my mission is to find Aquin. I can sleep while you go on. You don't need any sort of rest or anything, do you?'' he added considerately.

''Of course not. But what is your mission?''

''To find Aquin,'' Thomas repeated patiently. ''I don't know what details have been—what is it you say?—fed into you. But reports have reached His Holiness of an extremely saintly man who lived many years ago in this area—''

''I know I know I know,'' said the robass. ''His logic was such that everyone who heard him was converted to the Church and do not I wish that I had been there to put in a word or two and since he died his secret tomb has become a place of pilgrimage and many are the miracles that are wrought there above all the greatest sign of sanctity that his body has been preserved incorruptible and in these times you need signs and wonders for the people.''

Thomas frowned. It all sounded hideously irreverent and contrived when stated in that deadly inhuman monotone. When His Holiness had spoken of Aquin, one thought of the glory of a man of God upon earth—the eloquence of St. John Chrysostom, the cogency of St. Thomas Aquinas, the poetry of St. John of the Cross . . . and above all that physical miracle vouchsafed to few even of the saints, the supernatural preservation of the flesh . . . "for Thou shalt not suffer Thy holy one to see corruption . . .''

But the robass spoke, and one thought of cheap showmanship hunting for a Cardiff Giant to pull in the mobs . . .

The robass spoke again. "Your mission is not to find Aquin. It is to report that you have found him. Then your occasionally infallible friend can with a reasonably clear conscience canonize him and proclaim a new miracle and many will be the converts and greatly will the faith of the flock be strengthened. And in these days of difficult travel who will go on pilgrimages and find out that there is no more Aquin than there is God.''

"Faith cannot be based on a lie," said Thomas.

"No," said the robass. "I do not mean no period. I mean no question mark with an ironical inflection. This speech problem must surely have been conquered in that one perfect . . .''

Again he stopped in midsentence. But before Thomas could speak he had resumed, "Does it matter what small untruth leads people into the Church if once they are in they will believe what you think to be the great truths. The report is all that is needed not the discovery. Comfortable though I am you are already tired of traveling very tired you have many small muscular aches from sustaining an unaccustomed position and with the best intentions I am bound to jolt a little a jolting which will get worse as we ascend the mountain and I am forced to adjust my legs disproportionately to each other but proportionately to the slope. You will find the remainder of this trip twice as uncomfortable as what has gone before. The fact that you do not seek to interrupt me indicates that you do not disagree do you. You know that the only sensible thing is to sleep here on the ground for a change and start back in the morning or even stay here two days resting to make a more plausible lapse of time. Then you can make your report and—''

Somewhere in the recess of his somnolent mind Thomas uttered the names, ''Jesus, Mary, and Joseph!'' Gradually through these recesses began to filter a realization that an absolutely uninflected monotone is admirably adapted to hypnotic purposes.

''*Retro me, Satanas!*'' Thomas exclaimed aloud, then added, ''Up the mountain. That is an order and you must obey.''

''I obey,'' said the robass. ''But what did you say before that.''

''I beg your pardon,'' said Thomas. ''I must start teaching you Latin.''

The little mountain village was too small to be considered an inhabited area worthy of guard-control and passes; but it did possess an inn of sorts.

As Thomas dismounted from the robass, he began fully to realize the accuracy of those remarks about small muscular aches, but he tried to show his discomfort as little as possible. He was in no mood to give the modified *psi* factor the chance of registering the thought, ''I told you so.''

The waitress at the inn was obviously a Martian-American hybrid. The highly developed Martian chest expansion and the highly developed American breasts made a spectacular combination. Her smile was all that a stranger could, and conceivably a trifle more than he should ask; and she was eagerly ready, not only with prompt service of passable food, but with full details of what little information there was to offer about the mountain settlement.

But she showed no reaction at all when Thomas offhandedly arranged two knives in what might have been an X.

As he stretched his legs after breakfast, Thomas thought of her chest and breasts—purely, of course, as a symbol of the extraordinary nature of her origin. What a sign of the divine care for His creatures that these two races, separated for countless eons, should prove fertile to each other!

And yet there remained the fact that the offspring, such as this girl, were sterile to both races—a fact that had proved both convenient and profitable to certain unspeakable interplanetary entrepreneurs. And what did that fact teach us as to the Divine Plan?

Hastily Thomas reminded himself that he had not yet said his morning office.

It was close to evening when Thomas returned to the robass stationed before the inn. Even though he had expected nothing in one day, he was still unreasonably disappointed. Miracles should move faster.

He knew these backwater villages, where those drifted who were either useless to or resentful of the Technarchy. The technically high civilization of the Technarchic Empire, on all three planets, existed only in scattered metropolitan centers near major blasting ports. Elsewhere, aside from the areas of total devastation, the drifters, the morons, the malcontents had subsided into a crude existence a thousand years old, in hamlets which might go a year without even seeing a Loyalty Checker—though by some mysterious grapevine (and Thomas began to think again about modified *psi* factors) any unexpected technological advance in one of these hamlets would bring Checkers by the swarm.

He had talked with stupid men, he had talked with lazy men, he had talked with clever and angry men. But he had not talked with any man who responded to his unobtrusive signs, any man to whom he would dare ask a question containing the name of Aquin.

"Any luck," said the robass, and added "question mark."

"I wonder if you ought to talk to me in public," said Thomas a little irritably. "I doubt if these villagers know about talking robots."

"It is time that they learned then. But if it embarrasses you you may order me to stop."

"I'm tired," said Thomas. "Tired beyond embarrassment. And to answer your question mark, no. No luck at all. Exclamation point."

"We will go back tonight then," said the robass.

"I hope you meant that with a question mark. The answer," said Thomas hesitantly, "is no. I think we ought to stay overnight anyway. People always gather at the inn of an evening. There's a chance of picking up something."

"Ha, ha," said the robass.

"That is a laugh?" Thomas inquired.

"I wished to express the fact that I had recognized the humor in your pun."

"My pun?"

"I was thinking the same thing myself. The waitress is by humanoid standards very attractive, well worth picking up."

"Now look. You know I meant nothing of the kind. You know that I'm a—" He broke off. It was hardly wise to utter the word *priest* aloud.

"And you know very well that the celibacy of the clergy is a matter of discipline and not of doctrine. Under your own Pope priests of other rites such as the Byzantine and the Anglican are free of vows of celibacy. And even within the Roman rite to which you belong there have been eras in history when that vow was not taken seriously even on the highest levels of the priesthood. You are tired you need refreshment both in body and in spirit you need comfort and warmth. For is it not written in the book of the prophet Isaiah Rejoice for joy with her that ye may be satisfied with the breasts of her consolation and is it—"

"Hell!" Thomas exploded suddenly. "Stop it before you begin quoting the Song of Solomon. Which is strictly an allegory concerning the love of Christ for His Church, or so they kept telling me in seminary."

"You see how fragile and human you are," said the robass. "I a robot have caused you to swear."

"*Distinguo*," said Thomas smugly. "I said *Hell*, which is

certainly not taking the name of *my* Lord in vain.'' He walked into the inn feeling momentarily satisfied with himself . . . and markedly puzzled as to the extent and variety of data that seemed to have been ''fed into'' the robass.

Never afterward was Thomas able to reconstruct that evening in absolute clarity.

It was undoubtedly because he was irritated—with the robass, with his mission, and with himself—that he drank at all of the crude local wine. It was undoubtedly because he was so physically exhausted that it affected him so promptly and unexpectedly.

He had flashes of memory. A moment of spilling a glass over himself and thinking, ''How fortunate that clerical garments are forbidden so that no one can recognize the disgrace of a man of the cloth!'' A moment of listening to a bawdy set of verses of *A Space-Suit Built for Two*, and another moment of his interrupting the singing with a sonorous declamation of passages from the *Song of Songs* in Latin.

He was never sure whether one remembered moment was real or imaginary. He could taste a warm mouth and feel the tingling of his fingers at the touch of Martian-American flesh; but he was never certain whether this was true memory or part of the Ashtaroth-begotten dream that had begun to ride him.

Nor was he ever certain which of his symbols, or to whom, was so blatantly and clumsily executed as to bring forth a gleeful shout of ''God-damned Christian dog!'' He did remember marveling that those who most resolutely disbelieved in God still needed Him to blaspheme by. And then the torment began.

He never knew whether or not a mouth had touched his lips, but there was no question that many solid fists had found them. He never knew whether his fingers had touched breasts, but they had certainly been trampled by heavy heels. He remembered a face that laughed aloud while its owner swung the chair that broke two ribs. He remembered another face with red wine dripping over it from an upheld bottle, and he

remembered the gleam of the candlelight on the bottle as it
swung down.

The next he remembered was the ditch and the morning
and the cold. It was particularly cold because all of his
clothes were gone, along with much of his skin. He could not
move. He could only lie there and look.

He saw them walk by, the ones he had spoken with yesterday, the ones who had been friendly. He saw them glance at
him and turn their eyes quickly away. He saw the waitress
pass by. She did not even glance; she knew what was in the
ditch.

The robass was nowhere in sight. He tried to project his
thoughts, tried desperately to hope in the *psi* factor.

A man whom Thomas had not seen before was coming
along fingering the buttons of his coat. There were ten small
buttons and one large one, and the man's lips were moving
silently.

This man looked into the ditch. He paused a moment and
looked around him. There was a shout of loud laughter
somewhere in the near distance.

The Christian hastily walked on down the pathway, devoutly saying his button-rosary.

Thomas closed his eyes.

He opened them on a small neat room. They moved from
the rough wooden walls to the rough but clean and warm
blankets that covered him. Then they moved to the lean dark
face that was smiling over him.

"You feel better now?" a deep voice asked. "I know. You
want to say 'Where am I?' and you think it will sound
foolish. You are at the inn. It is the only good room."

"I can't afford—" Thomas started to say. Then he remembered that he could afford literally nothing. Even his few
emergency credits had vanished when he was stripped.

"It's all right. For the time being, I'm paying," said the
deep voice. "You feel like maybe a little food?"

"Perhaps a little herring," said Thomas . . . and was
asleep within the next minute.

When he next awoke there was a cup of hot coffee beside

him. The real thing, too, he promptly discovered. Then the deep voice said apologetically, "Sandwiches. It is all they have in the inn today."

Only on the second sandwich did Thomas pause long enough to notice that it was smoked swamphog, one of his favorite meats. He ate the second with greater leisure, and was reaching for a third when the dark man said, "Maybe that is enough for now. The rest later."

Thomas gestured at the plate. "Won't you have one?"

"No thank you. They are all swamphog."

Confused thoughts went through Thomas' mind. The Venusian swamphog is a ruminant. Its hoofs are not cloven. He tried to remember what he had once known of Mosaic dietary law. Someplace in Leviticus, wasn't it?

The dark man followed his thought. "*Treff*," he said.

"I beg your pardon?"

"Not kosher."

Thomas frowned. "You admit to me that you're an Orthodox Jew? How can you trust me? How do you know I'm not a Checker?"

"Believe me, I trust you. You were very sick when I brought you here. I sent everybody away because I did not trust them to hear things you said . . . Father," he added lightly.

Thomas struggled with word. "I . . . I didn't deserve you. I was drunk and disgraced myself and my office. And when I was lying there in the ditch I didn't even think to pray. I put my trust in . . . God help me in the modified *psi* factor of a robass!"

"And He did help you," the Jew reminded him. "Or He allowed me to."

"And they all walked by," Thomas groaned. "Even one that was saying his rosary. He went right on by. And then you come along—the good Samaritan."

"Believe me," said the Jew wryly, "if there is one thing I'm not, it's a Samaritan. Now go to sleep again. I will try to find your robass . . . and the other thing."

He had left the room before Thomas could ask him what he meant.

Later that day the Jew—Abraham, his name was—reported that the robass was safely sheltered from the weather behind the inn. Apparently it had been wise enough not to startle him by engaging in conversation.

It was not until the next day that he reported on "the other thing."

"Believe me, Father," he said gently, "after nursing you there's little I don't know about who you are and why you're here. Now there are some Christians here I know, and they know me. We trust each other. Jews may still be hated; but no longer, God be praised, by worshipers of the same Lord. So I explained about you. One of them," he added with a smile, "turned very red."

"God has forgiven him," said Thomas. "There were people near—the same people who attacked me. Could he be expected to risk his life for mine?"

"I seem to recall that that is precisely what your Messiah did expect. But who's being particular? Now that they know who you are, they want to help you. See: they gave me this map for you. The trail is steep and tricky; it's good you have the robass. They ask just one favor of you: When you come back will you hear their confession and say Mass? There's a cave near here where it's safe."

"Of course. These friends of yours, they've told you about Aquin?"

The Jew hesitated a long time before he said slowly, "Yes . . ."

"And . . . ?"

"Believe me, my friend, I don't know. So it seems a miracle. It helps to keep their faith alive. My own faith . . . *nu*, it's lived for a long time on miracles three thousand years old and more. Perhaps if I had heard Aquin himself . . ."

"You don't mind," Thomas asked, "if I pray for you, in my faith?"

Abraham grinned. "Pray in good health, Father."

The not-quite-healed ribs ached agonizingly as he climbed into the foam saddle. The robass stood patiently while he fed in the coordinates from the map. Not until they were well away from the village did it speak.

"Anyway," it said, "Now you're safe for good."

"What do you mean?"

"As soon as we get down from the mountain you deliberately look up a Checker. You turn in the Jew. From then on you are down in the books as a faithful servant of the Technarchy and you have not harmed a hair of the head of one of your own flock."

Thomas snorted. "You're slipping, Satan. That one doesn't even remotely tempt me. It's inconceivable."

"I did best did not I with the breasts. Your God has said it the spirit indeed is willing but the flesh is weak."

"And right now," said Thomas, "the flesh is too weak for even fleshly temptations. Save your breath . . . or whatever it is you use."

They climbed the mountain in silence. The trail indicated by the coordinates was a winding and confused one, obviously designed deliberately to baffle any possible Checkers.

Suddenly Thomas roused himself from his button-rosary (on a coat lent by the Christian who had passed by) with a startled "Hey!" as the robass plunged directly into a heavy thicket of bushes.

"Coordinates say so," the robass stated tersely.

For a moment Thomas felt like the man in the nursery rhyme who fell into a bramble bush and scratched out both his eyes. Then the bushes were gone, and they were plodding along a damp narrow passageway through solid stone, in which even the robass seemed to have some difficulty with his footing.

Then they were in a rocky chamber some four meters high and ten in diameter, and there on a sort of crude stone catafalque lay the uncorrupted body of a man.

Thomas slipped from the foam saddle, groaning as his ribs stabbed him, sank to his knees, and offered up a wordless hymn of gratitude. He smiled at the robass and hoped the *psi* factor could detect the elements of pity and triumph in that smile.

Then a frown of doubt crossed his face as he approached the body. "In canonization proceedings in the old time," he said, as much to himself as to the robass, "they used to have what they called a devil's advocate, whose duty it was to throw every possible doubt on the evidence."

"You would be well cast in such a role Thomas," said the robass.

"If I were," Thomas muttered, "I'd wonder about caves. Some of them have peculiar properties of preserving bodies by a sort of mummification . . ."

The robass had clumped close to the catafalque. "This body is not mummified," he said. "Do not worry."

"Can the *psi* factor tell you that much?" Thomas smiled.

"No," said the robass. "But I will show you why Aquin could never be mummified."

He raised his articulated foreleg and brought its hoof down hard on the hand of the body. Thomas cried out with horror at the sacrilege—then stared hard at the crushed hand.

There was no blood, no ichor of embalming, no bruised flesh. Nothing but a shredded skin and beneath it an intricate mass of plastic tubes and metal wires.

The silence was long. Finally the robass said, "It was well that you should know. Only you of course."

"And all the time," Thomas gasped, "my sought-for saint was only your dream . . . the one perfect robot in man's form."

"His maker died and his secrets were lost," the robass said. "No matter we will find them again."

"All for nothing. For less than nothing. The 'miracle' was wrought by the Technarchy."

"When Aquin died," the robass went on, "and put died in quotation marks it was because he suffered some mechanical defects and did not dare have himself repaired because that would reveal his nature. This is for you only to know. Your report of course will be that you found the body of Aquin it was unimpaired and indeed incorruptible. That is the truth and nothing but the truth if it is not the whole truth who is to care. Let your infallible friend use the report and you will not find him ungrateful I assure you.''

''Holy Spirit, give me grace and wisdom,'' Thomas muttered.

''Your mission has been successful. We will return now the Church will grow and your God will gain many more worshipers to hymn His praise into His non-existent ears.''

''Damn you!'' Thomas exclaimed. ''And that would be indeed a curse if you had a soul to damn.''

''You are certain that I have not,'' said the robass. ''Question mark.''

''I know what you are. You are in very truth the devil, prowling about the world seeking the destruction of men. You are the business that prowls in the dark. You are a purely functional robot constructed and fed to tempt me, and the tape of your data is the tape of Screw-tape.''

''Not to tempt you,'' said the robass. ''Not to destroy you. To guide and save you. Our best calculators indicate a probability of 51.5 per cent that within twenty years you will be the next Pope. If I can teach you wisdom and practicality in your actions the probability can rise as high as 97.2 or very nearly to certainty. Do not you wish to see the Church governed as you know you can govern it. If you report failure on this mission you will be out of favor with your friend who is as even you admit fallible at most times. You will lose the advantages of position and contact that can lead you to the cardinal's red hat even though you may never wear it under the Technarchy and from there to—''

''Stop!'' Thomas' face was alight and his eyes aglow with something the *psi* factor had never detected there before. ''It's all the other way round, don't you see? *This* is the triumph! *This* is the perfect ending to the quest!''

The articulated foreleg brushed the injured hand. ''This question mark.''

''This is *your* dream. This is *your* perfection. And what came of this perfection? This perfect logical brain—this all-purpose brain, not functionally specialized like yours—knew that it was made by man, and its reason forced it to believe that man was made by God. And it saw that its duty lay to man its maker, and beyond him to his Maker, God. Its duty was to convert man, to augment the glory of God. And it converted by the pure force of its perfect brain!

"Now I understand the name Aquin," he went on to himself. "We've known of Thomas Aquinas, the Angelic Doctor, the perfect reasoner of the church. His writings are lost, but surely somewhere in the world we can find a copy. We can train our young men to develop his reasoning still further. We have trusted too long in faith alone; this is not an age of faith. We must call reason into our service—and Aquin has shown us that perfect reason can lead only to God!"

"Then it is all the more necessary that you increase the probabilities of becoming Pope to carry out this program. Get in the foam saddle we will go back and on the way I will teach you little things that will be useful in making certain—"

"No," said Thomas. "I am not so strong as St. Paul, who could glory in his imperfections and rejoice that he had been given an imp of Satan to buffet him. No; I will rather pray with the Saviour, 'Lead us not into temptation.' I know myself a little. I am weak and full of uncertainties and you are very clever. Go. I'll find my way back alone."

"You are a sick man. Your ribs are broken and they ache. You can never make the trip by yourself you need my help. If you wish you can order me to be silent. It is most necessary to the Church that you get back safely to the Pope with your report you cannot put yourself before the Church."

"Go!" Thomas cried. "Go back to Nicodemus . . . or Judas! That is an order. Obey!"

"You do not think do you that I was really conditioned to obey your orders. I will wait in the village. If you get that far you will rejoice at the sight of me."

The legs of the robass clumped off down the stone passageway. As their sound died away, Thomas fell to his knees beside the body of that which he could hardly help thinking of as St. Aquin the Robot.

* * *

His ribs hurt more excruciatingly than ever. The trip alone would be a terrible one . . .

His prayers arose, as the text has it, like clouds of incense, and as shapeless as those clouds. But through all his thoughts ran the cry of the father of the epileptic in Caesarea Philippi:

I believe, O Lord; help thou mine unbelief!

TIGER BY THE TAIL

BY ALAN E. NOURSE (1928–   )
GALAXY SCIENCE FICTION, NOVEMBER

Alan E. Nourse was a practicing physician in Washington state from 1958 to 1964 before turning to full-time writing, and many of his stories reflect his expertise and experience with medical subjects. Perhaps his best known novel is The Bladerunner *(1974), (which has no relation to the later movie of similar name), although he has written more than a dozen books in the sf field, many of them for younger readers. He is also outstanding and underrated at the shorter lengths, and fortunately most of his best stories have been collected in* Tiger by the Tail *(1961),* The Counterfeit Man *(1963),* Psi High and Others *(1967), and* Rx for Tomorrow *(1971). These books also appeared as "juveniles," but make fine adult reading in every respect, and confirm Nourse's inventiveness and craftsmanship.*

"Tiger by the Tail" is a terrific little "other dimension" story, one of the first few he published.

—M.H.G.

Suppose you were asked if there were something you would want very much, or could always use and always be grateful for. What would it be? Or put it this way, suppose you were the legendary "man who has everything" (or woman), what could someone buy you? (Leave out abstractions like "health" and "happiness.")

I suspect that you could guess any number of times and you wouldn't ever guess anything half as useful, a tenth as useful as what I've finally come up with. I'll tell you what it is.

A hole! A bottomless hole! A really bottomless hole!

Imagine all the wastebaskets you've filled in your life; you've then had to dump them into a bigger container. People come along and dump them into a huge truck and that goes away and dumps it all onto some huge dump area.

Where does all the garbage go? Where does all the radioactive waste go? Where does all the dangerous chemical junk go?

We're filling all the waste spots on Earth with garbage and trash. We're overloading the ocean with garbage and sludge. We're going crazy thinking of where to put our radioactive waste.

All because we don't have a bottomless hole.

If there existed one bottomless hole on Earth, nations would fight wars to control it. If I owned a bottomless hole, I could charge anything I would wish for allowing others the use of it. It would be worth more to me than a gold mine, or an oil well.

But read the story. Read the story.

—I.A.

THE DEPARTMENT STORE was so crowded with the postseason rush, it was surprising that they spotted her at all. The salesgirl at the counter was busy at the far end, and the woman was equally busy at her own end, slipping goods from the counter into the large black purse. Kearney watched her in alarm for several minutes before calling over the other section manager.

"Look at that woman!" he said. "She's sorting that hardware like she owns the store."

"A klepto? What are we waiting for?" asked the other. "Let's have a talk with her."

Kearney scratched his head. "Watch her for a minute. There's something fishy—"

They watched. She was standing at the kitchenware counter, her hands running over the merchandise on the shelf. She took three cookie cutters and popped them into the pocketbook. Two large cake tins and a potato masher followed, then a small cake safe, two small pots and a large aluminum skillet.

The second man stared in disbelief. "She's taken enough junk there to stock a store. And she's putting it all into that pocketbook. Kearney, *she couldn't get all that junk into a pocketbook!*"

"I know," said Kearney. "Let's go."

They moved in on her from opposite sides, and Kearney took her gently by the arm. "We'd like to speak to you, madam. Please come with us quietly."

She looked up blankly. "What do you mean?"

"We've been watching you load that pocketbook for fifteen minutes."

"Pocketbook?" the woman said, bewildered.

Kearney took the pocketbook from her arm, unsnapped it, glanced inside, and shook it in alarm.

He looked up, eyes wide and puzzled. "Jerry, *look at this.*"

Jerry looked. When he tried to speak, there just weren't any words.

The pocketbook was empty.

Frank Collins parked his car in front of the Institute of Physics and was passed by fingerprint into the lab wing. Evanson met him in the corridor.

"Glad you got here," Evanson said grimly.

"Listen, John, what *is* this about a pocketbook? I hope it's not your idea of a joke."

"Not this gadget," Evanson promised. "Wait till you see it."

He led the way into one of the large lab sections. Collins eyed the shiny conrol panels uneasily, the giant generators and boosters, the duocalc relay board with its gleaming tubes and confusion of wiring. "I can't see what you want with me here. I'm a mechanical engineer."

Evanson walked into a small office off the lab. "You're also a trouble shooter from way back. Meet the research team, Frank."

The research team wore smocks, glasses, and a slouch. Collins nodded, and looked at the pocketbook lying on the table.

"Looks just like any other pocketbook to me," he said. He picked it up. It felt like a pocketbook. "What's in it?"

"You tell us," Evanson said.

Collins opened it up. It was curiously dark inside, with a dull metallic ring around the opening, near the top. He turned it upside down and shook it. Nothing came out.

"Don't reach around inside," Evanson cautioned. "It's not safe. One fellow tried, and lost a wrist watch."

Collins looked up, his bland face curious. "Where did you get this?"

"A couple of section managers spotted a shoplifter down in the Taylor-Hyden store a few days ago. She was helping herself to kitchen hardware, and was stuffing her pocketbook full. They nabbed her, but when they tried to get the hardware back out of the pocketbook they couldn't find any. One of them lost a wrist watch groping around in it."

"Yes, but how did *you* wind up with the purse?"

Evanson shrugged. "They turned the woman over to Psych, naturally. She denied ever seeing the purse. And when the Psych boys looked at the pocketbook they called us in a hurry. Here, I'll show you why."

Evanson picked up a meter stick and began to push it into the pocketbook. It went in about ten centimeters, to the bottom of the purse. . . .

And kept on going!

It didn't poke out the bottom. It didn't even bulge the purse.

Collins goggled at it. "Holy smoke, how'd you do that?"

"Maybe it's going somewhere else. Fourth dimension. I don't know."

"Nuts!"

"Where else, then?" Evanson laid the meter stick down. "Another thing about that pocketbook," he added, "no matter what you do, you *can't* turn it inside out."

Collins looked at the dark inside of the pocketbook. Gingerly he stuck his finger in, rubbed the metallic ring, scratched it with his nail. A shiny line appeared. "That's aluminum in there," he said. "An aluminum circle."

Evanson nodded, "All the stuff she was stealing was aluminum," he said. "That's one reason we called you. You're an engineer, and you know your metals. We've been trying for three days to figure out what's happening inside that purse. We still don't know. Maybe you can tell us."

"What have you been doing?"

"Pushing stuff into it. Checking it with all the instruments. X-ray, everything. Didn't tell us a thing. We'd like to know where that stuff that we push in goes."

Collins dropped an aluminum button into the purse. It went through the aluminum circle and vanished. "Say," he asked suddenly, scowling. "What do you mean, you can't turn this thing inside out?"

"It's a second-order geometric form." Evanson lit a cigarette carefully. "You can turn a first-order form, like a sphere or a rubber ball, inside out through a small hole in the surface. But you *can't* turn an inner tube inside out, no matter what you do."

"Hm. Why not?"

"Because it's got a hole in it. And you can't pull a hole through a hole. Not even an infinitesimal hole."

"So?" Collins said, frowning.

"So it's the same with that purse. We think it's wrapped around a chunk of another universe. A four-dimensional universe. And you can't pull a chunk of another universe through this one without causing a lot of trouble."

"But you *can* turn an inner tube inside out," Collins

protested. "It may stretch all out of shape, but you can pull it through the hole."

Evanson eyed the pocketbook on the table. "Maybe so. A second-order geometric under conditions of stress. But there's one hitch to that. *It won't be an inner tube any more.*"

He took another bit of aluminum and fed it into the purse. He shook his head tiredly. "I don't know. The stuff is going *somewhere.* He pushed a wooden ruler in, watched it pop right out again. "And it takes *only* aluminum. Nothing else. That detective had an aluminum military watch, which disappeared from his wrist, but he had two gold rings on the same hand, and neither one was touched."

"Let's play some thinking games," Collins said.

Evanson looked up sharply. "What do you mean?"

Collins grinned. "*Whatever* is on the other side of that pocketbook seems to want aluminum. Why? There's an aluminum ring around the mouth of the purse—all around it. Like a portal. But it isn't very big, and it doesn't use much aluminum. They seem to want lots more."

"They?"

"Whatever takes the metal but pushes back the wood."

"Why?"

"We could venture a guess. Maybe they're building *another* opening. A large one."

Evanson stared at him. "Don't be silly," he said. "Why—"

"I was just thinking out loud," said Collins mildly. He picked up the steel meter stick. Taking a firm grip on one end, he pushed the other end into the purse.

Evanson watched, puzzled. "They don't want it. They're trying to push it back."

Collins continued to push the stick in, perspiring a little. Suddenly the end appeared, curving back out. Like a flash Collins grabbed it and began tugging both ends at once.

"Watch it, watch it!" Evanson snapped. "You'll twist their universe to conform to our geometry!" The purse seemed to be sagging inward.

One end of the stick suddenly slipped out of Collins' hand.

He fell back, pulling it out of the pocketbook. It was straight again.

Collins stared at it, and his eyes narrowed. "Can you get a winch up here?"

"I think so," Evanson said.

"Good," said Collins. "I think I know how we can hook onto their universe."

The big three-inch steel bar rolled easily into the lab on a dolly. The end of the bar was covered with shiny aluminum tubing and bent into a sharp hook.

"Is the winch ready?" Collins asked.

"All set," Evanson said.

"Then slide the purse onto the end of the bar."

The end of the bar disappeared into the pocketbook.

"What are you trying to do?" Evanson asked uneasily.

"They seem to want aluminum, so we're going to give them some. If they're building another opening through with it, I want to hook onto the opening and pull it out into this lab. They'll be putting the aluminum on this bar with the rest. If we can hook onto what they already have, they'll either have to cut it free and let us retrieve it, or open it into this lab."

Evanson scowled. "But what if they don't do either?"

"They *have* to. If we pull a non-free section of their universe through the purse, it will put a terrific strain on their whole geometric pattern. Their whole universe will be twisted. Just like an inner tube."

The winch squeaked as Collins worked the bar to and fro inside the purse.

"Up a little," he said to the operator.

Evanson shook his head sourly. "I don't see—" he began. Th bar twanged under sudden pressure.

"Hold it! You've got it hooked!" Collins shouted.

The winch squealed noisily, the motor whining under the strain. The steel bar began sliding slowly out of the purse, millimeter by millimeter. Every ten minutes one of the technicians made a chalk mark on the bar by the mouth of the purse.

Frank Collins filled a pipe and puffed nervously. "The way I see it," he said, "these beings pried a small fourth-dimension hole into our universe, and somehow got that woman under control. Then they made her start collecting aluminum so they could build a bigger opening."

"But why?" Evanson poured coffee out of a thermos. It was late, and the whole building was silent and deserted except for this one lab section. The only noise in the room was the whine of the winch, tugging away at the other universe.

"Who knows? To get more and more aluminum? Whatever the reason, they want to get through to our universe. Maybe theirs is in some kind of danger. The reason may be so alien that we couldn't possibly understand it."

"But what's the idea of hooking onto them?" Evanson's eyes were worried.

"Control. We pull a non-free chunk of their universe into ours, and they can't use the opening. It'll be plugged up. The more we pull through, the more strain on the structure of their universe. They'll have to listen to *our* terms then. They'll have to give us their information so that we can build openings and examine them properly. If they don't, we'll wreck their universe."

"But you don't even know what they're *doing* in there!"

Collins shrugged, made another chalk mark on the bar. The bar was humming under the strain.

"I don't think we should take the risk," Evanson complained. "I didn't have permission to try this. I just let you go ahead on my own authority, on data—" he shuddered suddenly—"that's so vague it makes no sense at all."

Collins knocked out his pipe sharply. "It's all the data we have."

"I say it's wrong. I think we should release the bar right now, and wait till Chalmers gets here in the morning."

Collins eyed the winch with growing uneasiness. His fingers trembled as he lit his pipe again. "Don't be foolish," he said. "We *can't* release the bar now. The tapered sheaves are under too much tension. We couldn't even burn through that rod with an oxy torch in less than twenty minutes—and it would jolt the whole building apart when it broke."

"But the danger—" Evanson stood up, his forehead beaded with perspiration. He nodded toward the creaking winch. "You might be gambling our whole universe."

"Oh, calm down!" Collins said angrily. "We don't have any choice now. We're *doing* it, and that's all there is to it. When you grab a tiger by the tail, you've got to hang on."

Evanson crossed the room excitedly. "It seems to me," he said tensely, "that the tiger might have the advantage. If it went the wrong way, think what *they* could do to *our* universe!"

Collins rubbed his chin nervously. "Well, at any rate, I'm glad we thought of it first—" He trailed off, his face slowly turning white.

Evanson followed his stare, and his breath came in a sharp gasp. The thermos clattered noisily to the floor. He pointed at the second chalk mark, sliding slowly *into* the pocketbook.

"You mean you hope we did," he said.

WITH THESE HANDS

BY C. M. KORNBLUTH
GALAXY SCIENCE FICTION, DECEMBER

Cyril Kornbluth's second contribution to the best of 1951 is this stunningly ambitious story, barely science fiction, which the esteemed critic Damon Knight has described as an attempt to merge the mainstream with modern sf. It is a successful attempt, and remains one of the most interesting stories in the history of the field.

—M.H.G.

    I guess this is Cyril interpreting himself again.

    He was appreciated, but not by enough people and not sufficiently. I'm sure it bothered him.

    No, I never discussed it with him. Though we were both Futurians in the golden days of 1938 and 1939, and though we met on and off on very many occasions, we were never close.

    It was my fault, I'm sure. I'm very self-centered, very self-satisfied and happy, have no trouble with writing, no problem meeting deadlines, no familiarity whatsoever with the dread "writer's block," and it never occurs to me that others might have trouble.

    But then I read "With These Hands" and I think "That's

Cyril; that's how he saw himself—and I never knew—and I never paused to give him a kind word—or to see if there was some way I could help him." It doesn't exactly make me proud of myself.

The worst of it was that by the time it all penetrated my thick skin, it was too late. Cyril was dead.

—*I.A.*

I

HALVORSEN WAITED in the Chancery office while Monsignor Reedy disposed of three persons who had preceded him. He was a little dizzy with hunger and noticed only vaguely that the prelate's secretary was beckoning to him. He started to his feet when the secretary pointedly opened the door to Monsignor Reedy's inner office and stood waiting beside it.

The artist crossed the floor, forgetting that he had leaned his portfolio against his chair, remembered at the door and went back for it, flushing. The secretary looked patient.

"Thanks," Halvorsen murmured to him as the door closed. There was something wrong with the prelate's manner.

"I've brought the designs for the Stations, Padre," he said, opening the portfolio on the desk.

"Bad news, Roald," said the monsignor. "I know how you've been looking forward to the commission—"

"Somebody else get it?" asked the artist faintly, leaning against the desk. "I thought his eminence definitely decided I had the—"

"It's not that," said the monsignor. "But the Sacred Congregation of Rites this week made a pronouncement on images of devotion. Stereopantograph is to be licit within a diocese at the discretion of the bishop. And his eminence—"

"S.P.G.—slimy imitations," protested Halvorsen. "Real as a plastic eye. No texture. No guts. *You* know that, Padre!" he said accusingly.

"I'm sorry, Roald," said the monsignor. "Your work is better than we'll get from a stereopantograph—to my eyes, at least. But there are other considerations."

"Money!" spat the artist.

"Yes, money," the prelate admitted. "His eminence wants to see the St. Xavier U. building program through before he dies. Is that wrong, Roald? And there are our schools, our charities, our Venus mission. S.P.G. will mean a considerable saving on procurement and maintenance of devotional images. Even if I could, I would not disagree with his eminence on adopting it as a matter of diocesan policy."

The prelate's eyes fell on the detailed drawings of the Stations of the Cross and lingered.

"Your St. Veronica," he said abstractedly. "Very fine. It suggests one of Caravaggio's careworn saints to me. I would have liked to see her in the bronze."

"So would I," said Halvorsen hoarsely. "Keep the drawings, Padre." He started for the door.

"But I can't—"

"That's all right."

The artist walked past the secretary blindly and out of the Chancery into Fifth Avenue's spring sunlight. He hoped Monsignor Reedy was enjoying the drawings and was ashamed of himself and sorry for Halvorsen. And he was glad he didn't have to carry the heavy portfolio any more. Everything was heavy lately—chisels, hammer, wooden palette. Maybe the padre would send him something and pretend it was for expenses or an advance, as he had in the past.

Halvorsen's feet carried him up the Avenue. No, there wouldn't be any advances any more. The last steady trickle of income had just been dried up, by an announcement in *Osservatore Romano*. Religious conservatism had carried the church as far as it would go in its ancient role of art patron.

When all Europe was writing on the wonderful new vellum, the church stuck to good old papyrus. When all Europe was writing on the wonderful new paper, the church stuck to good old vellum. When all architects and municipal monument committees and portrait bust clients were patronizing the stereopantograph, the church stuck to good old expensive sculpture. But not anymore.

He was passing an S.P.G. salon now, where one of his

Tuesday night pupils worked: one of the few men in the classes. Mostly they consisted of lazy, moody, irritable girls. Halvorsen, surprised at himself, entered the salon, walking between asthenic semi-nude stereos executed in transparent plastic that made the skin of his neck and shoulders prickle with gooseflesh.

Slime! he thought. *How can they—*

"May I help—oh, hello, Roald. What brings you here?"

He knew suddenly what had brought him there. "Could you make a little advance on next month's tuition, Lewis? I'm strapped." He took a nervous look around the chamber of horrors, avoiding the man's condescending face.

"I guess so, Roald. Would ten dollars be any help? That'll carry us through to the twenty-fifth, right?"

"Fine, right, sure," he said, while he was being unwillingly towed around the place.

"I know you don't think much of S.P.G., but it's quiet now, so this is a good chance to see how we work. I don't say it's Art with a capital A, but you've got to admit it's *an* art, something people like at a price they can afford to pay. Here's where we sit them. Then you run out the feelers to the reference points on the face. You know what they are?"

He heard himself say dryly: "I know what they are. The Egyptian sculptors used them when they carved statues of the pharaohs."

"Yes? I never knew that. There's nothing new under the sun, is there? But *this* is the heart of the S.P.G." The youngster proudly swung open the door of an electronic device in the wall of the portrait booth. Tubes winked sullenly at Halvorsen.

"The esthetikon?" he asked indifferently. He did not feel indifferent, but it would be absurd to show anger, no matter how much he felt it, against a mindless aggregation of circuits that could calculate layouts, criticize and correct pictures for a desired effect—and that had put the artist of design out of a job.

"Yes. The lenses take sixteen profiles, you know, and we set the esthetikon for whatever we want—cute, rugged, sexy, spiritual, brainy, or a combination. It fairs curves from profile to profile to give us just what we want, distorts the profiles themselves within limits if it has to, and there's your portrait stored in the memory tank waiting to be taped. You set your ratio for any enlargement or reduction you want and play it back. I wish we were reproducing today; it's fascinating to watch. You just pour in your cold-set plastic, the nozzles ooze out a core and start crawling over to scan—a drop here, a worm there, and it begins to take shape.

"We mostly do portrait busts here, the Avenue trade, but Wilgus, the foreman, used to work in a monument shop in Brooklyn. He did that heroic-size war memorial on the East River Drive—hired Garda Bouchette, the TV girl, for the central figure. And what a figure! He told me he set the esthetikon plates for three-quarters sexy, one-quarter spiritual. Here's something interesting—standing figurine of Orin Ryerson, the banker. He ordered twelve. Figurines are coming in. The girls like them because they can show their shapes. You'd be surprised at some of the poses they want to try—"

Somehow, Halvorsen got out with the ten dollars, walked to Sixth Avenue, and sat down hard in a cheap restaurant. He had coffee and dozed a little, waking with a guilty start at a racket across the street. There was a building going up. For a while he watched the great machines pour walls and floors, the workmen rolling here and there on their little chariots to weld on a wall panel, stripe on an electric circuit of conductive ink, or spray plastic finish over the "wired" wall, all without leaving the saddles of their little mechanical chariots.

Halvorsen felt more determined. He bought a paper from a vending machine by the restaurant door, drew another cup of coffee, and turned to the help-wanted ads.

The tricky trade-school ads urged him to learn construction work and make big money. Be a plumbing-machine setup man. Be a house-wiring machine tender. Be a servotruck driver. Be a lumber-stacker operator. Learn pouring-machine maintenance.

Make big money!

A sort of panic overcame him. He ran to the phone booth and dialed a Passaic number. He heard the *ring-ring-ring* and strained to hear old Mr. Krehbeil's stumping footsteps growing louder as he neared the phone, even though he knew he would hear nothing until the receiver was picked up.

Ring-ring-ring. "Hello?" grunted the old man's voice, and his face appeared on the little screen. "Hello, Mr. Halvorsen. What can I do for you?"

Halvorsen was tongue-tied. He couldn't possibly say: I just wanted to see if you were still there. I was afraid you weren't there anymore. He choked and improvised: "Hello, Mr. Krehbeil. It's about the banister on the stairs in my place. I noticed it's pretty shaky. Could you come over sometime and fix it for me?"

Krehbeil peered suspiciously out of the screen. "I could do that," he said slowly. "I don't have much work nowadays. But you can carpenter as good as me, Mr. Halvorsen, and frankly you're very slow pay and I like cabinet work better. I'm not a young man and climbing around on ladders takes it out of me. If you can't find anybody else, I'll take the work, but I got to have some of the money first, just for the materials. It isn't easy to get good wood any more."

"All right," said Halvorsen. "Thanks, Mr. Krehbeil. I'll call you if I can't get anybody else."

He hung up and went back to his table and newspaper. His face was burning with anger at the old man's reluctance and his own foolish panic. Krehbeil didn't realize they were both in the same leaky boat. Krehbeil, who didn't get a job in a month, still thought with senile pride that he was a journeyman carpenter and cabinetmaker who could make his solid way anywhere with his toolbox and his skill, and that he could afford to look down on anything as disreputable as an artist—even an artist who could carpenter as well as he did himself.

Labuerre had made Halvorsen learn carpentry, and Labuerre had been right. You build a scaffold so you can sculpt up high, not so it will collapse and you break a leg. You build your platforms so they hold the rock steady, not so it wobbles and chatters at every blow of the chisel. You build your armatures so they hold the plasticine you slam onto them.

But the help-wanted ads wanted no builders of scaffolds, platforms, and armatures. The factories were calling for setup men and maintenance men for the production and assembly machines.

From upstate, General Vegetables had sent a recruiting team for farm help—harvest setup and maintenance men, a few openings for experienced operators of tankcaulking machinery. Under "office and professional" the demand was heavy for computer men, for girls who could run the I.B.M. Letteriter, esp. familiar sales and collections corresp., for office machinery maintenance and repair men. A job printing house wanted an esthetikon operator for letterhead layouts and the like. A.T. & T. wanted trainees to earn while learning telephone maintenance. A direct-mail advertising outfit wanted an artist—no, they wanted a sales-executive who could scrawl picture ideas that would be subjected to the criticism and correction of the esthetikon.

Halvorsen leafed tiredly through the rest of the paper. He knew he wouldn't get a job, and if he did he wouldn't hold it. He knew it was a terrible thing to admit to yourself that you might starve to death because you were bored by anything except art, but he admitted it.

It had happened often enough in the past—artists undergoing preposterous hardships, not, as people thought, because they were devoted to art, but because nothing else was interesting. If there were only some impressive, sonorous word that summed up the aching, oppressive futility that overcame him when he tried to get out of art—only there wasn't.

He thought he could tell which of the photos in the tabloid had been corrected by the esthetikon.

There was a shot of Jink Bitsy, who was to star in a remake of *Peter Pan*. Her ears had been made to look not pointed but pointy, her upper lip had been lengthened a trifle, her nose had been pugged a little and tilted quite a lot, her freckles were cuter than cute, her brows were innocently arched, and her lower lip and eyes were nothing less than pornography.

There was a shot, apparently uncorrected, of the last Venus ship coming in at LaGuardia and the average-looking explorers grinning. Caption: "Austin Malone and crew smile relief on safe arrival. Malone says Venus colonies need men, machines. See story on p. 2."

Petulantly, Halvorsen threw the paper under the table and walked out. What had space travel to do with him? Vacations on the Moon and expeditions to Venus and Mars were part of the deadly encroachment on his livelihood and no more.

II ·

He took the subway to Passaic and walked down a long-still traffic beltway to his studio, almost the only building alive in the slums near the rusting railroad freightyard.

A sign that had once said "F. Labuerre, Sculptor—Portraits and Architectural Commissions" now said "Roald Halvorsen; Art Classes—Reasonable Fees." It was a grimy two-story frame building with a shopfront in which were mounted some of his students' charcoal figure studies and oil still-lifes. He lived upstairs, taught downstairs front, and did his own work downstairs, back behind dirty, ceiling-high drapes.

Going in, he noticed that he had forgotten to lock the door again. He slammed it bitterly. At the noise, somebody called from behind the drapes: "Who's that?"

"Halvorsen!" he yelled in a sudden fury. "I live here. I own this place. Come out of there! What do you want?"

There was a fumbling at the drapes and a girl stepped between them, shrinking from their dirt.

"Your door was open," she said firmly, "and it's a shop. I've just been here a couple of minutes. I came to ask about classes, but I don't think I'm interested if you're this bad-tempered."

A pupil. Pupils were never to be abused, especially not now.

"I'm terribly sorry," he said. "I had a trying day in the

city." Now turn it on. "I wouldn't tell everybody a terrible secret like this, but I've lost a commission. You understand? I thought so. Anybody who'd traipse out here to my dingy abode would be *simpatica*. Won't you sit down? No, not there—humor an artist and sit over there. The warm background of that still-life brings out your color—quite good color. Have you ever been painted? You've a very interesting face, you know. Some day I'd like to—but you mentioned classes.

"We have figure classes, male and female models alternating, on Tuesday nights. For that I have to be very stern and ask you to sign up for an entire course of twelve lessons at sixty dollars. It's the models' fees—they're exorbitant. Saturday afternoons we have still-life classes for beginners in oils. That's only two dollars a class, but you might sign up for a series of six and pay ten dollars in advance, which saves you two whole dollars. I also give private instructions to a few talented amateurs."

The price was open on that one—whatever the traffic would bear. It had been a year since he'd had a private pupil and she'd taken only six lessons at five dollars an hour.

"The still-life sounds interesting," said the girl, holding her head self-consciously the way they all did when he gave them the patter. It was a good head, carried well up. The muscles clung close, not yet slacked into geotropic loops and lumps. The line of youth is heliotropic, he confusedly thought. "I saw some interesting things back there. Was that your own work?"

She rose, obviously with the expectation of being taken into the studio. Her body was one of those long-lined, small-breasted, coltish jobs that the pre-Raphaelites loved to draw.

"Well—" said Halvorsen. A deliberate show of reluctance and then a bright smile of confidence. "*You'll* understand," he said positively and drew aside the curtains.

"What a curious place!" She wandered about, inspecting the drums of plaster, clay, and plasticine, the racks of tools, the stands, the stones, the chisels, the forge, the kiln, the lumber, the glaze bench.

"I *like* this," she said determinedly, picking up a figure a half-meter tall, a Venus he had cast in bronze while studying under Labuerre some years ago. "How much is it?"

An honest answer would scare her off, and there was no chance in the world that she'd buy. "I hardly ever put my things up for sale," he told her lightly. "That was just a little study. I do work on commission only nowadays."

Her eyes flicked about the dingy room, seeming to take in its scaling plaster and warped floor and see through the wall to the abandoned slum in which it was set. There was amusement in her glance.

I am not being honest, she thinks. She thinks that is funny. Very well, I will be honest. "Six hundred dollars," he said flatly.

The girl set the figurine on its stand with a rap and said, half angry and half amused: "I don't understand it. That's more than a month's pay for me. I could get an S.P.G. statuette just as pretty as this for ten dollars. Who do you artists think you are, anyway?"

Halvorsen debated with himself about what he could say in reply:

An S.P.G. operator spends a week learning his skill and I spend a lifetime learning mine.

An S.P.G. operator makes a mechanical copy of a human form distorted by formulae mechanically arrived at from psychotests of population samples. I take full responsibility for my work; it is mine, though I use what I see fit from Egypt, Greece, Rome, the Middle Ages, the Renaissance, the Augustan and Romantic and Modern Eras.

An S.P.G. operator works in soft, homogeneous plastic; I work in bronze that is more complicated than you dream, that is cast and acid-dipped today so it will slowly take on rich and subtle coloring many years from today.

An S.P.G. operator could not make an Orpheus Fountain—
He mumbled, "Orpheus," and keeled over.

Halvorsen awoke in his bed on the second floor of the building. His fingers and toes buzzed electrically and he felt very clear-headed. The girl and a man, unmistakably a doctor, were watching him.

"You don't seem to belong to any Medical Plans, Halvorsen," the doctor said irritably. "There weren't any cards on you at all. No Red, no Blue, no Green, no Brown."

"I used to be on the Green Plan, but I let it lapse," the artist said defensively.

"And look what happened!"

"Stop nagging him!" the girl said. "I'll pay you your fee."

"It's supposed to come through a Plan," the doctor fretted.

"We won't tell anybody," the girl promised. "Here's five dollars. Just stop nagging him."

"Malnutrition," said the doctor. "Normally I'd send him to a hospital, but I don't see how I could manage it. He isn't on any Plan at all. Look, I'll take the money and leave some vitamins. That's what he needs—vitamins. And food."

"I'll see that he eats," the girl said, and the doctor left.

"How long since you've had anything?" she asked Halvorsen.

"I had some coffee today," he answered, thinking back. "I'd been working on detail drawings for a commission and it fell through. I told you that. It was a shock."

"I'm Lucretia Grumman," she said, and went out.

He dozed until she came back with an armful of groceries.

"It's hard to get around down here," she complained.

"It was Labuerre's studio," he told her defiantly. "He left it to me when he died. Things weren't so rundown in his time. I studied under him; he was one of the last. He had a joke—'They don't really want my stuff, but they're ashamed to let me starve.' He warned me that they wouldn't be ashamed to let *me* starve, but I insisted and he took me in."

Halvorsen drank some milk and ate some bread. He thought of the change from the ten dollars in his pocket and decided not to mention it. Then he remembered that the doctor had gone through his pockets.

"I can pay you for this," he said. "It's very kind of you,

but you mustn't think I'm penniless. I've just been too preoccupied to take care of myself.''

"Sure," said the girl. "But we can call this an advance. I
want to sign up for some classes."

"Be happy to have you."

"Am I bothering you?" asked the girl. "You said something odd when you fainted—'Orpheus.' "

"Did I say that? I must have been thinking of Milles's
Orpheus Fountain in Copenhagen. I've seen photos, but I've
never been there."

"Germany? But there's nothing left in Germany."

"Copenhagen's in Denmark. There's quite a lot of Denmark left. It was only on the fringes. Heavily radiated, but
still there."

"I want to travel too," she said. "I work at LaGuardia and
I've never been off, except for an orbiting excursion. I want
to go to the Moon on my vacation. They give us a bonus in
travel vouchers. It must be wonderful dancing under the low
gravity."

Spaceport? Off? Low gravity? Terms belonging to the
detested electronic world of the stereopantograph in which
he had no place.

"Be very interesting," he said, closing his eyes to conceal
disgust.

"I *am* bothering you. I'll go away now, but I'll be back
Tuesday night for the class. What time do I come and what
should I bring?"

"Eight. It's charcoal—I sell you the sticks and paper. Just
bring a smock."

"All right. And I want to take the oils class too. And I
want to bring some people I know to see your work. I'm sure
they'll see something they like. Austin Malone's in from
Venus—he's a special friend of mine."

"Lucretia," he said. "Or do some people call you Lucy?"

"Lucy."

"Will you take that little bronze you liked? As a thank
you?"

"I can't do that!"

"Please. I'd feel much better about this. I really mean it."
She nodded abruptly, flushing, and almost ran from the room.

Now why did I do that? he asked himself. He hoped it was because he liked Lucy Grumman very much. He hoped it wasn't a coldblooded investment of a piece of sculpture that would never be sold, anyway, just to make sure she'd be back with class fees and more groceries.

III

She was back on Tuesday, a half-hour early and carrying a smock. He introduced her formally to the others as they arrived: a dozen or so bored young women who, he suspected, talked a great deal about their art lessons outside, but in class used any excuse to stop sketching.

He didn't dare show Lucy any particular consideration. There were fierce little miniature cliques in the class. Halvorsen knew they laughed at him and his line among themselves, and yet, strangely, were fiercely jealous of their seniority and right to individual attention.

The lesson was an ordeal, as usual. The model, a musclebound young graduate of the barbell gyms and figure-photography studios, was stupid and argumentative about ten-minute poses. Two of the girls came near a hair-pulling brawl over the rights to a preferred sketching location. A third girl had discovered Picasso's cubist period during the past week and proudly announced that she didn't *feel* perspective.

But the two interminable hours finally ticked by. He nagged them into cleaning up—not as bad as the Saturdays with oils—and stood by the open door. Otherwise they would have stayed all night, cackling about absent students and snarling sulkily among themselves. His well-laid plans went sour, though. A large and flashy car drove up as the girls were leaving.

"That's Austin Malone," said Lucy. "He came to pick me up and look at your work."

That was all the wedge her fellow-pupils needed.

"*Aus*-tin Ma-*lone! Well!*"

"Lucy, darling, I'd love to meet a real *spaceman*."

"Roald, darling, would you mind very much if I stayed a moment?"

"I'm certainly not going to miss this and I don't care if you mind or not, Roald, darling!"

Malone was an impressive figure. Halvorsen thought: he looks as though he's been run through an esthetikon set for "brawny" and "determined." Lucy made a hash of the introductions and the spaceman didn't rise to conversational bait dangled enticingly by the girls.

In a clear voice, he said to Halvorsen: "I don't want to take up too much of your time. Lucy tells me you have some things for sale. Is there any place we can look at them where it's quiet?"

The students made sulky exits.

"Back here," said the artist.

The girl and Malone followed him through the curtains. The spaceman made a slow circuit of the studio, seeming to repel questions.

He sat down at last and said: "I don't know what to think, Halvorsen. This place stuns me. Do you *know* you're in the Dark Ages?"

People who never have given a thought to Chartres and Mont St. Michel usually call it the Dark Ages, Halvorsen thought wryly. He asked, "Technologically, you mean? No, not at all. My plaster's better, my colors are better, my metal is better—tool metal, not casting metal, that is."

"I mean *hand* work," said the spaceman. "Actually working by *hand*."

The artist shrugged. "There have been crazes for the techniques of the boiler works and the machine shop," he admitted. "Some interesting things were done, but they didn't stand up well. Is there anything here that takes your eye?"

"I like those dolphins," said the spaceman, pointing to a perforated terra-cotta relief on the wall. They had been commissioned by an architect, then later refused for reasons of economy when the house had run way over estimate. "They'd look bully over the fireplace in my town apartment. Like them, Lucy?"

"I think they're wonderful," said the girl.

Roald saw the spaceman go rigid with the effort not to turn and stare at her. He loved her and he was jealous.

Roald told the story of the dolphins and said: "The price that the architect thought was too high was three hundred and sixty dollars."

Malone grunted. "Doesn't seem unreasonable—if you set a high store on inspiration."

"I don't know about inspiration," the artist said evenly. "But I was awake for two days and two nights shoveling coal and adjusting drafts to fire that thing in my kiln."

The spaceman looked contemptuous. "I'll take it," he said. "Be something to talk about during those awkward pauses. Tell me, Halvorsen, how's Lucy's work? Do you think she ought to stick with it?"

"Austin," objected the girl, "don't be so blunt. How can he possibly know after one day?"

"She can't draw yet," the artist said cautiously. "It's all coordination, you know—thousands of hours of practice, training your eye and hand to work together until you can put a line on paper where you want it. Lucy, if you're really interested in it, you'll learn to draw well. I don't think any of the other students will. They're in it because of boredom or snobbery, and they'll stop before they have their eye-hand coordination."

"I *am* interested," she said firmly.

Malone's determined restraint broke. "Damned right you are. In—" He recovered himself and demanded of Halvorsen: "I understand your point about coordination. But thousands of hours when you can buy a camera? It's absurd."

"I was talking about drawing, not art," replied Halvorsen. "Drawing is putting a line on paper where you want it, I said." He took a deep breath and hoped the great distinction wouldn't sound ludicrous and trivial. "So let's say that art is knowing how to put the line in the right place."

"Be practical. There isn't any art. Not any more. I get around quite a bit and I never see anything but photos and S.P.G.s. A few heirlooms, yes, but nobody's painting or carving any more."

"There's some art, Malone. My students—a couple of them in the still-life class—are quite good. There are more across the country. Art for occupational therapy, or a hobby, or something to do with the hands. There's trade in their work. They sell them to each other, they give them to their friends, they hang them on their walls. There are even some sculptors like that. Sculpture is prescribed by doctors. The occupational therapists say it's even better than drawing and painting, so some of these people work in plasticine and soft stone, and some of them get to be good."

"Maybe so. I'm an engineer, Halvorsen. We glory in doing things the easy way. Doing things the easy way got me to Mars and Venus and it's going to get me to Ganymede. You're doing things the hard way, and your inefficiency has no place in this world. Look at you! You've lost a fingertip—some accident, I suppose."

"I never noticed—" said Lucy, and then let out a faint, "Oh!"

Halvorsen curled the middle finger of his left hand into the palm, where he usually carried it to hide the missing first joint.

"Accidents are a sign of inadequate mastery of material and equipment," said Malone sententiously. "While you stick to your methods and I stick to mine, *you can't compete with me.*"

His tone made it clear that he was talking about more than engineering.

"Shall we go now, Lucy? Here's my card, Halvorsen. Send those dolphins along and I'll mail you a check."

IV

The artist walked the half-dozen blocks to Mr. Krehbeil's place the next day. He found the old man in the basement shop of his fussy house, hunched over his bench with a powerful light overhead. He was trying to file a saw.

"Mr. Krehbeil!" Halvorsen called over the shriek of metal.

The carpenter turned around and peered with watery eyes. "I can't see like I used to," he said querulously. "I go over the same teeth on this damn saw, I skip teeth, I can't see the light shine off it when I got one set. The glare." He banged down his three-cornered file petulantly. "Well, what can I do for you?"

"I need some crating stock. Anything. I'll trade you a couple of my maple four-by-fours."

The old face became cunning. "And will you set my saw? My *saws*, I mean. It's nothing to you—an hour's work. You have the eyes."

Halvorsen said bitterly, "All right." The old man had to drive his bargain, even though he might never use his saws again. And then the artist promptly repented of his bitterness, offering up a quick prayer that his own failure to conform didn't make him as much of a nuisance to the world as Krehbeil was.

The carpenter was pleased as they went through his small stock of wood and chose boards to crate the dolphin relief. He was pleased enough to give Halvorsen coffee and cake before the artist buckled down to filing the saws.

Over the kitchen table, Halvorsen tried to probe. "Things pretty slow now?"

It would be hard to spoil Krehbeil's day now. "People are always fools. They don't know good hand work. Some day," he said apocalyptically, "I laugh on the other side of my face when their foolish machine-buildings go falling down in a strong wind, all of them, all over the country. Even my boy—I used to beat him good, almost every day—he works a foolish concrete machine and his house should fall on his head like the rest."

Halvorsen knew it was Krehbeil's son who supported him by mail, and changed the subject. "You get some cabinet work?"

"Stupid women! What they call antiques—they don't know

Meissen, they don't know Biedermeier. They bring me trash to repair sometimes. I make them pay; I swindle them good.''

"I wonder if things would be different if there were anything left over in Europe . . ."

"People will still be fools, Mr. Halvorsen," said the carpenter positively. "Didn't you say you were going to file those saws today?"

So the artist spent two noisy hours filing before he carried his crating stock to the studio.

Lucy was there. She had brought some things to eat. He dumped the lumber with a bang and demanded: "Why aren't you at work?"

"We get days off," she said vaguely. "Austin thought he'd give me the cash for the terra-cotta and I could give it to you."

She held out an envelope while he studied her silently. The farce was beginning again. But this time he dreaded it.

It would not be the first time that a lonesome, discontented girl chose to see him as a combination of romantic rebel and lost pup, with the consequences you'd expect.

He knew from books, experience, and Labuerre's conversation in the old days that there was nothing novel about the comedy—that there had even been artists, lots of them, who had counted on endless repetitions of it for their livelihood.

The girl drops in with groceries and the artist is pleasantly surprised; the girl admires this little thing or that after payday and buys it and the artist is pleasantly surprised; the girl brings her friends to take lessons or make little purchases and the artist is pleasantly surprised. The girl may be seduced by the artist or vice versa, which shortens the comedy, or they may get married, which lengthens it somewhat.

It had been three years since Halvorsen had last played out the farce with a manic-depressive divorcée from Elmira: three years during which he had crossed the mid-point between thirty and forty; three more years to get beaten down by being unwanted and working too much and eating too little.

Also, he knew, he was in love with this girl.

He took the envelope, counted three hundred and twenty dollars, and crammed it into his pocket. "That was your idea," he said. "Thanks. Now get out, will you? I've got work to do."

She stood there, shocked.

"*I said get out. I have work to do.*"

"Austin was right," she told him miserably. "You don't care how people feel. You just want to get things out of them."

She ran from the studio, and Halvorsen fought with himself not to run after her.

He walked slowly into his workshop and studied his array of tools, though he paid little attention to his finished pieces. It would be nice to spend about half of this money on open-hearth steel rod and bar stock to forge into chisels; he thought he knew where he could get some—but she would be back, or he would break and go to her and be forgiven and the comedy would be played out, after all.

He couldn't let that happen.

V

Aalesund, on the Atlantic side of the Dourefeld Mountains of Norway, was in the lee of the blasted continent. One more archeologist there made no difference, as long as he had the sense to recognize the propellor-like international signposts that said with their three blades, *Radiation Hazard*, and knew what every schoolboy knew about protective clothing and reading a personal Geiger counter.

The car Halvorsen rented was for a brief trip over the mountains to study contaminated Oslo. Well muffled, he could make it and back in a dozen hours and no harm done.

But he took the car past Oslo, Wennersborg, and Goteborg, along the Kattegat coast to Helsingborg, and abandoned it there, among the three-bladed polyglot signs, crossing to Denmark. Danes were as unlike Prussians as they could be, but their unfortunate little peninsula was a sprout off Prussia that radio-cobalt dust couldn't tell from the real thing. The three-bladed signs were most specific.

With a long way to walk along the rubble-littered highways, he stripped off the impregnated coveralls and boots. He had long since shed the noisy counter and the uncomfortable gloves and mask.

The silence was eerie as he limped into Copenhagen at noon. He didn't know whether the radiation was getting to him or whether he was tired and hungry and no more. As though thinking of a stranger, he liked what he was doing.

I'll be my own audience, he thought. *God knows I learned there isn't any other, not any more. You have to know when to stop. Rodin, the dirty old, wonderful old man, knew that. He taught us not to slick it and polish it and smooth it until it looked like liquid instead of bronze and stone. Van Gogh was crazy as a loon, but he knew when to stop and varnish it, and he didn't care if the paint looked like paint instead of looking like sunset clouds or moonbeams. Up in Hartford, Browne and Sharpe stop when they've got a turret lathe; they don't put caryatids on it. I'll stop while my life is a life, before it becomes a thing with distracting embellishments such as a wife who will come to despise me, a succession of gradually less worthwhile pieces that nobody will look at.*

Blame nobody, he told himself, lightheadedly.

And then it was in front of him, terminating a vista of weeds and bomb rubble—Milles's Orpheus Fountain.

It took a man, he thought. Esthetikon circuits couldn't do it. There was a gross mixture of styles, a calculated flaw that the esthetikon couldn't be set to make. Orpheus and the souls were classic or later; the three-headed dog was archaic. That was to tell you about the antiquity and invincibility of Hell, and that Cerberus knows Orpheus will never go back into life with his bride.

There was the heroic, tragic central figure that looked mighty enough to battle with the gods, but battle wasn't any good against the grinning, knowing, hateful three-headed dog it stood on. You don't battle the pavement where you walk or the floor of the house you're in; you can't. So Orpheus, his face a mask of controlled and suffering fury, crashes a great chord from his lyre that moved trees and stones. Around him the naked souls in Hell start at the chord, each in its own way: the young lovers down in death; the mother down in death; the musician, deaf and down in death, straining to hear.

Halvorsen, walking uncertainly toward the fountain, felt something break inside him, and a heaviness in his lungs. As he pitched forward among the weeds, he didn't care that the three-headed dog was grinning its knowing, hateful grin down at him. He had heard the chord from the lyre.

A PAIL OF AIR

BY FRITZ LEIBER (1910–   )
GALAXY SCIENCE FICTION, DECEMBER

Regular readers of speculative fiction know that Fritz Leiber is one of the most versatile writers in the business, known for his supernatural horror, his sword and sorcery, and his socially satirical science fiction. But we tend to forget that he can also write carefully extrapolated "hard" science sf with the best of them, as in his long novel The Wanderer *and the present selection. "A Pail of Air" combines serious scientific speculation with excellent writing, and turns the tending of a routine chore in an unpleasant future into a memorable example of* science *fiction.*

—M.H.G.

In the years after 1945, it seemed that every science fiction writer tried his hand at a post-holocaust story. The first nuclear bombs were bound to give rise to that. What happens after the world we know is destroyed one way or another (nuclear war, overpopulation, disease, astronomical accident)?

Generally, I couldn't endure such stories because they seemed to take pleasure in describing the misery, the violence, the degradation—all of which might be exactly what would happen, but I couldn't enjoy it. And I never, never

274

wrote one myself. I suppose Pebble in the Sky *came close but it was long, long, post-holocaust.*

However, one story in this category I liked when it came out, and I still like it. It is truly unique, I think. Here is a world that is all but dead, and it contains love and hope and human effort and the promise of rebirth.

I'm not at all surprised that Fritz Leiber wrote it because he is, and always has been, a civilized man who can't help but be upbeat about humanity because he can't make himself believe that others are not as decent and as indomitable as he is himself.

No one story reflects a writer because individual stories can always be atypical. However, the entire corpus of work of a prolific writer cannot help but portray the artist very exactly, and I think Leiber's does, and it reflects most favorably upon him.

—I.A.

PA HAD SENT me out to get an extra pail of air. I'd just about scooped it full and most of the warmth had leaked from my fingers when I saw the thing.

You know, at first I thought it was a young lady. Yes, a beautiful young lady's face all glowing in the dark and looking at me from the fifth floor of the opposite apartment, which hereabouts is the floor just above the white blanket of frozen air four storeys thick. I'd never seen a live young lady before, except in the old magazines—Sis is just a kid and Ma is pretty sick and miserable—and it gave me such a start that I dropped the pail. Who wouldn't, knowing everyone on Earth was dead except Pa and Ma and Sis and you?

Even at that, I don't suppose I should have been surprised. We all see things now and then. Ma sees some pretty bad ones, to judge from the way she bugs her eyes at nothing and just screams and screams and huddles back against the blankets hanging around the Nest. Pa says it is natural we should react like that sometimes.

When I'd recovered the pail and could look again at the
opposite apartment, I got an idea of what Ma might be feeling
at those times, for I saw it wasn't a young lady at all but
simply a light—a tiny light that moved stealthily from window to window, just as if one of the cruel little stars had
come down out of the airless sky to investigate why the Earth
had gone away from the Sun, and maybe to hunt down
something to torment or terrify, now that the Earth didn't
have the Sun's protection.

I tell you, the thought of it gave me the creeps. I just stood
there shaking, and almost froze my feet and did frost my
helmet so solid on the inside that I couldn't have seen the
light even if it had come out of one of the windows to get me.
Then I had the wit to go back inside.

Pretty soon I was feeling my familiar way through the
thirty or so blankets and rugs and rubbery sheets Pa has got
hung and braced around to slow down the escape of air from
the Nest, and I wasn't quite so scared. I began to hear the
tick-ticking of the clocks in the Nest and knew I was getting
back into air, because there's no sound outside in the vacuum, of course. But my mind was still crawly and uneasy as I
pushed through the last blankets—Pa's got them faced with
aluminum foil to hold in the heat—and came into the Nest.

Let me tell you about the Nest. It's low and snug, just
room for the four of us and our things. The floor is covered
with thick woolly rugs. Three of the sides are blankets, and
the blankets roofing it touch Pa's head. He tells me it's inside
a much bigger room, but I've never seen the real walls or
ceiling.

Against one of the blanket-walls is a big set of shelves,
with tools and books and other stuff, and on top of it a whole
row of clocks. Pa's very fussy about keeping them wound.
He says we must never forget time, and without a sun or
moon, that would be easy to do.

The fourth wall has blankets all over except around the
fireplace, in which there is a fire that must never go out. It
keeps us from freezing and does a lot more besides. One of

us must always watch it. Some of the clocks are alarm and we can use them to remind us. In the early days there was only Ma to take turns with Pa—I think of that when she gets difficult—but now there's me to help, and Sis too.

It's Pa who is the chief guardian of the fire, though. I always think of him that way: a tall man sitting crosslegged, frowning anxiously at the fire, his lined face golden in its light, and every so often carefully placing on it a piece of coal from the big heap beside it. Pa tells me there used to be guardians of the fire sometimes in the very old days—vestals, he calls them—although there was unfrozen air all around then and a sun too and you didn't really need a fire.

He was sitting just that way now, though he got up quick to take the pail from me and bawl me out for loitering—he'd spotted my frozen helmet right off. That roused Ma and she joined in picking on me. She's always trying to get the load off her feelings, Pa explains. He shut her up pretty fast. Sis let off a couple of silly squeals too.

Pa handled the pail of air in a twist of cloth. Now that it was inside the Nest, you could really feel its coldness. It just seemed to suck the heat out of everything. Even the flames cringed away from it as Pa put it down close by the fire.

Yet it's that glimmery blue-white stuff in the pail that keeps us alive. It slowly melts and vanishes and refreshes the Nest and feeds the fire. The blankets keep it from escaping too fast. Pa'd like to seal the whole place, but he can't—building's too earthquake-twisted, and besides he has to leave the chimney open for smoke. But the chimney has special things Pa calls baffles up inside it, to keep the air from getting out too quick that way. Sometimes Pa, making a joke, says it baffles him they keep on working, or work at all.

Pa says air is tiny molecules that fly away like a flash if there isn't something to stop them. We have to watch sharp not to let the air run low. Pa always keeps a big reserve supply of it in buckets behind the first blankets, along with extra coal and cans of food and bottles of vitamins and other things, such as pails of snow to melt for water. We have to go way down to the bottom floor for that stuff, which is a mean trip, and get it through a door to outside.

You see, when the Earth got cold, all the water in the air froze first and made a blanket ten feet thick or so everywhere, and then down on top of that dropped the crystals of frozen air, making another mostly white blanket sixty or seventy feet thick maybe.

Of course, all the parts of the air didn't freeze and snow down at the same time.

First to drop out was the carbon dioxide—when you're shoveling for water, you have to make sure you don't go too high and get any of that stuff mixed in, for it would put you to sleep, maybe for good, and make the fire go out. Next there's the nitrogen, which doesn't count one way or the other, though it's the biggest part of the blanket. On top of that and easy to get at, which is lucky for us, there's the oxygen that keeps us alive. It's pale blue, which helps you tell it from the nitrogen. It has to be colder for oxygen to freeze solid than nitrogen. That's why the oxygen snowed down last.

Pa says we live better than kings ever did, breathing pure oxygen, but we're used to it and don't notice.

Finally, at the very top, there's a slick of liquid helium, which is funny stuff.

All of these gases are in neat separate layers. Like a pussy caffay, Pa laughingly says, whatever that is.

I was busting to tell them all about what I'd seen, and so as soon as I'd ducked out of my helmet and while I was still climbing out of my suit, I cut loose. Right away Ma got nervous and began making eyes at the entry-slit in the blankets and wringing her hands together—the hand where she'd lost three fingers from frostbite inside the good one, as usual. I could tell that Pa was annoyed at me scaring her and wanted to explain it all away quickly, yet I knew he knew I wasn't fooling.

"And you watched this light for some time, son?" he asked when I finished.

I hadn't said anything about first thinking it was a young lady's face. Somehow that part embarrassed me.

"Long enough for it to pass five windows and go to the next floor."

"And it didn't look like stray electricity or crawling liquid or starlight focused by a growing crystal, or anything like that?"

He wasn't just making up those ideas. Odd things happen in a world that's about as cold as can be, and just when you think matter would be frozen dead, it takes on a strange new life. A slimy stuff comes crawling toward the Nest, just like an animal snuffing for heat—that's liquid helium. And once, when I was little, a bolt of lightning—not even Pa could figure where it came from—hit the nearby steeple and crawled up and down it for weeks, until the glow finally died.

"Not like anything I ever saw," I told him.

He stood for a moment frowning. Then, "I'll go with you, and you show it to me," he said.

Ma raised a howl at the idea of being left alone, and Sis joined in, too, but Pa quieted them. We started climbing into our outside clothes—mine had been warming by the fire. Pa made them. They have triple-pane plastic headpieces that were once big double-duty transparent food cans, but they keep heat and air in and can replace the air for a little while, long enough for our trips for water and coal and food and so on.

Ma started moaning again, "I've always known there was something outside there, waiting to get us. I've felt it for years—something that's part of the cold and hates all warmth and wants to destroy the Nest. It's been watching us all this time, and now it's coming after us. It'll get you and then come for me. Don't go, Harry!"

Pa had everything on but his helmet. He knelt by the fireplace and reached in and shook the long metal rod that goes up the chimney and knocks off the ice that keeps trying to clog it. Once a week he goes up on the roof to check if it's working all right. That's our worst trip and Pa won't let me make it alone.

"Sis," Pa said quietly, "come watch the fire. Keep an eye on the air, too. If it gets low or doesn't seem to be boiling fast enough, fetch another bucket from behind the blankets. But mind your hands. Use the cloth to pick up the bucket."

Sis quit helping Ma be frightened and came over and did as she was told. Ma quieted down pretty suddenly, though her eyes were still kind of wild as she_watched Pa fix on his helmet tight and pick up a pail and the two of us go out.

Pa led the way and I took hold of his belt. It's a funny thing, I'm not afraid to go by myself, but when Pa's along I always want to hold on to him. Habit, I guess, and then there's no denying that this time I was a bit scared.

You see, it's this way. We know that everything is dead out there. Pa heard the last radio voices fade away years ago, and had seen some of the last folks die who weren't as lucky or well-protected as us. So we knew that if there was something groping around out there, it couldn't be anything human or friendly.

Besides that, there's a feeling that comes with it always being night, *cold* night. Pa says there used to be some of that feeling even in the old days, but then every morning the Sun would come and chase it away. I have to take his word for that, not ever remembering the Sun as being anything more than a big star. You see, I hadn't been born when the dark star snatched us away from the Sun, and by now it's dragged us out beyond the orbit of the planet Pluto, Pa says, and is taking us farther out all the time.

We can see the dark star as it crosses the sky because it blots out stars, and especially when it's outlined by the Milky Way. It's pretty big, for we're closer to it than the planet Mercury was to the Sun, Pa says, but we don't care to look at it much and Pa won't set his clocks by it.

I found myself wondering whether there mightn't be something on the dark star that wanted us, and if that was why it had captured the Earth. Just then we came to the end of the corridor and I followed Pa out on the balcony.

I don't know what the city looked like in the old days, but

now it's beautiful. The starlight lets you see it pretty well—there's quite a bit of light in those steady points speckling the blackness above. (Pa says the stars used to twinkle once, but that was because there was air.) We are on a hill and the shimmery plain drops away from us and then flattens out, cut up into neat squares by the troughs that used to be streets. I sometimes make my mashed potatoes look like it, before I pour on the gravy.

Some taller buildings push up out of the feathery plain, topped by rounded caps of air crystals, like the fur hood Ma wears, only whiter. On those buildings you can see the darker squares of windows, underlined by white dashes of air crystals. Some of them are on a slant, for many of the buildings are pretty badly twisted by the quakes and all the rest that happened when the dark star captured the Earth.

Here and there a few icicles hang, water icicles from the first days of the cold, other icicles of frozen air that melted on the roofs and dropped and froze again. Sometimes one of those icicles will catch the light of a star and send it to you so brightly you think the star has swooped into the city. That was one of the things Pa had been thinking of when I told him about the light, but I had thought of it myself first and known it wasn't so.

He touched his helmet to mine so we could talk easier and he asked me to point out the windows to him. But there wasn't any light moving around inside them now, or anywhere else. To my surprise, Pa didn't bawl me out and tell me I'd been seeing things. He looked all around quite a while after filling his pail, and just as we were going inside he whipped around without warning, as if to take some peeping thing off guard.

I could feel it, too. The old peace was gone. There was something lurking out there, watching, waiting, getting ready.

Inside, he said to me, touching helmets, "If you see something like that again, son, don't tell the others. Your Ma's sort of nervous these days and we owe her all the feeling of safety we can give her. Once—it was when your sister was born—I was ready to give up and die, but your

Mother kept me trying. Another time she kept the fire going a
whole week all by herself when I was sick. Nursed me and
took care of the two of you, too.

"You know that game we sometimes play, sitting in a
square in the Nest, tossing a ball around? Courage is like a
ball, son. A person can hold it only so long, and then he's got
to toss it to someone else. When it's tossed your way, you've
got to catch it and hold it tight—and hope there'll be someone
else to toss it to when you get tired of being brave."

His talking to me that way made me feel grown-up and
good. But it didn't wipe away the thing outside from the back
of my mind—or the fact that Pa took it seriously.

It's hard to hide your feelings about such a thing. When we
got back in the Nest and took off our outside clothes, Pa
laughed about it all and told them it was nothing and kidded
me for having such an imagination, but his words fell flat. He
didn't convince Ma and Sis any more than he did me. It
looked for a minute like we were all fumbling the courage-
ball. Something had to be done, and almost before I knew
what I was going to say, I heard myself asking Pa to tell us
about the old days, and how it all happened.

He sometimes doesn't mind telling that story, and Sis and I
sure like to listen to it, and he got my idea. So we were all
settled around the fire in a wink, and Ma pushed up some
cans to thaw for supper, and Pa began. Before he did, though,
I noticed him casually get a hammer from the shelf and lay it
down beside him.

It was the same old story as always—I think I could recite
the main thread of it in my sleep—though Pa always puts in a
new detail or two and keeps improving it in spots.

He told us how the Earth had been swinging around the
Sun ever so steady and warm, and the people on it fixing to
make money and wars and have a good time and get power
and treat each other right or wrong, when without warning
there comes charging out of space this dead star, this burned-
out sun, and upsets everything.

You know, I find it hard to believe in the way those people

felt, any more than I can believe in the swarming number of them. Imagine people getting ready for the horrible sort of war they were cooking up. Wanting it even, or at least wishing it were over so as to end their nervousness. As if all folks didn't have to hang together and pool every bit of warmth just to keep alive. And how can they have hoped to end danger, any more than we can hope to end the cold?

Sometimes I think Pa exaggerates and makes things out too black. He's cross with us once in a while and was probably cross with all those folks. Still, some of the things I read in the old magazines sound pretty wild. He may be right.

The dark star, as Pa went on telling it, rushed in pretty fast and there wasn't much time to get ready. At the beginning they tried to keep it a secret from most people, but then the truth came out, what with the earthquakes and floods—imagine, oceans of *unfrozen* water!—and people seeing stars blotted out by something on a clear night. First off they thought it would hit the Sun, and then they thought it would hit the Earth. There was even the start of a rush to get in a place called China, because people thought the star would hit on the other side. Not that that would have helped them, they were just crazy with fear. But then they found it wasn't going to hit either side, but was going to come very close to the Earth.

Most of the other planets were on the other side of the Sun and didn't get involved. The Sun and the newcomer fought over the Earth for a little while—pulling it this way and that, in a twisty curve, like two dogs growling over a bone, Pa described it this time—and then the newcomer won and carried us off. The Sun got a consolation prize, though. At the last minute he managed to hold on to the Moon.

That was the time of the monster earthquakes and floods, twenty times worse than anything before. It was also the time of the Big Swoop, as Pa calls it, when the Earth speeded up, going into a close orbit around the dark star.

I've asked Pa, wasn't the Earth yanked then, just as he has done to me sometimes, grabbing me by the collar to do it, when I've been sitting too far from the fire. But Pa says no, gravity doesn't work that way. It was like a yank, but nobody felt it. I guess it was like being yanked in a dream.

You see, the dark star was going through space faster than the Sun, and in the opposite direction, and it had to speed up the world a lot in order to take it away.

The Big Swoop didn't last long. It was over as soon as the Earth was settled down in its new orbit around the dark star. But the earthquakes and floods were terrible while it lasted, twenty times worse than anything before. Pa says that all sorts of cliffs and buildings toppled, oceans slopped over, swamps and sandy deserts gave great sliding surges that buried nearby lands. Earth's blanket of air, still up in the sky then, was stretched out and got so thin in spots that people keeled over and fainted—though of course, at the same time, they were getting knocked down by the earthquakes that went with the Big Swoop and maybe their bones broke or skulls cracked.

We've often asked Pa how people acted during that time, whether they were scared or brave or crazy or stunned, or all four, but he's sort of leery of the subject, and he was again tonight. He says he was mostly too busy to notice.

You see, Pa and some scientist friends of his had figured out part of what was going to happen—they'd known we'd get captured and our air would freeze—and they'd been working like mad to fix up a place with airtight walls and doors, and insulation against the cold, and big supplies of food and fuel and water and bottled air. But the place got smashed in the last earthquakes and all Pa's friends were killed then and in the Big Swoop. So he had to start over and throw the Nest together quick without any advantages, just using any stuff he could lay his hands on.

I guess he's telling pretty much the truth when he says he didn't have any time to keep an eye on how other folks behaved, either then or in the Big Freeze that followed— followed very quick, you know, both because the dark star was pulling us away very fast and because Earth's rotation had been slowed by the tug-of-war and the tides, so that the nights were longer.

Still, I've got an idea of some of the things that happened from the frozen folk I've seen, a few of them in other rooms in our building, others clustered around the furnaces in the basements where we go for coal.

In one of the rooms, an old man sits stiff in a chair, with an arm and a leg in splints. In another, a man and woman are huddled together in a bed with heaps of covers over them. You can just see their heads peeking out, close together. And in another a beautiful young lady is sitting with a pile of wraps huddled around her, looking hopefully toward the door, as if waiting for someone who never came back with warmth and food. They're all still and stiff as statues, of course, but just like life.

Pa showed them to me once in quick winks of his flashlight, when he still had a fair supply of batteries and could afford to waste a little light. They scared me pretty bad and made my heart pound, especially the young lady.

Now, with Pa telling his story for the umpteenth time to take our minds off another scare, I got to thinking of the frozen folk again. All of a sudden I got an idea that scared me worse than anything yet. You see, I'd just remembered that face I'd thought I'd seen in the window. I'd forgotten about that on account of trying to hide it from the others.

What, I asked myself, if the frozen folk were coming to life? What if they were like the liquid helium that got a new lease on life and started crawling toward the heat just when you thought its molecules ought to freeze solid forever? Or like the electricity that moves endlessly when it's just about as cold as that? What if the ever-growing cold, with the temperature creeping down the last few degrees to the last zero, had mysteriously wakened the frozen folk to life—not warm-blooded life, but something icy and horrible?

That was a worse idea than the one about something coming down from the dark star to get us.

Or maybe, I thought, both ideas might be true. Something

coming down from the dark star and making the frozen folk move, using them to do its work. That would fit with both things I'd seen—the beautiful young lady and the moving, starlike light.

The frozen folk with minds from the dark star behind their unwinking eyes, creeping, crawling, snuffing their way, following the heat to the Nest, maybe wanting the heat, but more likely hating it and wanting to chill it forever, snuff out our fire.

I tell you, that thought gave me a very bad turn and I wanted very badly to tell the others my fears, but I remembered what Pa had said and clenched my teeth and didn't speak.

We were all sitting very still. Even the fire was burning silently. There was just the sound of Pa's voice and the clocks.

And then, from beyond the blankets, I thought I heard a tiny noise. My skin tightened all over me.

Pa was telling about the early years in the Nest and had come to the place where he philosophizes.

"So I asked myself then," he said, "what's the use of dragging it out for a few years? Why prolong a doomed existence of hard work and cold and loneliness? The human race is done. The Earth is done. Why not give up, I asked myself—and all of a sudden I got the answer."

Again I heard the noise, louder this time, a kind of uncertain, shuffling tread, coming closer. I couldn't breathe.

"Life's always been a business of working hard and fighting the cold," Pa was saying. "The earth's always been a lonely place, millions of miles from the next planet. And no matter how long the human race might have lived, the end would have come some night. Those things don't matter. What matters is that life is good. It has a lovely texture, like some thick fur or the petals of flowers—you've never seen those, but you know our ice-flowers—or like the texture of flames, never twice the same. It makes everything else worthwhile. And that's as true for the last man as the first."

And still the steps kept shuffling closer. It seemed to me

that the inmost blanket trembled and bulged a little. Just as if they were burned into my imagination, I kept seeing those peering, frozen eyes.

"So right then and there," Pa went on, and now I could tell that he heard the steps, too, and was talking loud so we maybe wouldn't hear them, "right then and there I told myself that I was going on as if we had all eternity ahead of us. I'd have children and teach them all I could. I'd get them to read books. I'd plan for the future, try to enlarge and seal the Nest. I'd do what I could to keep everything beautiful and growing. I'd keep alive my feeling of wonder even at the cold and the dark and the distant stars."

But then the blanket actually did move and lift. And there was a bright light somewhere behind it. Pa's voice stopped and his eyes turned to the widening slit and his hand went out until it touched and gripped the handle of the hammer beside him.

In through the blanket stepped the beautiful young lady. She stood there looking at us the strangest way, and she carried something bright and unwinking in her hand. And two other faces peered over her shoulders—men's faces, white and staring.

Well, my heart couldn't have been stopped for more than four or five beats before I realized she was wearing a suit and helmet like Pa's homemade ones, only fancier, and that the men were, too—and that the frozen folk certainly wouldn't be wearing those. Also, I noticed that the bright thing in her hand was just a kind of flashlight.

Sinking down very softly, Ma fainted.

The silence kept on while I swallowed hard a couple of times, and after that there was all sorts of jabbering and commotion.

They were simply people, you see. We hadn't been the only ones to survive; we'd just thought so, for natural enough reasons. These three people had survived, and quite a few others with them. And when we found out *how* they'd survived, Pa let out the biggest whoop of joy.

They were from Los Alamos and they were getting their heat and power from atomic energy. Just using the uranium and plutonium intended for bombs, they had enough to go on for thousands of years. They had a regular little airtight city, with airlocks and all. They even generated electric light and grew plants and animals by it. (At this Pa let out a second whoop, waking Ma from her faint.)

But if we were flabbergasted at them, they were double-flabbergasted at us.

One of the men kept saying, "But it's impossible, I tell you. You can't maintain an air supply without hermetic sealing. It's simply impossible."

That was after he had got his helmet off and was using our air. Meanwhile, the young lady kept looking around at us as if we were saints, and telling us we'd done something amazing, and suddenly she broke down and cried.

They'd been scouting around for survivors, but they never expected to find any in a place like this. They had rocket ships at Los Alamos and plenty of chemical fuel. As for liquid oxygen, all you had to do was go out and shovel the air blanket at the top level. So after they'd got things going smoothly at Los Alamos, which had taken years, they'd decided to make some trips to likely places where there might be other survivors. No good trying long-distance radio signals, of course, since there was no atmosphere, no ionosphere, to carry them around the curve of the Earth. That was why all the radio signals had died out.

Well, they'd found other colonies at Argonne and Brookhaven and way around the world at Harwell and Tanna Tuva. And now they'd been giving our city a look, not really expecting to find anything. But they had an instrument that noticed the faintest heat waves and it had told them there was something warm down here, so they'd landed to investigate. Of course we hadn't heard them land, since there was no air to carry the sound, and they'd had to investigate around quite a while before finding us. Their instruments had given them a wrong steer and they'd wasted some time in the building across the street.

* * *

By now, all five adults were talking like sixty. Pa was demonstrating to the men how he worked the fire and got rid of the ice in the chimney and all that. Ma had perked up wonderfully and was showing the young lady her cooking and sewing stuff, and even asking about how the women dressed at Los Alamos. The strangers marveled at everything and praised it to the skies. I could tell from the way they wrinkled their noses that they found the Nest a bit smelly, but they never mentioned that at all and just asked bushels of questions.

In fact, there was so much talking and excitement that Pa forgot about things, and it wasn't until they were all getting groggy that he looked and found the air had all boiled away in the pail. He got another bucket of air quick from behind the blankets. Of course that started them all laughing and jabbering again. The newcomers even got a little drunk. They weren't used to so much oxygen.

Funny thing, though—I didn't do much talking at all and Sis hung on to Ma all the time and hid her face when anybody looked at her. I felt pretty uncomfortable and disturbed myself, even about the young lady. Glimpsing her outside there, I'd had all sorts of mushy thoughts, but now I was just embarrassed and scared of her, even though she tried to be nice as anything to me.

I sort of wished they'd all quit crowding the Nest and let us be alone and get our feelings straightened out.

And when the newcomers began to talk about our all going to Los Alamos, as if that were taken for granted, I could see that something of the same feeling struck Pa and Ma, too. Pa got very silent all of a sudden and Ma kept telling the young lady, "But I wouldn't know how to act there and I haven't any clothes."

The strangers were puzzled like anything at first, but then they got the idea. As Pa kept saying, "It just doesn't seem right to let this fire go out."

Well, the strangers are gone, but they're coming back. It hasn't been decided yet just what will happen. Maybe the

Nest will be kept up as what one of the strangers called a "survival school." Or maybe we will join the pioneers who are going to try to establish a new colony at the uranium mines at Great Slave Lake or in the Congo.

Of course, now that the strangers are gone, I've been thinking a lot about Los Alamos and those other tremendous colonies. I have a hankering to see them for myself.

You ask me, Pa wants to see them, too. He's been getting pretty thoughtful, watching Ma and Sis perk up.

"It's different, now that we know others are alive," he explains to me. "Your mother doesn't feel so hopeless any more. Neither do I, for that matter, not having to carry the whole responsibility for keeping the human race going, so to speak. It scares a person."

I looked around at the blanket walls and the fire and the pails of air boiling away and Ma and Sis sleeping in the warmth and the flickering light.

"It's not going to be easy to leave the Nest," I said, wanting to cry, kind of. "It's so small and there's just the four of us. I get scared at the idea of big places and a lot of strangers."

He nodded and put another piece of coal on the fire. Then he looked at the little pile and grinned suddenly and put a couple of handfuls on, just as if it was one of our birthdays or Christmas.

"You'll quickly get over that feeling, son," he said. "The trouble with the world was that it kept getting smaller and smaller, till it ended with just the Nest. Now it'll be good to start building up to a real huge world again, the way it was in the beginning."

I guess he's right. You think the beautiful young lady will wait for me till I grow up? I asked her that and she smiled to thank me and then she told me she's got a daughter almost my age and that there are lots of children at the atomic places. Imagine that.

DUNE ROLLER

BY JULIAN MAY (1932–   )
ASTOUNDING SCIENCE FICTION, DECEMBER

"Dune Roller" was the amazing debut story of 21-year-old Julian Chain May, who later married the noted science fiction anthologist Ted Dikty. And except for a minor short story, "Star of Wonder" in the February 1953 Thrilling Wonder Stories, *that was all the sf published by this talented woman until the early 1980s, when she returned to the field with the very successful and entertaining "Saga of Pliocene Exile" series of novels, beginning with* The Many-Colored Land *and continuing with* The Golden Torc *and* The Nonborn King, *and concluding in 1984 with* The Adversary. *The four books neatly blend science fiction and fantasy and have enjoyed great commercial success. It's a little sad to think about what she might have produced during that silent quarter-century, but we will have more books to look forward to in the future.*

—M.H.G.

I had a distant connection with Julian May, or as I knew her, Judy Dikty. Back in 1965, she was working for Follett Publishing company in Chicago. She wrote to me, saying that we had met at a convention in Chicago, and that she was the wife of Ted Dikty (who had in the past anthologized a couple of my stories).

Well, I knew we had never met in Chicago, because I had never attended a science fiction convention in Chicago (and still haven't as of today), but I assumed we must actually have met somewhere else and she just mis-remembered it as Chicago. Besides, I had met Ted Dikty a couple of times, and he had anthologized me—so when Judy asked me to do a book for Follett for old time's sake, I couldn't say "No." (One of my big problems is not being able to say "No" to anyone who can be identified as a friend.)

I wrote a little book entitled The Moon *for Follett (really for Judy). It was the kind of book that could be written in a weekend, and was—December 10-12, 1965, if you're curious. I then proceeded to write seven more equally little books on astronomical subjects over the next nine years—even after Judy had left the firm.*

They were nice little books, and I enjoyed writing them, and while they didn't make a lot of money, they made a little money, and I was always grateful to Judy for pushing the project my way. Like Marty, I am glad she is back in science fiction now, and wish she hadn't left it for all those years.

                                                          —I.A.

THERE WERE ONLY two who saw the meteor fall into Lake Michigan, long ago. One was a Pottawatomie brave hunting rabbits among the dunes on the shore; he saw the fire-streak arc down over the water and was afraid, because it was an omen of ill favor when the stars left the heaven and drowned themselves in the Great Water. The other who saw was a sturgeon who snapped greedily at the meteor as it fell—quite reduced in size by now—to the bottom of the fresh water sea. The big fish took it into his mouth and then spat it out again in disdain. It was not good to eat. The meteor drifted down through the cold black water and disappeared. The sturgeon swam away, and presently, he died. . . .

*   *   *

Dr. Ian Thorne squatted beside a shore pool and netted things. Under the sun of late July, the lake waves were sparkling deep blue far out, and glass-clear as they broke over the sandbar into Dr. Thorne's pool. A squadron of whirligig beetles surfaced warily and came toward him, leading little v-shaped shadow wakes along the tan sand bottom. A back-swimmer rowed delicately out of a green cloud of algae and snooped around a centigrade thermometer which was suspended in the water from a driftwood twig.

3:00 P.M., wrote Dr. Thorne in a large, stained notebook. *Air temp 32, water temp*—he leaned over to get a better look at the thermometer and the back-swimmer fled—28. *Wind, light variable; wave action, diminishing. Absence of drifted specimens.* He dated a fresh sheet of paper, headed it *Fourteenth Day*, and began the bug count.

He scribbled earnestly in the sun, a pleasant-faced man of thirty or so. He wore a Hawaiian shirt and shorts of delicious magenta color, decorated with most unbotanical green hibiscus. An old baseball cap was on his head.

He skirted the four-by-six pool on the bar side and noted that the sand was continuing to pile up. It would not be long before the pool was stagnant, and each day brought new and fascinating changes in its population. *Gyrinidae, Hydrophilidae*, a *Corixa* hiding in the rubbish on the other end. Some kind of larvae beside a piece of water-logged board; he'd better take a specimen or two of that. *L. intacta* sunning itself smugly on the thermometer.

The back-swimmer, its confidence returned, worked its little oars and zig-zagged in and out of the trash. *N. undulata*, wrote Dr. Thorne.

When the count was finished, he took a collecting bottle from the fishing creel hanging over his shoulder and maneuvered a few of the larvae into it, using the handle of the net to herd them into position.

And then he noticed that in the clear, algae-free end of the pool, something flashed with a light more golden than that of mere sun on water. He reached out the net to stir the loose sand away.

It was not a pebble or a piece of chipped glass as he had supposed; instead, he fished out a small, droplike object shaped like a marble with a tail. It was a beautiful little thing of pellucid amber color, with tiny gold flecks and streaks running through it. Sunlight glanced off its smooth sides, which were surprisingly free of the surface scratches that are the inevitable patina of flotsam in the sand-scoured dunes.

He tapped the bottom of the net until the drop fell into an empty collecting bottle and admired it for a minute. It would be a pretty addition to his collection of Useless Miscellanea. He might put it in a little bottle between the tooled brass yak bell and the six-inch copper sulfate crystal.

He was collecting his equipment and getting ready to leave when the boat came. It swept up out of the north and nosed in among the sand bars offshore, a dignified, forty-foot Matthews cruiser named *Carlin*, which belonged to his friend, Kirk MacInnes.

" 'Hoy, Mac!" Dr. Thorne yelled cordially. "Look out for the new bar the storm brought in!"

A figure on the flying bridge of the boat waved briefly and howled something unintelligible around a pipe clamped in its teeth. The cruiser swung about and the mutter of her motors died gently. She lay rocking in the little waves a few hundred feet offshore. After a short pause a yellow rubber raft dropped over the stern.

Good old Mac, thought Thorne. The little ex-engineer with that Skye terrier moustache and the magnificent boat visited him regularly, bringing the mail and his copy of the *Biological Review*, or bottled goods of a chemistry designed to prevent isolated scientists from catching cold. He was a frequent and welcome visitor, but he had always come alone.

Previous to this.

"Well, well," said Dr. Thorne, and then looked again.

The girl was sitting in the stern of the raft while MacInnes paddled deftly, and as they drew closer Thorne saw that her hair was dark and curly. She wore a spotless white playsuit.

and a deep blue handkerchief was knotted loosely around her throat. She was looking at him, and for the first time he had qualms about the Hawaiian shorts.

The yellow flank of the raft grated on the stony beach. MacInnes, sixty and grizzled, a venerable briar between his teeth, climbed out and wrung Thorne's hand.

"Brought you a visitor this time, Ian. Real company. Jeanne, this gentleman in the shorts and fishing creel is Dr. Ian Thorne, the distinguished writer and lecturer. He writes books about dune ecology, whatever that is. Ian, my niece, Miss Wright."

Thorne murmured politely. Why, that old scoundrel. That sly old dog. But she was pretty, all right.

"How engaging," smiled the girl. "An ecologist with a leer."

Dr. Thorne's face abruptly attempted to adopt the protective coloration of his shorts. He said, "We're really not bad fellows at heart, Miss Wright. It's the fresh air that gives us the pointed ears."

"I see," she said, in a tone that made Thorne wonder just how much she saw. "Were you collecting specimens here today, Dr. Thorne?"

"Not exactly. You see, I'm preparing a chapter on the ecology of beach pool associations, and this little pool here is my guinea pig. The sand bar on the lake side will grow until the pool is completely cut off. As its stagnation increases, progressive forms of plant and animal life will inhabit it—algae, beetles, larvae, and so forth. If we have calm weather for the next few weeks, I can get an excellent cross section of the plant-animal societies which develop in this type of an environment. The chapter on the pool is one in a book I'm doing on ecological studies of the Michigan State dunes."

"All you have to do is charge him up," MacInnes remarked, yawning largely, "and he's on the air for the rest of the day." He pulled the raft up onto the sand and took out a flat package. "I brought you a present, if you're interested."

"What is it? The mail?"

"Something a heck of a lot more digestible. A brace of

sirloins. I persuaded Jeanne to come along today to do them up for us. I've tasted your cooking.''

"I can burn a chop as well as the next man," Thorne protested with dignity. "But I think I'll concede the point. I was finished here. Shall we go right down to the shack? I live just down the shore, Miss Wright, in a place perched on top of a sand dune. It's rugged but it's home.''

MacInnes chuckled and led the way along the firm damp sand near the water's edge.

In some places the tree-crowned dunes seemed to come down almost to the beach level. Juniper and pines and heavy undergrowth were the only things holding the vast creeping monster which are the traveling dunes. Without their green chains, they swept over farms and forests, leaving dead trees and silver-scoured boards in their wake.

The three of them cut inland and circled a great narrow-necked valley which widened out among the high sand hills. It was a barren, eery place of sharp, wind-abraded stumps and silent white spaces.

"A sand blow," said Thorne. "The winds do it. Those dunes at the end of the valley in there are moving. See the dead trees? The hills buried them years ago and then moved on and left these skeletons. These were probably young oaks.''

"Poor things," said the girl, as they moved on.

Then the dismal blow was gone, and green hills with scarcely a show of sand towered over them. At the top of the largest stood Thorne's lodge, its rustic exterior blending inconspicuously into the conifers and maples which surrounded it on three sides. The front of the house was banked with yew and prostrate juniper for sand control.

A stairway of hewn logs came down the slope of the dune. At its foot stood a wooden bench, a bright green pump and an old ship's bell on a pole.

"A dunes doorbell!" Jeanne exclaimed, seizing the rope.

"Nobody home yet," Thorne laughed, "but that's the shack up there.''

"Yeah," said MacInnes sourly. "And a hundred and thirty-three steps to the top.''

Later, they sat in comfortable rattan chairs on the porch while Thorne manipulated siphon and glasses.

"You really underestimate yourself, Dr. Thorne," the girl said. "This is no shack, it's a real home. A lodge in the pines."

"Be it ever so humble," he smiled. "I came up here to buy a two-by-four cabin to park my typewriter and microscopes in, and a guy wished this young chalet off on me."

"The view is magnificent. You can see for miles."

"But when the wind blows a gale off the lake, you think the house is going to be carried away! It's just the thing for my work, though. No neighbors, not many picnickers, not even a decent road. I have to drive my jeep down the beach for a couple of miles before I can hit the cow path leading to the county trunk. No telephones, either. And I have my own little generating plant out back, or there wouldn't be any electricity."

"No phone?" Jeanne frowned. "But Uncle Kirk says he talks to you every day. I don't understand."

"Come out here," he invited mysteriously. "I'll show you something."

He led the way to a tiny room with huge windows which lay just off the living room. Radio equipment stood on a desk and lined the walls. A large plaster model of a grasshopper squatting on the transmitter rack wore a pair of headphones.

"Ham radio used to be my hobby when I was a kid," he said, "and now it keeps me in touch with the outside world. I met Mac over the air long before I ever saw him in the flesh. You must have seen his station at home. And I think he even has a little low-power rig in the cruiser."

"I've seen that. Do you mean he can talk to you any time he wants to?"

"Well, it's not like the telephone," Thorne admitted, "the other fellow has to be listening for you on your frequency. But your uncle and I keep a regular schedule every evening and sometimes in the morning. And hams in other parts of the country are very obliging in letting me talk to my friends and colleagues. It works out nicely all the way around."

"Uncle Kirk had represented you as a sort of scientific anchorite," she said, lifting a microphone and running her fingers over the smooth chrome. "But I'm beginning to think he was wrong."

"Maybe," he said quietly. "Maybe not. I manage to get along. The station is a big help in overcoming the isolation, but—there are other things. Shall we be getting back to the drinks?"

She put down the microphone and looked at him oddly. "If you like. Thank you for showing me your station."

"Think nothing of it. If you're ever in a jam, just howl for W8-Dog-Zed-Victor on ten meters."

"All right," she said to him. "If I ever am." She turned and walked out of the door.

The casual remark he had been about to make died on his lips, and suddenly all the loneliness of his life in the dunes loomed up around him like the barren walls of the sand blow. And he was standing there with the dead trees all around and the living green forever out of reach. . . .

"This Scotch tastes like iodine," said MacInnes from the porch.

Thorne left the little room and closed the door behind him. "It's the only alcohol in the house, unless you want to try my specimen pickle," said Thorne, dropping back into his chair. "As for the flavor—you should know. You brought the bottle over yourself last week."

The girl took Thorne's creel and began to arrange the bottles in a row on the table. Algae, beetles and some horrid little things that squirmed when she shook them. Ugh.

"What's this?" she asked curiously, holding up the bottle with the amber drop.

"Something I found in my beach pool this afternoon. I don't know what it is. Rock crystal, perhaps, or somebody's drowned jewelry."

"I think it's rather pretty," she said admiringly. "It reminds me of something, with that little tail. I know—Prince Rupert drops. They look just like this, only they're a bit smaller and have an air bubble in them. When you crack the little tail off them, the whole drop flies to powder." She shrugged vaguely. "Strain, or something. I never saw one that had color like this, though. It's almost like a piece of Venetian glass."

"Keep it, if you like," Thorne offered.

MacInnes poured himself another finger and thumb of Scotch and scrupulously added two drops of soda. In the center of the table, the small amber eye winked faintly in the sunlight.

Tommy Dittberner liked to walk down the shore after dinner and watch the sand toads play. There were hundreds of them that came out to feed as soon as dusk fell—little silvery-gray creatures with big jewel eyes, that swam in the mirror of the water or sat quietly on his hand when he caught them. There were all sizes, from big fellows over four inches long to tiny ones that could perch comfortably on his thumbnail.

Tommy came to Port Grand every August, and lived in a resort near the town. He knew he was not supposed to go too far from the cottage, but it seemed to him that there were always more and bigger toads just a little farther down the shore.

He would go just down to that sand spit, that was all. Well, maybe to that piece of driftwood down there. He wasn't lost, like his mother said he would be if he went too far. He knew where he was; he was almost to the Bug Man's house.

He was funny. He lived by himself and never talked to anyone—at least that's what the kids said. But Tommy wasn't too sure about that. Once last week the Bug Man and a pretty lady with black hair had been hiking in the dunes near Tommy's cottage and Tommy had seen him kiss her. Boy, that had been something to tell the kids!

Here was the driftwood, and it was getting dark. He had been gone since six o'clock, and if he didn't get home, Mom was going to give it to him, all right.

The toads were thicker than ever, and he had to walk carefully to avoid stepping on any of them. Suddenly he saw one lying in the sand down near the water's edge. It was on its back and kicked feebly. He knelt down and peered closely at it.

"Sick," he decided, prodding it with a finger. The animal winced from his touch, and its eyes were filmed with pain. But it wasn't dead yet.

He picked it up carefully in both hands and scrambled over the top of the low shore dune to the foot of the great hill where the Bug Man lived.

Thorne opened the door to stare astonished at the little boy, and wondered whether or not to laugh. Sweat from the exertion of climbing the one hundred and thirty-three steps had trickled down from his hair, making little stripes of cleanness on the side of his face. His T-shirt had parted company from the belt of his jeans. He held out the toad in front of him.

"There's this here toad I found," he gasped breathlessly. "I think it's sick."

Without a word, Thorne opened the door and motioned the boy in. They went into the workroom together.

"Can you fix it up, mister?" asked the boy.

"Now, I'll have to see what's wrong first. You go wash your face in the kitchen and take a Coke out of the icebox while I look it over."

He stretched it out on the table for examination. The abdomen was swollen and discolored, and even as he watched it the swelling movement of the floor of its mouth faltered and stopped, and the animal did not move again.

"It's dead, ain't it?" said a voice behind Thorne.

"I'm afraid so, sonny. It must have been nearly dead when you found it."

The boy nodded gravely. He looked at it silently for a moment, then said: "What was the matter with it, mister?"

"I could tell if I dissected it. You know what that is, don't you?" The boy shook his head. "Well, sometimes by looking inside of the sick thing that has died, you can find out what was wrong. Would you like to watch me do it?"

"I guess so."

Scalpel and dissecting needle flashed under the table light.

Thorne worked quickly, glancing at the boy now and then out of the corner of his eye. The instruments clicked within the redness of the incision and parted the oddly darkened and twisted organs.

Thorne stared. Then he arose and smiled kindly at the young face before him. "It died of cessation of cardiac activity, young fellow. I think you'd better be heading for home now. It's getting dark and your mother will be worried about you. You wouldn't want her to think anything happened to you, would you? I didn't think so. A big boy like you doesn't worry his mother."

"What's a cardiac?" asked the boy, looking back over his shoulder at the toad as Thorne led him out.

"Means 'pertaining to the heart,' " said Thorne. "Say, I'll tell you what. We'll drive home in my jeep. Would you like that?"

"I guess so."

The screen door slammed behind them. The kid would forget the toad quickly enough, Thorne told himself. He couldn't have seen what was inside it anyway.

In the lodge later, under the single little light, Thorne preserved the body of the toad in alcohol. Beside him on the table gleamed two tiny amber drops with tails which he had removed from the seared and ruptured remains of the toad's stomach.

The marine chronometer on the wall of Thorne's amateur station read five-fifteen. His receiver said to him:

"I have to sign off now. The missus is hollering up that she wants me to see to the windows before supper. I'll look for you tomorrow. This is W8GB over to W8DVZ, and W8GB is out and clear. Good night, Thorne."

Thorne said. "Good night, Mac. W8DVZ out and clear," and let the power die in his tubes.

He lit a cigarette and stood looking out of the window. In the blue sky over the lake hung a single, giant white thunderhead; it was like a marble spray billow, ponderous and sullen. The rising wind slipped whistling through the stiff branches of the evergreen trees on the dune, and dimly, through the glass, he could hear the sound of the waves.

He moped around inadequately after supper and waited for something to happen. He typed up the day's notes, tidied the workroom, tried to read a magazine, and then thought about Jeanne. She was a sweet kid, but he didn't love her. She didn't understand.

The sand walls seemed to be going up around him again. He wasn't among the dead trees—he was one of them, rooted in the sand with the living greenness stripped from his heart.

Oh, what the hell. The magazine flew across the room and disappeared behind the couch in a flutter of white pages.

He stormed into the workroom, bumped the shelves and set the specimens in their bottles swaying sadly to and fro. In the second bottle from the end, right-hand side, was a toad. In the third were two small amber drops with tails, whose label said only:

YOU TELL ME—8/5/57

Interest stirred. Now, there was a funny thing. He had almost forgotten. The beads, it would seem, had been the cause of the toad's death. They had evidently affected the stomach and the surrounding tissues before they had had a chance to pass through the digestive tract. Fast work. He picked up the second bottle and moved it gently. The pale little thing inside rotated until the incision, with all the twisted organs plainly visible inside, faced him. Willy Seppel would have liked to see this; too bad he was across the state in Ann Arbor.

Idly, Thorne toyed with the idea of sending the pair of drops to his old friend. They were unusual looking—he could leave the label on, write a cryptic note, and fix Seppel's clock for putting the minnows in his larvae pail on their last field trip together.

If he hurried, he could get the drops off tonight. There was a train from Port Grand in forty-five minutes. As for the storm, it was still a long way off; he doubted that it would break before nightfall. And the activity would do him good.

He found a small box and prepared it for the mails. Where was that book of stamps? The letter to Seppel: he slipped a sheet of paper into the typewriter and tapped rapidly. String— where was the string? Ah, here it was in the magazine rack. Now a slicker, and be sure the windows and doors are locked.

His jeep was in a shed at the bottom of the dune, protected by a thick scrub of cottonwood and cedar. Since there was no door, Thorne had merely to reverse gears, shoot out, swing around, and roar over the improvised stone drive to the hard, wet sand of the beach. Five miles down the shore was an overgrown but still usable wagon trail which led to the highway.

The clouds were closing ranks in the west as Dr. Thorne and his jeep disappeared over the crest of a tall dune.

Mr. Gimpy Zandbergen, gentleman of leisure, late of the high sea and presently of the open road, was going home. During a long and motley life, Mr. Zandbergen had wandered far from his native lakes to sail on more boisterous waters; but now his days as an oiler were over, and there came into his heart a nostalgic desire to see the fruit boats ship out of Port Grand once more. Since he possessed neither the money for a bus ticket home, nor the ambition to work to obtain it, he pursued his way via freight cars and such rides as he was able to hook from kindly disposed truck drivers.

His last ride had carried him to a point on the shore highway some miles south of his goal, at which he had regretably been invited to continue his journey on foot. But Mr. Zandbergen was a simple soul, so he merely shrugged his shoulders, fortified himself from the bottle in his pocket and trudged along.

It was hot, though, as only Michigan in August can be, and the sun baked the concrete and reflected off the sand hills at the side of the road. He paused, pulled a blue bandanna handkerchief from his pocket, and mopped his balding head under his cap. He thought longingly of the cool dune path which he knew lay on the other side of the forest, toward the lake.

It had been a long time, but he knew he remembered it. It would lead to Port Grand and the fruit boats, and would be refreshingly cool.

When the storm came, Mr. Zandbergen was distinctly put out. He had not seen the gathering storm through the thick branches, and when the sky darkened he assumed that it was merely one of the common summer sun showers and hoped for a quick clearing.

He was disturbed when the big drops continued to pelt down among the oak trees. He was annoyed as his path led him out between the smaller and less sheltering evergreens. He swore as the path ended high on a scrubby hill.

Lightning cut the black clouds and Mr. Zandbergen broke into a lope. He had taken the wrong turning, he knew that now. But he recognized this shore. He dimly remembered a driftwood shanty which lay near an old wagon road somewhere around here. If he made that, he might not get too wet after all.

He could see the lake now. The wind was raging and tearing all the waves, whipping the once placid waters of Michigan into black fury. Mr. Zandbergen shuddered in the driving rain and fled headlong down a dune. Great crashes of thunder deafened him and he could hardly see. Where was that road?

A huge sheet of lightning lit the sky as he struggled to the top of the next dune. There it was! The road was down there! And trees, and the shanty, too.

He went diagonally across the dune in gigantic leaps, dodging the storm-wracked trees and bushes. The wind lulled, then blasted the branches down ferociously, catching him a stinging blow across the face. He tripped, and with an agonized howl began to roll straight down the bare face of the sand hill. He landed in a prickly juniper hedge and lay, whimpering and cursing weakly, while the rain and wind pounded him.

The greenery ripped from the trees stung into him viciously

as he tried to rise, gave up, and tried again. On the black beach several hundred feet away, waves leaped and stretched into the sky.

Then came another lull and a light appeared out in the lake. It rose and fell in the surf and in a few moments the flattened and horrified little man on the shore could see what it was. A solemn thunderclap drowned out his scream of terror.

Shouting wordless things, he stumbled swaying to his feet and clawed through the bushes to fall out onto the road. It saw him! He was sure it saw him! He struggled along on his knees in the sand for a short distance before he fell for the last time.

The wind shrilled again in the trees, but the fury of the storm had finally passed. The rain fell down steadily now on the sodden sand dunes, and dripped off the cottonwood branches onto the quiet form of Mr. Zandbergen, who would not see the fruit boats go out again after all.

The sheriff was a conversational man. "Now I've lived on the lake for forty years," he said to Thorne, "but never— *never* did I see a storm like today's. No sir!" He turned to his subordinate standing beside him. "Regular typhoon, eh, Sam? I guess we won't be forgetting that one in a hurry."

Dr. Thorne, at any rate, would not forget it. He could still hear in his mind the thunder as it had rolled away off over the dunes, and see the flaring white cones of his headlights cutting out his way through the rain. He had gone slowly over the sliding wet sand of the wagon road on his way home, but even at that he had almost missed seeing it. He remembered how he had thought it was a fallen branch at first, and how he got out of the car then and stood in the rain looking at it before he wrapped his slicker around it and drove back to town.

And now the rain had stopped at last, and the office of the Port Grand physician who was the county medical examiner was neat, dim, and stuffy with the smell of pharmaceuticals and wet raincoats. Over the other homely odors hung the stench of burnt flesh.

Snip, went the physician's bandage shears through charred cloth. Thorne lit a cigarette and inhaled, but the sharp, sickening other smell remained in his nostrils.

"According to his Seamen's International card, he was George Zandbergen of Port Grand," said the sheriff to Sam, who carefully transcribed this information in his notebook. To Thorne he said, "Did you know him, mister?"

Thorne shook his head.

"I remember him, Peter," said the physician, experimentally determining the stiffness of the dead fingers before him. "Appendicitis in 1946. Left town after that. I think he used to be an oiler on the *Josephine Temple* in the fruit fleet. I'll have a file on him around somewhere."

"Get that, Sam," said the sheriff. He turned to Thorne, standing awkwardly at the foot of the examination table. "We'll have to have your story for the record, of course. I hope this won't take too long. Start at the beginning, please."

Gulping down his nervousness and revulsion, Thorne told of returning from town about nine o'clock and finding the corpse of a man lying in the middle of a deserted side road. Dr. Thorne recalled puzzling at the condition of the body, for although it had been storming heavily at the time, portions of the body had been burned quite black. Thorne had found something at the scene also, but failing to see that it had any connection with the matters at hand, prudently kept his discovery to himself. The sheriff would hardly be interested in it, he told himself, but nevertheless he hoped that the bulge it made in his pocket wasn't too noticeable.

Officer Sam Stern made the last little tipped-v that stood for a period in his transcription and looked nervously about him. His chief peered approvingly—even if uncomprehendingly—at the notes and then said:

"How does it look, doctor?"

"Third degree burns on fifty percent of the body area, seared to the bone in some parts of the face and about the right scapula. How did you say he was lying when you found him, Mr. Thorne?"

"In an unnatural kind of sprawled position, on the right side."

The physician yawned, rummaged in a cabinet and produced a sheet with which he covered the charred body. "Pretty obvious, Peter, with these burns and all. Verdict is accidental death. The poor devil was struck by lightning. Time of death was about eight P.M." He tucked the sheet securely around the head. "That lightning's pretty odd stuff, now. Can blow the soles off a man's shoes without scratching him, or generate enough heat to melt metal. You never know what tricks it's going to play. Take this guy here: one side of him's broiled black and the other's not even singed. Well, you never know, do you?"

He picked up his phone and conversed briefly with the local undertaking parlor. When negotiations for the disposition of the unfortunate Mr. Zandbergen had been completed, he replaced the receiver and shuffled toward the door. Thorne could see that he had bedroom slippers on under his rubbers.

"You can finish up tomorrow, Peter," he resumed. "My wife was kinda peeved at me coming out this way. You know how women are, ha-ha. Good night to you, Mr. Thorne. I think there's an old overcoat in that closet I could let you take. You'll be wanting to send yours to the cleaners."

There was a genial guffaw from the sheriff. "We won't keep you any longer tonight, Mr. Thorne. Just let me know how I can get in touch with you."

"Through Kirk MacInnes on River Road," said Thorne. "He'll be glad to contact me through his amateur station." He edged through the door into the quiet night. The sheriff came close behind.

"So you're a ham, eh?" he said warmly. "Well, can you tie that! I used to have a ticket myself in the old days."

Polite noises. How about that? Kindred souls. Sorry about all this sloppy business, old man. Tough luck you had to be the one to find him. Really nothing, old man. *Why* didn't he stop talking? The weight in Thorne's pocket seemed to grow.

"You know, I'll be dropping in to see your rig some one

of these days if you don't mind. I'll bet you could use a little company out there in the dunes, eh?''

No, why should he mind? Delighted, old man. Any time at all.

The thing in his pocket seemed to sag to his ankles. It would rip the pocket and fall out. And it had bits of charred cloth on it. Why didn't they go? They couldn't possibly suspect that he hadn't—

Oh, yes, he was on ten meters. Phone. Oh, the sheriff had done c.w. on 180? Well, wasn't that nice.

They walked to the cars under the big old elm trees that lined the comfortable street. A few stars came out and down where the street dead-ended into the river, they could see lights moving toward the deepwater channel that connected the river with the lake.

"Well, good night, Sheriff," Thorne said. "Good night, Mr. Stern. I hope next time we'll meet under more pleasant circumstances.''

"Good night, Mr. Thorne," said Sam, who was thoroughly bored with talk he didn't understand, and anxious to get home to his wife and baby.

The police got into their car and drove off. Thorne sat quietly behind the wheel of the jeep until he was sure they were gone, then gingerly removed the weight from his pocket and unwrapped the handkerchief that covered it.

This one was the size of a closed fist and irregular in shape. He had found it flattened under the black char that had once been a man's shoulder, glowing with a bright yellow light in its heart. It looked the same as the three small drops he had previously seen, but he saw that what he had mistaken for golden flecks inside of it was really a fine network of metallic threads which formed a web apparently imbedded a few centimeters below the thing's surface.

The damn thing, he thought. There was something funny about it, all right.

Around him, the lights of the quiet houses were going out one by one. It was eleven o'clock. A few wet patches still glistened on the street under the lamps, and a boat motor on the river pulsed, then stilled.

Thorne looked around him quickly, then got out of the car and laid the thing on the curb. The wet leaves in the gutter below it reflected yellow faintly.

It was funny that a mere matter of shape could change his feeling toward it so radically. The smaller drops had been rather beautiful in their droplike mystery, but this one, although it was made of the same wonderful stuff, had none of the beauty. The irregular cavity in its side that would fit a human shoulder blade made it a thing sinister; the dried blood and ashes made it monstrous.

He took a tire iron out of the tool kit and tapped the glowing thing experimentally. It was certainly stronger than it looked, at any rate. When harder taps failed to crack it, he raised the iron and brought it down with all his strength. The tool bounced, skidded and chipped the concrete curbstone, but the thing flew undamaged into the gutter.

Throne bent down and poked it incredulously. And suddenly, with a cry of agony, he dropped the tire iron. It was hot! The tool arced down and lay sizzling sullenly among the little drops of water that still clung to the grass blades. His hand— He clenched his teeth to keep from crying out.

But the glowing thing in the gutter was not hot. Steam rose from the iron in the grass, but the little rivulets bathing the glowing thing were cool. He seemed to remember something, but then the shocked numbness coming over his hand took his attention and he forgot it again.

Down among the leaves and trash, the thing that was not shattered by the strength of Dr. Thorne grew, momentarily, more golden; and with a deliberate, liquid ripple the ugly bulges on its surface smoothed and it assumed the perfect drop shape of its predecessors.

200000 AU PLUS PLENTY WATTS. TELL ME PRETTY MAIDEN ARE THERE ANY MORE AT HOME LIKE YOU? ARRIVE NOON THURSDAY. LOVE, SEPPEL.

"You think you're pretty smart, don't you?" said Thorne.

"Yep," said Willy Seppel smugly, smirking around the edge of his beer. He put down the glass and the smirk expanded to a grin. "Smart enough to see what those drops were that you sent me for a gag. That was a great little trick of yours, you know. I was all set to throw them out after reading that note of yours. The only thing that saved them was Archie Deck. He thought they might be Prince Rupert drops and tried to crack the tails off with a file."

"Aha," said Dr. Thorne.

Seppel looked at him with bright blue, innocent eyes. He was a large, pink-faced, elegantly dressed man with an eagle-beak nose and a crown of fine, blond hair.

"You don't have to look at me like that," said Thorne. "I've been able to find out a little bit more about them myself."

"Tell me," said the pink face complacently.

"They generate heat. And I found out the same way as Archie Deck probably did." He gestured with one bandaged hand. "Only I managed it the hard way." He swept up the empty glasses and beer bottles with a crash and disappeared into the kitchen. His voice continued distantly:

"I found those two I sent you inside the stomach of a toad. Or at least what was left of the stomach of a toad. Look in the lab room, the big shelf; second bottle from the end on the right-hand side."

Wiping his good hand on his trousers, he returned to Seppel, who stood looking thoughtfully into the toad's bottle. "It ate the drops," Thorne said shortly.

"Mm—yes," he mused. "The digestive juices might very possibly be able to—"

"Come on, Willy. What is it?"

"You were almost right when you said it generated heat," Willy said. "I brought one of them here to show you." He left the room and returned in a minute with a large cowhide briefcase.

"This thing's in a couple of pieces," Seppel apologized.

"You'll have to wait until I set it up. Have you got a step-down transformer?"

Thorne nodded and fetched it from the bookcase.

"Now this little drop here may look like a bead, but it has some singular properties." He removed the thing from a box which had been heavily sealed and padded, and set it in a nest of gray, woolly stuff in the middle of the table.

"It gives off long infrared, mostly stacked up around 200,000 Angstroms. But their energy is way out of proportion from what you'd expect from the equation. This little gadget is something Deck and I rigged up to measure it crudely. Essentially, it's a TC130X couple hooked up to a spring gun. You put the drop in here, regulate the tension of the spring and firing the gun releases this rod which delivers the drop an appropriate smack." His fingers with their immaculately groomed nails worked deftly. "We don't get a controlled measurement, of course, but it'll show you what I mean. . . . Where do you hide your outlets?"

"Behind the fish tank. Be careful not to disconnect the aerator."

"The screen on that end will show you the energy output. Watch now."

The horizontal green line on the little gray screen bucked at the firing of the spring, then exploded into an oscillating fence of spikes.

"Mad, isn't it?" remarked Dr. Thorne. "Hit it again, but lower the tension of the spring."

If anything, the spikes were even higher.

"The smack-energy ratio isn't proportional," said Seppel. "Sometimes a little nudge will set it off like a rocket. And again, after we tapped it for a week at Ann Arbor figuring out what it was, it showed a tendency to sulk and wouldn't perform at all after awhile."

"The energy output," Thorne said. "It's really quite small, isn't it?"

"Yes, but still surprising for an object this size." He removed the drop from the device and put it back into its little box. "We think that glowing heart has something to do with it. And those gold threads—they are gold, you know—come in there too. Old Camestres, the Medalist himself, was visiting the University, and he says that glow is something that'll have the physicists crawling the walls."

"Oh, come now," said Dr. Thorne broadly.

"You just wait," said Seppel. "We haven't done the analysis yet, but we expect great things. The glow," he added, "isn't hard radiation, if that's what you're thinking."

Willy was proud of it, Thorne thought. It was really his discovery after all, not Thorne's, and Seppel, who found challenge and stimulation in the oddest places, had hit the heights with the little golden drops.

But Thorne was remembering a larger drop, the size of a man's fist, and the charred body of a dead man.

"I found another specimen," he said, turning to a drawer in the worktable. "A larger one." He took out Mr. Zandbergen's drop.

"This is wonderful!" Seppel cried. "It's almost the size of a grapefruit! Now we can—"

Thorne cut him off gently. "I want to tell you about this one. Then I'll turn it over to you. When I first found it, it was irregularly shaped. Lumpy. Ugly. It's smooth now, just like the others, but it changed before my eyes. It just seemed to run fluid, then coalesce again into the drop shape. And there's something else."

He told Seppel about the attempt to crack the thing and the abrupt heating of the tire iron.

"Yes, that could be," Seppel decided. "It's easily possible that a larger specimen such as this one could cause a metal object near it to become perceptibly warm. Infrared rays aren't hot in themselves, but when they penetrate a material their wave length is increased and the energy released heats the material. In the case of the tire iron, the conductivity of the metal was greater than that of your hand, and you felt the warm iron before the skin itself was affected."

"The iron wasn't warm, Willy. It was damn hot. And in a matter of seconds."

Seppel shook his head. "I don't know what to say. It's the funniest thing I've ever run across."

"The dead man who lay down on it didn't think it was funny," said Thorne.

"You don't think this little thing killed him, do you? He was charred to a cinder all along one side of him. Do you know what kind of infrared could do a thing like that? None."

"I didn't say I thought *this* one killed him," said Thorne, with a cue that Seppel chose to ignore. "I just said the body was right on top of it."

"Too wild for me," said Seppel. He got up, stretched leisurely, and glanced at the clock. "And anyhow, it's sack time. We can worry about it tomorrow, eh?"

Thorne had to smile. Good old Willy. No little glowing monster was going to keep *him* from his sleep.

"We'll put grapefruit back in the drawer," Seppel suggested, "have ourselves a snack, and go to bed."

"Wouldn't the big one be better off in a pail of ice?" asked Thorne, half laughingly.

"If it did decide to give out, it would probably melt the pail before it melted the ice. And besides," he added with dapper complacency, "they never radiate unless they're disturbed."

In the dream, there was sand all around him. He was in it, buried up to his neck. There was a sun overhead that was gold and transparent, and a wind that never seemed to reach his feverish face threw up little whirls of yellow sand.

Sometimes the familiar face of a woman was there. He cried her name and she was gone. And after that, he forgot her, for small shapeless things gamboled out on the sand into the sunlight, only to be burnt black as the rays struck them. . . .

For the fifth time that night, it seemed, Thorne awoke, his eyes staring widely into the darkness. He cursed at himself and turned the perspiration-soaked pillow over, pummeling it into a semblance of plumpness. Seppel lay beside him, snoring gently.

Somewhere in the lodge a timber creaked, and he felt the fear come back again, and saw the black, huddled heap lying before his headlights, and felt the pain renewed in his slowly healing hand. Of the dream, strangely enough, there was no memory at all.

Only the fear.

But why should he be afraid? There was nothing out there. Nothing out there at all.

But the heap in the road. Lightning. *But the little one had burned. So what? The little one was too small to burn a man seriously.* I know that. *He was burned.* Lightning, you silly fool! *He was burned!* Shut up. *One of them burned him.* Shut up! Shut up! *There's another one out there tonight.*

No. Nothing out there at all.

Nothing but the dunes and the lake. Nothing.

The wind squalls strummed the pine branches out there, and swirls of sand borne up the bluff from the beach below tickled faintly at the window. The waves of Michigan were roaring out there—but there was nothing else.

Finally, he was able to sleep.

It was nearly dawn when he woke again, but this time he was on guard and alert as he lowered his bare feet softly to the floor. His hand closed over the barrel of a flashlight on the chest of drawers, and he moved noiselessly so that he would not wake the sleeper beside him.

He tiptoed slowly through the workroom and the living room. Something was on the porch.

As he came through the doors, he said sharply: "Who's there?"

An odor of burned wood hit his nostrils. He exclaimed shortly under his breath and shone the light down near the sill of the outside door. There was a round black hole in the door, smoking and glowing faintly around the edges.

He raced back into the workroom and pulled out the drawer that had held the grapefruit-sized drop. It was empty, and a hole gaped in the bottom of it. The hard wood was still burning slowly.

He yanked out the drawer, put it in the kitchen sink and

turned on the water. Then he filled a pan and soaked the hole in the door thoroughly.

They never radiate unless they're disturbed! That was a laugh. Not only had it radiated, but it had somehow focused the radiation. Dr. Thorne was no physicist, but he began to wonder whether the meter had told the whole story of the little glowing drop.

He unlocked the door and slid out into the night. Below the stair was a small, almost imperceptible track in the sand. He followed it down the ridge of the dune, lost it momentarily in a patch of scrub, then found it again in the undisturbed expanse of the sand blow.

He went down into the silent valley, the bobbling yellow light from his flash throwing the tiny track into high relief. When he reached the center of the bowl, he stopped among the long shadows of the gaunt spiky trees.

There was another track in the sand, meeting and merging with the little one. And the track was three feet wide.

He followed it as if in a dream to the crest of the first low shore dune and stood on its summit among the sharp grass and wild grape. The moon's crescent was low over the water and orange. He saw the track go down the slope and disappear into the waves which were swirling in a new depression in the sand.

The wind whipped his pajama shirt about his back as he stood there and knew that he was afraid of that track in the sand, and that no lightning had killed the little tramp.

It was not until he had locked the door of the lodge behind him that he realized he had run all of the way back.

Friday was a quiet day in the dunes country, but the police did receive three minor complaints. A farmer charged that someone had not only made off with and eaten three of his best laying hens, but had burned the feathers and bones and left them right in the chicken yard. The Ottawa County Highway Commission wanted to know who was building fires in the middle of their asphalt roads and plastering the landscape with hot tar. And a maiden lady complained that the artists in the local summer colony must be holding Wild Orgies again from the looks of the lights she had seen over there at three A.M.

Dr. Thorne bent down over the tracks in the sand. It certainly looked to him as though the big one had been waiting for Mr. Zandbergen's drop.

Seppel said, "Get out of the way there," and snapped his Graflex. "These sand tracks won't last long in the winds around here. And I frankly tell you that if I hadn't seen it with my own eyes, I would never have believed it." He circled the point of conjunction, laid his fountain pen beside it for size reference, and the Graflex flashed again.

"We'll want the door, too," he said, putting the camera aside and scrawling in his notebook.

Thorne howled.

"Well, just the part with the hole in it then," Seppel conceded. "Did you find out where the large track came from?"

"I tracked it to the woods. The ground there is too soft and boggy to hold a wide track like that, and I finally lost it."

Seppel struggled to his feet and retrieved his coat, which he had hung for safety's sake on the white peg branch of a skeleton tree. "Just imagine the size of an object which would make a three-foot track in soft sand!" he exclaimed. "And to think it's been in the lake for heaven knows how long and this is the first time it's come into evidence!"

"I wouldn't be too sure about that—about this being the first time, I mean. There have been some funny stories told along these shores. I heard one myself from my grandmother when I was about twelve. About the dune roller that was bigger than a schooner and lived in the caves at the bottom of the lake. It came out every hundred years and rolled through the dune forest, leaving a strip of bare sand behind it where it had eaten the vegetation. They said it looked for a man, and when it found one, it would stop rolling and sink back into the lake."

"Great Caesar," said Seppel solemnly. "I can see it now— the great glowing globe lurking deep in the caverns where the sun never shines and there is no life except a few diatoms drifting in the motionless waters."

Thorne gaped at his friend for a minute, and then spied a suspicious twinkle in one blue eye.

"This is no laughing matter, you Sunday supplementist!" he said sharply.

"Hmp," said Willy Seppel, and brushed a few grains of sand from the sleeve of his handsome suit.

It was late when Miss Jeanne Wright got out of the movie in Muskegon—so late that she barely had time to do the shopping which had, ostensibly, been her reason for taking *Carlin* out. "You just can't buy decent dresses in Port Grand, Uncle Kirk," she had pleaded, and he really wouldn't mind if she took the boat, would he? MacInnes had growled indulgently from the depths of his new panadaptor and said he certainly did, confound it, and what was the matter with using the car? But he had tossed her the keys just the same.

The street lights of the city were going on when, laden with bundles, she finally hailed a cab and drove to the yacht basin. It was a beautiful evening, with soft-glowing stars in a sky that was still red-purple in the west. *Carlin* slipped majestically out among the anchored craft into Muskegon Lake.

A bonfire blazed cheerfully on the shore and singing voices from some beach party floated melodiously out over the water. They shouted a jocular greeting to *Carlin* and Jeanne blew a hail to them with the air horn. Her heart was light as she led the cruiser through the channel into the lake and headed for home.

A secretive smile danced on her lips, and she thought kindly about a certain stern-faced young biologist. He was a strange man, occasionally even rude in an unintentional sort of way, and preoccupied with such dreary things as plant cycles and environmental adaptations. But he had walked with her in the dunes one day and changed for a little while, and kissed her once, very gently, on the lips. And after that she had known what she wanted.

He would be sitting in his workroom now, looking over the day's bugs and not thinking of her at all. Or perhaps he would be talking to her uncle over the radio.

She hummed dreamily to herself. The cruiser's speed increased to twenty, and it rocked momentarily in a trough, setting the little good luck charm hung up over the wheel to bobbing like a pendulum. Ian had given that to her. She loved it because of that.

After a while she turned on the short wave receiver that sat on one of the lockers in the deckhouse and listened to Ian and her uncle.

"I have a colleague of mine out from Ann Arbor," Thorne was saying. "About that amber drop we found. Remember my telling you about it? I gave one to Jeanne for a souvenir. My friend is a biophysicist and thinks the drops are a great scientific discovery. His name is Willy Seppel. Say something, Willy."

"Gambusia," said Seppel, recalling the minnows in the larvae pail.

Jeanne listened absently. Ian was telling how the drops gave off hot light when they were disturbed. How he thought there might be bigger drops around that could really grind out the energy 40db. above S9. (What in the world did *that* mean?) Thorne and this Willy person would look for the bigger drops.

"Is it really hot?" Jeanne wondered, staring curiously at the pendant drop, swinging above the binnacle in its miniature silver basket. It didn't seem to be. But then Ian had said the little ones didn't radiate very much. Only enough to tickle something-or-other.

Far out in the lake, the lights of an ore boat twinkled. She passed the little village of Lake Harbor and put out a bit farther from shore. There would be no more towns now until Port Grand.

Over the radio, her Uncle Kirk's voice, homely and kind, was describing the great things in store for the new panadaptor. Ian would put in a comment here and there, but she noticed that he sounded tired, poor darling.

Cleanly, powerfully, *Carlin* sliced though the waves, pursuing the shadow of herself. The shadow was long, and very black. A boat with a searchlight, thought Jeanne, and looked astern.

It was there, riding high in the dark, choppy water: a great glowing globe of phosphorescence not twenty yards off the stern. It was coming after her, rapidly overtaking the cruiser.

She screamed then, and when the thing came on, she opened the throttle and attempted to outmaneuver it. But the great glowing monster would pause while she veered and spiraled, then overtake her easily when she tried to run away. The motors of the Matthews throbbed in the hull beneath her feet as she tried to urge them to a speed they were never meant for.

The thing was drawing closer. She could see trails of water streaming from it. What was it? What would it do if it caught her?

Bigger ones! Her eyes turned with horror to the tiny drop on its silver chain. Its glow was the perfect miniature of the monstrous thing in the water behind her. She sobbed as she wrenched *Carlin*'s wheel from side to side in hysterical frenzy. Across the cabin, the quiet voice of Ian was telling MacInnes how to rig the panadaptor as a frequency monitor.

Ian!

And if you're ever in a jam. . . .

With tears streaming down her cheeks she set the automatic pilot and fumbled with the little amateur transmitter that had been built into the locker. She had seen her uncle use it only once. That turned it on, she thought, but how did she know it was set right? Or did you set these things?

The little panel wore three switches, two knobs, a dial and a little red light. Naturally Kirk MacInnes had not labeled the controls of an instrument he had built himself. The panel was innocent of any such clutterment.

Carlin tore through the night. The glowing thing was less than fifteen yards behind.

Jeanne wept wildly and the placid voices over the receiver

spoke sympathetically of the ruining of Thorne's beach pool by the storm.

Oh, those knobs and switches! This one, then this one, she thought. No—that wouldn't be right. The transmitter might not even be on the air at all. Or she might be in some part of the band where Ian and her uncle would fail to hear her. But what was she supposed to do? And she couldn't read this funny tuning scale.

"I've got a swell mobile VFO in *Carlin*," said MacInnes.

"What's VFO?" said Seppel.

"In Mac's case, it means Very Frequently Offband."

Laughter.

Oh, what difference would it make? What could he do to help her? The brilliance of the huge thing was lighting up the water for yards around.

The calm voices floated from the receiver and the globe drew closer than it had ever been.

She clawed at the stand-by switch of the radio and suddenly her sobs and the beat of the engines were the only sounds in the deckhouse. She would try. That was all. She would try to reach Ian, and pray that her uncle had left the transmitter set to the correct frequency.

"Ian!" she cried, then remembered to press the button on the side of the little hand microphone. Forcing back her tears, she said, "Ian, Ian—can you hear me?"

Trembling, her hand touched the receiver.

"Jeanne!" the sound burst into the deckhouse. "Is that you? What are you doing?"

"It's after me, Ian!" she screamed. "A glowing sphere fifteen feet high! It's chasing the boat!"

"The boat," came MacInnes' voice numbly. "She took it to Muskegon."

"Jeanne! Listen to me. I don't know whether this will do any good, but you must try. You must do exactly as I say. Do you hear me?"

"I hear you. Ian! That thing is almost on top of the boat!"

"Listen. Listen to me, darling. You have that little amber drop somewhere in the boat. Do you remember? The little

amber drop I gave you. Get it. Take it and throw it over-
board. Throw it as far as you can. The amber drop! Now tell
me if you heard me.''

''Yes. I hear you. The drop. . . .''

The drop. It danced on its little silver chain and the light in
its core was bright and pulsating and warm. She tore it from
its place over the wheel and groped back to the open cockpit
of the cruiser. She clung for a full minute to the canopy
stanchion, blinded by the golden light.

And then the small drop arced brightly over the water,
even as a meteor had, many centuries past.

The light, reflecting off the walls painted a flat, clinical
white, was full of blurred, fuzzy forms. They might have
been almost anything, Thorne thought. And he shuddered as
he thought of what they might have been. A table, for
instance, with a burden that was sprawled and made black all
along one side.

Without moving his head or changing his expression he
squeezed his eyes shut very slowly and opened them again.
But it was not the medical examiner's office. It was the
waiting room of the little local hospital, and Willy Seppel
was sitting beside him on the leather couch. Through the
open window behind lowered blinds, a clovery night breeze
stirred, parting the smoke that filled the room and turning a
page of the magazine that Seppel was staring at.

A young man of twenty-five or so sat across the room from
them and ate prodigious quantities of Lifesavers. ''My wife,''
he had grinned nervously at them. ''Our first.''

The persons in the waiting room could see through the
open door to a room at the end of the hall. People in white
would periodically enter and leave this room, but another,
grimmer group which had entered nearly an hour ago had not
come out.

''Willy, I'm going nuts,'' Thorne burst out at last. ''What
are they doing in there? You'd think they'd at least let me
know—let me see her.''

''Easy. It'll be any minute now.'' He proffered a gold

cigarette case, but Thorne shook his head. "Why don't you lie back and try to relax?" Seppel said. "You've been crouching there staring at the floor until your eyes look like a pair of burned-out bulbs. What good do you think you're going to do her in that kind of shape?"

Thorne sank back and lay with the back of his hand shading his eyes. If he could have been there when they brought her in! But it takes time to find where an unmanned boat has drifted. Time while he sat before his receiver with nothing to do but wait. The hands of the clock had wound around to one A.M. before the call finally came and he knew she was saved.

It was three-thirty now. MacInnes and his wife were in there with her. He looked despairingly down the white corridor, and waited.

The sound of her voice, made broken and breathless with weeping, rose again in his mind. She had said the thing was fifteen feet high. The big one itself. And it could have—

This wouldn't do at all. The memory of his dream the previous night stood out in his mind with horrible clarity. The bright golden sun and the little burned things. But infrared doesn't burn. The bright golden sun.

"Sun," said Dr. Thorne to himself, very quietly.

"Mm'mm?" said Seppel.

"Sun," he repeated firmly. "Willy, do you always think the same way?"

"Nope."

"If I hit you, how do you think?"

"Mad," said Seppel, with a winning smile.

"But if you figure the best way to sneak out of here without being seen, how do you think?"

"Rationally."

"I've been thinking about the drops again. You know, we've got a pretty serious discrepancy in the so-called properties of the things. We've proved the infrared emission, but infrared doesn't sear flesh."

"That's what I've been trying to tell you," said Seppel, with patience.

"Nonetheless, I'm convinced that the big one Jeanne saw is the thing that did in the tramp. Now what if the energy emitted is not always infrared? What if the infrared is a sort of involuntary result of the blows we gave the drop, while ordinarily when it's aroused it gives off another wave length? Say something in the visible with a lot of energy, that that drop shape could focus into a beam."

Seppel didn't say a thing.

Silence precipitated heavily. The young man in the chair opposite them shifted his position and stared at them with gaping awe. Scientists!

There was a starchy swish and a nurse appeared in the doorway. Thorne started to his feet. "Can we—"

"Mr. DeAngelo," she beckoned coolly. "It's a boy. Will you follow me, please?"

The young man gave a joyous, inarticulate cry and rushed out of the room.

Thorne dropped back. "Ye gods," he muttered.

"You've really got it bad, haven't you?" Seppel marveled.

"Oh, Willy, shut up. You know I'm only interested in her because of the thing that chased her. And wipe that look off your face. Between you and MacInnes a man doesn't have a chance."

Seppel looked slightly hurt.

"I'm sorry," Thorne apologized briefly. He walked around the room. The young man with the new son had been so anxious to leave that he had forgotten his Lifesavers. Thorne ate one. It was wintergreen. He hated wintergreen.

Seppel yawned delicately, then leaned forward and glanced out the door. "Someone's coming," he warned softly.

A tall man in a uniform of summer tans had left the room at the end of the corridor and walked purposefully toward the waiting room.

Seppel rose to his feet as the man entered the room. He said: "Good evening—or rather, good morning. Is there something I can do?"

"My name is Cunningham, commander of the Coast Guard cutter *Manistique*. Are you Mr. Ian Thorne?"

"My name is Seppel. This is Mr. Thorne. Won't you sit down?"

"Thanks, I will." To Thorne, who stood with his hands rudely clasped behind his back, he said briskly: "Mr. Thorne, at nine this evening your amateur station contacted our base with information that the cruiser *Carlin* was in difficulty off the mainland somewhere between Port Grand and Muskegon."

"It wasn't me, it was Kirk MacInnes." Thorne was not interested in brisk, nautical gentlemen.

"We found the cruiser drifting, out of gas, some seven miles off the Port Grand light. Miss Wright, the operator of the craft, was found lying unconscious on the cockpit floor. I've just seen her—"

"How is she?" Thorne cut in.

"The doctors say she is suffering from shock, but other than that, they can't find a thing wrong with her. Now what I'd like to know—"

"Is she conscious? Has she been able to talk?"

"She's very weak and what she says makes no sense. I thought perhaps you might be able to help us on that score."

Thorne looked at the Coast-Guardsman narrowly. "We were conversing with her over the radio, when she suddenly seemed to become disturbed and evidently fainted."

"Didn't MacInnes tell you anything?" asked Seppel.

"No."

"Quiet, Willy," Thorne said.

"She seemed to be trying to tell us that someone was chasing her," Cunningham persisted. "Are you sure she said nothing in her talk with you that could give us a hint of the trouble?"

"I knew there was something wrong from the sound of her voice. That's all. When she didn't answer, Mr. MacInnes radioed the Coast Guard."

"And we found her after a four-hour search. That young lady was very lucky that she ran out of gas. Her automatic pilot had the cruiser headed straight out into the middle of the lake."

"There was—nothing else on the water near her?"

"The lake was empty." Cunningham paused, then said casually, "Was there something you expected us to find, Dr. Thorne?"

"Certainly not. I was just wondering."

"I see." The officer got to his feet. "I don't mind telling you gentlemen that I think there's something you're not letting me know. My job is done, and it's true that legally I have no business questioning you at all. But my business *is* keeping the waterways safe. The young lady in the room down the hall didn't faint from nervous exhaustion or hunger. Something scared the hell out of her out there on the lake. If you know what it was, I wish you'd tell me!"

"Have you ever read any science fiction, Commander Cunningham?" Seppel asked, toying with his gold cigarette case. Rather belatedly, he said, "Cigarette?"

The Coast-Guardsman took one with suspicious thanks. "Are you trying to tell me that the little green Martians have put outboards on their rocket ships and are chasing the pleasure craft on our lake?"

Thorne said harshly: "What Dr. Seppel means is this. We have reason to believe that a highly unusual occurrence was responsible for tonight's unpleasantness. I don't like to mince words, Commander. I think I *do* know what was out there last night, but I'm not going to tell you. I can't begin to prove my suspicions, and I have a rather intense aversion to being laughed at."

"I have no intention of laughing, Mr. Thorne. But if you have information relative to marine safety, let me remind you that you have an obligation to report it to the proper authorities."

"Proper authorities are not notorious for their sympathy. They'd laugh in my face. No, thank you, Commander. Until I have proof, I say nothing."

The door at the end of the corridor opened once more, and closed softly. Kirk MacInnes and his wife came down toward the waiting room. Thorne started up.

"She wants to see you, son," MacInnes said tiredly. "She's

a little stronger now, and she asked for you. I'm taking Ellen back home. This has been pretty raw for her.''

"I'm all right," his wife said stiffly. She clutched a damp, tightly balled lace handkerchief, but her features were immobile.

"Will Jeanne be all right?" Thorne asked brokenly.

"She'll be fine," said MacInnes, clapping him on the back. "Now get down there and see her before those medics decide she can't have any more visitors."

"I'm there now. And—thanks, Mac." He disappeared down the corridor. The engineer and his wife left quietly.

"Thorne is a good man," Seppel said, "even if he is a trifle mule-headed." His bright blue eyes looked humorously into the half-angry face of the Coast Guard officer. He laughed, moved over on the leather couch, and said: "Sit down here, Commander. Have another cigarette. Have a Lifesaver. I'm going to tell you a singular story."

It was shortly before lunchtime in Thorne's dune lodge, but the bubbling beaker on the range that Willy Seppel was stirring exuded a decidedly unappetizing aroma. Pungent, acidic in an organic kind of way, with noisome and revolting overtones, the fumes finally brought indignant remarks from Thorne.

"Look," he said, peering in the doorway, and holding his nose. "I'm the last one to criticize another man's cooking, but will you tell me what in heaven's name that is?"

"Oh, just a bit of digestive juice," said Seppel cheerily, turning off the gas and removing the beaker with a pair of pot holders. He carried his foul-steaming container into the workroom. Thorne fled before him.

"I suppose I'd better not ask where you got it," he said, from the sanctuary of the radio room.

"Don't be silly," said Seppel. "I merely raided your enzymes and warmed up a batch. Just an idea."

He took the little drop out of its container and set it on the table beside the beaker. "I thought since digestive juice provoked it into emitting once, it might do it again."

Thorne regarded him dubiously.

"I only wish," Seppel went on to say, "that the grapefruit-sized one hadn't escaped." He set the drop in a loop of plastic and dipped it into the brew.

"Take it easy with that one, Willy. It's the only link we have with the big one."

"So you think they can communicate, too," said Seppel without looking up.

"I don't know whether it's communication or sympathetic vibration or the call of the wild. But that thing did follow Jeanne because of the little drop in the boat, and it disappeared when it got what it wanted. The grapefruit heard mama, too, and got away. I'll bet if that little one had been strong enough to get through your fancy insulation, it would have disappeared along with the other one."

"And the two tracks merged into one," said Seppel, testing the soaked drop in the thermocouple. Nothing happened. "As the rustic detective was heard to remark, 'They was two sets o' footsteps leadin' to the scene of the crime, and only one set leadin' away.' I wonder what kind of a molecular bond that transparent envelope has?" He felt the drop with his finger, shrugged and put it back into the juice.

"The big globe killed the tramp, if my idea is correct," said Thorne. "He must have seen the thing coming out of the lake, turned to beat it, and fell on his face. And I think he picked exactly the wrong place to fall."

"On grapefruit," Seppel agreed. "All mama wanted to do was to pick up her offspring. She couldn't help it if there was a body in the way."

"But she killed just the same," said Thorne. "Those old dune roller stories hint that she may have done it before." He fished the miniature drop out of the liquid and looked into its yellow heart meditatively.

"And Willy," he said abstractedly, "unless something is done soon, she'll do it again."

During the days that followed, Dr. Thorne went about his work with quiet preoccupation; and this in itself was enough to make Seppel more than a little suspicious. He rarely mentioned the drops, although he visited Jeanne every day, carrying sheaves of flowers and boxes of candy and fruit. Seppel went along on these pilgrimages for the ride, but almost always tactfully declined visiting the sickroom and hiked out instead to the Coast Guard station for a parley with his new ally, Commander Cunningham.

Anxiety furrowed Seppel's pink forehead as he paced up and down the officer's quarters. "He's got something up his sleeve," he maintained. "He goes off in the jeep in the morning and doesn't come back until noon. When I ask him where he's been, he says he just went into town to see Jeanne. But visiting hours are from two to four! If he doesn't go to the hospital, where does he go?"

Cunningham shrugged, and picked up a folded newspaper that lay on the table. "Have you seen this, Willy? It might explain a few things."

Mystified, Seppel read aloud: "We pay CASH for certain unusual minerals. Highest prices, free pickup. Samples wanted are round, semi-transparent, amber colored with metallic veining. HURRY! Write today, Box 236, Port Grand, Michigan."

Seppel stared aghast.

"I take it you weren't acquainted with this," the officer said. He walked to the window and looked down at a fruiter steaming through the channel. "Do you know what he plans to do?"

"No, but I know what I'd do. There's some kind of an attraction between the big globe and the drops—a force that draws the little ones home to mama when they get her call. We found that out with a drop at Thorne's lodge. But that attraction is so great that it works the other way too. Little Miss Wright told you that. If the drops can't come, if we hold them back, mama comes after her children. That's what Thorne will probably count on."

It was Cunningham's turn to stare. "You mean he'll use the drops from the ad for *bait?*"

Seppel said gently: "What's a man to do, Rob? He can't let it go free. The fellow that finds the monster has three choices: he can run home and hide under the bed, and pretend he didn't see it at all, he can try to inform the proper authorities, or he can attempt to dispose of the monster himself. Thorne knows nobody will believe his dune roller story so he just doesn't waste time convincing people.''

Cunningham turned abruptly from the window and said violently: "You aren't going to start on me too, are you, Willy? Sure. Here I am, one slightly used but still serviceable authority. I believe your damn dune roller yarn for some reason or other. But it doesn't do any good. I'd earn the biggest haw-haw from here to the Straits of Mackinac if I tried to initiate an official search for a round glowing thing fifteen feet high. The world won't unite simply because Michigan has itself a monster, you know. And what can I do, even if I take the *Manistique* out? Maybe Ian Thorne knows how to catch monsters, but I certainly don't.''

"You want to let him go on, I suppose," Seppel said. He added a trifle wistfully, "I hate to see him get his hide fried off when he's just beginning to think about settling down.''

"You watch him. That's all. And let me know when you think he's going to pull something. I'll do everything I can." He glanced at his watch. "I have to get out of here now, Willy. Keep your eyes open. All *we* can do is wait.''

"And that," said Seppel, with dark doubt shading his pleasant voice, "seems to be all there is to say.''

The drops glowed on the kitchen table. "Seven!" said Ian Thorne triumphantly. "How do they look to you, Willy? From the size of a pea to a tennis ball. Seven little devil eyes.''

"What are you going to do with them?" asked Seppel. He wore an old lab apron over his trousers and wiped the breakfast dishes. It was very early in the morning.

"Just a little experiment. I got a bright idea the other day while I was visiting Jeanne. You can have the drops after I'm finished if you like, but I want to try this thing out first.''

"I wish you'd let me help you.''

"No, Willy.''

"Cunningham believes you, too," Seppel went on recklessly. "Why don't you tell us what you're going to do?"

"No." He scooped the drops into a bakelite box. "I'll be gone most of the day. I have some collecting to do out in the dunes."

He vanished into the bedroom and came out wearing hiking boots and a heavy leather jacket. An empty knapsack dangled over his arm. He put the bakelite box into the buckled pouch on the outside of the sack, and took a paper packet from the sink and stuffed it into his back pocket.

"Oops! Almost forgot my collecting bottles," he laughed, and went into the radio room.

Seppel put down the dish towel and stepped softly after him. There were no collecting bottles in the radio room. He was just in time to see Thorne drop a handful of little metal cylinders and a black six-inch gadget into the knapsack.

Thorne did not seem at all abashed to find Seppel standing there. He brushed past and went out the kitchen door.

"So long, Willy. Keep the homes fires burning. Send out the posse if I'm not back before dark." The screen door slammed.

After waiting a minute, Seppel grabbed up the binoculars from the china shelf and glided silently through the sandy yard, past the generator building to the path that led down the side of the dune to the shed where the jeep was kept.

The early morning mist still curled around the trees and settled in the hollows, and a distant bird call echoed down on the forest floor. At a bend in the steep path, Seppel caught a glimpse of Thorne's broad back dappled by the pale sun rising through the fog.

The path turned sharply and cut off diagonally down the dune toward the shed. Instead of continuing, Seppel stepped off the path, and treading cautiously, circled across through the woods to arrive at a point on the slope directly above the garage. Then he removed his apron, spread it on the twiggy, dew-wet ground and stretched out among the bushes, bringing his binoculars to bear on the man below.

Thorne removed a small wooden crate from the rear of the jeep. It bore the red-stenciled inscription:

G. B. VANDER VREES & SONS
—HIGHWAY CONSTRUCTION

There were other words, too, but Thorne stood in the way of Seppel's vision. He quickly transferred the contents of the crate to his knapsack, and with a·single look around him, set off down the dune trail that ran through the forest, parallel to the lake shore.

As soon as Thorne was out of sight, Willy Seppel scrambled heavily to his feet and went back up the path to the lodge. There he addressed some intense words to the microphone of the amateur station, an operation which would have been frowned upon by the FCC, which discourages the use of such equipment by unlicensed persons.

He would have maintained his disinterest and scientific detachment if he had been asked about it, but the truth was that Dr. Ian Thorne deeply loved the dunes. He had lived in them during his childhood, grown up and gone away, and come back to find them substantially the same. He recalled that had surprised him little. You expected the dunes to change, they were like a person, though only one who has known the heights and swamps of them can explain the curious sleeping vitality of the sands under the forest. Things with a smaller life than the dunes would flutter and creep and stalk boldly through them until you might think of them as dead and tame. But Dr. Thorne had seen the traveling dunes shifting restlessly before the winds and felt a kinship with the great never-lasting hills.

The path he strolled along was an old friend. He had pursued the invertebrate citizens of the forest along its meandering length, waded in the marshy interdunal pools which it carefully skirted, and had itched from encounters with the poison ivy that festooned the trunks and shrubs beside it. The path wound along the shore for a good five miles—

horizontally, at least—and he did not hurry. The knapsack
was too heavy, for one thing, and the still air was warming
slowly as the sun rose up through the pines and oak trees. An
insect chirred sleepily in a gorge on his right, and as if at
some prearranged signal, an excursion of mosquitoes bobbed
out to worry the back of his neck.

The path took him through a clearing in the sand covered
with patches of dusty, green grass and scarlet Indian weed.
On the lee side of a great bare dune at the edge of the clearing
stood a single, short cottonwood, half buried in the sand. But
the tree had grown upward to escape, modifying its lower
branches into roots. The tree was one of the few forms of life
that defied the dunes—by growing with them—and its branches
were brave and green.

Thoughtfully, Thorne passed on again into the dimmer
depths of the forest.

It was nearly noon when he reached the foot of a cluster of
sand dunes, the principal peak of which rose some hundred
and fifty feet above the floor of the woods. It was the highest
point for many miles along the shore, and its name was
Mount Scott. The path circled its eastern slope and then
continued on, but Thorne stepped off onto the faintly defined,
spider-web-laced trail leading to the summit.

The going was rough. Thornapple branches probed after
his eyes, and as the ascent grew steeper, sudden shifts in the
dirty sand under his feet brought him to his knees. The tree
roots across the path had partially blocked the sand, forming
crude natural steps in the lower reaches of the dune; but as he
climbed higher, the trees were left behind while the sand
grew cleaner and hotter, and the wild grape, creeper and
ubiquitous poison ivy became the prevalent greenery.

He was winded and perspiring when he finally stood on the
peak of the dune. He glanced briefly about him and selected a
spot partially shaded by a scrub juniper as his campsite. He
sat down, shucked the knapsack and his heavy jacket and lit a
cigarette.

The hills below rolled away in gentle, green waves toward
the farmlands and orchards in the east and the brilliant blue

lake in the west. He could see the spires of the town of Port Grand poking out of the haze a few miles down the shore, and some white sails appeared off the promontory that hid the entrance to the river harbor.

He turned his attention to Mount Scott itself. The summit of the dune was really composed of two shallow humps, with a depression on the lakeward side in which Thorne had made his camp. Below this, a sheer, fairly clean slope of sand swept down to the low tangle of woods which lay between him and the shore.

He looked cautiously in the knapsack and removed the seven small drops, grouping them in a circle on the white sand of the lake slope. After that, he retreated to his hollow and settled down as comfortably as he could.

The paper packet in his pocket yielded three ham-and-pickle sandwiches, slightly soggy, which he consumed leisurely. A short foray around the peak brought dessert in the form of a handful of late blueberries. After his meal he employed himself at length with the contents of the knapsack. When the job was finally done, he sat down under the juniper tree and began to wait.

The shade of the tree diminished, disappeared as the sun climbed higher, and then reappeared on the other side of the tree, leaving Thorne with the sun in his face and a monumental thirst. The blueberries, unfortunately, were all gone.

At last, at four P.M., the largest drop began to move.

It rolled slowly out of the shallow hole in the sand that cupped it and moved down the hill. Thorne watched it roll *up* a small pile of sand that blocked its path and disappear into the woods at the foot of the hill.

At 4:47 one of the smaller drops followed in the track of the first. It had a little trouble when it came to the pile of sand—which was one of several strung across the face of the dune—but it negotiated the obstacle at last and disappeared.

Just as the sun was beginning to redden the water, a third drop began its descent. Quietly, Thorne rose and replaced it in its hole. The faint gleam within it might have grown a bit brighter when he interfered, but perhaps it was only the reflection of the sun.

The five remaining drops were grouped in a horseshoe, downward pointing, and the drop whose elopement had just been foiled reposed at the end of one prong. A few minutes later, the larger drop at the other prong attempted to roll down the hill. Thorne put it back and rapped sharply on each of the others with his cigarette lighter, tamping them down further into the sand. He was strained forward alertly now, with his eyes on the strip of forest below. The sun slipped grudgingly behind the flat lake, and a tang of pine washed up the slope. The drops did not move again.

With the departure of the sun, the glow in the heart of each alien thing leaped higher and higher, until the string of them was like a softly glowing corona in the sand—a strange earthbound constellation.

But their glow was not beauty, Thorne reminded himself. It was death. Death had dwelt in their great, glowing mother who had already called two of her incredible children home. Death that rolled seeking through the lake and the dune forest. . . .

His cigarette end made a dimmer eye in the dusk than the glow of the drops. There was still enough light to see by—the sky was red around him and the dune forest was silent.

He wondered idly what long forgotten power had strewn the drops along the shore. They were not terrestrial, he was almost sure of that. Perhaps they had been a meteor that had exploded over the lake, and the life of the great thing—if it was life—had been patiently gathering up its scattered substance ever since, assimilating the fragments during its long rests at the bottom of the lake.

From the size of it, it must have been growing for hundreds of years, collecting a drop of itself here and there, from roadbeds and sand dunes and farmyards, responding to those who imprudently hindered it with the only defense it knew.

And now he was to destroy it. It had killed a man. Perhaps before this, even, men had found the drops attractive and carelessly put them in their pockets . . . and the dune roller sought a man. It had killed the little tramp, and almost killed Jeanne. He couldn't take a chance of letting it go again.

The image of Jeanne rose in his mind. The memory of the time they had walked down the winding forest path, and of a twig caught in her sandal. She had had grains of sand on her tanned arms, and a bright yellow flower stuck crazily in one dark curl. She had laughed when he plumped her down on the moss-soft root of an old oak and took the twig out, but she had not laughed when he kissed her.

Around him, the forest was still.

A cold breath whispered along his skin. The forest was still. Not a bird, not an insect, not an animal noise. The forest was still.

He felt like yelling at it: *Come on out, you!* Come out and chase me like you chased her!

He fingered the stud of the little black instrument in his hand. He would show it. Let it dare to come out.

Come out!

It came.

He had never dreamed it would be so big.

It had made no noise at all. In a fascination of horror he watched it roll to the foot of the tall dune. It vanished among the trees, but a warm yellow radiance lit the undersides of the fluttering leaves as it moved beneath them. The light blazed as it emerged from the brush and came straight toward him, rolling up the hill.

The small drops pulsed in their sandy snares and he gave each one a savage rap. As if it, too, shared the insult, the great globe flared, then subsided sullenly. But its ponderous ascent was alarmingly rapid.

He could not take his eyes away from it. The smaller drops were rocks, were mere bits of oddly glowing crystal; but this great thing before him seemed the most beautiful and the most terrible thing he had ever seen in his life. And it was alive. No man could have looked upon it and said that it was not alive. The brilliant golden heart in it swelled and blazed upon the golden veining that closed it in.

There were noises now from the winding path in the forest

below, and the twinkling pinpoint lights of men. But Thorne did not hear them, nor see any light except the great one before him. He could not move. Sweat stood out on his face and the instinct to flee dissolved into terror that folded his legs like boneless things. He half-crouched on hands and knees and stared . . . and stared.

The thing was closer now, nearly up to the line of sand humps that Thorne had worked so hard on. He had to get away. There was no more time. He forced his paralyzed hands and feet to tear into the loose sand of the side of the depression and pull him up. He had to get on the other side of the hill.

In the last instant, his numbed fingers pressed the stud of the little transmitter that would activate the firing caps of the nitro buried in the sand.

But the monster must have realized, somehow. Because he felt—when he flung himself out over the peak with the deep red sky around him—a searing, mounting pain that started on the inside and flooded outward. He rolled unconscious over the far side of the hill just as the five solemn detonations blasted the golden glowing globe to bits.

There were white, gauzy circles around the place where his eyes looked out. He was vaguely surprised to see six people with the eyes—three sets of two. He made the eyes blink and the six people changed into Seppel, MacInnes and Jeanne. He tried to raise an arm and was rewarded by a fierce jab of pain. The arm was thick and bandaged, like the rest of him.

The six—three—people had seen his eyes open and they moved closer to him. Jeanne sat down beside the bed and leaned her head close.

"I hope that's you in there," she said, and he was amazed to see there were tears in her eyes.

"How am I?" he mumbled through the bandages.

"Medium rare," said Seppel. "You doggone crazy fool."

"We almost got to the top, anyway," said MacInnes gruffly. "But you went and beat us to it."

"Had to," Thorne said painfully.

"You would," Jeanne said.

"Is it gone?" he asked. There were six people again and he felt very tired.

"Shivered to atoms," said Seppel with finality. "You should see the crater in the sand. But we'll still have small ones to study. Your ad brought in four more today. I was talking to Camestres on the phone, and he says he's sure he can swing a nice fat research grant for us as soon as you're able to get out of that bed—"

Thorne groaned.

"He says," Jeanne translated firmly, "that he's sticking to *Ecological Studies of the Michigan Dunes*, Chapter Eight. No more dune rollers, thank you."

MacInnes laughed and wagged his gray old head. "You'd better surrender, Dr. Seppel. Jeanne's got her mind made up. And one thing about her—whatever she says, she'll always be Wright."

"Don't be too sure about that," she said pertly, laying her two small hands gently on Thorne's bandaged arm. It didn't hurt a bit.

High on a dune above the lake, the moon rode high over a blackened crater in the sand. Two of the grains of sand, which gleamed in the moonlight a bit more golden than the rest, tumbled down together into a sheltered hollow to begin anew the work of three hundred years.

DAW

**Unforgettable science fiction
by DAW's own stars!**

M. A. FOSTER

☐	THE WARRIORS OF DAWN	UE1994—$2.95
☐	THE GAMEPLAYERS OF ZAN	UE1993—$3.95
☐	THE MORPHODITE	UE2017—$2.95
☐	THE DAY OF THE KLESH	UE2016—$2.95

C.J. CHERRYH

☐	40,000 IN GEHENNA	UE1952—$3.50
☐	DOWNBELOW STATION	UE1987—$3.50
☐	VOYAGER IN NIGHT	UE1920—$2.95
☐	WAVE WITHOUT A SHORE	UE1957—$2.50

JOHN BRUNNER

☐	TIMESCOOP	UE1966—$2.50
☐	THE JAGGED ORBIT	UE1917—$2.95

ROBERT TREBOR

☐	AN XT CALLED STANLEY	UE1865—$2.50

JOHN STEAKLEY

☐	ARMOR	UE1979—$3.95

JO CLAYTON

☐	THE SNARES OF IBEX	UE1974—$2.75

DAVID J. LAKE

☐	THE RING OF TRUTH	UE1935—$2.95

NEW AMERICAN LIBRARY
P.O. Box 999, Bergenfield, New Jersey 07621

Please send me the DAW Books I have checked above. I am enclosing
$_____ (check or money order—no currency or C.O.D.'s).
Please include the list price plus $1.00 per order to cover handling
costs.

Name _____

Address _____

City _____ State _____ Zip Code _____
Please allow at least 4 weeks for delivery

DAW

The really great fantasy books are published by DAW:

Andre Norton

☐ LORE OF THE WITCH WORLD   UE2012—$3.50
☐ HORN CROWN   UE1635—$2.95
☐ PERILOUS DREAMS   UE1749—$2.50

C.J. Cherryh

☐ THE DREAMSTONE   UE2013—$3.50
☐ THE TREE OF SWORDS AND JEWELS   UE1850—$2.95

Lin Carter

☐ DOWN TO A SUNLESS SEA   UE1937—$2.50
☐ DRAGONROUGE   UE1982—$2.50

M.A.R. Barker

☐ THE MAN OF GOLD   UE1940—$3.95

Michael Shea

☐ NIFFT THE LEAN   UE1783—$2.95
☐ THE COLOR OUT OF TIME   UE1954—$2.50

B.W. Clough

☐ THE CRYSTAL CROWN   UE1922—$2.75

NEW AMERICAN LIBRARY
P.O. Box 999, Bergenfield, New Jersey 07621

Please send me the DAW Books I have checked above. I am enclosing
$_____ (check or money order—no currency or C.O.D.'s).
Please include the list price plus $1.00 per order to cover handling
costs.

Name _____

Address _____

City _____ State _____ Zip Code _____
Please allow at least 4 weeks for delivery

DAW

Presenting JOHN NORMAN in DAW editions . . .

- [ ] **HUNTERS OF GOR** (#UE2010—$2.95)
- [ ] **MARAUDERS OF GOR** (#UE2025—$3.95)
- [ ] **TRIBESMEN OF GOR** (#UE2026—$3.50)
- [ ] **SLAVE GIRL OF GOR** (#UE2027—$3.95)
- [ ] **BEASTS OF GOR** (#UE2028—$3.95)
- [ ] **EXPLORERS OF GOR** (#UE1905—$3.50)
- [ ] **FIGHTING SLAVE OF GOR** (#UE1882—$3.50)
- [ ] **ROGUE OF GOR** (#UE1892—$3.50)
- [ ] **GUARDSMAN OF GOR** (#UE1890—$3.50)
- [ ] **SAVAGES OF GOR** (#UE1715—$3.50)
- [ ] **BLOOD BROTHERS OF GOR** (#UE1777—$3.50)
- [ ] **KAJIRA OF GOR** (#UE1807—$3.50)
- [ ] **PLAYERS OF GOR** (#UE1914—$3.50)
- [ ] **MERCENARIES OF GOR** (#UE2018—$3.95)
- [ ] **TIME SLAVE** (#UE1761—$2.50)
- [ ] **IMAGINATIVE SEX** (#UE1912—$2.95)
- [ ] **GHOST DANCE** (#UE2038—$3.95)

With close to four million copies of DAW's John
Norman books in print, these enthralling novels
are in constant demand. They combine heroic adventure, interplanetary peril, and the in-depth de-
piction of Earth's counter-orbital twin with a
special charm all their own.

**DAW BOOKS are represented by the publishers of Signet and
Mentor Books, NEW AMERICAN LIBRARY.**

NEW AMERICAN LIBRARY
P.O. Box 999, Bergenfield, New Jersey 07621

Please send me the DAW BOOKS I have checked above. I am enclosing
$_____ (check or money order—no currency or C.O.D.'s).
Please include the list price plus $1.00 per order to cover handling
costs.

Name _____

Address _____

City _____ State _____ Zip Code _____
Please allow at least 4 weeks for delivery